A FLICKER OF STEEL

I1056404

ALSO BY STEVE McHUGH

The Hellequin Chronicles

Crimes Against Magic

With Silent Screams

Born of Hatred

Prison of Hope

Lies Ripped Open

Promise of Wrath

Scorched Shadows

Infamous Reign

The Avalon Chronicles

A Glimmer of Hope

A Flicker of Steel

A FLICKER OF STEEL

STEVE McHUGH

47NORTH

This is a work of fiction. Names, characters, organizations, places, events, and incidents are either products of the author's imagination or are used fictitiously. Any resemblance to actual persons, living or dead, or actual events is purely coincidental.

Text copyright © 2018 by Steve McHugh
All rights reserved.

No part of this book may be reproduced, or stored in a retrieval system, or transmitted in any form or by any means, electronic, mechanical, photocopying, recording, or otherwise, without express written permission of the publisher.

Published by 47North, Seattle

www.apub.com

Amazon, the Amazon logo, and 47North are trademarks of Amazon.com, Inc., or its affiliates.

ISBN-13: 9781542047081
ISBN-10: 1542047080

Cover design by @blacksheep-uk.com

Cover illustration by Larry Rostant

Printed in the United States of America

For Ben

1

Domme, Louisiana. USA.

"I'd like to point out that this is an astonishingly bad plan," Layla Cassidy said. There was no one in the parked red Ford Mustang GT with her, no one anywhere near the car for that matter. She wore a small communication device in her left ear that allowed her to talk to, and hear, the other three people in her team. Two of them had switched theirs off while they went to work, leaving Layla only able to talk to her best friend, Chloe Range.

Chloe made a slight grunting noise in response, signaling that she couldn't exactly talk at the moment.

Layla tapped her fingers against the steering wheel and wondered if there had been a better way to get the information they were here to retrieve. There had to be a safer one, but then Chloe had seen a chance to gain more than just information and no one was going to talk her out of it.

Originally, they'd arrived in Louisiana to speak to one of Tommy Carpenter's contacts about finding the people who were supplying spirit scrolls to Nergal. The influx of spirit scrolls was a serious concern to those who stood against Arthur and his version of Avalon: a version in which you vanished if they no longer deemed you an ally. Tommy's people had tracked the spirit scrolls to an unnamed port in the south of Louisiana. Once they were offloaded, the scrolls were taken to an unknown destination somewhere in America. All Tommy's contacts had managed to ascertain was that there was a stopover in Domme.

Domme was a small settlement close to a port. It wasn't on any maps. It officially didn't exist. Avalon at work once again. Domme consisted of several dozen miles of swamp and a few buildings dotted around. One such building was only a mile up the road from where Layla had parked. She looked out of the window at the cypress trees. The sun had begun to set a short time ago, and Layla found the trees to be simultaneously creepy and pretty. The swamp was close by, and she'd had to park the car on muddy ground. Thankfully it was firm enough that she hadn't needed to worry about getting stuck, but if it decided to rain then that idea might be shot to hell.

The plan to get information and tail the smugglers had changed when Layla and Chloe had started looking around the port and found that there was a lot more being trafficked than old scrolls. People. Dozens of people. Marched off fishing boats at gunpoint, thrown into the backs of trucks and driven away. Layla didn't know what they were being used for, or where they'd come from, but both she and Chloe knew they had to find out more. It turned out that apart from grabbing people who were brought in by boat, the smugglers also kidnapped any-one unlucky enough to be hitchhiking in the area. There had been mul-tiple missing persons reports throughout the surrounding towns, and nearly all of them pertained to people who were last seen hitchhiking.

"You still there?" Chloe whispered.

"Of course. I'm waiting for you to get your ass out of there. Where is there, anyway?"

"An old house, or more accurately a mansion. I've been locked in the cellar with several other humans. We're all kept in separate cells.

They drugged me—didn't realize I wasn't human, so I had to go along with it. Most of the others are still out cold."

"Any idea why they're taking people?"

"No, but there's never been a kidnapping ring that's done it for good reasons."

"Not exactly what I meant, Chloe."

"I know. It's just been a long day. I haven't heard anything about the scrolls. One of these kidnappers has a Confederate flag tattooed on the back of his hand. But it's the old version of the flag, with the circle of stars in the top left corner. He seems to be in charge. I think he was there. As in, actually there during the Civil War. I saw a picture on a wall with him and several others who the tattooed guy said were Confederate guerillas. One of them was Jesse James."

"The bandit? How can you know that?"

"That's the one. And I know it because the tattooed guy told me. His name is Alfred. He saw me look at it, picked it up, and showed it to me. Made a big deal about how he knew Jesse."

"So, at least one isn't human. Any idea what he is?"

"No. I count eight. All men. I doubt many of them aren't human, although obviously I can't tell without fighting them."

"Please don't fight them."

"I wasn't planning on it. I'd like to hurt a lot of them, though. Some of the people I saw coming in—" Chloe paused, as if fighting off a deeply troubling memory. "They keep them drugged out of their minds in other rooms around the house. I heard screams, even through the walls. My drenik wants me to hurt people. It's the closest I've come to just letting it out for a long time."

Apart from drenik being the base of the power that umbras could wield—a power that was random for every umbra—they were also capable of taking temporary control of the host body. In that time, the drenik had access to the entire reserve of power it possessed, making it an enemy to be feared by even the most powerful foe. Unfortunately, allowing the drenik control in such a way had the unfortunate side effect of giving it a greater chance of taking control of its human host for good. For that reason, most umbra and their drenik came to an agreement about how they could work together. Layla knew that Chloe hadn't allowed her drenik to take control for over a year; for her to be considering it now meant she was deeply angry.

"We'll take the whole lot of them down," Layla assured her friend. She looked at the wooden bracelet on her right wrist and the runes carved into it. Everyone who lived at the compound and worked with Hades and his people wore one. The bands were linked to a blood curse mark on the back of their shoulders.

A blood curse mark was created using blood magic. Most curses did awful things to people, like remove their powers or memories, but some were more benign. Everyone had been told that their marks linked to the runes on the bracelets, and only those with both could enter and leave the compound safely. No one had argued against this, but it had been the topic of much discussion.

"Do you still have your bracelet on?" Layla asked Chloe.

"Yes, they left it on me, although I'm not sure that it would have done anything if they'd removed it."

"Better safe than sorry. Have you heard from the others?"

"No, reception is spotty at best. Diana is around somewhere, though. Remy, too. I'm sure you'll be able to hear their bickering before they get to you."

Chloe chuckled, although there was little humor in it. Layla wished they hadn't decided on their plan a day ago, but it was too late for regret. Now they had to see it out.

"You okay, Chloe?"

"I'm fine. Angry. Unbelievably angry. Other than that, I'll be okay. These are the bad guys I've always wanted to stop. I've got to go—if you don't hear from me in a few hours you know what to do."

"Guns blazing."

"Nuke the site from orbit, just to be sure."

Layla smiled at the line and exhaled. A lot had happened to her in the last two years. She'd been kidnapped because Nergal had wanted to get to her father, she'd seen her friends murdered in front of her in horrific ways she could barely have imagined before and on top of all that she'd bonded with a spirit scroll and become an umbra. She had accepted the three spirits and Terhal—her drenik—who were in the scroll and gained mastery over her abilities.

Six months into her new life, the world had turned to shit. Avalon—a group who controlled the world from the shadows—gained a new boss: King Arthur. The same King Arthur who had been comatose for several centuries, who everyone now thought of as some kind of messiah sent to save them. Layla could remember the day when the world had discovered the existence of magic, monsters, and the fact that the people from mythology were real. Hundreds of thousands had died in attacks all over the world, causing panic and fear in the human population.

That panic and fear were exactly what Arthur had wanted. He'd stepped into the limelight, bringing the entire world of non-humans with him whether they wanted to follow him or not, and announced to humanity that he would ensure their safety. Publicly, Avalon now kept the evil at bay and made sure humans slept soundly in their beds. Privately, Avalon hunted down those who would oppose them, murdering thousands in order to hold on to power. Arthur and his people had taken control of the entire world, and humanity had welcomed them with open arms.

Some still opposed Arthur and continued to fight against his regime. That was the reason that Layla was in Louisiana. To hurt Arthur and Avalon, you had to hurt those who were helping him, and Nergal was considered an integral part of Avalon's organization. He controlled the parts of Avalon that used to protect people, like the LOA—the Law of Avalon—and used what was meant to be a law informant agency as his own personal secret police. The majority of people wouldn't even notice that the world had become a totalitarian state until Arthur had succeeded in wiping his enemies from the earth so he could turn his full attention to everyone else. And if that ever happened, there was never going to be a chance to fight back.

"You okay?" Rosa said from the passenger seat of the Mustang.

Layla turned toward the spirit beside her. Rosa had once used her powers as an umbra to deliver vengeance in the name of Queen Victoria. She had been an assassin of exceptional talent, and of the three spirits inside the scroll, she was the one Layla spoke to the most. Their friendship was something both Layla and Rosa cherished.

"A lot has happened in a short period of time," Layla said.

"I didn't see Arthur as the villain," Rosa said. "Everyone thought he was the best of us. He'd been comatose for hundreds of years when I was born; everyone spoke about the time he'd wake and take us to a better future. I don't think anyone, outside of those who knew the real Arthur, expected him to wake up and decide to kill everyone who opposed him."

Layla nodded, but wanted to move the conversation away from melancholy. "I can't get used to you not wearing the appropriate clothes."

Rosa looked down at her black-and-red dress and white trainers. Her dark hair had once been long and braided, but was now much shorter and closer to green in color. "I get to look how I like. You know this. Not sure why you still find it strange. We spirits can wear whatever the current period deems acceptable, or whatever you deem acceptable. I like it."

"The others wear clothes from their own time."

"The other two have sticks up their butts," Rosa said with a smile. "And I know you have steered the conversation away from your concern."

"Chloe is in the house of horrors. Yes, it worries me. I know she can take care of herself, but if they figure out what, or who, she is, she'll be on her own until backup arrives."

Rosa looked around the small parking area. "Lots of thick woods, bit of swamp. How did you know about this place?"

"Diana spoke to someone in New Orleans. They told us about the old mansion. No one goes there, to the best of my knowledge. Used to be a smugglers' drop, but it's too out-of-the-way for that these days."

"That and the lack of people smuggling hooch."

"Hooch?" Layla asked with a slight smile.

Rosa shrugged. "I just like the word."

"How long would it take you to get to Chloe from here?" a man's voice asked from the back seat of the car.

Layla turned to look at the praefectus legionis. His name was Servius Tullius, and he was a huge man, well over six feet in height and probably weighing two of Layla. The Roman had dark skin, short black hair, and a small beard—the only thing that had changed about him in the two years since Layla had become an umbra.

"You don't have to wear the uniform," Layla said, ignoring his question.

Servius looked down at his armor. "Yes, I do," he said softly. "It's who I am."

Layla sighed; she'd had the same conversation with him many times in the last year. Servius just wasn't comfortable enough to adapt his habits. He was a soldier. That's who he was, how he defined himself. To change his clothing was an act he considered to be a waste of time and effort. Layla knew he had a point, but she still wished he would relax a bit more.

"Have you scoped out the place?" Servius asked.

"Diana and Remy are moving around the area now," Layla said. "They're both a lot quieter than I am."

"Remy?" Rosa asked doubtfully.

"He can be quite stealthy."

"He's sometimes quiet?" Servius asked.

"Did you just make a joke?" Layla asked.

"I'm a soldier, not a robot," Servius said with a smile.

"You sure you're not both?" Rosa asked.

"You were a lot less chatty when you were the umbra," Servius said. "I remember those times fondly."

Rosa laughed.

"Where's Gyda?" Layla asked. "Still ignoring me?"

"Yes," a woman spoke from outside the car.

Layla turned to say something to Gyda, but she'd already disappeared. "Damn it, Gyda."

"She thinks you're becoming a monster," Rosa said. "She believed the same of me. You won't go crazy and murder everyone if you accept the drenik, but Gyda will glare at you a lot. Difficult choice."

"It's easy to mock," Servius said.

"Yes, it is," Rosa replied. "That's why I do it."

"The drenik murdered her family, friends, and her entire village," Servius reminded everyone. "It can't be easy for Gyda to have remained for so long as a spirit, having to deal with the drenik being so close all the time."

Layla knew that Gyda's transformation into an umbra had been difficult, and she had never properly dealt with what had happened to her, preferring to remain judgmental and aloof from those who had taken the scroll after her death. She had also been the first spirit and had spent the last several thousand years telling everyone else that she knew best. Even when it was clear she didn't.

"Stop arguing," Layla said. "It gives me a headache."

"Your ability to heal will get rid of that quickly," Servius said.

Layla rested her forehead against the steering wheel and wondered if it was possible to have some of the spirits gagged. It was a beautiful thought.

"I heard that," Servius said.

Layla sighed. There were no secrets between the umbra and the spirits in the scroll. While both could dig around in the memories of the other, Layla and the spirits had agreed that it was less invasive to ask questions. Sometimes the information was taken without thought, but for the most part their agreement worked. However, all current thoughts were open between spirits and umbra. Layla thought of as many rude words as she could in as short a time as possible.

Rosa laughed.

"Very mature," Servius said.

Layla looked back at the Roman and smiled. "I thought so."

Servius tried to mask a grin before vanishing from sight.

"Are you feeling better now?" Rosa asked.

Layla nodded. "A little, thank you."

"Can I ask something important?"

Layla knew what was coming, but waved for Rosa to continue anyway.

"How are you sleeping?"

"Fine," she lied.

"I know when you're lying. And not because I live in your head, but because I know you."

"Okay, mostly fine. I still have the occasional nightmare, but I completed my counseling and I'm in a good place. When I first became an umbra I was worried that Terhal's presence was going to corrupt me, but in all honesty she was helpful. I was scared she'd lead me down a path to make me like my father, to murder and torture without remorse. And then when I did kill someone . . ."

"We're at war. Sometimes that means you have to take a life to save others."

Layla nodded. "I know. He was butchering people. He was hunting and slaughtering them, and he wasn't going to stop. He wasn't going to get better. He'd been turned into a werewolf, but he chose to behave like a monster. And so I killed him. It's been sixteen months, and I've killed more during that time. Always in battle; always because it was them or me, or my friends. Or for someone else who didn't deserve to die."

9

"But the werewolf was different."

Layla nodded, remembering when she'd refused to kill him at first, refused to take a life. The werewolf had escaped and killed three more innocents before she'd caught him again. Three lives she could have saved if she hadn't hesitated. She dreamed about them more than she did of her father. She dreamed about her own failure. "I took his life because there was no one else to do it. I had to make a choice, and it wasn't an easy one. But I dealt with it: I'm not him. I see that. I understand that. Nevertheless, somewhere inside of me, I still wonder if I'm going down a road that I can't turn back from. And that scares me."

"I've killed countless people," Rosa said. "I don't even remember their names. Not all of them, anyway. I remember those who died because I wasn't quick enough to save them, and I remember those who died because I didn't do the right thing. Those ones lay heavy on your soul, as they should. They show us that we need to do better. That we have to constantly strive to be better."

"At killing people," Layla said.

"Sometimes, yes. The others you killed, you don't think about them. You don't dream about them."

Layla stared out of the car window, looking into the distance as she spoke. "You probably already know, but I was in a firefight about a year ago. Thirty men and women were shooting assault rifles at the six of us. I killed two of them, because I was unwilling to let the bastards hurt my friends: people like Tommy, Diana, Remy, and Chloe. They've killed for the cause, too. I think Terhal helps my mind deal with what I need to do. I think she allows me to, if not outright accept, at least digest the actions I've had to take to keep my friends and innocent people alive.

"We are at war with Avalon. With Arthur and anyone who would crush those who dare oppose them. It's a war with no end in sight, and I'm a criminal to those people. The LOA want us found and arrested. Or killed. I doubt they care much one way or the other. It feels like everything has been flipped around since Arthur declared open season on his enemies. Since he woke up, took charge of Avalon, and began massacring anyone who opposed him. How many thousands died in those early days? How many humans and non-humans alike?

"I doubt I've killed for the last time. But I don't want to reach the point where I kill and feel nothing for it. Taking a life should mean something. I'm only twenty-three and I've become a soldier in a war I didn't want any part of. One that I never asked to be a part of, but a war I will fight to the bitter end to keep people safe. Arthur brought this fight into our lives, and we will end it."

Rosa stared at Layla for several seconds. "You were a bit all over the place there. You feel better?"

Layla nodded. "If I'm right, and Terhal is helping me deal with the other lives I've taken, that's probably for the best. I don't have the luxury of freezing or second-guessing myself. These people aren't human, and they will destroy or take whatever they want. It's our job to stop them. Like I said, a lot has happened in the last two years."

"You know you can talk to me, right? I mean, I know you do, but about anything."

Layla smiled. "I know. And I'm happy to talk to you, but you chose to kill people for a living. I find that idea . . ."

"Abhorrent?"

"I was going to say alien."

"That too. I was trained from a young age to take life. That was my destiny. I was good at it. And I didn't mind doing it. At least not until I actually sat down and thought about it, but by then I was in far too deep and had already become an umbra. I hadn't completely grasped what my life was going to change into once I'd agreed to kill for Queen and Country. Although I agree that it sounds like I had a choice.

"You're not like me, Layla. You're not cold. You're not capable of ignoring your emotions enough to kill a man in his bathtub while his family are eating in the room next door. You don't want to become that person, and you won't, I promise you. You're a good person. Better than

I ever was. Better than Servius, and better even than Gyda, who was never the goodie-two-shoes her judgmental arse likes to believe she was. She forgets we all know one another's sordid little life stories. You're a good person, Layla. But sometimes, good people have to do bad things. Just look at Chloe. She's a good person, but she's more than capable of pushing that aside to get the job done. You want to know the real difference between you and your father?"

"He was insane?"

"Apart from that."

Layla nodded.

"He enjoyed taking life. He loved it. I've the same memories of his interviews and information that you do." Rosa tapped the side of her head. "You know it's true. You know that you don't like hurting people, but that sometimes you have to do what you need to do. You're not him, Layla. Don't ever think you are."

"Do you regret anything?" Layla asked, wanting to move away from the topic of her father.

"Lots of things," Rosa said. "But mostly that I never got to go to all of these amazing places for anything other than to remove a stain on humanity; that I didn't get to enjoy my visits. I just did my job and left. Even when I stopped working for Queen Victoria and essentially vanished, I was always looking over my shoulder. I wish I'd have just taken some time to enjoy the world."

"Damn it, I thought you were going to say something frivolous, and then I was going to mock you. I can't mock you for sounding so heartfelt," Layla said with a smirk.

"Would you prefer that I said I wish I'd eaten more cake? Do you want to tell me what quip you had ready?"

"Not now. You ruined it with your words of bitter, bitter honesty."

Rosa laughed. "I'm clearly a monster."

Layla was about to say more when Diana's voice entered her ear. "I'm close to the mansion. I'll keep the irritating little thing on for now."

"You're not talking about Remy, are you?"

Diana chuckled as Chloe's voice started in Layla's ear. "You there?"

"What's up?" Layla asked, her attention immediately focused.

"Our contact is in the house. He's in a building near the one where we're being kept. I saw them dragging him outside. My cell has a small window that looks out onto the back garden. It's barred, but I heard them talking about him as some sort of traitor to his kind. I think they're going to kill him."

"You need help?"

"I'm not talking to anyone," Chloe said, followed by the muffled sounds of someone talking to her.

"Chloe, what's going on?"

Layla heard Chloe's heavy breathing, and a minute later her friend's earpiece went dead.

"Chloe's in trouble," Layla said.

"I heard," Diana said in her ear. "We're approaching the house now. Meet us as soon as you can."

Layla switched on the Mustang's ignition and sped away. She wasn't going to lose another friend. Not here, not now, and certainly not to people who would help abduct innocents for Nergal and his cronies to experiment on.

2

Layla stopped the Mustang on the side of the main road and began jogging through the darkness up the dirt path toward the mansion. Large gates barred her entrance to the property, and the white stone wall that surrounded it was at least fifteen feet high and topped with razor wire. She needed to find another way inside. Or fight her way through her enemies inside. She wasn't sure she could do that and get people out alive, so she looked to the side of the building to try to find a way around it.

The pathway was difficult to spot at first, and Layla only discovered it after pushing aside several thin branches, which gave way and tore down some of the overgrown vines that covered it.

Layla ducked under the remaining branches and followed the trail around to the side of the mansion. She glanced back through the thick deterrent of thorny bushes that separated her from the main road where she'd parked the car. There was no way anyone could get straight through it without a machete. Either the estate had become the creepiest place on Earth by sheer accident, or someone had purposefully made sure it looked that way.

The path turned into a slope, and Layla was careful not to slip on the muddy ground. By the time she reached the bottom, the skies had begun to open and rain quickly slicked the ground around her.

"Guess I'm not getting out that way without some luck," she said to herself, removing a hairband from her pocket and tying up her long hair in a ponytail. When she'd first gained her abilities as an umbra, Layla's hair had been dark blue, but once she'd finally come to accept what she'd become, she decided to change it slightly, so her hair was now dark blue on top and lighter blue the further down it went, ending in a more aqua color.

"We'll just have to use the front door then," Diana said as she stepped out of the undergrowth, the razor-sharp claws on her fingers retracting. Some people were lucky enough that they came with their own set of machetes.

Layla sighed with relief. Diana was over six feet tall, with olive skin and dark hair. She was a warrior through and through and had spent the last two years training Layla to fight and defend herself. Their friend Harry once suggested that she would make a great Wonder Woman, which was fitting since Diana had once been considered the goddess of the hunt, the moon, and nature by the Romans.

"Where's Remy?" Layla asked when it was apparent that Diana was alone.

"He went around the other side of the building. Don't worry, if he'd been captured the building would be on fire. There would be screams, and panic; generally, he's a liability who shouldn't be allowed out."

Layla smiled. That sounded par for the course where Remy was concerned.

"Chloe still in there?" Diana asked. "I thought about just going through the wall, but there's no telling who, or what, is waiting for us. This forest does not make for easy navigation in human form. Nor does the fact that we're pretty close to a swamp. The mansion's grounds begin fairly close to the water, so we're going to have to figure out a way to get through it if we want to get around to the rear of the grounds."

Layla sighed. "This was meant to be an easy mission: track the spirit scrolls and get them out of circulation. Then we find kidnapped people, and who knows what else. It's turning shitty, just like everything else Nergal has his grubby fingers in."

"Let's shut this all down then," Diana said.

"I'm glad you're here," Layla told her.

"Me too. You know Chloe is good, though, right? There's no way she's anything more than mildly irritated at the moment."

Layla nodded, despite her uncertainty. "Even so, we can't let her have all the fun."

"Oh, heavens no," Diana agreed. "That's just rude."

Despite their jovial tones, it was obvious that Layla and Diana were concerned for Chloe, and they were soon on their way again, moving further and further around the property and finding that it bordered more and more swampland dense with cypress trees.

"What's that?" Layla asked as they turned a corner and found the remains of what appeared to be an old hut. The door was no longer attached, and most of the front wall looked as though it might collapse at any moment.

Diana walked over to a hole in the wall and looked in. "Shit."

Before Layla could ask what was wrong, Diana tore huge chunks out of the wood, tossing them aside and ignoring the falling roof as it landed all around her.

Layla stepped back and let Diana work. It was easier than trying to interfere and getting hit with flying pieces of wood.

A few seconds later, the front wall of the hut, along with the roof, was all but demolished, revealing a blue Ford SUV.

"That looks new," Layla said.

Diana stepped over a pile of debris and peered into the Ford's rear window. "Looks new inside, too. There are rucksacks in here." Diana's fingernails grew several inches and became razor sharp. She tapped them against the glass of the rear window, which behaved as though it had been hit with a safety hammer. Diana reached in and pulled out one of the rucksacks, throwing it to Layla.

Layla emptied the contents onto the ground and found several forms of identification for a young woman by the name of Samantha Daze. "She's nineteen," Layla said.

Diana joined her with four more bags, dumping their contents beside Layla. "Five kids out driving. Looks like these people grabbed them. Wasn't long ago, either. There are tire tracks leading away from the hut. I think the hut was staged to look decrepit. Looks like someone didn't expect visitors here. Maybe they stashed the vehicle until they could dispose of it?"

"Why not put it in the compound?"

Diana shrugged. "Maybe this was done not long ago, and there are police out looking for the occupants. If it's on the land and law enforcement or snooping people turn up, it could jeopardize whatever is happening here."

"You think the occupants of the SUV are the captives Chloe mentioned?"

"I hope so," Diana said.

"It's a big risk to just take people from the road."

"Maybe five lost kids were too good an opportunity to pass up. They come to the house, ask for directions, and before they know it, they're permanent residents of the place."

Layla stared at the smiling face of Samantha Daze; her big blue eyes and blonde hair, the easy-going expression she wore, the fact that she had her whole life before her. Layla was only a few years older than Samantha, but it felt like there was a lifetime between them. "We need to get in there," she said without looking up from the girl's picture.

"There has to be a back way in," Diana said. "The car tracks go through that path over there." Diana sniffed the air. "No one has been this way for a few days, maybe longer. It's rained since then, too. Difficult for me to pick up scents."

"Follow the trail it is then," Layla said, getting back to her feet and pocketing the I.D. She was going to ask the smugglers where the young people were, and if she didn't like their answers, then she was going to do everything in her power to find them. Layla wasn't sure what else she was going to do if she didn't get answers she liked.

The pair continued to follow the increasingly inhospitable path around the mansion until it became more swamp than dry land. Large trees grew out of the water, alongside damaged and broken stumps that jutted out from the surface of the swamp, as if coming up for breath. Green ferns—overgrown and wild—spilled over the banks of land. It was impossible to know what lay just beneath the surface of the murky water.

"You think there are alligators in there?" Layla asked. "Because I'd rather not get eaten today."

Diana pointed across the swamp to a small jetty. "That's where we need to be. It looks like it leads into a boathouse at the rear of the property."

"Why not use this place to drop off any illicit cargo?"

"My guess is that it's too dangerous to get it from the sea to here." Diana picked up a fist-sized rock and hurled it into the swamp. "No alligators," she said after a few seconds of watching the water ripple.

"No alligators in that spot," Layla said. "Lots of other spots."

"They're not like crocs," Diana said. "Not as aggressive."

"Doesn't mean they won't try to eat us if we go swimming with them."

Diana picked up another rock and threw it into a separate part of the swamp. Yet again, nothing stirred. "It's fifty feet to the jetty. Do you have a better idea?"

Layla reached out with her power, hoping to find something useful. Layla's umbra ability allowed her to manipulate metal. She could melt it, change its shape, move it around, and one of the other tricks she'd learned over the last few years was the ability to sense large enough amounts of it from a distance. She focused her efforts around the jetty and the small building beside it and got a hit of metal almost immediately.

"There's a boat in there," she said, pointing to the boathouse. "Not a big boat—it's only large enough for two or three people—but it's better than swimming."

"You think you can pull it over here?"

Layla reached out again, this time wrapping her power around the metal in the boat, and immediately began to drag it out from where it was moored. But after a few feet, the boat stopped moving. Layla concentrated as she moved her power to try to find the source of the resistance. If there was a rope attached, then it would mean swimming was their best option, but as she searched she discovered the metal chain that moored the boat.

With a quick flare of power, Layla tore the boat free and felt the surge of movement as she navigated the small vessel out of the hut and into the swamp. It wasn't easy to do when she couldn't see the boat, and it took a lot of physical effort, but soon it became visible and easier to manipulate.

"Nice going," Diana said when the boat had reached the shore and she climbed in.

"Thanks," Layla said, also stepping in and sitting down, glad to take a breather.

The boat's metal hull was painted white. It had an outboard motor and two wooden benches and that was it. It was only about eight feet long, and Layla was almost certain that it would be of zero help if the waters became choppy, but using the two wooden paddles also resting inside, it was good enough for a short voyage.

About halfway across the swamp, the boat was hit by something that quickly swam away, leaving the wake of a large tail as it vanished into the gloomy water. Layla continued to paddle without a word.

"Okay," Diana said. "You were right."

"I didn't say anything."

"But you're thinking it."

They reached the jetty and climbed out, using a piece of rope to tie up the boat.

The pair entered the small hut, which was dark and had an unpleasant smell of stale water. The two windows had been boarded up, and its only light came in through the missing wall, which also meant that the place was covered in leaves and rotting vegetation.

Diana reached the door inside the hut and crouched in front of it, pushing it slowly open with one hand while peering into whatever lay beyond. She pointed to Layla and then pointed outside, and Layla went through the open door, keeping low and moving quickly until she reached a large nearby tree. She stayed behind it as Diana followed the same route.

"The mansion is a few hundred feet up that slope," Layla said.

"I see other buildings up there. I can smell people too, at least three. Two of them are in that long building. Looks like it used to be a guest house, or something. The other one is walking around to the far left of the main building—he's smoking an incredibly awful cigarette."

"You smell anyone else?"

Diana sniffed. "No, I can only smell the two in the long building because they just went inside. There's too much interfering with my nose out here. A lot of crap in the air."

"We clear out the buildings as we go?"

"That's the plan."

"I'll take the guy on his own near the hut over there. You take the two in the guest house?" said Layla.

"Sounds like a plan. Be careful." Diana took off in a crouched sprint, moving from tree to tree until she was quickly out of sight. Layla couldn't run anywhere near as quickly, but she was still faster than any human, and moved through the trees with speed and grace until she reached the final one before a small hut. It sat at the side of the huge garden at the rear of the mansion, halfway between the tree line and the guesthouse. The overgrown vegetation at the end of the garden allowed them to move toward their destinations without being spotted.

Layla faced the rear of the hut, and occasionally she saw the cigarette smoke from the guard who stood outside it. The hut itself was covered in moss and vines, which looked as though they were keeping it from falling down.

She looked across the expansive yard and saw Diana creep around to the rear of the guest house. Layla took that as her cue and slowly moved to the side of the hut; the smell of cigarette smoke was evident even to her human level sense of smell.

She glanced around the corner of the small hut and saw the guard stood outside the front of it. He was just under six feet tall and wore jeans and a white t-shirt. A rifle was slung over his left shoulder, and a leather holster with a pistol of some kind sat on his hip. He leaned against a white wooden post, close to a dark brown door. He faced away from Layla and blew smoke up into the air.

Layla crept around the hut and, the moment she was close enough, launched herself at the guard, wrapping her arms around his neck and tightening her grip as she leaned back, taking them both to the ground. With her enhanced strength, it was only seconds until the man passed out. She grabbed hold of his rifle and dropped it by the wall of the small building, along with the pistol a few seconds later. Layla then grabbed the man by his lapel and dragged him over to the hut, depositing his unconscious body out of sight.

Layla walked back to the door, just as it opened and a heavy-set man stepped outside, his shotgun aimed at Layla.

Layla considered her options and was about to take control of the metal gun when a second man followed him into the garden. This one was skinny, with a large beard and long, mousy hair. It looked like he hadn't washed in a considerable amount of time and he smelled of stale cigarette smoke. He held a baseball bat.

"We got us a visitor," the bat-wielding man said.

"You here for some fun, girl?" the larger man asked, his voice a deep baritone.

Both men sniggered.

Layla reached for metal in the shotgun, but before she could do anything she caught a blur of movement in the corner of her eye and a small, red, fox-like creature leapt at the larger of the two men. The man's eyes widened as the sword the fox-man carried opened his throat; a sword that was then quickly buried in the chest of the skinny man. Both were on the ground and dead in seconds.

The fox-man stood up to his full three-and-a-half-foot height and cleaned his two specially designed, basket-hilted swords on the skinny man's clothes, removing the blood from the blades before returning them to the sheaths he wore on his back.

"I could have dealt with them, Remy," Layla said, happy to see her friend.

"I know. But I've been watching these assholes for a few hours and wanted to kill them the first chance I got. Tell you what, the next cockwomble we come across is all yours."

Layla chuckled despite herself.

Remy had once been human, although that part of his life had ended when he crossed a coven of witches who decided to turn him into a fox and hand him over to a hunt. As it turned out, their spell hadn't quite worked, and Remy had ended up with a dozen witch souls inside his new hybrid form.

"I dealt with the others. How many more?" Diana asked as she joined the pair.

"Eight inside, that I could see. Chloe is in the basement with other captives. Two guards." Remy paused. "It's not great in there. I came close to just slaughtering as many of the bastards as I could before you arrived. Had to take a breather. They drug those they kidnap. And some are taken to the bedrooms upstairs."

Layla didn't want to hear any more.

"They abuse them?" Diana asked, her voice hard.

"If you mean experimenting or sexual, I don't know," Remy said. "Only noticed the state of them. I saw the aftermath of one guy taking a hell of a kicking, so it's not making a huge leap to imagine none of the prisoners here are treated well. He's in the room to the north. He needs medical attention."

"I'll go get Chloe," Layla said.

"We'll deal with the rest," Remy said, drawing one of his swords. "I removed the guard from the rear doors just before I spotted you. These bastards are about to learn how pissed off a fox can get."

Layla picked up the pistol she'd taken from the unconscious man and emptied it of bullets, throwing the parts in opposite directions. She then picked up the rifle and used her ability to tear it in half.

"Still don't like guns?" Remy asked.

"I'm good without them," Layla said.

The group moved toward the mansion, where Diana opened the door, allowing Layla in to the main building first. Remy followed soon after, with Diana last, closing the door behind her.

"Basement is down there," Remy said, pointing to a set of stairs. "There must be a few rooms below, from the number of small ground level windows I saw around the mansion. Chloe is in the left one facing the house. Be careful. Like I said, I only saw two guards. Could be more."

Layla nodded and slowly descended the nearby staircase, feeling the dread inside her grow with every step. When she reached the bottom, she pushed open a door and stepped into a corridor.

The walls were made of large, gray, concrete slabs, and the floor of pure stone in a variety of dingy colors. The hollow structure made Layla concerned about causing echoes as she walked to the first junction and looked around the corner. There were two doors off the corridor, and a sizable open room at the end. She considered taking off her boots, but figured she'd spend more time doing that than just creeping slowly along.

Layla stopped at the first door and tried the handle. It opened with ease, revealing nothing more than a supply cupboard. The door on the opposite side of the corridor contained the same thing: food, water, cleaning supplies, and a host of bedding. They'd certainly maintained a good stock, and Layla wondered just how many people had been through this mansion on their way to Nergal's clutches.

She pushed the thought aside and left the small room, moving toward the end of the corridor. The open room beyond contained several washing machines and a few sinks. Clothes had been hung up in one corner, dripping water into a drain.

Taking a few steps into the room, Layla realized that it was much larger than she'd thought. There was a set of double doors at its far end, behind a large pillar that had obscured them from the entrance.

Layla crossed the area and pushed the doors open, revealing a set of dimly lit stairs. She immediately heard voices somewhere in the distance, although they were muffled. When she reached the bottom step, she looked around the corner and saw eight cells, each one with a barred metal door. The cells faced one another across a large space. Through an open door at the end of the room, Layla could hear two guards talking about the previous night's baseball game at a volume that suggested they'd been drinking. She ignored them and crept away from the staircase, looking into each cell as she went. Of the first six she passed, most were empty, but two had occupants—one male and one female—both of whom appeared to be asleep. Neither of them was Chloe. Layla moved to the other side of the room, closer to one set of cells and out of view of the doorway, and spotted Chloe in the cell closest to the guards. She sat on a bed, looking out through the bars as Layla approached.

Chloe smiled, and Layla held a finger to her lips. She tapped the bars. Tearing them apart wouldn't be a problem, but she had a better idea. She held up a finger to communicate that she'd be back in a moment and then walked into the center of the room, between the two rows of cells. And she whistled.

The two men looked out of the doorway in a state of confusion.

"Hey, I'm a bit lost," Layla said. "Wondered if there's a toilet around here? Oh wait, you guys would call it a bathroom. I still get confused with the English versus American thing. Which is weird, as I was born in New York."

Both men staggered toward her, batons in their hands.

"No guns?" Layla asked with a slight shrug. "I sort of expected guns."

"We don't need guns," the closest of the two men said. "Not for a little thing like you."

Layla nodded, her expression deadly serious. "You should have brought guns."

There were several loud creaks, and the two guards looked slightly worried as Layla stretched out her power to grip the bars of several of the cells.

"Really should have brought guns," she repeated, and tore the bars from the closest two cells free with a horrific noise. Pieces of stone and mortar filled the air as Layla threw the metal rods at the guards with enough force to send the men reeling. Moving her hands, Layla then wrapped the steel bars around them until they were unable to move.

"How very X-Men of you," Chloe said with a slight laugh.

"I've been wanting to try that since Harry showed me those films," Layla told her. She went over to the guards and melted part of another liberated bar in front of them. She wrapped the metal around her fist in a gauntlet and punched both men in the face hard enough to break bone and knock them out. Like Rosa had said, Layla took no enjoyment from hurting the two guards. It just needed to be done. She turned back to Chloe and concentrated on the bars of her friend's cell, tearing out enough of them to free her.

"You okay?" Chloe asked.

Layla nodded, leaning against the wall and taking a few deep breaths. "I think I'm meant to ask you that. Tearing those bars from solid stone took a lot out of me. That was considerably more metal than I'm used to throwing around in such a short time. Usually, I can only manipulate the same amount as me, size-wise."

The pair found the keys to the other cells and unlocked the two that were occupied. The man and woman within were beaten, dehydrated, and scared, but were otherwise okay. They were able to walk under their own power, although Layla wouldn't want them around to help out in a fight.

"So, what happens now?" Chloe asked, raising her wrist to show the sorcerer's band.

"Now we find Diana and Remy and see how much carnage they've caused."

3

With the sorcerer's band on her wrist, Chloe was unable to heal the injuries she'd sustained at the hands of her captors. She said she didn't think that any were serious, but to Layla it looked like she'd been hit hard a few times.

"Someone knew I was here," Chloe said as they reached the top of the basement stairs. The two injured men followed just behind them.

"Any idea who?"

Chloe shook her head. "I'd like to find them and make them see the error of their ways, though."

You and me both, Layla thought, and Rosa agreed inside her head.

Any fighting carried out by Diana and Remy had finished by the time Layla and Chloe found them in the main living room. Both sat on chairs, and several people lay around them in various states of consciousness. All had their hands tied behind their backs with plastic cable ties.

Layla helped Chloe sit on one of the couches and motioned for the man and woman to get comfortable.

"We found a drawer full of them," Remy said, pointing to the ties, as if aware of what Layla was thinking.

"There were nine of them," Diana said, getting to her feet. "We haven't searched the top floor bedrooms yet, but according to our friend in the next room, this is everyone involved. We wanted to make sure that none of these assholes could do anything to jeopardize the rest of the captives."

"You believe him?" Chloe asked.

Diana nodded. "He's a sorcerer. Low-level stuff. Turned out he had a bunch of sorcerer's bands just hanging around. Most of them were for umbras, but we found a few that worked for other species. He's been quite compliant since we switched his magic off."

"I'm going to the bedrooms," Layla said. "Do we know how many captives are up there?"

"He said nine. Three in each room. All out of their minds on whatever cocktail of shite these people have fed them."

Layla prepared herself for the worst and set off to find the survivors of Nergal's influence.

"You still want to kill him, don't you?" Rosa said as Layla reached the halfway point on the large staircase.

"Nergal? He killed my mom."

"Not exactly an answer."

"Would you want to kill him?"

"I'd flay the skin from his bones. But I'm not you."

Layla stopped walking. "Yes, I want him dead. But I'll settle for his punishment. How many lives has that man ruined? How many families has he torn apart? He deserves to go before an Avalon court and be tried and convicted. But seeing how Avalon is currently Nergal's biggest fan, I'm guessing that's not going to happen for a considerable amount of time."

Layla reached the top of the stairs and stepped into the hallway. To her left was a window overlooking the front of the mansion, and to her right a corridor that snaked around the first floor. Several doors were set along one side of the wall only a few feet apart, and she opened them as she went, finding the first two only contained beds, a TV, several fans, and some chests of drawers.

"The guards stayed here," Layla whispered, picking up a shotgun that rested against one of two single beds. She emptied its shells onto the mattress before turning its metal into a molten puddle. She left the room and crept along cautiously as she turned the first corner of the hallway, in case she met another kidnapper waiting to strike.

The third door wore a macabre wreath made from the bones of small birds. "That is some Silent Hill level shit," Chloe said as she turned the corner and stood beside Layla.

"How are you feeling?" Layla asked.

Chloe raised her wrist. "We found a key for my sorcerer's band. I healed up fairly fast after that. Thought you could use a hand."

"Thanks." Layla opened the door and the smell of urine and sweat greeted her. There were several filthy mattresses in the room, placed on the ground next to one another with barely enough space between them to see the linoleum-covered floor. Two men and a woman occupied three of the beds, and they appeared to be sedated. None of the captives looked older than their mid-twenties, and all were disheveled and dirty.

Chloe and Layla checked each of them and found no evidence of needle marks or drug paraphernalia. And other than looking like they were on another planet, the young people didn't appear to have any obvious injuries.

"What were they given?" Layla asked.

"We need Diana or Remy up here—maybe their noses will help. It's as if they're in some sort of trance. It reminds me of those old films when they show opium dens where everyone is just stoned out of their gourd with not a care in the world. And now I know exactly what those dens smell like, and it's disgusting."

"Go get one of them. I'll check the next room," Layla said. She walked around another bend in the hallway and saw a set of stairs at its far end, next to one final door. Like the previous one, it wore a wreath of small animal bones, and Layla braced herself before opening it. She discovered the same set up. Except this room held a man and two women, all in the same condition as the others.

Layla checked each of the captives and, like before, found no evidence of drug use. She left the room and ascended the stairs to a landing above, which held two doors. Neither had anything on them, but she opened the first with a sense of trepidation about how much more awful things could possibly get. The curtains in the room had been drawn, keeping out the last rays of sunlight, but Layla could easily make out the double bed and the single occupant upon it.

She flicked on the light and forced herself not to turn away. A young man, no older than those in the rooms downstairs, lay on the bed. He was unconscious and hooked up to various medical machines. A heart monitor beeped at regular intervals and Layla spotted a catheter bag, and a drip one that fed him nutrients. A third bag appeared to collect the man's blood, and after a few seconds there was a slight noise as blood ran out of the tube hooked up to the man's arm and into the bag.

"What the hell is going on?" Layla said.

She left the patient's room and opened the only other door on the landing. A huge four-poster bed sat in the center of the bedroom. Black and red velvet drapes hung all around it, blocking the bed from Layla's view. The window drapes were made of the same material. A dressing table next to the window was covered in gold leaf, and its mirror sparkled with various stones. The chair in front of it matched the gold theme.

"Money doesn't buy taste," Layla said, looking around at the gaudy furniture, variety of stuffed animals, and, on one wall, several muskets.

A noise from the bed immediately grabbed Layla's attention. "You can come out, or I can come get you, but I'm certain you won't like the latter."

A slender hand moved one of the drapes aside, revealing three women lying on the bed. All wore white negligees that did little to cover them and black high-heeled shoes.

"What the hell is going on?" Layla asked.

"Where's Alfred?" one of the women asked, sounding slightly worried.

"He's currently downstairs, under arrest, as is everyone who works for him. Who are you?"

"I'm Amber," said one of the women. She had long, blonde hair, in contrast to the two dark-haired women with her. "This is Daisy and Veronica."

"You're going to have to explain a bit more than that," Layla said.

"We were given an option," Veronica said. "We either stay in here, or we get to go downstairs with the others."

A cold rage built up inside Layla's chest. "Where are you from?"

"Daisy and I are from Texas," Veronica said.

"I'm from New Orleans," Amber said.

"How long have you been here?"

Daisy burst into tears and Veronica comforted her, exposing the bruises on her back.

"Six months," Amber said. "Daisy and Veronica arrived a month ago. We were put in with the others at first, but, like I said, Alfred gave some of the women a choice: join him or stay there. There were others when I was brought here, but . . ." Amber closed her eyes and shook her head sadly.

"He has two guns," Daisy said. "Two revolvers. Old things. He uses them to play Russian roulette with us."

Layla followed Daisy's gaze and spotted the twin revolvers on top of the chest of drawers next to the open bathroom door.

"They're Colt Army Model 1860," Veronica said, with anger etched on her face. "My daddy has one."

Layla picked up the revolvers and found them empty of bullets. She searched the drawers and soon found some and began loading the guns with purpose.

"Can you all move?" Layla asked the three women. They nodded. "Right, let's get you out of here. Do you know what they're doing to the man next door?"

"He's an umbra," Veronica said. "That's what Alfred called him. Said he secretes the drug they use to keep us docile, so that we can be easily handed over to someone else."

"Do you know who?" Layla asked.

"Negal, Nergan? Something like that," Daisy said.

"Nergal?" Layla suggested.

Veronica nodded. "That's the one. They drug them before driving them away. Alfred brags about it, about sending scrolls on from here so that they can create more of those . . . umbra. Is it true that they get you to bleed on them, and then you merge with a demon?"

"Not exactly. Based on the fact that you don't know what they are, I assume none of you have been given a scroll?" Layla asked, suddenly concerned that she hadn't checked before. She would need to inspect the other captives, although the chance that any of them had been given a scroll was low, considering she hadn't seen anyone wearing a sorcerer's band, and she doubted that they'd just allow a powered-up umbra prisoner to sit around without one.

All three women shook their heads.

"Alfred said he wouldn't let us," Amber said.

"I'm sorry this happened to you," Layla said, unsure of what else to say. She wanted to hurt Alfred and anyone else who was involved.

"You going to kill him?" Daisy asked. "I want you to kill him."

"He'll die one way or another," Layla assured her. She wanted to tell the young women it would be okay, that they would be okay, but she didn't believe it. She couldn't bring herself to spout some ridiculous, shallow words after what they'd gone through. All three of them had hardened themselves and done what they'd had to do to survive. Eventually that hurt would surface, and Layla could only hope that they were able to deal with it.

"I'm going to take you down to the ground floor," Layla said. "There's a dining room no one is using. You won't have to see Alfred or his people ever again."

"Is he hurt?" Daisy asked.

"Yes. I don't know how badly—the woman who stopped him wasn't gentle."

"Good," Daisy said, gripping Veronica and Amber's hands as they left the room.

Layla looked down at the revolvers and then back at the room. She wanted to set it on fire, but there might be things in it they needed, information on where the captives were taken. The notion of Chloe being brought up to the room filled her with a rage that threatened to consume her.

"He deserves to die," Terhal said from behind her.

"Not now," Layla told the drenik without turning around.

"He deserves pain and suffering. Those women deserve vengeance."

"I'm not disagreeing with you, I just don't want to talk about it." Layla turned to see Terhal.

Drenik could alter their gender when they felt like it, but Terhal preferred to remain in female form. Her species were as close to demonic appearance as it was possible to get. Terhal's light-red skin was tight over her skull, and a pulsing orange ridge circled her head. It gave the impression that she wore a crown of fire. The drenik's eyes were large, and orange-and-red flames spilled out of her eye sockets. She had no nose, just a dark hole, and there was no skin or muscle around her mouth, allowing you to see her jawbone.

Terhal's black tongue licked her dozens of shark-like teeth. Just below her chin, two-foot-long silver tendrils occasionally pulsed red and orange. She wore a black business suit, and her two black, tattered wings were currently folded away.

When Layla had first seen Terhal, it had been a frightening experience, but over time she'd come to accept the drenik, and eventually the pair had entered into something that was, if not a friendship, then an understanding. The drenik were a species that valued the survival of the fittest over any other attribute. They did what needed to be done, no matter how awful it might seem to outsiders. When someone wronged Layla, or those she cared about, Terhal's first response was usually a desire to tear out their throat and show them who's in charge.

"I could take over and flay him for you?" Terhal said with a smile.

"No." Layla declined her offer. Both times she'd let Terhal take control had resulted in the deaths of their enemies, and both times Layla had been dismayed to see how much the drenik reveled in the chaos and destruction.

"Just an offer," Terhal said. "The part of your mind that is mine has become a pleasant home. I know it's not real there, but it's nice, and I can satisfy my need to hunt and kill. You should allow the women who were wronged to do as they like with Alfred. Drenik would never subjugate another of our kind in this manner. It's unnecessarily cruel."

"Again, not disagreeing."

"You're still holding those revolvers. Planning on using one of them?"

"I'm considering forcing him to play my own version of Russian roulette." Anger burned inside Layla and she fought it down; now was not the time to allow her own desire for vengeance to win out.

Terhal laughed. "That is an excellent idea."

"There's an umbra next door. They're using his blood to drug these people."

"Every umbra's power is different, and not all of your kind are powerful enough to resist people like this Alfred."

"Why didn't the man's drenik take control? I thought your kind did that if your human host was unable to defend itself."

"Pumping enough drugs into your body would stop me from doing anything. Also, you're assuming he got to bond with his drenik. They could have made him an umbra, and once they realized what his power was, drugged him and stuck him in there. The drenik wouldn't have had time to gain a foothold, although it's probably in there screaming to get out."

"Either way, it sounds horrific. That man has been tortured so that Nergal can claim his guinea pigs and these people can stay in Nergal's pocket. Frankly, this whole place should be burned to the ground and salt poured on the ashes."

Terhal's expression brightened.

"No, I'm not going to do that," Layla said.

Terhal vanished, and Layla headed off after the three prisoners, making sure they found their way downstairs okay. She helped the young women into the empty dining room and told them that someone would come to talk to them soon, and that shortly afterwards they'd be taken as far away from the mansion and the people inside it as possible.

Layla found Diana outside the room, waiting for her. "They okay?"

"No," Layla said. "Not even slightly."

"You okay?"

Layla shook her head.

"Yeah, well it's about to get much worse. If that's possible."

Layla's heart felt suddenly heavy. "How?"

"Remy's outside. I'll stay here."

Layla walked past the main living area where the occupants of the house remained tied up on the floor, along with the guards who had been brought up from the basement. She stepped out into the garden at the rear of the property, and immediately wished that the aircon could be switched on outside, too.

35

Remy stood at the center of the large lawn, sniffing loudly, with Chloe beside him. Every time he pointed to the ground, she planted a piece of metal pipe. Many pipes already sprouted from the grass.

"What did you find?" Layla asked.

"Bodies. Lots of bodies," Remy said. "Over two dozen. I wouldn't want to start digging through the earth to count them. We contacted Tommy and he said some people would be on their way in the next hour or so. Until then, I'm just trying to figure out roughly how many people these assholes have murdered."

Layla cursed under her breath.

"We also found our contact," Chloe said. "He was in one of the ground floor rooms next to the front door. We untied him, removed the sorcerer's band, and left him where he was. He'll live, but he's hurt."

"I'll go talk to him. I get the impression that they knew we were coming, Chloe."

Chloe nodded. "Yep. They knew we were looking for the scrolls, and they knew that we were here. I think they were looking for anyone out of the ordinary, a spy, and I fit the bill. We have a leak somewhere. We were just lucky they didn't have time to prepare better."

"One more blasted thing after another." Layla re-entered the house, glad for the air conditioning that someone had cranked up as high as possible. She found the room Chloe had spoken about. Their contact was a small, thin man, with a large beard and long hair, both of which were brown and speckled with gray.

"Hi," the man said with a Southern States accent, although Layla couldn't have placed it any closer than that.

"I'm Layla," she said as she entered the room.

The man rose from his chair and offered her his hand, which she took. "Joseph Lee," he said. "Thanks for getting me out of this situation."

"Did they hurt you?"

"Some. Looks like someone ratted me out. They came for me this morning. Brought me in here and gave me a beating. I didn't tell them anything, if that's what you're wondering."

"I'm not," Layla said honestly. "They also knew we were coming, though."

"You've got a leak."

Layla nodded. "One more problem in an endless stream of them."

Joseph smiled. "I've known Alfred for a long time. Served with him in the Confederate army." He pointed to the shelf on the wall behind him where an old black-and-white framed photo sat.

"The one of Jesse James?"

Joseph nodded. "Sorry, I just don't want you to think that we're all like Alfred. He changed during that war. We all did. But he never got over losing. Jesse was the same: he decided to punish the union by robbing them. Alfred decided to punish everyone because he felt he was owed something."

"You stayed with him?"

"Oh no. I hadn't seen Alfred in a century. Just happened that he found me and offered me a job. Said we'd be working for Nergal, bringing in spirit scrolls. Easy pay, easy job. I didn't care about Avalon politics. All those 'gods' born to the right species, at the right time, in the right place made no difference to me.

"We brought the scrolls in and sent them on their way for about four years, but I didn't know where they were being sent. It was all very secretive. And then about a year ago we started taking people, too. And that I had a problem with. It took me a long time to figure out who I needed to talk to about it. I couldn't leave those people here, that would just be awful, so I stayed and helped some escape when I could and stopped others from being assaulted when possible. Eventually, I managed to contact Tommy, who I'd met a century ago, and told him about what was happening. He asked me to stay here and report back."

"You were our contact all this time? How did Alfred ID Chloe as a spy?" Layla asked.

"He got a call," Joseph said. "No idea who from. But he got a call and immediately made sure she was secure. Sorry I can't be of more help."

"What about you? How'd you get caught?"

"When I knew your people were coming, I thought it best not to be in the line of fire. I told Alfred I was done with this, and he decided that quitting wasn't an option."

"What about the women Alfred took upstairs?"

"I tried," Joseph said, his eyes welling up. "Goddamn it, I tried. I got three of them out. In one go, about two months past. He caught them, had them killed. I could have intervened, could have gotten myself killed. But how would I have been able to save anyone else if I was dead? So, I sold a little bit more of my soul to the devil so that I could help save others. I heard the abuse, but I knew if I stopped it, we'd all die. Everyone held captive here would die, and this place would simply be set up somewhere else."

Layla placed a hand on Joseph's shoulder and squeezed. She knew about the type of things that had happened in the mansion all too well. "You were put in a difficult position."

"Doesn't help me sleep at night. Doesn't help the people who were taken. Doesn't help those women who were abused by Alfred. Nothing will ever help them. I want to stop this. All of this. I want it to end."

"It will. Stay here, rest, and heal. Tommy is sending some people. Do you know anything else that might help?"

"Nergal is planning something. More scrolls have come into port in recent months, and they all get shipped out fast. No idea where to—that's information that Alfred keeps to himself."

"So, I need to get Alfred to talk?" Layla asked.

"Won't be easy. He's not exactly someone who will give up information without a fight."

Layla smiled. "Some of the people here can be incredibly persuasive. We'll find out where those scrolls go before they end up in Nergal's dirty hands. Thank you for your help."

Joseph nodded. "It would be my pleasure to end Nergal, Alfred, and anyone else who helped put this horror show together."

4

Layla left Joseph alone and went to the room where Alfred was being held. It was opposite the dining room where the three conscious women were currently staying, and Layla immediately had an urge to take them as far away from Alfred as possible. A few walls were not enough separation.

Diana stood outside of Alfred's room, leaning against the wall with her arms crossed over her chest. "You here to kill him?" she asked, with no hint of humor in her voice.

"Not sure yet," Layla answered honestly. "I'm not convinced that killing him isn't being too kind."

Diana shrugged. "You talk to him and see for yourself. I managed four minutes before I had to leave or put him in traction. Remy managed a full thirty seconds."

"I'll try not to kill him," Layla promised.

"Good luck with that. I've been told we should have more people here within the hour. Sounds like they're making this place a priority. We still need to uncover where those scrolls are being sent."

"I'll see if I can get anything out of Alfred. Maybe the realization that he can talk to me, or talk to someone like Hades, will get him to cooperate."

"Rather you than me."

Layla grabbed the doorknob and took a deep breath before using it and stepping inside the dining room. There was a long wooden table at its center. Five of its six chairs were nowhere to be seen. Two glass-door cupboards along one wall revealed various pieces of crockery, and two Winchester rifles hung on the far wall with a plaque under them proclaiming their supposedly important owner. Opposite them, double doors overlooked the back garden.

Alfred sat on the only chair in the room, his hands cuffed behind his back. He might have been wearing a sorcerer's band, but even without his magic he was still dangerous. He wore black jeans, cowboy boots, and a white t-shirt that was now partially blood stained. He had long, light-brown hair that cascaded over his shoulders, and a short goatee. A scar cut across his cheek, ending just above his top lip.

"Did you model yourself on General Custer?" Layla asked. "Or did you just assume that his hair and beard never went out of style? Maybe you grew the goatee to hide the scar?"

"I look good," he said.

"You don't have a southern drawl. That's a surprise. I assume you've spent a lot of time trying to lose your accent so you don't get caught for one reason or another. I kinda like the southern lilt—it's sexy—so I'm glad someone like you doesn't get to ruin it for me."

"I'll be whatever you want me to be, darlin'," he said with a smirk and wink.

Layla repressed the need to gag. "Oh, don't do that. There's a fine line between charming and creepy, and you crossed that line at high speed some time ago."

Alfred's eyes narrowed. "What do you want?"

"I want to know where you send the spirit scrolls. I want to know where you were going to send those people, and then I want to know whether you'd like a jail cell with a view of the front yard or back."

"I ain't going to jail."

"Death or jail. It's not a great choice, but it's all you've got."

"You gonna kill me, little girl?"

Layla sighed. "I've never killed anyone handcuffed to a chair before, but you speak to me like that again, and we're going to test how many bones of yours I can break."

Alfred smiled. "I've killed many. Hundreds. Maybe more. I'm good at it. Good at a few things, as it turns out. Killin', that's just one of them."

"How many are buried in the garden?"

"Few dozen. Some were thrown into the swamp to let nature take its course. It's easier. But the girls, well, I needed them close to me. I needed to feel them between my toes as I walked around outside on crisp mornings. I needed to keep our connection. They were no longer of use to me in the physical world, but the spiritual one? Well, now, that's a whole different matter."

"You really like the sound of your own voice, don't you?" Layla leaned against the nearest wall. "Where do you send the people and scrolls?"

"To Nergal."

"And where is he?"

"Here and there. I'm not going to tell you anything. Not one of you has the balls to force the information out of me. Not the big woman, not you, and certainly not the sexy little kitty-cat I caught. Pretending to be a kidnap victim, that was very brave. I was going to find out how brave she really was when I got her upstairs."

Layla wanted to kill him, but she pushed the thought aside and sighed. "You're not hurting anyone. Not now, not ever again."

The door opened, and a young woman stepped inside the room. Her name was Mapiya, but everyone called her Sky. She had been born several centuries earlier to a Sioux Chief father and a European Missionary mother, but when both had been murdered, Sky had been adopted by a friend of her parents: Hades. Layla had only met the man a handful of times, but, along with his wife Persephone, Hades was one of the few people who made her a bit nervous.

Sky smiled at Layla. "The helicopter landed just up the road a short time ago. I'm not too late for the interrogation, am I?"

"No, darlin', you're just in time," Alfred said. "Interrogate away, bitch."

Layla punched him in the jaw, snapping his head to one side. "I don't like that word," she told him as he spat blood onto the floor.

"Nice punch. I see that Diana has been teaching you," Sky said with a slight chuckle. "You want to hit him again?"

"Can I?" Layla asked.

"We don't need him alive. I can drag the information out of his soul. Being a necromancer helps."

"Beatin' a defenseless man," Alfred said. "If you had any courage, you'd untie me and we'd settle this properly. I see you've found my guns. You dare come into a man's home and take his guns? You bitches have no idea what I want to do to you. But you could just go ask those other three. They'll give you lots of ideas." He winked.

Layla removed the two revolvers from her belt, placing both of them on the table. "You want those cuffs removed? Okay." She turned to Sky. "Can you get the key to the handcuffs?"

Sky smirked and left the room, returning a moment later with Diana, who unlocked Alfred's cuffs.

"Do you know what you're doing?" Diana asked Layla.

Layla nodded and retrieved the two revolvers. "Trust me."

"Always."

"If any of this piece of crap's prisoners here want to see this, let them. Bring out our prisoners whether they like it or not."

Layla opened the double doors to the garden, allowing in the breeze, and then motioned for Alfred to leave the room.

Alfred now eyed the three women with concern, but swaggered into the garden as if he were still king of his castle. "I buried the first one right here," Alfred proclaimed.

Chloe and Remy stopped walking around the garden and stared at Alfred. Chloe took a step forward, but Remy stopped her, shaking his head a little.

Layla saw the anger on Chloe's face and walked over to her. "Sorry, I didn't see you still out here."

"That's okay," Chloe said. "You think you can get any answers from him?"

"That's not why I brought him out here." Layla walked over to Alfred and tossed one of the revolvers on the grass by his feet. "Pick it up. You seem to think you're a cowboy. Let's see how good you are against an itsy-bitsy girl."

Alfred smiled and reached for his revolver, keeping one eye on Layla the whole time. He checked the bullets. "We drawing? Like it's high noon? You don't look much like Clint Eastwood."

"I'm going to give you a chance," Layla said. "You outdraw me, and I'll give you an hour's head start. You all agree to that, yes?"

Everyone nodded.

"What if you have silver bullets in that gun?" Alfred asked.

"This isn't to kill you. This is to make a point. A man like you only thinks of women as things to abuse. Things to control. You think you're invincible. That Nergal and his allies will swoop in and save you. They won't. You're going to get shot and bleed all over this lawn while I go inside and have a nice cold drink of lemonade."

Diana stepped outside of the house with several prisoners in tow, all forced to kneel and watch. Daisy, Veronica, and Amber joined her, but stood well away from Alfred's accomplices. Diana and Sky stood between the two groups.

"I don't have a holster," Alfred shouted.

Diana threw one in front of him, and a second on the ground in front of Layla, who put it on immediately. She holstered her revolver. "I want all of you to understand that this man is nothing," Layla said to Alfred's people. "I want you to understand that helping us to locate the people he kidnapped is a far better thing to do than believing that people like Alfred will ever get to you. You shouldn't be afraid of people like him."

"You ready, girl?" Alfred asked. "I get an hour's head start?"

Layla nodded. "One hour. And we will hunt you."

"You'll be bleeding all over the grass, so I might not bother running. Maybe just the sight of you in pain and agony will be enough to know that I won."

"Last chance," Layla said. "You want to just help us? You want to do something right for a change?"

"I want to shoot you."

Layla shrugged.

"You gonna count?" Alfred asked.

"Nope. Just gonna wait for you to—" Alfred went for his revolver, but Layla was quicker and drew hers smoothly, shooting him twice in the chest.

Alfred looked down at the red spreading across his t-shirt, dropped the gun, and slumped to his knees. Layla walked over and crouched in front of him. "If you ever touch, look at, or speak badly about any woman ever again, without their express permission, I will end you. Your bullets aren't silver, so you'll live, even with that sorcerer's band on. I just want you to know that the pain you're feeling is nothing compared to what I'll do to you if we ever cross paths again. You will answer any and all of our questions. Am I clear?"

Alfred didn't respond, so Layla shot him in the stomach, just above his groin. He screamed and collapsed on the grass. "Remember that pain," Layla said. "Remember what happened here, and what I could have done to you. Do you understand?"

Alfred nodded.

Layla held the revolver and watched as it twisted into a ball, the bullets dropping harmlessly onto the grass. She bumped fists with Sky as she walked past.

"Feel better?" Diana asked.

"Much," Layla said as she re-entered the house.

"You think they'll talk now?" Daisy said from behind Layla.

Layla turned toward the young woman, who stood in the doorway to the rear of the property. "I hope so. Or it'll make them think twice about crossing us."

Daisy left the house again, and Rosa appeared beside Layla. "I am genuinely shocked. I didn't think you would challenge someone like that."

"I cheated."

"What? How?"

"I moved the metal around the gun, which allowed me to draw it quicker. I couldn't be sure I'd do it any other way. I was also going to stop the bullets from hitting me if he'd fired first."

Rosa laughed. "That's quite devious."

"Yes, it's clear you're rubbing off on me. I couldn't let him get away with what he'd done. He knew that no one here would talk; his people are too scared of him to do anything but wait for the cash to fall their way."

"Not complaining. I'd have aimed a little lower."

Layla stared at Rosa for several seconds. "I know that parts of our personalities will merge, but I'd quite like it if the penis-removing stayed with you."

Rosa was still laughing as Chloe entered the room, walked up to Layla, and hugged her. "Thank you for what you did. Seeing him there all smug and confident was making me feel a bit ill."

"He's not worth killing. It pains him more to live and be reminded of his failures."

The front door to the mansion opened and a man stepped inside. He was over six feet tall, had a bald head, and wore a pair of dark trousers with a white shirt. He came across as a kind, gentle person who cared deeply for those he loved, but Layla had seen the other side of this man, the side that appeared when someone crossed him, or when they threatened his people. There were good reasons that Hades was feared as one of the most powerful beings on the planet.

"Hades," Chloe said. "Your daughter is already here."

Hades crossed the room and hugged Chloe before doing the same to Layla. "It's good to see you both. How did things go?"

Layla gave him a quick rundown, and when she got to the part about Alfred and the three young women, she saw Hades' eyes narrow in anger. When she'd finished, he walked to the window and looked out over the garden to where Alfred remained on the ground.

"I'd have aimed a little lower," he said, causing Chloe to laugh. "Anyone who has been hurt by these people will be given all the help they need. I'll see to it myself. Until then, there's a ride for Remy and Diana to get back to Tommy and Olivia. I'm sure we'll run more missions together before this is all over."

"Has everyone in your employ started to evacuate from Canada now?" Layla asked.

Hades had a large secret compound in Greenland, a place that no one but his closest allies knew about. It was where he staged all of their operations, and it was where Layla currently called home. Hades also owned large pieces of land in Canada, territory that Avalon would go after sooner or later. He had shown Avalon more than once that he was not on board with their ideas, and so it was just a matter of time before Arthur turned his considerable war machine on Hades' influence in Canada.

"We've already started on some of the bigger cities," Hades said. "Those east of Sault Ste. Marie are pretty much empty of my people, so we'll head west next and evacuate Red Rock and Thunder Bay. The people there are under orders to start leaving within the next few days, but I'll have to leave a small contingent in each city so that it doesn't look like we've just fled. By the time Arthur finally gets around to dealing with me—and he's in no hurry, I assure you—we'll be more than ready to strike back."

"You need to come out here," Sky said, entering the mansion and waving at her dad.

Everyone left the building and followed Sky back outside where Alfred was still prone. Standing over Alfred, Remy leaned forward and shook Hades' hand. "So, the 'B' team has arrived. Time to go home."

Hades smiled. "I have half-a-dozen people coming to help scour this entire place. Nothing will be left unattended. A car is waiting for you all outside—Diana too, when she finishes tending to Alfred's wounds."

"You mean we can't just let him bleed out on the grass?" Remy asked. "Because, honestly, that would get my vote."

"I can tell you where they're being sent," Alfred said through gritted teeth.

"Where what is being sent?" Sky asked. "Be really specific."

"The scrolls and the people," Alfred answered. "Get me a map. I'll show you."

Diana used the map on her phone and Alfred pointed out the exact place.

"It's about four hours from here," Diana said. "Shoal Point, Texas."

"There's a warehouse close to the beach. There's a small dock nearby. The supplies are driven through to Galveston Bay and shipped over to Shoal Point. Someone else then picks them up."

"Who picks them up?" Hades asked.

When Alfred didn't speak, Remy pressed one paw down on the man's hip, causing him to cry out.

"I don't know," Alfred snapped. "That's where my role in our agreement with Nergal ends."

"If you're lying to us . . ." Diana said.

"I'm not," Alfred told her. "Do I get some kind of lesser sentence for helping you?"

Layla's anger bubbled over and she went for the prone man, but was stopped by Sky. "We need him at the moment. Or at least we need his information. My dad and I could kill him and take all of his memories, but, speaking for myself, I don't want to. I really don't want to. Okay?"

Layla nodded and walked back inside. "Is this ever going to end?" she asked, feeling suddenly tired.

"One day, I hope so," Hades said, following her. "Arthur can't fight us all forever. And every bit of damage we do against his organization helps everyone who isn't a part of it."

"Avalon," Remy said, entering the house. "If you can still call it that."

Hades shook his head. "I've worked with Avalon for thousands of years. What Arthur has turned it into is not the real Avalon. It's a vile corruption of what Avalon was created for. I refuse to call it such."

"How about giving it a new name?" Chloe asked as she joined them in the house.

"The Lodge of Dickbags," Remy suggested. "The Bushel of Cocks. Cockwombles United. You know, if you want, I can keep going?"

Chloe and Layla turned away to try to stop laughing, and a smile tugged at Hades' lips.

"I like the last one best," Remy said. "I just need to come up with two more words to complete the acronym."

"I think we should go now," Layla said.

Chloe's chuckles turned into laughter just as Diana and Sky entered the room and looked at them quizzically.

"It's Remy's fault," Hades said by way of explanation. "All of you need to go home and rest. Sky, I assume you'll be staying with me?"

Sky nodded. "I have a few questions for Alfred and his people."

"I want to go to the warehouse," Layla said. "I need to see this through."

"I'm going with her," Remy said.

Chloe and Diana also wanted to join them, and Hades said that he'd arrange for the armed personnel who'd arrived with him to accompany the team on one of his three helicopters, while he stayed behind with Sky to see what else they could find out.

A short time later, Layla, Remy, Chloe, and Diana were onboard the customized Black Hawk helicopter heading toward Shoal Point. Layla watched the land pass far below her and wondered just how many of the humans down there knew how much danger they were in. Arthur and his people had taken great pains to reveal the non-human species to the world, and then gone to even greater lengths to make humanity afraid of them. And Nergal had been beside him every step of the way.

At some point Layla knew she was going to find Nergal, and she was going to have to stop him. And if that meant killing him, then so be it. But how could you kill someone that powerful? How did you kill someone who was once considered a god?

Eventually, she drifted off to sleep, but her dreams were filled with images of those she cared about being hurt by an unknown force. Layla awoke with a jolt as the helicopter landed, feeling concerned about exactly what the future held.

5

"That is not a warehouse," Diana said as the group stood on the beach at Shoal Point and stared at what was meant to be a large warehouse. It was large, but it was more barn-like than they expected.

Chloe tapped the screen of her phone a few times. "Is it just me, or is it super-creepy that my map doesn't have that building on it?" She showed everyone the screen, and sure enough the large wooden barn wasn't there.

The six soldiers moved across the beach in well-practiced formation. They'd told Layla, Remy, Diana, and Chloe to stay back and let them do their job. They had to tell Remy this three times. In Layla's mind this was because . . . well, it was Remy.

The group consisted of four men and two women, and Layla didn't know any of them beyond a few first names. They were considered by everyone who worked with Hades as dangerous people—Special Operations in all but name—and they kept to themselves even outside of missions.

The soldiers moved into the barn, their silver-bullet-loaded weapons raised and ready to engage as necessary. A few seconds later one returned to the beach and waved Layla's team over.

"It's safe," he called out. "No one home."

"I'm glad they're here," Remy said. "I don't know what we would have done if they hadn't searched the empty barn first."

"They're just doing their jobs," Chloe said with a roll of her eyes.

"I could have searched the barn," Remy told her. "I could have told them there was no one in there from way back on the beach."

"Why didn't you?" Diana asked, a sly smile on her lips.

Remy shrugged. "Didn't want them to feel useless."

"You're pouting," Chloe told him as they reached the barn entrance.

"Foxes don't pout," Remy said, crossing his arms before catching himself in the action and dropping them to his sides.

"So you've tried?" Layla asked.

"I'm suddenly feeling hatred for some of my friends," Remy told them.

"Remy, I know you like to get . . . involved," Layla said, trying to put it diplomatically, "but Hades wants his people more engaged in stuff like this. The only reason they weren't kicking in the mansion door with us back in Louisiana is because it was meant to be a simple job."

Remy kicked a stone across the barn, striking the wall. "Sure, I guess. I just don't like waiting around for things to happen."

"No, you prefer causing things to happen," Diana said.

Before Remy could answer, the soldiers' commander stopped the search of the huge open barn and looked back toward the group. "Nothing here."

Layla turned 360 degrees, taking in her surroundings. The floor was covered in hay and the stables were currently empty of everything except more hay. A ladder went up to the next level, and a soldier peered over the railing high above them. He confirmed that there was nothing up there but more hay and a large quantity of spiders.

"What kind of spiders?" Remy asked. "Do we need to burn this whole place?"

"Not a fan of spiders?" Layla asked.

"I met some very large ones a while ago," Remy said.

Diana shivered. "That was not a fun experience."

"How large?" the soldier called out.

"Bigger than you," Chloe called back.

The soldier looked over his shoulder and climbed down the ladder a lot faster than he'd climbed up it. "Yeah, they're not that big," he said as he walked past them.

"So, we got screwed," said the commander. The leader of the soldiers was a woman who looked like she was in her mid-thirties, but could have been hundreds of years old, depending on her species. Like the rest of her team, she wore dark body armor with runes inscribed on it to deflect or absorb at least a portion of magical attacks. "I'll contact Hades and let him know."

"Wait," Layla told her, and reached out with her power. "There's a small dock on the beach, and an empty barn full of hay. Why would someone put a barn here?"

"It looks pretty old," Diana said. "A century, at least. Who knows what someone thought back then."

Layla continued to push out her power, sensing all of the screws and rivets that sat in the timber around her. She pushed a little further and felt as if her power had vanished. She simply couldn't see past a certain point.

Layla frowned. "That's weird."

"We back to talking about Remy again?" Diana asked.

"That was a low blow," Remy said with mock indignation.

Diana apologized and looked back at Layla. "Go on."

Layla explained about her vanishing power. "It's under the barn. There's something under here that's stopping me reaching down further. There are metal pieces down there, screws and hinges, and something else, like a door, a metal door, but past it . . . there's nothing. Like a void. I can't tell you where the entrance is, but it's under us."

"So there's an underground lair?" the commander asked. "Okay, people, we're looking for a secret entrance to something underneath here. Rip the place apart. No magic, powers, or bullets; we don't want anything being set off. Old-fashioned brute strength only."

The soldiers went back to the helicopter and returned with several axes, before they set about destroying a large part of the barn in their effort to find the way to get beneath it. It didn't take long before the soldiers found a metal door and a set of stairs leading to it, below the large hole they'd made in the barn floor.

"There was no secret entrance or anything," the commander said.

"They must use an earth elemental, or someone with earth magic to move the floor about," Remy said.

"There are marks here," Diana told everyone, pointing to them on the floor. "The boards can be lifted as one, but they must get scratched as they're moved. I imagine whoever did this isn't an old hand at using their power."

It didn't take long for the rest of the floor to be removed, exposing the stairs in their entirety.

"We'll go first," the commander said.

"I think you might need me to open that door," Layla said, pointing to the dark red runes that were inscribed on its surface.

The commander looked at her team and then back down at the door. She turned to Layla. "I think you're probably right. You can read the runes?"

Layla shook her head.

"They block magic," Diana said. "That's all I can tell you. I'm not a rune expert by any means."

Layla descended the narrow stone staircase and stood in front of the door. It was ten feet tall, but about as wide as a normal-sized entrance. There was a brass handle, which Layla tried just because she didn't want to be one of those people who forced open a door that was actually unlocked, but it refused to budge.

As an umbra, Layla's power wasn't based on the laws of magic. It came from the energy supplied by the drenik and the words written in the scroll. She wasn't sure if her ability would let her bypass the security on the door, but it was better than just standing around while everyone twiddled their thumbs.

Layla placed her hand on the door and reached out. She still felt nothing beyond it, but she pushed her power all over the front of the door until it was covered. Layla then clenched her fists and pulled her power in two directions at once. The door tore in half with a horrific noise. It bent back on itself, twisting and turning until it was unrecognizable and nothing more than a metal outline to a large hole. Layla made sure there were no sharp edges and looked inside.

Lights flickered in the distance, and Layla, stepping through the hole, noted the stone floor beyond the doorway. The lights in the room instantly came to life, showing it for what it was: a library. A cavernous library.

"Holy shit," Remy said as he stood beside Layla. "That's a lot of scrolls."

There were hundreds and hundreds of metal bookshelves, which stretched from the floor to a ceiling twenty feet above them. Each one held hundreds of scrolls.

"It's a football field in length," Chloe said. "British football, that is."

"Get Hades here," the commander said to one of her people. "Get him here now." Two soldiers ran off to do as they were told, while the rest stood guard at the entrance to the cave.

Layla reached out with her power and realized that with the door gone, she could feel the metal all around her. It was oddly comforting. She sighed. "I'm glad I'm not powerless in here," she said. "There are a lot of things that could be hiding in the shadows."

Everyone shared a glance.

"Why in the name of Satan's testicles would you say that?" Remy asked, hurriedly sniffing the air, before visibly relaxing. "I've got nothing. Mildew and old scents. Nothing obvious that could be considered a threat."

The group started looking through the piles of scrolls and found that most of them were blank, or about something other than umbras. It took them a few hours to walk the cave's length, looking around as they tried to get a good idea of the number of scrolls they'd need to remove.

"Tens of thousands," Diana said.

"That's not quite as scientific as I'd hoped," Remy said.

"At least thirty thousand scrolls," Chloe said, looking up from her phone. "That's based on how many scrolls were on one shelving unit, multiplied by the number of shelving units in this whole place. There's not actually as many as I thought. Most of the cave is empty."

"That's still an awful lot of scrolls," Layla said. "We need to get them out of here. And we're going to need something huge to transport them."

"There's a large port near here," the commander said. "Maybe we can figure something out. Do you think this is all of them?"

"No," Remy said. "I was told that hundreds of thousands of scrolls have been made. I think that this is a large number of them, but Nergal wouldn't put all of his eggs in one basket."

"Even so, this is a big score for us," Diana said. "If only half of these are spirit scrolls, that's a considerable amount of danger removed from the hands of Avalon."

Hades arrived on a second Black Hawk soon after, with more heavily armed soldiers. He walked around the cave, picking up the occasional scroll, unfurling it, and replacing it before moving on. Layla felt oddly nervous, as if her teacher was examining her homework and about to grade it in front of everyone.

Hades met with the team at the mouth of the cave. "This here is a big deal, people," he said with a smile. "You did good today. We'll sort out the logistics of getting all of this removed, but to be honest I'd rather hide them all in a deep, dark pit somewhere."

"You can't," Layla and Chloe said in unison.

Hades raised an eyebrow. "Why?"

"There are spirits trapped in there," Layla said. "We don't know what happens to them once the scrolls are destroyed."

Hades looked thoughtful. "You're right. We'll check with the people who helped make these things and find out what to do. It's my belief that the scroll spirits aren't actively aware of time in the same way as you and me, and so I don't think they would feel anything if the scrolls were destroyed. They'd just vanish into the ether with the normal spirits, but it's worth looking into."

"Besides, we could have an immense level of power here," the commander said.

"It's too hard to create an army with them," Hades said. "Nergal knows that only too well. People don't always adjust to having the spirits and drenik inside of them. Any umbras on Earth have remained hidden for thousands of years. It's only since Nergal started trying to make an army out of them, in the last decade or so, that we've come into contact with them on a regular basis. Getting a human, the spirits, and a drenik to bond is a lot of work. We can't use these ones as soldiers. We're lucky to have Chloe and Layla."

"So, what do we do with them?" Layla asked. "The amount of knowledge in some of these scrolls could shed light on so much history. And not just human history."

Hades looked back at the scrolls. "You're right. I just need to figure out how I'm meant to put them to good use. First thing is getting them back to the base. Second thing is finding out how many of these are actually still usable. I saw several that weren't even spirit scrolls. One was a Babylonian recipe for cheese. After that we figure out where to go. In the meantime, I'm ordering you all back to base."

Diana raised an eyebrow. "Ordering?"

"Sorry, I meant suggesting," Hades said. "Strongly suggesting."

Diana nodded and smiled. "That, I can live with."

"You all need rest. And by rest, I mean sleep, food, and actual rest. I'm sure we'll have new missions soon enough, so please don't spend all of your time training."

"What about Alfred?" Layla asked as everyone made their way back to the sunlit beach.

"He's being exceptionally cooperative. Sky has a way with people like Alfred."

"She scares them," Remy said.

"Not all of them," Hades said. "Just the ones who need scaring."

"And the prisoners we found?"

"Deposited at hospitals in and around Louisiana, all of which are secretly helping those of us who don't think Avalon is particularly healthy at the moment. They'll be looked after and put in contact with loved ones as needed. They all have a long road ahead of them, but we can help them. Mental health professionals are in attendance to aid their recovery, too."

"I'm glad to hear it," Layla said as they all reached the Black Hawks. Four identical helicopters now sat on the beach, and Layla wondered if it wouldn't look like an invasion force to anyone who accidentally came across them.

"Those three women you saved," Hades said. "They wanted me to say thank you. They're strong people and, I won't lie, they're going to have to be even stronger to get through it, but right now they are very happy to be free from Alfred. I'm glad you decided to stick with the team when Arthur declared us all enemies. Stuff like what you did today really makes a difference."

Layla climbed aboard the helicopter with the others. "Keep an eye on them, okay? I want to make sure they do well."

Hades nodded. "I will."

Layla felt the power of the helicopter's engine, and they were about to take off when Layla spotted someone walking up the beach. She signaled to Hades, who turned around as Diana told the pilot to cut the engine.

A few seconds later, they jumped out of the Black Hawk and walked toward the young woman, who was being screamed at by the soldiers to lie face down on the beach. She obeyed them without a word as one of the female soldiers patted her down.

"Nothing," the soldier said as she got back to her feet, her MP5 pointed at the woman, who got up slowly and held her hands where everyone could see them.

"I'm not here to hurt anyone," the woman said, complying with the orders barked at her.

"She has no scent," Diana said.

"And that means?" Layla asked.

"Nothing good," Remy whispered.

The woman was about five-and-a-half feet in height and looked athletic. She wore some kind of fitness band on her wrist that was turquoise in color. She had shoulder-length, dark hair that was tied into pigtails. Layla assumed that she was trying to look innocent, but it didn't come off well. The woman's blue eyes were just . . . wrong. Layla couldn't put a finger on it, but something about the newcomer reminded her of her father.

"And you are?" Hades asked.

"My name is Kristin Tusk," she said. "I told Nergal not to leave so many of his scrolls here, but he doesn't listen to me."

Anyone watching the woman who might have relaxed was instantly woken up at the mention of Nergal's name.

"Where did you come from?" Remy asked.

"Oh, I was on my way here when your helicopters arrived. I didn't want to cause a scene, so I stopped at the end of the island and walked over. It's a nice day for a walk."

"You work for Nergal?" Diana asked, a low growl leaving her throat.

Kristin nodded. "I live here. I take care of the scrolls and things. Make sure the rats don't eat them. We had a rat problem a while ago. Massive buggers."

"How did you get down into the cave?" Chloe asked.

"Oh, there's a rune in the barn," she said, as if telling everyone was no big deal. "I assume you just tore it apart? Shame. They used to use an earth elemental to lift it, but the man was an idiot, so I had to slit his throat and push him into the water."

The ease with which she admitted killing visibly startled several people. Layla took a step toward her.

"Why don't you have a scent?" Remy asked.

Kristin shrugged. "Never considered it before. Does it make you afraid of me?"

"Things with no scent either means magic, or that you're not real," Diana finished. "I see no evidence of magic, and you're definitely real."

"Maybe I'm something new?" Kristin said with a laugh.

"You're coming with us," Hades said. "We'll question you further in a more secure location."

"I think I'm meant to know you," Kristin said to Layla, ignoring Hades. "But it's been a while since I was back home, so I'm not sure."

"Lucky me," Layla said, trying to figure out if the woman was telling the truth and, if so, where she might have met her. She couldn't come up with anything. And judging by the strangeness Kristin exuded, Layla was pretty sure she'd have remembered the woman if they had met.

"Depends on your definition of luck," Kristin told her. "Well, this has been pleasant, but I really do need to get going."

Kristin turned to walk away, and several soldiers moved to stop her. One of them got too close and Kristin quickly grabbed the man, getting behind him and holding his pistol against his temple.

"Don't," Hades said. "You don't need to hurt him."

Kristin laughed. "Hurt him? No, you've got it all wrong. I don't plan on hurting any of you. Did you notice the runes inside the library? Spirit scrolls can't be torn, or burned, or broken. Normally, anyway." She pushed the man forward, placed his gun under her chin, and pulled the trigger. The blast removed a portion of Kristin's skull and brain, and she collapsed lifeless to the sand as the soldier scrambled away.

A second later a massive explosion ripped through the air as the barn collapsed and the ground rumbled. The commander removed the fitness band from Kristin's wrist and turned it over. "It was linked to her heartbeat," she said. "She killed herself to blow up the cave. We're lucky none of our people were inside."

"What kind of person sacrifices her own life just to destroy a bunch of scrolls?" Remy asked.

"The kind that doesn't have a scent," Layla said.

"That was strange," Diana replied, sniffing the air. "Still nothing from her. It's odd. And we've lost all of those scrolls."

"Better they are destroyed than allowed to be used by the likes of Nergal," one of the soldiers said.

"All of those spirits . . . gone," Layla said. "How many people were in those scrolls? How many spirits . . . how much knowledge have we just lost?"

The soldier shrugged and walked away.

"He has a point," Diana told her.

"We'll get down there and search for any scrolls that survived," Hades said. "If they've discovered a way to destroy spirit scrolls, I'd like to know about it."

Layla looked over at the smoking ruin of the barn. She wondered if the scrolls inside the cave were totally destroyed, or if any of them had survived the blast. She didn't feel lucky. She felt that fighting Avalon was like going one step forward, and two steps back.

6

Kristin had been happy working for Nergal. She'd been happy doing as she was told, going on missions for Avalon and removing threats as needed. Right up until she'd discovered something awful: that someone who was meant to be dead, wasn't.

She'd come across the information by accident. The woman in question was living under a new name, in a part of the country that Kristin had never been to. But by complete chance, a news channel had been interviewing a man about a recent storm when the woman had walked behind him. Kristin's first reaction had been surprise. Then doubt. But after making a few calls, she discovered that the woman on the TV and the woman who was meant to be dead were one and the same, and Kristin's reaction had changed to pure rage.

Unfortunately, Nergal was not one to allow his employees time to deal with their own problems, so it took several months for Kristin to slowly and surely arrange what needed to be done.

She found herself parked in a black BMW X5, watching a woman who was meant to be dead, now called Madison Grace, walk down her driveway to her silver C Class Mercedes and drive away.

"Madison," Kristin said. "Madison. Do you think she chose that name? I remember her as Ava. Pretty little Ava with the fake smile. It's quite late in the evening to be working, but she was wearing a suit. I wonder where she's going."

Kristin had intended to watch the woman for several days before doing anything, but the urge to kill her was too great, and she wasn't sure she'd be able to keep it together for that long.

"Nergal cannot know," said the voice in her head.

"He won't," Kristin assured them. "She deserves to die. She should have stayed dead."

"Make it right."

The voice stopped, and Kristin smiled. She looked in the rearview mirror and noticed her bright green eyes. They'd never been green before. "Weird," she said.

She had considered killing the woman's family—after all, she'd been responsible for ensuring that Kristin never got her happy ever after—but she had decided against it: too messy, too many variables that could go wrong. Better to make it look like a random act of violence, to leave her family to grieve, just like Kristin had been forced to do all those years ago.

"I can't believe she changed her name," Kristin said, setting off after the Mercedes.

"She was given help by the government," the voice said. "New name, new identity."

Kristin pulled up at a red light and watched the Mercedes make a right down the next road toward the center of town. Kristin beamed as the light turned green, and she set off again. "He deserved to die. Him and his bitch."

"Yes, they did."

"The whole family hid their relationship from us. Hid what they were doing. They all deserved to die."

"And they did. And once Madison is dead, the world can go back to being complete."

Kristin forced herself to remain calm. "She's still pretty."

"She is. She's lived years longer than she was meant to. Release will be our gift to her. It is almost her birthday, after all. Do you have any ideas about how you're going to accomplish your task?"

"I was going to kill her on the street, but I'll see how I feel. I brought guns. However I do it, there will be nothing to trace it back to us, back to Nergal."

"Excellent. Contact me when it's finished."

Kristin felt the voice switch off for the second time, leaving her alone in the car. She watched as Madison parked her Mercedes outside of an Italian restaurant and went inside. Kristin pulled the BMW into a nearby alley and switched off the engine. Out of the rear window she could see Madison being taken to a table where five other people already sat—four men and another woman—all wearing suits, all with alcoholic drinks in their hands. They raised them toward Madison when she came over.

"Celebration time," Kristin said. She got out of the BMW as a young policeman came over to her.

"You can't park here," he said, his expression stern. "You need to move."

"Sorry, officer," Kristin said, walking around to the front of the car, away from anyone passing by on the sidewalk outside of the alley. "I'm just a little lost and wanted to take a look at my sat nav without driving. Do you happen to know where Bene Italia is?"

The officer walked over to Kristin. "It's just there," he said, pointing to the restaurant where Madison currently sat. Kristin darted forward, stabbing her dagger under his chin. She held the policeman tightly while he died, before dragging him over to a dumpster and throwing him in. Being an umbra meant having more strength than a normal human; it was one of the most fun things about it.

Kristin went back to the car and took a Glock .22 from a bag under the passenger seat. She removed the holster and put it on, before placing the gun inside. Two daggers then went into a knife belt that she put around her waist. She grabbed her coat and put that on, too, concealing the weapons.

When she'd first discovered that her boyfriend was cheating on her and made the decision to punish not only him, but also the woman in question and her family for hiding it, Kristin had used two revolvers and a dagger hammer. She'd wielded the hammer to great effect and wished she'd kept it as a memento of the occasion. She would have liked to use it now, to finish the job she'd started so long ago, but she needed this to be quick. If not quiet.

"I want her to know it's me," Kristin said in her head.

"What do you have planned?"

"She's in a restaurant. I'm considering waiting, but I'm not feeling awfully patient." Kristin opened the huge car boot and climbed inside, sitting up against the rear seats to watch the restaurant through the window. "I should have brought a rifle," she said to herself.

After a few hours of observing Madison and her friends eating and drinking their way through the restaurant's menu, Kristin noticed that the number of people inside had dropped. It was getting late, and she saw that few people remained in the establishment. She opened the trunk of the BMW and stepped out into the crisp night air. The weight of the gun under her jacket made her feel a level of contentment she hadn't experienced since before she discovered that Madison—Ava—hadn't died on that fateful day.

Despite being shot in the chest and hit with a hammer, the woman had still managed to survive. The one survivor out of the fourteen Kristin had killed over the space of two days. "The Christmas Day Massacre," the media had called it. She'd hated that headline at the time, as most of the deaths had actually happened on Christmas Eve. The police had found her on Christmas Day, and that hadn't been fun at all. Kristin hadn't liked being tasered, or the way that they'd dragged her semiconscious form out of the house after she'd attacked one of the responding officers with her bloody hammer.

Kristin crossed the road, feeling the beat of her heart as she prepared herself for what was to follow. She opened the door of the restaurant and savored the aroma that greeted her. A man in his early twenties walked over to her. "Table for one?"

"Please," Kristin said, and glanced over at Madison, feeling an almost overwhelming urge to kill her.

The young man took Kristin to a table at the opposite end of the restaurant to where Madison and her friends sat. She declined to remove her coat and ordered some coffee and a pepperoni pizza for one.

Kristin drank the coffee and continued to watch her target as the pizza arrived. She took her time eating, although she didn't really care what the food was like. She wasn't there for the cuisine. She didn't want to finish before Madison was ready to go.

Three cups of coffee later, Madison got up from her seat and went to the bathroom. Kristin followed her, her heart almost skipping a beat as she opened the door and stepped into the large room. Only one stall was occupied, so she entered a cubicle near to it and waited.

A flush of the toilet, the sound of a stall door opening, and Kristin pushed open her door and walked up behind the woman at the wash basin.

"Hello, Madison," Kristin said.

The woman turned around, her eyes wide and fear spreading across her face as she realized who she was in the bathroom with.

"Kristin?" Madison asked, a mixture of shock and panic on her face. "I thought you were in jail."

"I've been out for a while now. I thought you were dead."

"You don't have to do this." Madison then paused. "Why do you have green eyes?"

"Long story," Kristin said. "Long, beautiful story. That was marked like the pox when I discovered you weren't where you belonged. You betrayed me."

"None of us betrayed you."

"You kept his cheating a secret. You liked her better than me."

"That's not what happened," Madison said. "Mia was our sister. You're my sister. I would never betray you. He broke up with you a year before he got together with her. A year. You went to hospital because you had a break down."

"You all sent me there so he could have his way with that bitch," Kristin snapped.

"He dated you for three weeks in college. It wasn't even a relationship."

"You all betrayed me," Kristin snapped again. "I loved you all, and you help him cheat on me. Helped him cheat on me with our sister."

Madison's expression hardened. "I always wanted to tell you this, Kristin: you're a monster. A vindictive, evil little parasite, who never should have been allowed to live with people like our family. Mom and Dad should have had you locked away when you were a child. You even killed someone in college; can you remember that? Do you remember why you had to go away?"

"She deserved it. She stole from me."

"She stole nothing. You're just a monster. You always were. You hurt people, you hurt innocent people, and you like it. You enjoyed killing the people I love. You even enjoyed thinking you'd killed me. I always wondered what I'd say if I saw you again, what I'd do if you were to stand before me."

The door to the bathroom opened, and Madison screamed a warning at the woman who stepped inside. Kristin drew one of the guns from her hip holster, aimed at the newcomer, and fired twice, catching her both times in the chest. Madison hit Kristin around the head, shoving her off balance, and ran for the bathroom door.

Kristin fired at her sister, but missed and took out a piece of the door instead. "Damn it," she snapped.

"Get after her already," said the voice in her head.

She ran toward the door, barreling through it, and shot a man on the other side who'd come to investigate the commotion. He fell back onto the nearest table with a loud crash as other people inside the restaurant either hid under their tables or fled.

Kristin looked over at the table where Madison had been and saw the woman she had eaten with scramble to her feet. Kristin shot her in the shoulder, spinning her around and dropping her to the floor. She walked over to the woman as she began to crawl away. "Where's Madison?"

"She ran out," the woman said.

Kristin put two rounds into the back of her head and ran out of the restaurant to see Madison's car pull away as quickly as possible. She fired twice, ignoring the screams of bystanders, and only hit the rear of the car, but she had a pretty good idea where Madison was going.

Kristin jogged across the road, got into her BMW, and drove out of the alley, joining the traffic on the other side. Sirens wailed somewhere in the distance, but she was soon on her way back to Madison's house. If Madison wasn't there, Kristin would make sure whoever was there got her back. She wondered if Madison would care, especially when she didn't even give a shit about her own sister.

Kristin ejected the Glock's magazine and loaded a fresh one as she drove. She neared the house and spotted Madison's Mercedes parked half in the road. Kristin stopped the BMW a few houses away and got out, keeping her Glock ready by her side.

She stood by a large tree just outside of Madison's house and looked at the two-story building to try to figure out where there might be people. The front door was closed, and she saw no lights on.

Kristin hurried across the perfectly manicured lawn and placed a hand against the door handle, twisting it slightly. She pushed open the unlocked door. Big mistake, sister, Kristin thought to herself. She stepped into the hardwood hallway and felt the force of the shotgun blast hit her in the chest. Kristin looked down at her top as it rapidly turned red, before dropping to her knees.

"You should have stayed away," Madison said, walking out of the darkness with a shotgun in her hands.

Kristin tried to lift her Glock, but a second blast from the shotgun ended her life.

Several hundred miles away another Kristin sat up with a gasp. She'd been lying down, hoping to hear the good news of her sister's demise, but instead had been powerless to stop her own murder. Or, at least, the murder of her clone: Kristin was an umbra, with the ability to make up to nine clones. Whether she made them all at once, one at a time, or several together was entirely up to her, although she had to deal with the amount of energy it took to do so. It had taken a long time to send one across the country to kill her sister.

"Damn it," she snapped, rubbing the spot on her chest where she'd felt the shotgun pellets hit. Kristin swung her legs out of bed and took a moment to compose herself. The clone had failed. They were no more durable than a human, but Kristin hadn't been able to deal with Madison personally. It was a choice she now regretted.

She went into the bathroom of her suite in Nergal's Texas compound and splashed water on her face. Kristin looked at her normal brown eyes in the mirror. No clone was perfect, and while she could imbue them with a fraction of her power, each clone would be changed from the original in a small way. Eye color, hair color or length, height, weight, the list went on. They possessed a percentage of autonomy and were able to live separate lives, but Kristin had final control. Should she want them to do something, they would do it without pause.

She would have to make sure that Nergal didn't discover her little off-the-books excursion. Now her face would be recognizable in the area, and the police would be involved. The body of the clone would be identified as Kristin's, and people would think she was dead. Let Madison live her life for a few more months until she'd become accustomed once again to not looking over her shoulder. Then, and only then, would Kristin strike. And next time she wouldn't use a clone.

The door to her room opened and one of Nergal's aides stepped inside. Kristin didn't know her name and simply called her Sycophant Three.

"Hello," Kristin said, drying her face. "I'm not certain, but aren't you meant to knock?"

The woman sneered as Kristin walked past her to the bed. "You're a pet. You don't get that level of courtesy."

Kristin picked up a glass of water on the bedside table and drained it. She sat on the mattress, put on her black boots, and then walked back toward the bathroom, glass in hand, as if to refill it. But as she passed, Kristin smashed the glass into the side of the woman's head, embedding shards into the aide's face. Kristin then kicked her opponents' knee, snapping the joint and forcing the aide to drop to the ground, and stamped on her head over and over until something crunched.

Kristin looked down at the bloody mess that was the face of Nergal's aide. She had no idea what species the woman was, but she wore a sorcerer's band on one wrist, so was incapable of using her powers. "You had a message for me?" Kristin asked.

The aide made a gurgling noise.

"No matter," Kristin said. She knew she couldn't kill the woman—that wouldn't be considered polite—but she could hurt her. Nergal didn't mind that. In fact, he almost encouraged it.

Kristin picked up the aide's mobile phone and dialed Nergal, who answered on the first ring. "My lord, your aide said you had a message," she said.

"She was to bring you to me," Nergal replied.

"Yes, well, she appears to have suffered a case of being rude. She'll take a few days to heal."

Nergal tutted his disapproval. "Do not kill her, Kristin. Good help is hard to find. And, yes, I want to see you. Hades and his people have taken Alfred and disrupted my supplies."

"I'll be there shortly, my lord," Kristin said, and hung up, dropping the phone onto the aides' chest. "If you ever speak to me in such a condescending tone again, I'm going to keep you as a play thing and peel the skin off your face. I don't know, or care, what species you are. This compound isn't big enough to hide from me. Are we clear?" The woman made a sound that Kristin took to be her agreement, and she stepped over the aide and left her bedroom.

Pain suddenly laced through her body and brought Kristin to her knees, and she knew that she'd lost the clone on Shoal Point. That meant someone had found the scrolls there, presumably Hades or someone who worked for him. Alfred had talked. Kristin got back to her feet. Nergal would not be happy, but hopefully this would urge him to finally do something about Hades and his little group. Maybe the day wasn't going to be a complete bust after all.

7

Layla, Diana, Chloe, and Remy had been ordered back on the helicopter heading to the base in Greenland about twenty minutes after Kristin killed herself on the beach. Hades and his people had work to do and had decided to stay behind. With the modifications to the Black Hawk, that meant a very long trip, but not one that required stopping for refuelling.

Everyone fell asleep during the ride, and Layla only woke when the Black Hawk landed and the open doors allowed freezing cold air into the helicopter cabin.

"Get some rest," Tommy Carpenter said as he greeted Remy, Layla, Chloe, and Diana.

They entered the compound, walking past dozens of heavily armed soldiers and more than a few pieces of artillery that Layla hoped would never be used.

"You did good today." Tommy wasn't terribly tall, but he was broad-shouldered and cut an imposing figure as he spoke to them. He had a long, graying beard, pale skin, and short dark hair, and the middle and fourth fingers on his right hand were missing from the knuckles. There was a rumor that he'd lost them during the Hundred Years War, when the French attacked Soissons during 1414. It was thought that Tommy had been an archer for the English army, and when captured had been mutilated by one of the French commanders who thought it entertaining.

Layla had thought that the practice of taking fingers was a myth, that it had never happened, but then Tommy had appeared in her life and a lot of things she thought were myth turned out to have at least a nugget of truth to them. She'd considered asking Tommy but didn't want to risk making him relive something awful to sate her curiosity. And asking Tommy's wife, Olivia, or daughter, Kasey, just seemed rude.

Tommy stopped next to Layla. "You okay?"

"Are you going to ask me that every time we do something? I've worked for you for years now. I think I'll be fine."

Tommy nodded. "I know. But I heard about what you found in that mansion. And what happened on Shoal Point. It's a lot to deal with in a short time. And I know that I speak for myself, but some of us haven't always dealt with awful stuff in the best way."

"Even you?"

Tommy nodded. "When I was your age, I wasn't what you'd call well-adjusted. You've thrown yourself into mission after mission, and though I'm all for that, you need downtime, too. You still need to go out and be twenty-three years old."

"Not easy to do when a large number of people either want to experiment on me or kill me."

"I never said it was easy. I just don't want you to burn out. Take a few days off, rest, relax, and have fun. Not necessarily in that order."

Layla sighed. "I get it. I'm not going to burn out. I'm not going to let everything pile up until I can't bear the weight. I get your concern, and I thank you for it, but throwing myself into work is how I deal with the awful stuff. It's how I've always dealt with it. It's comforting. And now I get to punch people, too. That's therapeutic."

"Now that, I agree with," Tommy said with a laugh. "There's been too much misery and sadness around here since Arthur decided to turn us into enemies of the state."

"Do you need to take your own advice?" Layla asked.

"Yep. That's why I have to make sure that no one else is pushing themselves too hard. I know what it's like to take comfort in the work. I've been there, seen it done. Olivia, too. It took us both a long time to figure out how to relax."

"What happened to the people we found in the mansion?" Layla asked.

"They're being taken care of, and Alfred is in the process of telling us everything he knows. He's recounting his life story at the moment—it's a bit like living that scene with Chunk in *The Goonies*."

Layla recalled the time Sky had sat her down and almost forced her to watch the film, calling it a classic. She hadn't been wrong. It was a happy memory.

"What about the scrolls?" Layla asked.

"Well, we haven't been able to search all of the cave because the explosion essentially destroyed it, and what we've found isn't great. None of the scrolls had any spirits left in them. They're just burned paper now."

"What does that mean for my team?"

"It means you're on standby until we figure out what Alfred knows. You were searching for the scrolls, we found a lot of them, and they're destroyed. Right now, you deserve some time off."

Layla nodded. She was upset that the scrolls had been destroyed, and that she'd spent so long working with her team to find them only to have them torn from her grasp. But on the other hand, they'd saved a lot of lives over the last few years and helped those who were in danger of falling under Avalon's crushing machine. That was something she was proud of.

"Do you think we'll ever be able to leave this place for something more than a mission?" Layla asked.

Tommy looked around the huge hangar at the dozens of people running about, working to ensure that the compound continued to function without problems and everyone was kept safe. "We're on it."

"That sounds very secretive," Layla said as the pair reached the door to a stairwell leading to the offices and rooms underground. Diana, Remy, and Chloe had used it moments earlier, presumably to go and shower off the stench of Alfred and his people. The stairs also reached the walkway above the hangar, which allowed people to walk out onto the mountain.

The part of the compound above ground had become Layla and her friend's temporary home and was officially a research station. The people who worked at the complex lived there, too, but they also shared a large village that had been built into and around the mountain. The settlement housed thousands, but to reach it you had to go through the hangar. It just so happened that inside the hangar were enough heavily armed people to give any invading force second thoughts.

"I'm going home," Layla said. "I'm going to sleep for a day, eat a lot of cake, and watch truly awful films. Try not to have an emergency in that time."

"I miss awful films," Tommy said. "I miss good films, too. I have such a backlog that, frankly, it's embarrassing."

Before Layla could touch the door, it was opened from the other side, revealing Olivia and Kasey, or "Kase" as she was known. Kase smiled and hugged Layla tight.

"Kase, mind my bones," Layla said as the woman lifted her off the ground.

"You'll be fine," Kase said with a laugh. She had inherited her father's werewolf powers and the water elemental powers of her mother.

She was the same age as Layla and had grown up best friends with Chloe. The three women were usually sent on missions together, and Kase had taken exception to being left out of the trip to Louisiana.

Kase put Layla back on the ground. "I have time off."

"Me too," Layla said.

"I'm glad the mission went well," Olivia said. She was a little shorter than Kase, and her hair was dyed a dark red, while Kase kept hers brown. Olivia was several centuries old but could have passed for Kase's only slightly older sister: one of the benefits of having a lifetime measured by centuries and not decades. In hundreds of years' time, Kase would probably look only slightly older than she did now.

The thought made Layla sad. She might have been an umbra, but her lifespan was only a few times that of a human, and not the dozens and dozens that were possible for some of the other species that resided on the planet.

"Thanks," Layla said. "I've had more fun, but we did what needed to be done."

"Go rest," Olivia said to Layla before turning to Kase. "You've both got a few days, so use them as wisely as twenty-three-year-olds usually do. Don't pass out anywhere stupid."

Kase saluted before she walked through the door with Layla, causing Olivia to roll her eyes and Tommy to stifle a laugh.

A few minutes later, the two young women were on the travelator heading to the rear of the hangar where the windows on the walkway showed several groups of people in training.

"You think this will ever end?" Layla asked. "All the training, missions, evading capture."

Kase shrugged. "I hope so. Greenland is a lovely place, but I miss England. I miss that my country is no longer a place I'm able to feel safe in. I miss proper chocolate. The American stuff they keep shipping in is not chocolate. It's . . . odd."

"You know I'm half-American, right? There's nothing weird about American chocolate—it took me a while to get used to how sweet your stuff is."

"And your bacon is weird. It's not proper bacon. What you eat is streaky bacon."

Layla paused. "Okay, I'll give you that one."

Kase threw her hands in the air. "You can't make a bacon sandwich with streaky god damn bacon. Frankly, I'm considering taking helicopter lessons just so I can steal one, fly to England, buy several pigs worth of smoked back bacon, and bring it here."

"I'll be right there with you." They were quiet for a few seconds until curiosity got the better of Layla. "Why did you have to stay behind?"

"Ah, my mum felt I hadn't passed my weapons training tests."

"Why?"

"Because I hadn't taken them. I've been training to fight with a variety of weapons since I was old enough to hold them, so I kind of started to skip some training sessions. She made it clear that I still had to attend, even if I've already mastered them. Twenty-three and still having to make sure I go to class on time."

"You know your mom wasn't doing it to just wind you up."

"My mum is a disciplinarian. She has always been a ball-buster, but I know why she does it. She doesn't want people saying that I get any kind of privilege for being the daughter of one of the people in charge."

"Ball-buster?"

"The term still fits. Balls are fragile and easily bruised and vagina-buster just sounds . . . you know, weird."

Layla laughed so hard she started to cough. "Please don't use that term again."

"Can I ask you something?" Kase asked, suddenly serious.

"Any time," Layla said.

"Do you ever get freaked out about the blood curse we all have? About the link to the bracelet?"

Layla considered it. "Not really. I've removed mine outside of the compound. It didn't blow up, and I could still use my powers, so as it also lets us use our powers here, I'm not really sure what it does."

"That's my point. Blood curse marks aren't known for their pleasantness."

"You spoken to your mom or dad about it?" Layla asked.

"Yeah, but they said I was fine. Dad can't lie for shit, so I'm sure he's telling the truth, but I really do find it strange."

They got off the travelator after several hundred meters and stepped out into a large open area with a helipad to one side. The village stretched out before them. Layla wasn't sure exactly when the mountainside had been changed to accommodate the settlement, but work had already been underway when she'd arrived. All she knew was that a cave had been excavated and turned into what many would consider paradise.

A ten-foot-wide river of glacial water bisected the area and several stone bridges connected the two halves of the village.

"Still takes your breath away, doesn't it?" Kase said from beside her. "You get elementals to work with sorcerers, and this is the kind of magic they create. It's still the most beautiful place I've ever been to in this or any other realm."

Layla had been schooled about the realms: how the Earth was at their center and that from here, portals led to the other realms. For the most part, each doorway led only to one realm, so if you wanted to go to a different one, you had to travel back through Earth.

Layla had been told that there were hundreds, if not thousands, of realms, ranging from the familiar ones, like Asgard or Tartarus, to some known only to those who had grown up under Avalon, like Shadow Falls. She hadn't left Earth, although hoped that one day she would be able to travel. It was a dream that had helped her get through the tougher moments.

Not only were the gods, goddesses, and creatures of all mythology real, but the places Layla had only read about in stories as a child were too. Not all of them were accurate descriptions from what she'd heard, but since the same could be said for the gods, goddesses, and creatures she'd met, that wasn't too surprising.

The crater in the middle of the mountain range was large enough to house several thousand people. At night, runes glowed around the tips of the mountain high above and kept them hidden from anyone flying over. Runes, magic, glyphs, sorcerers, werewolves, vampires, and elementals were only the tip of the iceberg of what Layla had discovered in the last year. For a while, she had felt there would always be something new, something incredible, to learn. That was slowing down now, although she still occasionally found a species, or type of power, that she'd never encountered before.

Before a lunatic with the need to make everyone kneel to him had run Avalon, the organization had kept a fairly tight lid on the existence of other species. Now that was done. Over. But Layla was impressed that they'd kept it secret for so many years, as gods turned into myth and legend and humanity stopped believing that magic existed.

Layla lived in a seven-bedroom house close to the entrance of the village. It reminded her of the mansion in England where she'd stayed while coming to terms with her abilities, before it had been deemed too dangerous to remain. She shared it with Harry, Chloe, Kase, Remy, and Diana, who she assumed was only there to make sure the rest of them behaved. Or to make sure Remy did.

Kase tapped Layla on the shoulder. "You sort of zoned out there for a minute."

Layla blinked. "Sorry, I was miles away. I still can't believe so much has happened in such a small amount of time."

Layla and Kase walked down the slope toward the village and, reaching their home, stepped into a sparsely decorated foyer. A hallway stretched to the right and left, leading to the many rooms on the ground floor. A large staircase in the middle of the foyer was the only way for residents to get to the bedrooms above. Space was at a premium, so there were no gardens in the settlement and very few people had a home to themselves, but Layla was happy to have her own bedroom, bathroom, and more than one person in the house who knew how to cook.

Harry Gao appeared in the corridor to Layla's right, talking on his mobile phone. Harry was human, and seemingly had no interest in changing that fact. He was born to a Chinese-American general in the US Army and an English mother who was a doctor. Harry had helped the group hunt and stop Elias Wells, Nergal's last psychotic employee. "Gotta go, Mum, see you soon." He ended the call and hugged Kase and Layla. "Glad to have you home safe."

"Your mum and dad still checking up on you?" Kase asked.

Harry rubbed a hand over his almost bald head. He was several inches taller than Layla, and his build was what Kase had once described as wiry. "They think I'm working a marine biology job in Greenland. I'm sure my dad would be calling in favors from his old military buddies to drag me home if they realized what I was actually doing. I love my parents, but protective doesn't even begin to describe it."

"We any closer to finding out where Nergal has established his main base of operations?" Kase asked. Harry had been trying to get a handle on Nergal's location since they'd all moved to Greenland.

"No. Not even a little bit." Harry replied. "And, seeing how I'm on a bad news kick, we've also received word that Avalon forces are searching for Hades' hidden compound in Canada. At the moment, Hades doesn't seem to be worried, but Persephone is still running interference with Avalon, trying to make them think whatever she wants them to think.

"And, I'd like to take this chance to say that as one of the few pure humans living here, it's still weird as hell to work with people I read about in stories as a child. Does that ever go away?"

"Eventually," Layla said. "You just need to train with a few more of them. Trust me, the awe disappears when they're kicking your ass."

"I'll keep that in mind," Harry said in a tone that suggested he didn't want to do anything of the sort. "Jared is in your room, by the way."

Layla smiled. After being forced to leave England, Layla and Jared had grown close, and had eventually decided to start a relationship. It hadn't always been easy to maintain with both of them playing active parts in the operation to bring down Avalon, but they managed to steal a moment here and there.

"I'm going to go say hi," Layla said.

Kase punched her on the shoulder. "I'm not sure if that's the correct response when someone's friend is about to see their boyfriend for the first time in two weeks, but it was that or wolf-whistle, and as a were-wolf, I feel like I'm meant to be offended by that term."

"Really?" Harry asked.

"Honestly, I'm not sure. I just know that I don't like people doing it at me."

Harry and Layla shared a glance. "What did you do?" Layla asked.

"Well, there was some wolf-whistling, and cat-calling, and then shortly after, they found a giant werewolf standing in front of them. After that, there was a lot of pants-pissing, followed by running and screaming."

Layla turned away and smiled, while Harry chuckled. "I would pay to see that on film."

"It was pretty cathartic."

Layla left Harry and Kase to chat and bounded up the stairs to her room, which was one of two at the rear of the building. Harry's room was opposite hers, which was quite useful when they stayed up late to drink vodka and watch whatever film their housemates had managed to acquire. Movie night was about as close to normal as they got.

Layla opened the door to her room and found Jared lying on her bed reading a book. His long, dark hair was tied back in a ponytail, and he looked up at her with piercing blue eyes and a warm smile.

"Now that is sexy," Layla said.

"Me lying on your bed?" He had a slight Irish accent.

"No, you reading."

"Ah, I found it in the library. Did you know this place has a library? I heard some of our residents were unhappy at the lack of books, so people have been acquiring them and bringing them in. I also heard you were coming back today, so I thought I'd wait. Hope you don't mind."

Layla walked over and kissed Jared on the lips, lingering there for a few seconds. "I need a shower," she said, pulling away.

Jared sniffed. "Yes, yes you do."

Layla hit him playfully on the arm. "I can't believe you sniffed me. You're not meant to agree I stink."

"Oh, I'm sorry, you smell divine. Or swampy. I get the two confused. How did the mission go?"

"Saved some people, found a bunch of Nergal's scrolls. Then lost the latter when someone killed themselves and blew them all up."

Jared opened his mouth to speak and then closed it again.

"Yep," Layla said. "It's been a weird day."

"How long are you off for now?"

"Not sure. I guess until someone tells me otherwise. At some point, all of this hornet-nest-kicking is going to get Avalon's attention." Layla walked into the bathroom and switched on the shower before undressing and turning back to Jared with a smile on her face. "So, you feel like washing my back for me?"

Jared placed the book on the bed and almost ran to the bathroom.

8

Layla was fast asleep when the door to her bedroom was flung open and someone shouted for her to get up. She opened one eye, saw the time on the bedside clock, and was about to tell them where they could stick their 3:27 a.m. wake-up call when she saw that it was Sky standing in the doorway. It couldn't be even slightly good. Layla sat up. "Why are you here?" she asked.

"Because someone drew the short straw to get everyone in this place up, and that someone was me. You first, then I'll wake everyone else."

"Why me first?"

"You want to keep asking questions or would you rather come talk to my dad, Olivia, and the others to find out what's going on?"

"Others?" Layla still felt a little groggy. She had stayed up late with Jared, watching a movie, before he'd gone home, but now she wished she'd gone to sleep earlier.

Sky crossed over to the bed and handed Layla a mug of coffee; the smell removed any remaining semblance of sleep almost immediately. "I'm up," Layla said, putting the coffee on the table and getting out of bed.

"Downstairs in five," Sky said. "Wear something suitable for a mission. Weaponry will be given to you when you leave."

"Leave?"

Sky crossed her arms.

"I'm up," Layla said, standing. "I'm up, and completely awake, Captain Sleepkill."

"That was awful." Sky chuckled and left the room to go wake the others. Layla almost felt bad for her having to get Remy out of bed, but she looked at the clock again and any near-empathy vanished.

Layla got dressed in a pair of jeans and some heavy black boots and pulled a black hoodie over a t-shirt. If she needed body armor she'd be given some, along with weapons, by the quartermaster of the main compound. She went out the front door to the sounds of Remy being woken, and she pictured his unhappy reaction. Chloe, Harry, and Kase were already outside when Layla arrived.

"Any idea what's going on?" Harry asked. "It's too early to be this cold."

Chloe hopped from one booted foot to the other. "It's never the time to be this cold."

"I'm okay," Kase said with a smile. "Werewolves are hard to freeze, even in human form."

"Are all werewolves as smug as you?" Layla asked.

"No. Just me," Kase said, and started walking toward the village exit.

"Doesn't it strike you as odd that, apart from the guards on duty, no one else is awake?" Harry asked.

"Cruel," Chloe replied. "The word is cruel."

It didn't take long for the four friends to reach the walkway, and as the travelator took them across the compound, Layla began to run through the possible reasons for their early wake-up call. Had someone been hurt on a mission? No, if that was the case, why wake up their whole household?

"I don't have any idea, either," Chloe said to Layla. "I assume that's what you're thinking about."

Kase sighed. "I just don't know what else could possibly go wrong at this point. We're fugitives from Avalon and we live in a hollowed-out mountain in Greenland. Are they going to cut our Wi-Fi now? Did you download too much music and films, Harry?"

Harry shrugged. "Define 'too much'. We're not under attack: they'd need more than us for that."

They reached the end of the walkway and were greeted by Tommy and Olivia. "I'm sorry for the early rise," Tommy said.

"Liar," Kase replied. "You're beaming inside."

"Unfortunately, not this time," Tommy said with a solemn expression.

"Dad, what's going on?" Kase asked.

"We'll explain in a minute," Olivia assured them as they ushered the group through the compound and into an elevator, which took them down to the third of over a dozen floors, where several large offices were located.

The hallway was covered with the same gray brick as the rest of the compound, although here someone had at least tried to make it look slightly more inviting by painting the walls an eggshell-blue color. The floor was white, and it made Layla imagine she was walking on a cloud, which probably wasn't what the designers were going for. Or maybe it was, after all; she wasn't particularly up on her interior decorating dos and don'ts.

They stopped outside the third door on the left and Olivia went in first, revealing the massive room. It was fifty feet long and twenty feet wide and contained nothing but chairs: forty of them, all pointing toward the far wall. The room was closer to a hall than an office.

Most of the chairs were occupied by people Layla knew by name and by face, but they weren't the folk she usually hung out with. The majority of them were professional soldiers: people who had worked for Hades or one of the other big names, representing all who had joined together to fight when shit had well and truly hit the fan. Jared sat at the far end of the hall and he waved in Layla's direction. He had completed a lot of training in order to be invited onto one of the military teams and Layla was exceptionally proud of his progress. She waved back and watched as Jared's hair was tussled by a large man sitting behind him. Laughter broke out on that side of the room as the people he worked with teased him.

Other familiar faces were present. Nabu and Irkalla, once considered Mesopotamian deities, had worked with Nergal many centuries ago. Diana was already with them, talking to Irkalla. The pair were close friends, and Layla was surprised to see Irkalla wave her over to a chair beside them.

Layla, Chloe, Harry, and Kase all sat in the row with Diana, Irkalla, Nabu, and several people who Layla didn't know.

"How are your umbra powers coming along?" Irkalla asked as Layla sat next to her. Irkalla was roughly Layla's height and build, with dark brown skin and long, dark-purple hair that was currently in a bun. Her deep-brown eyes always held a sparkle of mischief, which was probably why she got on so well with Remy.

"Good, thanks," Layla said, not sure how to respond.

She saw Zamek, the Norse dwarf—his battle-ax strapped across his back—enter the room and sit in the front row. He turned around to face Layla and the others. "Any idea what's going on?" he asked.

"None," Irkalla told him. "Hades and Persephone told me to be here, so here I am. That's all the information I was given."

"Do you sleep with that thing on?" Harry asked Zamek. "I don't think I've ever seen you without it."

"I sleep with it, but I don't wear it," Zamek said with a wink. "I spent hundreds of years in a place where blood elves tried to eat my face at a moment's notice. You met them, didn't you, Layla?"

Layla nodded. "They worked for Nergal. It wasn't a fun time in their company."

The blood elves had once been called shadow elves, before a civil war between them and the sun elves had resulted in a loss for them. Their imprisonment in one of the Norse dwarf realms had caused them to become something feral, vicious, and evil. Layla had seen many of them over the years, and the experience never got any better.

"Ladies and gentlemen, my thanks to you for coming," Persephone said as she entered and moved toward the front of the room. "I know it's short notice, and I know it's blasted freezing outside, but this is important."

Despite the sleep-deprived state of pretty much everyone in the room, Persephone had their undivided attention.

"About an hour ago, we managed to get intel from one Alfred Carter: Nergal is mobilizing a force to attack Thunder Bay."

There were murmurs throughout the room.

"Yes, I know what you're all thinking: we've been expecting this, but how can we believe the words of a lying piece of crap? Well, we have checked in with Copper Harbor and Sault Ste. Marie, and the latter has already fallen to Avalon forces. It's being kept off the news and the fighting there was minimal as we pulled our people some time ago. We knew this was going to happen sooner or later. We're going to war."

There were more murmurs, this time tinged with regret, sadness, and more than a little anger. Everyone in the room knew what being held prisoner by Nergal meant. They'd all seen the results of his hospitality, and the aftermath of the brutal methods he used. If he took prisoners, they would not be treated well, non-combatant or otherwise.

"What do you need us to do?" Zamek asked.

"We'll get to that," Persephone said. "But first, Layla, I need you to go with Hades." She pointed at the door. "I think you're going to want answers I can't provide."

Chloe took hold of Layla's hand and squeezed it slightly as Layla got to her feet and walked over to the office door where both Sky and Hades stood.

"You okay?" Sky asked.

"I don't know," Layla told her honestly. "What's the rest of the meeting about?"

"We'll explain, I promise," Hades said softly. "But you're going to have questions that no one else in this room needs to hear."

"This is to do with my dad, isn't it?"

Hades nodded.

Layla knew it. Whenever something awful happened, she always wondered if her father was involved. He'd been in jail for years, but he still managed to cause her problems. Caleb Cassidy was the All-American Ripper, a title bestowed on him by the media after he had murdered people in almost every state. Over three hundred people died at his hands, and each of them had committed a crime and gotten away with it. On the outside, Caleb Cassidy had been an FBI agent with an exemplary record, while on the inside he'd used his position to murder those he deemed to have escaped justice.

Her father was an umbra with the ability to track anyone down, anywhere. All he needed was something they'd used and he was able to see where they were: the longer the personal connection to the item, the more powerful the vision. Caleb used his power not only to locate his victims, but also watch them go about their lives, meeting loved ones, doing other mundane things. He could stalk people from any distance without them sensing him watching them. It was a power that both Nergal and Avalon wanted to use to track down their enemies. And something Tommy, Hades, and the others very much wanted to avoid.

Layla walked with Sky and Hades back toward the elevator, which they then took up to the main floor of the compound. They entered a spacious room with windows that overlooked the mountain range. Sometimes Layla forgot how beautiful the place was.

Tommy and Olivia were already seated on one side of the large table. Both got up to greet Layla, motioning for her to sit. Hades and Sky sat beside the young woman who now just wanted answers.

"After the whole issue with Nergal and Elias," Tommy began, reminding Layla of the man who had kidnapped her in the hope that she would put him in touch with her father. Nergal had then murdered her friends and been responsible for her finding a spirit scroll and becoming an umbra; then he'd tried to murder her and everyone she cared for. In short, they weren't good memories. "Your father was moved. We couldn't have anyone discovering where he was. We asked you if you wanted to know the location."

Layla remembered her reply. "I said no, and to bury him somewhere he'll never be found."

"Well, only two people knew his new location," Olivia said. "I was one."

"And I was the other," Tommy replied. "We felt it was safer if it never went further. Your father was placed in a human prison that contained a wing covered in runes and used as a stop-gap for criminals with more-than-human characteristics. He was only meant to be there for a short time, but circumstances changed and the new political landscape made moving him a dangerous proposition."

"So you left him there?" Layla asked. It wasn't a criticism; it was, quite frankly, what she would have done.

Tommy nodded. "Safest place for him. He couldn't hurt anyone, he couldn't get out, and he certainly wasn't about to draw attention to himself."

"Does Nergal know where he is?" Layla asked.

"We don't know," Tommy admitted. "But the prison where your father is being housed is unfortunately close to Thunder Bay."

"We're putting together two teams," Olivia said. "One will go to the prison to retrieve your father, and the second is a strike force to provide support should the need arise."

"You want me to go in there," Layla said. It wasn't phrased as a question.

"We need you to, yes," Tommy said. "We have only one person he trusts at our disposal. And that's you. We could only move him without you last time because we gave him something he wanted."

"What?"

"His wedding ring," Olivia said. "That was his one request."

"Why not just drug him?" Layla asked.

"He's an umbra with what appears to be a high level of power," Hades said. "Unfortunately, we have no way of accurately gauging how powerful while he's in the rune inscribed room. And we don't want to take him out of it without some measure of assurance that he won't do something stupid."

"Hence me," Layla said.

"If we knew he'd cooperate, or that we could drug him, we would have moved him here, but no one saw Arthur turning into a monster coming," Hades said. "And by the time he had, we figured it'd be best not to draw attention to Caleb. That judgment has changed."

"Do you think that Nergal's forces will be waiting for us?" Layla asked. It was something she'd always been concerned about. Nergal wanted her father and had kidnapped and tortured Layla to try to get her to cooperate with him, too. Two years ago, his people had murdered her friends and destroyed her life. So she'd become an umbra and agreed to help Tommy fight against Avalon's enemies. And six months later, Avalon became the enemy. Arthur and his allies had seen to that. Layla wasn't about to let what had happened to her be for nothing.

"That's why we're sending you in with a team," Tommy said. "Nergal wants Caleb, and he's about to march on Thunder Bay. Once he takes the city, he'll head toward Red Rock, where Nergal knows we have a realm gate. Alfred said as much. But Alfred also said that Nergal wasn't going to war until the next batch of scrolls had been delivered, so apparently we've been moved up his schedule. It's possible that Nergal's forces will be there. We're unsure if they know about Caleb's location, or if you'll just encounter them, but either way we can't leave it to chance."

"I've known Nergal for many years," Hades said. "Caleb is the prize he wants above all others: a way to find all those who oppose Arthur; a way to remove problems before they arise. It's a nightmare scenario."

One thought occurred to Layla, and it wasn't one she really wanted to consider. But it needed to be asked. "What are your strike teams' orders if Nergal's people get hold of my dad?"

"If the members of the team can help him to escape, we go with that option," Sky said.

"And if we can't?" Layla asked, knowing where it would lead, but wanting to hear them say it.

"We kill him," Hades said without pause. "He either comes with us, or he dies. There's no third option."

Layla hated her father. He had ruined everything she'd ever loved as a child, forced her to undergo intensive training at a young age, and taught her to hurt people. Her father had done everything in his power to make her a weapon, although she still had no idea why, beyond his paranoid delusions about people coming to get them. It had taken Layla a long time to get over the crap that he'd stuck in her head, and even longer to talk about him with a detached coolness that only just betrayed the anger she felt at his continued existence. But despite the anger, and hatred, and resentment, she couldn't kill him. And that was something she needed the others in the room to understand. "My father is a monster. But I don't think I can kill him," she said. "Who's going to be in my team?"

"Diana, Kase, Chloe, Remy, Irkalla, and Zamek," Olivia said. "It's a good mix of skills, and you've worked with all but Zamek and Irkalla before. Commander Fenix will lead the second group. I believe Jared is part of the strike team. We wanted people you knew and trusted to be with you. The strike team will accompany you to the cell area and wait for you to collect your father."

Each of them was a good person who Layla trusted. "So, who gets the job of killing my father?"

"Irkalla will take his spirit," Sky said. "That way, any information he has will be retained."

Layla sighed. She liked Irkalla a lot and knew she would kill Caleb without hesitation should the need arise. "I hope Irkalla knows what she's got herself into."

"She is a last option," Hades said. "She won't do it unless it's completely necessary. We'd rather we got your father back here so we can talk to him."

"You want him for the same reasons as Nergal," Layla said. "Two sides of the same coin."

"We won't use the information to slaughter innocent people," Olivia said. "You know that, right?"

Layla knew Olivia was telling the truth. But the idea of using her father for anything sat badly with her. She didn't want her father to help either side; she didn't want him to do anything but sit in a small room with a tiny window and watch the world pass him by. She wanted him to be punished and allowing him to use his power didn't seem like a punishment, especially considering that Caleb wouldn't just hand over that information for free. He would want something in return to play ball. "I'm finding it hard to comprehend that I'm discussing the murder of my father with Hades, his daughter, and my best friend's parents. It's . . . disturbing."

"I understand that," Olivia said.

"I don't think you do," Layla told her. "I'm not sure there's anything else in the world that's quite as strange as having this conversation."

"You're right," Tommy said. "This is weird and messed up, and an absolutely shitty thing to put on your shoulders. To bring you in here, ask you to retrieve your dad, and tell you that we'll kill him if he falls into enemy hands, or refuses to leave . . . that's shitty, and I wish that it didn't have to be this way. I wish this could be resolved without death, and without your involvement. But you're a smart woman and a massive asset to our organization. If we'd misled you, or secretly kept information from you, you'd have felt betrayed and hurt, and none of us here want that. We've told you the worst-case scenario because we feel that we owe you the truth. Part of the reason Avalon is now in the state it's in is because of all the hidden deals and shady bullshit that happened over the centuries. When we defeat Arthur and his Avalon—and we will—we'll need something better to replace it, and frankly, I don't want to start whatever it will be by lying to our allies and friends."

Everyone stared at Tommy.

"What he said," said Sky before she turned to Tommy. "Have you been working on that speech?"

"No," Tommy told her. "I'm just naturally eloquent, and I read a lot of science fiction and epic fantasy. There are many stirring monologues in those kinds of books."

Olivia smiled. "I married such a huge geek."

"So, Layla," Hades said, bringing the conversation back on track. "Can you help us?"

"What if I say no?" Layla asked.

"Then we'll keep you here, send the teams, and see what happens. We'd rather it didn't come to that, primarily for the reasons we've already stated, but also because we value your place on our team. Removing a key piece means the others can't function quite as well."

Layla took a deep breath and let it out slowly. "I'll do it. I'll help get my dad out of prison and back here. But there are two provisos to this. One: you don't kill him unless there is no other option. If we're under attack, I don't want someone immediately killing him to just deal with it."

"Deal. No one would ever do that," Olivia said. "Okay, some would. But no one we're sending with you."

"What's the second condition?" Sky asked.

"When he's here, I don't want to know his location in the compound. I don't want to know how he's doing, or what information he's providing. I just want to hand him over to you, so I can go back to never thinking about him."

"What if he agrees to help, but only if you are involved?" Hades asked.

"We'll come to that if he says it." Layla sighed; she knew he'd make that deal. "Fine, yes, then I'll have to be involved."

"Anything else?" Olivia asked.

Layla shook her head. "Actually, yes. If Harry wants to be involved, I'd like him on comms and intel in the field. He's smart, he knows my team, and I trust him one hundred percent."

"He's only human," Hades said. "I mean that without disrespect."

"I know, but he's been trying to get put in the field for a year. And you know he's passed every single test you've thrown at him. The only thing that sets him apart is his humanity. You want to lead a new Avalon? One without secrets? Then start by involving humans in what you do. Harry is probably the best of them."

"Deal," Tommy said without a second thought.

"You sure about this?" Hades asked.

Tommy nodded. "Harry is a damn genius, and I like him, but more importantly, Layla's right; we have thrown every obstacle at the man and he climbs them all. He tried to create his own Green Lantern power ring at one point, using those damn magic crystals from Shadow Falls. Almost blew his hand off. He'll be fine running comms with Fenix and Diana beside him. Would you want to go through Diana to get to someone?"

Hades shook his head. "Not if I wanted to keep all of my limbs." He looked at Layla. "Seems like you've got yourself a deal. Go get kitted out and prepare for Minnesota."

"So, where is this prison exactly?" Layla asked.

"In the middle of a forest, near a small village by the name of Sawbill," Olivia said. "Everyone who lives in the village works at the prison, and they were all loyal to me when I was Director of the LOA."

"They're still loyal to you?" Layla asked.

"Not everyone moved over to work with Arthur's Avalon," Olivia told her. "There are some people who want nothing to do with Arthur's plan."

"And you put my father there?"

Olivia nodded. "It was perfect for him. And for us."

"There is one problem," Hades said. "As you know, Nergal is going to attack Thunder Bay. We assume he wants access to the realm gate at Red Rock. I've ordered an evacuation, but if this does go wrong, head for Red Rock. I'll have people waiting there just in case. It's a bit of a trek, so you might need to get some transport."

"If it comes to that, I'll figure something out," Layla said. "Hopefully, this will be as smooth a job as we've ever done." Even as she said the words, she knew she didn't believe them one hundred percent. Nothing involving her father was ever simple.

9

It didn't take long for everyone to get ready to collect the man who Layla had hoped never to see again. If her father was the lesser of two evils, things must really be bad.

Their modified Black Hawk flew the whole group through the night until they landed in a large field a few miles away from the village of Sawbill. The helicopter's occupants disembarked and were met by four black Audi Q7's, all parked in a neat row.

"It's a good job that we still have people who can sort out things like this, despite being on Avalon's most wanted list," Remy said. Like everyone else, he now wore combat armor and wielded several weapons, although, unlike everyone else, his weapons consisted of his sword and two custom-designed revolvers that hung from his hips.

A young woman walked over to Diana and hugged her. "No Sky this time?" the woman asked with a hint of a Southern accent.

"She got to stay home in the warm," Diana told her, before turning to everyone else. "This is Felicia Hales. She's responsible for supplying us with these vehicles."

"And a few extra things in the trunks," Felicia said, running an elegant hand through her long hair, which was varying shades of green.

"Thank you," Layla said.

"I knew your dad," Felicia told her. "When he worked for the FBI. I didn't know he was . . ."

"Evil?" Layla guessed.

"I'm not sure evil is the right word," Felicia said. "He was always very professional and helpful. He didn't know I was a vampire, and he certainly didn't tell me what he was, but then, when I worked with him, the word umbra wasn't known. I'm sorry he turned out to be much more dangerous than I imagined. And I'm even more sorry that your life got turned upside down because of it."

"Thank you," Layla said as everyone made their way toward the SUVs.

"Can I give you a piece of advice?" Felicia asked.

Layla nodded. "Sure, but if you're about to tell me to forgive him because he's my father and I'll miss him when he's gone, you're going to be disappointed."

Felicia laughed. "No, not even slightly. I'm a vampire, a very powerful one. Not in a bragging, look-at-how-awesome-I-am sense. It's just as a fact. I've dealt with many people over the centuries and not all of them have been nice. I like to consider myself a good judge of character, but your father is one of the few I was wrong about. I thought he was just someone who loved his family and job, and he managed to hide the dark side of himself so well that I found it genuinely terrifying."

"You're not the only one."

"No, I don't suppose I am. I know you're probably very conflicted about this whole thing, but my advice is that if you need to put him down, do it. I've read the report on his crimes—don't ask how—and I've met people like him over the years, people who hide that side of themselves so well you don't get a glimpse of their real personality until it's too late. Your dad may love you, but the second he gets the chance to revert to his old ways, he'll jump at it, and if you're in the way, there's a possibility he'll consider you an obstacle to remove."

"I've wondered that myself," Layla said with a sad sigh. "Would he hurt me to get to someone else? I'd like to think not. I'd like to think that despite everything else he's done, it would matter that I'm his daughter. But, honestly, I doubt it would. I don't think he would consider me anything other than an obstacle. Thanks for the advice. I'm not sure I could put my dad down, despite everything, but hopefully it's something I'll never find out."

Felicia offered her hand, which Layla shook. "Take care out there," Felicia said. "I don't want to read how we've lost another of our side to Avalon's evil. We've lost too many already, and I'm going to try everything I can to stop adding to that total."

"I'll do my damnedest to make sure I'm not one of them." Layla got into the nearest SUV and buckled herself into the seat next to Remy as the cars moved out of the park.

"Everything okay?" Remy asked.

"I hope so," Layla said. "Felicia just reminded me how much we've lost in the last few years. She didn't want me to be added to it."

Remy patted Layla on the hand. "We'll get this done and then we'll get back to our frozen paradise where we can all sit around, drink margaritas, and talk about the good old days."

"Talk about the good old days?"

"Those days when we look back with the rosiest colored glasses and decide that the young whippersnappers have it too easy, or aren't respectful enough, or have music that's strange and confusing."

"I'm twenty-three," Layla said. "I think I have a while before I get there."

"I'm several hundred years old," Remy replied. "I think I've always been there. I'm definitely wiser than my years."

"Are you bollocks," Chloe said, causing everyone to laugh.

"See, whippersnappers," Remy said with a tut.

The conversation continued with its usual jovial tone for the rest of the short journey until the car stopped. Layla looked out of the window at the dense forest all around them. There was a turning off the main road a few hundred feet from where she sat, and a dirt road appeared to disappear into the trees. Three buildings sat between her and the turn-off, all two stories tall, with white fences and small yards. They obstructed her view of the dirt road until they were level with the houses, when they stopped and several of the strike team got out to talk to the residents of the houses.

"That's Sawbill," Kase said, nodding toward the hamlet. "Small place, but they have a big job. We need them to talk to those working at the prison so that the gates can be opened. They might be expecting us, but if Sawbill doesn't let them know we're on our way, they won't take kindly to us just arriving."

"So, are these guards all human?" Chloe asked.

"Yep, pretty much," Irkalla answered from her position in the shotgun seat. "The prison is a human prison, after all; we just use a part of it to put people we want out of the way until we can move them somewhere more permanent. It's not a huge place—only a few hundred inmates—but it's high security, so we play nice with those who work there, provide protection to its employees, and we get to come and say hello without having to deal with Avalon or its newfound dislike of us."

"Sounds fair to me," Zamek said as the SUV started up again.

"They didn't make this place easy to get to, did they?" Chloe said, just before the convoy turned down the dirt trail that Layla had spotted earlier. Huge trees towered over them from either side, putting the occupants of the car into shadow.

"They aren't good people here," Irkalla said. "But if you break out of this jail, you're going to face several hundred square miles of nothing all around you. It's just forest, rivers, mountains, and, in winter, death. And that's ignoring the bears, wolves, and other assorted wildlife that will make your escape more difficult. And those are just the obstacles for humans. For the supernatural prisoners, there are runes of various types; some just remove powers, and some are designed to cause injury.

We had a werewolf escape a few years ago. He got to the outer perimeter, ignited a rune, and it turned the wall to gas. A rather unpleasant cocktail if I remember correctly. It almost killed him."

"They should put that in the prison brochure," Remy said.

"Anything else we should know?" Layla asked.

"Technically, this place still falls under the jurisdiction of the LOA. Thankfully, Olivia kept its existence off the official record because she's paranoid like that. Her predecessor did the same, presumably because working for Avalon for too long makes you distrust a lot of people. From what Olivia told me, the prison's location is known only to the director of the LOA. When she was kicked off Team Avalon, she made a few calls to let those loyal to her know what was happening. Also, she never gave up any information about places like this to her successor."

"Who's her successor?" Layla asked.

"Not sure who's in charge now," Irkalla said. "It was Ares after Olivia, but he came down with a bad case of pissing-off-the-wrong-sorcerer, and he's now dead. As for this prison, I have no idea. Avalon has more important things to do, and if the information I gathered about the prison is right, Avalon doesn't know they exist. So, it's a win all around, although if this goes well, we might want to send them some money to keep them happy."

"So long as Nergal doesn't know about this place," Remy said.

"We can only hope at the moment," Irkalla told him.

Half an hour later, the convoy stopped outside of the prison, which loomed over its surroundings. The walls were thirty-foot-tall concrete with four guard towers and a guard post with several armed personnel. They passed the first hurdle and were allowed onto the prison grounds where there were more towers and a parking area that led to the prison offices. Both teams got out of the SUVs and waited as two guards left the building and walked over to the group.

"Which one is in charge?" the older of the two men asked as he rubbed his hand across his graying beard.

"That would be her," Irkalla said, pointing to Layla.

"Sorry, what?" Layla asked, surprised by the announcement.

"He's your father and you're the only one he might listen to, so you're in charge," Irkalla told her.

"Surprise," Remy said, raising his hands and then, palms out, wiggling them about.

"Did you just do jazz hands?" Kase asked.

Remy smiled.

"You done with the show?" the guard asked. "My name is Captain Malcolm Turner and I'm in charge here. We've dealt with Avalon and its people a few times over the years, but I've always had Olivia as my main contact, and frankly I trust her more than whoever now has her job. Besides, I hear that Avalon is less interested in our prisoners and more interested in executing everyone, which puts me out of a job. So, I'm on your side."

"I like you," Remy said.

"I don't give a shit," Malcolm countered. "It's my job to keep you people safe, and to keep the inmates secure. Many of them are about as close to animals as people can get, but they're my animals, and I take my job seriously. You will not engage with any inmate. You will not rile them up or make fun of them. And you sure as hell won't touch them in any way. If, during your time in the prison, any inmate other than the one you're cleared to engage with says anything to you, you will ignore it. If they whip out their dicks and start pissing on you, you will continue as if nothing is happening. We will deal with the prisoners, not you. I don't care how many guns and how much magic you've brought with you. Am I clear?"

"Yes," Layla said.

"Your father, Caleb, is about as model a prisoner as we get here; until you put him with the general population, and then he tends to reduce their numbers. He is not to be underestimated, not even by his own daughter. He's in solitary. There are four other inmates in the same unit. Again, do not engage with them. We go in, get your father, and leave. That is the only way this works."

"Anything else?" Irkalla asked.

"Caleb Cassidy scares the living shit out of everyone who deals with him. Because his power allows him to track anyone, anywhere, so long as he has something they've touched, he was able to see where some of the guards went in the evenings. We were not meant to keep people like your father here for long-term care. The wing he's in was only meant to be a stop-gap before they could move him on. Unfortunately, that turned to shit, and we got stuck with him. We do our best, but we were never equipped to deal with someone like him. Most of the non-human prisoners we have here are only capable of minor power displays.

"Caleb would find a hair from one of his guards, or steal things like a pencil, and he would use that item to investigate the owner's world. Caleb would ask about their families, about mistresses and drug use. It was like some kind of screwed up game for him."

"He's a real charmer then," Remy said.

"When he was first arrested, Caleb was placed in general population. We knew that he was dangerous and arranged for greater security. Before those arrangements could be completed, he escaped his cell. He beat one inmate with a chair leg so badly most of the bones in his face were crushed." Malcolm looked toward his younger colleague. "This is Cody. He was the one who had to stop your dad."

"Took four guards to pull him away," the younger man said. "We threatened to shoot him, but he just laughed. Was he like that before he went in, Miss?"

Layla shook her head. "I never saw that side. Not until they arrested him, and his crimes were exposed for all to see."

"He was perfectly pleasant to talk to," the younger guard said. "Even when he said things about our lives—he'd mention that it looked like our kids were having a nice time playing a particular game, or that it must have been good to have our parents visit—it never seemed like he was being malicious or cruel, just like he was making conversation. Like he wanted to keep his power in use and was interested in what we did. He seemed surprised that we were upset with him."

"You'd better take us to him then," Irkalla said. "And we're keeping our weapons, so don't even ask."

Malcolm stared at Irkalla for several seconds before nodding. "With or without guns, there's not a lot we can do if you start killing people."

Layla and the rest of her team were led around to the side of the prison with the strike team bringing up the rear. Including the two guards, fourteen people passed through several security checkpoints as they moved through the prison.

Eventually they reached a set of heavy-duty doors, where four more men stood guard. Their station was filled with security controls, a locker that Layla imagined must contain weapons, and a few chairs. A second door lay a little further along the hallway. The prison captain turned to the group. "Only Layla and her team will go through these doors. You were informed of this, yes?"

"Yes," the commander of the strike team said.

Layla felt bad that she didn't even know the man's name. Her nerves had begun to kick in, but Jared stood behind her and squeezed her hand slightly, making her feel a little better about what was going to happen once those huge doors were opened.

The strike team commander turned toward Layla. "We'll be right here if you need us."

Jared gave Layla's hand another little squeeze, and she watched him walk away with his team. One of the guards swiped his keycard over the reader, while a second hit a switch to open the heavy security doors, which regained Layla's attention as the doors began to slowly part.

"How do you get back out?" Remy asked.

"Security keycard," Malcolm told him, showing him the keycard on his belt. "You need to use two different cards within a set time frame—one at the first set of doors, and one at the second—and a key code. It's the only way to get in or out of this wing. Thankfully."

"Has anyone outside of the facility been in contact with my father?" Layla asked.

"Do you mean in person?" Malcolm replied. "No. We get a lot of correspondence for him, though. Love letters from men and women, and occasionally messages that'd make a porn star blush. Officially he's still in a maximum-security prison north of New York, so they forward us all of his mail. I trust the people there—you don't need to worry about them."

"Can I read those?" Remy asked. "For purely scientific reasons."

"You disturb me," Diana said.

"You just figuring that out now?" Remy replied. "Seriously, though, people send him that stuff?"

"Some people love danger, or death, or are drawn to things that aren't quite right," Malcolm told everyone. "And some of those people think that talking to a serial killer is sexy."

"They should try being the child of one, and see how much fun that is," Layla said.

When the doors opened, Cody remained behind, and the group followed Malcolm down a brightly lit corridor to another set of doors at the far end. Malcolm swiped his card over the reader and input a six-digit combination code, opening the door a moment later and leading the team into another corridor. It didn't take long for them all to reach the solitary area. After clearing another security checkpoint with two more guards, they stepped into a horseshoe-like portion of the prison. Layla wondered how the strike team felt being so far away from them. She knew that the people with her would fight if anything happened, so she wasn't concerned.

Layla could see two levels to the solitary area, each with six cells. Those on top were set further back than those on the bottom level, and a glass dome covered the whole facility, letting in a lot more light than she had expected. Layla had imagined her father's prison to be a dark, dank, and frankly very unpleasant place, but it was light and airy, even though it felt cooler than necessary. She rubbed her arms, even feeling the chill through her jacket.

"We've learnt that being cold makes people less likely to be assholes," Malcolm said. "Not freezing, but just cold enough to feel uncomfortable. Don't know if that's science or some shit, but it seems to work here. And there are the runes, too. They work on anyone inside the cells, but we've been told that the power leaks out to here too, so don't take too long."

Layla looked over at the rest of her team, most of whom shrugged in response. "Which one is my dad in?" she asked their guide.

"Top floor, second from the left," Malcolm told her. "All of the cells have reinforced doors, their own bathrooms, and a few modern conveniences: our inmates may be among the worst people on earth, but the more pleasant their stay, the less likely they are to gut the guards."

"Just tell them to open the cell and leave," Layla said. "I know it's not protocol, but I'd rather do this as quickly and easily as possible."

Malcolm activated the walkie-talkie on his lapel. "Gary, can you open Caleb's cell? Don't worry about the shackles—apparently his daughter doesn't think he'll need them."

Gary's swearing was muffled by Malcolm's hand, but it was still obvious that the guard wasn't thrilled about the idea.

The cell door clicked before making a hissing noise.

"It's all yours," the guard told Layla.

"Thank you," Layla said, before slowly ascending the metal stairs to the floor above. She walked along the landing, every step ringing a million decibels in her ears, and stopped outside her father's cell. She'd rehearsed the things she'd wanted to say to him and imagined their first meeting a million times since the night he was arrested so many years earlier. Layla had believed she'd have a handle on the hurt and anger she felt, but she was wrong. She wanted to punch him, more than anything else in the world, and had to force herself to remain calm.

"Am I allowed to leave now?" her father called out as Gary left his cell, walking past Layla at a quick pace. Caleb had lost none of his Brooklyn accent in the years since she'd last heard his voice. It stirred memories she'd long since pushed deep inside.

"Hi Dad," Layla said, taking a step toward the cell.

Her father was almost six feet tall, bald, with a short blonde beard and deep-green eyes. Layla had thought of him as a giant, both in height and width, but the truth didn't quite reflect the memory of a child. He was still broad-shouldered, but was much more muscular than she remembered, his massive arms strained against his orange prison jumpsuit.

"Layla, is that you?" Caleb asked, disbelief on his face.

"We need to talk," she said.

Caleb took a step forward, and Layla's hand fell to the Glock against her hip. Caleb froze and took a step back. "You scared of your pa?"

"I know what you did, Dad. I know what you did and who you did it to. I am not the little girl who hid under her bed when the FBI came to arrest you in the middle of the night, terrified that the bad guys had found us. You cross me now, and I'll put you down. No screwing around."

Caleb Cassidy held Layla's gaze for several seconds before nodding. "Okay, my little hawk. Your call."

"Don't call me that. Just don't. You lost that right a long time ago."

Caleb nodded again. "Okay. Anything else I'm not allowed to do?"

"Piss me off."

Caleb's eyes narrowed. "I didn't bring you up to use that kind of language with your father."

"You didn't bring me up at all," Layla snapped, before forcing herself to be calm.

Caleb opened his mouth to say something, but closed it again after he saw Layla's team standing behind her. "You here for more than a catch up then?"

"We're here to take you somewhere more secure."

"You going to stick me in Fort Knox? Or have they re-opened the Tower of London for little old me?"

"Nergal is coming for you."

Fear flickered over Caleb's face. It was the first time Layla could ever remember her father seeming afraid of anything.

"You know who he is, I assume?"

Caleb nodded. "He's not a man whose acquaintance I'd like to make."

"You know why he wants you?"

"Yes, he wants me to track down his enemies so he can kill them. I assume Avalon has been unable to stop him."

"Avalon is under new management. The kind that considers Nergal a friend, and me a fugitive."

"You're an umbra, aren't you?"

Layla nodded.

"I never wanted that for you. I never wanted this life."

"You trained me to fight. You didn't do that because you wanted to save me from your life."

"I trained you to be better. That was all."

Layla was about to reply, but decided against it. "We . . . I need you to come with us."

"On one condition."

"I don't think you're in any position to make demands. It's not like you want to be found by Nergal."

"I'll develop a sudden case of power blockage."

"Fine, what do you want?"

"To be a part of your life."

"I tell you what, you come back with me, without any trouble, and we'll talk. Actually sit down and talk. But that's all I'm agreeing to."

A wicked smiled creased Caleb's lips. "Please do lead on then." He glanced up at the bullet-proof glass dome above the prison, and Layla followed his gaze as he spoke. "I always thought that when someone freed me of this place, they would burst through that ceiling. It's a huge design flaw."

"Sorry to disappoint. We're just going to go sit in a car and drive away. Nice and boring."

Caleb walked back into his cell and picked up a small jewelry box.

"What's that?" Layla asked.

"It's the one thing that I would like to take with me."

He passed it to Layla, who opened it and saw a white-gold ring. "This is what Tommy gave to you, isn't it?"

"It was your mother's."

Layla closed the box and passed it back to her father. She escorted him over to the group and Gary placed handcuffs on him. Layla couldn't help but look up at the sky through the glass dome as Irkalla added a sorcerer's band. She hoped they'd be able to get him someplace safe before the drenik inside Caleb started to gain control. Things were going far too easily.

10

"I'm sorry to lose you," Malcolm Turner said to Caleb as he opened the door leading out of the solitary area. "You were quiet for the most part. I like quiet prisoners."

"Malcolm, you never did anything exciting enough for me to want to know about your life outside of work," Caleb told him. "No affairs, no drugs, no gambling: a family man, who honestly loved being a family man, and did his job because he was good at it. There should be more like you."

"Ah, shucks," Malcolm said. "You're going to make me all misty-eyed."

They reached the second set of thick doors, and Malcolm brushed his keycard over the pad to unlock them, but the keypad blinked red. "Damn it." Malcolm activated his radio. "Cody, what the hell is going on back there?" There was silence for several seconds. "Cody, can you hear me, damn it?"

"Yes, boss. There's some sort of electrical problem. We had to reboot the system."

"Damn it," Malcolm said. "Just hurry."

"This happen a lot?" Irkalla asked.

"Not a lot, but sometimes when we get some bad weather, it makes the electrics go a bit crazy. Good job all the systems aren't connected, or we'd have to reboot the whole prison every few weeks."

"Good thing you don't use the electric chair," Remy said.

Malcolm chuckled. "It would be cheaper to tie people to the lightning rod and let nature do the job for us."

There was a slightly uncomfortable silence.

"It's a joke," Malcolm said. "We're primarily a human prison. Minnesota doesn't have the death penalty, and I'm not about to start executing Avalon prisoners."

"I can attest to that," Caleb said.

The door hissed, followed by an audible click as it slowly moved open to reveal Cody, the other guards and the strike team.

"Hey, can you hear me?" Harry said on the comm device that Layla wore in her ear.

"What's up?" Layla asked.

"We think we saw movement just outside the prison perimeter."

"You think you saw movement?" Chloe asked.

"It's gone," Diana told her. "It could have been a bear or something, but just be careful when you get out of the prison."

"Thanks for the warning," Layla said as the mood changed between those who had heard the concern in Harry and Diana's voices.

"Problems?" Malcolm asked.

"Probably nothing," the strike team commander said as he arrived with several of his people. He turned to Layla. "You ready to go?"

"Yes, thank you." She looked at her dad. "We're going to take you to a SUV. I will not be in that car with you. These fine ladies and gentlemen with the large guns will be in the vehicle. They are much less tolerant than I am. Do not make me regret anything I've done today."

"I gave my word."

"You're a serial killer," Layla told him. "Your word means exactly jack and shit."

"I see we have a long way to go before we can talk candidly," Caleb said.

"Sure, whatever gets you to behave," Layla told him. She passed her father off to the strike team, who led him out of the prison while Layla and her team followed alongside Cody and Malcolm.

"You hate him, don't you?" Cody asked Layla.

She shrugged, unwilling to be drawn into a conversation about her relationship with her father by a complete stranger.

The remainder of the walk was done in silence, and Layla could feel how on-edge everyone was. They'd all expected Nergal's people to try something, and with the possibility of movement outside the perimeter of the prison, Layla felt like every part of her umbra-enhanced senses was working overtime.

"I don't like this," Servius said, appearing beside her. "There's a bottleneck coming up that would make for a good place to attack."

"I know," Layla said.

"You know what?" Kase asked.

"Bottleneck coming up. High on both sides. Guard tower there, too. If someone is here, that's the place they'll try to get us."

No one joked. Not even Remy tried to make light of the situation. Everyone was too busy making sure they didn't miss something as they walked through the outer perimeter of the prison, under the guard tower.

"You see anything?" Chloe asked.

Layla looked up at the wall of the prison and then over at the high roof of the main building. Nothing. She stopped, turned, and glanced up at the guard tower at the exact same moment that Irkalla did.

"There's no one there," Irkalla said. "I sense no spirits."

"Up there, or anywhere?"

"Anywhere. No life nearby. That includes us."

"What does that mean?"

"Nothing good. At first, I thought it might have been the runes around the building, but it's something else. This is a block of my power."

Layla looked back at the others, who had all stopped. The SUVs were in the distance, and Caleb was thirty feet from them when she heard the sound of a whistle.

"What the hell is that?" Kase asked, looking around to try to find the culprit.

"That," Remy said, pointing up at a huge mass falling incredibly fast from the sky. It smashed into the closest SUV, demolishing it. Fragments of the vehicle were flung all around as the strike team hustled Caleb back behind the closest wall.

A second mass struck part of the perimeter wall, which vanished in a cloud of smoke and dust.

"What the hell was that?" Remy shouted as part of an SUV bounced out of the cloud of debris that had been created by the wall's destruction.

It was quickly followed by gunfire as the strike team engaged the first creature, just as the second ran back through the hole it had created in the wall.

"Oni," Irkalla said. "Shit."

The oni was almost exactly how Layla had assumed one of them would look. It was eight feet tall, with a huge muscular body, and wore black leather armor across its lower body. Its feet were bare, showing the talons at the tip of each of its toes. It had deep-red skin that reminded Layla of Terhal. The oni had two huge, white horns jutting from its forehead, and a black egg-shaped spot between its eyes. As the creature opened its mouth and roared, its sharp teeth protruded from a mouth that was never designed to fully close.

Layla looked toward the second oni, which was identical to the one closest to her, except that its skin was a putrid yellow, and unlike the large black mace of the red oni, it carried a vicious-looking curved sword.

"Did they drop them out of a plane?" Chloe asked.

"They absorb kinetic energy to grow stronger," Irkalla said. "Physical attacks will just make things worse. And the spot on their forehead is their only weakness, but it takes a lot of power to crack. Do not let the creature headbutt you."

"I'll try my damnedest," Remy said. "Anything else?"

"Don't die," Irkalla said, and used her necromancy to reach out to the nearest oni—the one with the curved sword. "You should not have come here."

The oni laughed, right until Irkalla bolstered her power with the spirits inside her, turning them into pure force, and used it to blast the oni in the face, knocking it back through the wall with a loud crash.

"I will keep this one busy," Irkalla said. "Get your father to safety."

Layla ran past Irkalla straight into another fight, as the oni with the mace cleaved an unfortunate prison guard in half as it tried to get closer to the main gate. The strike squad had moved to cover behind a prison wall, along with everyone in the second team.

"So, any ideas on how to kill an oni if you're not Irkalla?" Remy asked.

"Power," Zamek told everyone. "Not bullets, just pure power. Any chance you have an elemental or sorcerer among your number?"

The commander shook his head.

"Well, I for one wish we had a sorcerer right now," Remy said, with a touch of sadness in his voice.

"Crack the crystal. Not a problem," the commander said, then turned around the wall and fired two rounds directly into the oni's forehead.

The large creature roared in anger.

"Not with a gun," Zamek shouted. "Not even silver will hurt that thing."

"It absorbs kinetic energy, yes?" Chloe asked.

"Yes," Zamek said.

"Excellent. Me too." Chloe ran out from behind the wall and charged at the oni, who was tearing apart the main gate with its bare hands. It looked back at the woman running toward it and laughed. When she was only a few feet away, Chloe changed. Her skin cracked as red-and-orange power leaked out of it, her hands became claw-like, and her fingernails grew sharp as talons.

Layla watched as her friend allowed the drenik inside of her to take control, and as the oni pulled back and punched Chloe with a fist the size of her head. The drenik-Chloe was forced back several feet before she unleashed all of the power she'd gathered from the punch. Layla had seen it before, seen the power Chloe had inside of her, but, even so, it was incredible to witness her friend unleash enough power to knock an oni off its feet, screaming in pain as its crystal cracked.

"That's our cue," Zamek said, and the strike team swarmed over the injured creature. One of them turned into a werebear mid-leap and landed on its chest, tearing out huge chunks as a second strike team member—an alchemist—placed a hand on the wall beside the beast and collapsed it on the oni's head. The rock smashed with several times more force than gravity alone would have managed. The spirit inside the oni left its body, which dissolved.

An SUV crashed through the remains of the wall close to the puddle that was the dead oni, and Diane, Jared, and several more strike team members jumped out, ready to fight.

Layla sprinted around to where Irkalla had been and saw her rip the crystal out of the curved-sword-carrying oni's head. The woman shivered slightly, and Layla knew that she was absorbing the oni's spirit.

Layla walked up to Irkalla, who kneeled on the ground, her eyes closed, concentrating on what she'd just absorbed. "Irkalla?" she said softly.

"Too much power at once. The oni are powerful in a very specific way; their spirits are essentially pure energy. They are difficult to absorb." She gasped. "It was young. A mere child in oni terms. No wonder we defeated them so easily."

Caleb stood beside Layla as the rest of the group made their way toward them.

"The vehicles are done. And this isn't over," Layla said.

"The radios are out," Malcolm said. "What have you brought down on us?"

Before Caleb could reply, the sound of banging drums floated over the air, malignant and foreboding.

"Nergal really wants you," Remy said to Caleb.

"Yeah, that's come up before."

Layla looked at the sky, which had become dark since she'd entered the prison. "Dawn isn't for a few hours." She removed the phone from her pocket. "No reception, no nothing. We're out here by ourselves."

"Many people here don't deserve to be caught up in this," Kase said. "We need to get Caleb away from here."

"We'll buy you time," Diana said. She'd changed into her werebear form and towered over everyone.

"Irkalla, can you move?" Layla asked.

Irkalla got to her feet, albeit shakily. "I do not think I can contain more spirits. And frankly I'm not sure that if I expel the oni's spirit, the power won't just destroy indiscriminately. It will take me time to reduce its power to manageable levels. I say we keep to our original teams. Is there another way out of this place?"

"There's a maze of tunnels underground," Cody said. "They were here when the prison was built. They run from the town to here, and then from here up to the mountains. It's not a short walk, but it's much safer than running through the woods."

"We'll keep them here," Jared said, taking hold of Layla's hand. "Give you time to escape."

"I'll take the woods," Remy said. "I can get through them quicker than you lot, and frankly I'd rather let Hades know what's going on. I can get out of range of this comms block, get hold of our people, and hopefully have reinforcements here before we have to play Butch and Sundance."

"If they want Caleb this badly," Diana said, "they're going to tear this place apart looking for him unless we make a stand here."

Layla and Jared looked at one another and nodded.

"Okay," Layla said. "Let's get out of here."

"Hello," a voice called out through a megaphone at the front of the jail. "Is Layla there?"

"I'll go," Layla said. "Keep my dad here."

"We're coming," Kase and Chloe said in unison.

"You need me?" Remy asked.

Layla shook her head.

"I'll catch you up. Be safe." He took off out of the hole in the perimeter wall and vanished from sight in the dense and dark forest.

Layla, Kase, and Chloe walked toward the corner of the prison yard so they could see whoever was talking. When they arrived, Layla noticed that Harry was next to her.

"Harry, you're human," she whispered through gritted teeth.

"And you're my friend. Not letting you do this alone."

"You could get hurt," Layla told him.

"So could you," Harry said, not breaking her stare.

"I don't have all day," the megaphone-enabled voice said.

"I'm here," Layla shouted, stepping from the corner of the building with her hands raised. "What do you want?"

A woman stood just inside of the ruined gate. She didn't look to be too much older than Layla and wore black body armor over jeans and a t-shirt, and carried a sheathed sword against her hip. Layla recognized her as the same woman who had killed herself on the beach only yesterday.

"How are you alive?" Layla shouted. "Kristin, wasn't it? I watched you blow yourself up."

"I'm very special," Kristin said. "Just so you know, this sword isn't made from metal. Don't want you getting any ideas."

A man stepped over the rubble and leaned against the guard tower.

"You killed the guards in those towers?" Layla asked.

Kristin smiled. "Of course. They died the second you stepped inside the prison."

"And the rest of the guards?"

She shrugged. "You're less freaked out than I expected."

"You're either an umbra or something I haven't met before," Layla said. "Nothing to freak out over."

"It's a pleasure to meet you again. Sorry about the loss of the spirit scrolls, but we couldn't have them falling into your hands."

"Where are the rest of the guards?" Layla asked again, more forcefully.

"We've known about your father for a few days now. But we wanted to wait and get as many of Hades' little friends as possible into the bargain."

"You're not answering my question."

"Fine. The guards are mostly still alive. Can't say how long that's going to last, though. How'd you like the oni? To be honest, I was expecting them to be more impressive."

"Irkalla says they're young."

"Yes, the older they get the less likely they are to take orders from those they don't like. Or anyone. Solitary creatures by nature, so you have to get them young to make them work for you."

Layla resisted the urge to run back to the rest of the group and tell them what she'd heard, and looked up at the nearest guard tower. She saw a blood elf watching her.

"Blood elves, again?" Layla asked.

"They're just good cannon fodder," Kristin said. "They take orders like champs and they really like killing people—sometimes a bit too much, you know? No rifles up there. We weren't sure just how powerful you've become, so we didn't want to take any chances with metal, hence the ceramic sword. It's not just ceramic, you understand—that would be bad, if my high school science lessons were accurate. No, this is something we managed to cook up in Nergal's laboratories. Smart people work for him. Less smart people stand against him."

"What do you want? Apart from my dad?"

"Oh, there's no back-and-forth here? I was expecting more banter. Okay, if that's how you want it, you will all stand down and come with us, or we will slaughter you and Caleb comes with us anyway. That's it."

"Or we kill you?" Chloe asked.

Kristin laughed and pointed to a middle-aged man, who stepped over the rubble accompanied by a blood elf, who held a sword to the man's neck. Blood elves have purple skin, with blotches of lighter or darker purple across their bodies. The one in front of Layla had a bald head and wore blood-red leather armor. Its sword was black, and she knew from experience that the creature would happily use it to torture rather than killing quickly. Like all of its kind, the blood elf had black eyes, and its teeth were small, sharp triangles, like those of a piranha.

It pushed the man forward slightly, and he stumbled, waving his arms in an effort to keep from falling to the ground.

"This is subject 4942, I think," Kristin said, turning to the man. "Is that right?"

"Yes," the man said softly.

"He's an umbra with a very distinct power. He can block electronic communications for several hundred meters in all directions. That means landlines, too. And he can screw with the electrical signals that people give off, making us invisible. It's quite impressive. There's no call for help, no cavalry coming, and the only people who can save you are locked up for horrific crimes. Oh, actually that's a lie. I have a few dozen blood elves currently slaughtering every living thing inside that prison. They started the second you left solitary. You were all so busy with the onis, with no comms, they didn't stand a chance."

"So, our choices are surrender or die?" Layla asked.

"Yep. Nergal wants your father, but he also wants you. I think you might have pissed him off a bit. I tell you what, I'll give you five minutes to talk to your friends, and then all of you can lay down your weapons and leave. Or we can start butchering you, and I get my cardio for the day."

"Or, like I said earlier, we kill you first," Chloe repeated.

"We have a horde of blood elves. I don't even know how many that is, but it's a lot. And we have a few other surprises, too. I'm looking forward to you watching them in action. A gargoyle—have you ever seen a gargoyle? They used to be sorcerers and basically screwed up their bodies with blood magic and turned themselves into monsters. They're a bit messed-up, and they really like hurting people."

The bullet came from beside Layla. Chloe had fired without a word. Kristin collapsed to the floor with a hole in her forehead.

Layla aimed toward the nearest blood elf, instinctively firing twice as it advanced, hitting the creature in the throat and chest. It dropped to the ground and subject 4942 fell upon its body, pounding on it with his fists. The elf wasn't quite dead and drove a dagger into the man's throat; both of them died a moment later.

"We need to get back to the others," Harry said. "Because . . ."

The doors to the prison opened and dozens of blood elves poured out. Chloe shot two in the chest, knocking them to the floor despite their leather armor. Kase had changed into her werewolf form and was flinging blood elves around as if they were made of paper, while everyone else fired at anything that moved.

Layla looked for Harry and discovered him fighting an elf. The elf clearly thought that attacking a human would be easy, but Harry had been trained by the best and carried two batons—Harry called them eskrima sticks—he'd spent time working with. He'd converted one of them to give a massive electric shock upon impact, as the elf quickly discovered when Harry smashed the stick into its jaw. The creature collapsed to the ground, convulsing for a second before lying still.

As more elves left the prison, the four friends turned and ran back toward the rest of the group, who were dealing with an even larger number of blood elves. The strike force was putting them down in huge numbers, using the silver-rounded Heckler and Koch MP5s to deadly effect as everyone made their way toward the hole in the perimeter wall.

Layla noticed that Cody and Malcolm were in the thick of the fighting and ran to their side as Caleb calmly avoided any blood elf that got too close, never lifting a finger to fight them or protect himself.

"We need to get out of here now," Layla said.

"Go," the strike team commander shouted. "We've got these."

"Go!" Diana ripped the head clean off one blood elf and tossed it at another close by.

Malcolm and Cody led Irkalla, Chloe, Kase, Harry, and Layla to the rear of the prison as blood elves on the towers starting firing at them. Jared killed two of the creatures and ran toward the group.

"Let's get out of here," he said. "Fenix is going to hold them back before joining us."

"Didn't know freedom was so close," Caleb said as Zamek brought him over to the group.

Everyone ignored him as Cody and Malcolm pushed aside overgrown vegetation to reveal a metal door. Layla moved her hands and the lock spun with incredible force. A second later the door opened by itself.

The group ran into the dark tunnels beyond, with Layla last so that she could shut the door. She paused as Jared stood guard, firing at any blood elves who got too close.

"You coming with us?" Layla asked.

Jared shook his head. "My place is here with the team. We'll catch you up, I promise. Now go."

"Be careful," Layla said as she closed the door. There was no point in arguing with Jared. He had made up his mind, and she needed to get everyone to safety. She pulled the metal around the door, making it impossible for anyone to follow unless they had a blowtorch or another oni.

The sounds of fighting were heavier now, and she hoped that everyone who'd stayed behind just so they could get Caleb to safety would be okay.

She turned to the rest of the group.

"They'll be okay," Irkalla said. "No one out there is going to let Nergal and his friends win."

Layla nodded. "Let's get going. We have a lot of distance to cover and not a lot of time to do it."

"We can stop off at a town close to the border," Cody said. "It's called Winterborn. It's the only big town between here and Red Rock."

"At least we will be able to rest, get some supplies, and check in with your friends to see if they're okay," Malcolm said. "And I can check with my family. They're going to be worried."

"Sounds like as good a plan as we've had so far," Chloe said.

The group set off down the dark tunnels; the occasional hanging bulbs the only lights to guide them.

11

"Two clones in two days," Kristin said angrily. "I'm beginning to get really fed up with it." She stood just outside of the prison grounds in a makeshift command center that consisted of a few SUVs and a truck that had been parked together.

"And we lost some elves," Abaddon said from beside her.

Abaddon had insisted on coming with Kristin, which she didn't mind so much as find confusing. She didn't know the ancient necromancer well, and honestly wasn't sure if anyone could claim to, but she knew that Abaddon wasn't overly fond of Nergal. She didn't want it to turn into a pissing contest, but Abaddon had never seemed interested in throwing Nergal from the inner circle of New Avalon—as it had been named internally, a title which Kristin personally hated. She was more about pointing and laughing when it all went wrong.

"More importantly, we lost Layla and Caleb," Abaddon said without any kind of mocking or anger, just stating facts.

"They'll go to the closest city," Kristin said. "Winterborn."

"If that's the case, they'll want to head to an area that Hades controls, such as Red Rock. The exact place Nergal is trying to take."

Kristin nodded. "And that's fine. We control Winterborn."

"We must take Red Rock," Abaddon said.

"Why?" Kristin asked.

"Because I say so," Abaddon told her, making it known that the conversation was closed.

Kristin shrugged and continued toward a black BMW SUV parked at the rear of the assembled military vehicles that Nergal had deployed. She paused at the car and looked back. For the first time, it struck her that Nergal wasn't using his own people. Most were blood elves that Abaddon had brought with her, and they outnumbered Nergal's forces two-to-one.

"Something funny?" Abaddon asked from beside her.

Kristin sighed and turned to face the necromancer. "No," she said. "I'm going to make a call."

"To Nergal?" Abaddon asked. "I'd like to be in on that."

Kristin tried not to snap. She'd been told to offer Abaddon every courtesy in their dealings together, and Kristin knew how deadly the necromancer was. There were good reasons why people feared her. She hadn't seen Abaddon cut loose herself, but she'd heard stories from people she trusted. The necromancer had murdered people who used to be considered gods. She stood at the right hand of Arthur. She hadn't accomplished those things through luck.

Kristin climbed into the rear of the SUV and dialed Nergal's number.

"How did it go?" he asked as Abaddon sat beside Kristin, placing a finger to her lips as if to ask Kristin to remain quiet about her presence.

Kristin thought for a second. Give up Abaddon, or deal with the necromancer's anger. It wasn't much of a choice. "They both escaped," Kristin said. "Along with several more of their group."

"Goddamn it," Nergal snapped, which was followed by the sounds of things being flung around. "I knew you were useless, but I figured you'd at least be able to take them down without making this more complicated."

Kristin chose to ignore his unpleasantness. "Their only choice is to head toward Winterborn."

"Unless they use the river."

"They won't use the river," Kristin said, adding *idiot* in her head. "We'll see if we can shepherd them along toward Winterborn. We can take them there with few problems. They won't fight us when innocents are in the way."

"You hope."

"They're weak like that," Kristin said. "That Layla woman didn't shoot me when she could have. She hesitated. The same can't be said for all of them, but if we can separate them from the pack, we can take them."

"Get it done. Don't screw up again." Nergal ended the call.

Kristin took a deep breath, climbed out of the BMW, removed her sword, and used it to smash the windows of the vehicle. She walked around the SUV, breaking the lights at the front and rear, puncturing the tires, and doing as much damage as she could until her rage had dissipated.

"You done?" Abaddon asked. She leaned up against one of the smashed windows. "He doesn't treat you with the respect you're due."

Kristin tossed her sword onto the ground.

"He blames you for his failure," Abaddon continued. "How many of his people did he send to help you do this? Too few. I know you were thinking the same. He relied on my blood elves to do the job. Unfortunately, they're mostly reanimated blood elves, and they lack that extra bit of something living blood elves have, that extra bloodlust. He sent you to fail so he could lord it over you."

Nergal had been upset with Kristin's predecessor for his loss of blood elves, so Nergal had made a deal with Abaddon. She'd reanimate the corpse of every dead blood elf that they could bring back. They would only follow rudimentary orders and killing was their only goal, but they were useful fodder. Unfortunately, Nergal appeared to think that Abaddon clawed her way a little further into his organization with every blood elf she reanimated. Kristin didn't think Abaddon could get any further into Avalon than she already had. Not unless she wanted to kill Arthur, and that was never going to happen.

As far as Kristin was concerned, Nergal's problem was that no one else on their side was as powerful as Abaddon in terms of necromancy, so he had to use her. They'd tried to reanimate blood elf corpses with some less powerful necromancers, but the results had been disappointing and, on one particularly gruesome occasion, incredibly gooey. It meant that Abaddon was a wonderful ally, but one who made Nergal more and more resentful with every success that she was part of.

Kristin shook her head. "Allowing me to fail seems like a lot of effort on his part."

"Nergal does not believe that women are his equal," Abaddon said, walking over to Kristin and placing a hand on her shoulder. "He will never believe that, no matter how much we show to the contrary. And it wasn't about you failing. It was about me failing."

"You're suggesting that Nergal set me up so that he could lord one over you when it went wrong?"

Abaddon nodded.

Kristin opened her mouth to argue, but thought better of it. Would Nergal have done that? Yes, there was no doubt in her mind that he would have sacrificed her to make someone else look bad. But she'd always thought that he had given her abilities because he saw something special in her. The idea that Nergal would use her as any other disposable entity, just to make a point, stung more than she cared to admit. She turned and walked away without another word.

Kristin made her way through the ranks of blood elves, which were sprinkled with several species, and enjoyed the sounds of the battle taking place inside the prison grounds. She wondered how many reanimated blood elves were dead. Until today it hadn't mattered, not in her eyes. They were expendable. But now the idea that Nergal was using their failure as a way to gain more favor with Avalon had been placed in her head, it was all she could think about.

"How's it going?" Kristin asked one of the living blood elves, one of only a dozen that had come with the group.

"A lot of them fled," the elf said, its voice raspy and deep. "We caught a few."

"How many are alive?"

The blood elf shrugged.

Kristin stepped over the rubble of the prison entrance and the sounds of fighting died away, replaced with an awful silence that she felt was almost oppressive. She was used to battle, she was used to noise, to the din all around her, but not to silence. Kristin didn't like silence. It left her alone with her own thoughts, and she was of the opinion that no one should be burdened in such a way. And at the moment she had more thoughts to deal with than she considered healthy.

She walked around the corner of the prison and found several dead bodies belonging to other species, including human, among the dozens of dead blood elves. She stopped walking. "Are these blood elves dead, or re-dead?" she asked Abaddon, who she knew was walking behind her.

"How do you do that?" Abaddon asked.

"I have another clone in that tower behind you. What she sees, I see. I'm younger than you, Abaddon, but I'm not new at this."

Kristin continued on and found the remains of the force Hades and his people had sent to find Caleb around another corner. Two were dead, leaving only four alive: two men, one much older than the other, and two women, one about the same age as Kristin and the other currently in the shape of a werebear. All three were on their knees with looks of anger etched on their faces.

"You let Layla and her kin escape," she said to the blood elf commander next to the oldest of the three prisoners.

"They fought well," the blood elf said.

"Commander Fenix," Kristin said. "You plan on introducing me to your friends here?"

"I have no idea who you are," Fenix said.

"My name is Kristin," she told him. "Nergal has a file on you. You were human until you had a run-in with a werewolf in Germany in 1944. You worked for the military at the time, but you left when Hades made you a better offer than stalking the woods of a country you were only there to liberate. No wife, no children, no family of any kind. I hear you're not that powerful a werewolf, but we can't all be Tommy or Kase Carpenter, now can we? So, who are your friends?" Kristin slapped the younger male across the face. "Your name, soldier."

"Jared Bray," he said.

"Well, Jared, you're going to behave, yes? I would so hate to slice up that pretty face of yours."

"What did you do to me?" Fenix asked.

Kristin's attention refocused on the commander. "Ah, not being able to turn into a seven-foot werewolf beginning to concern you? And with no sorcerer's band. Well, do you remember a few years ago when Arthur had humans slaughtered in their thousands so he could jump out and save them all? Well, that's the thing about humans: they work well under pressure. So, after Arthur . . . persuaded their best and brightest to work for him, he asked them to come up with new ways to deploy the sorcerer's band." Kristin motioned for the blood elf to pass her the rifle he held. Once she had it, she showed it to Commander Fenix.

"It's a rifle."

"It's a specially-designed rifle." Kristin emptied the weapon and passed it back to the blood elf, keeping the magazine in her hand. She ejected the final round and showed it to the three prisoners.

"A tranquilizer dart?" the werebear asked.

"That's right. And you are?"

"Diana," the werebear said. The silver cuffs she wore around her wrists must have been incredibly painful, yet she didn't return to her human form.

"Ah, well, Diana. Now we have a celebrity in our midst," Kristin said with a mocking curtsey. "This little dart is exceptional. You see, when it exits the chamber, the casing is designed to fall away, leaving just this tiny needle. It travels just fast enough that when it hits something not human, it'll puncture the skin and inject the enzyme. Don't ask me how, I'm not a scientist. You fire this at a human, it'll kill them. Basically, they managed to distill those bracelets into a chemical compound. They don't perform completely right yet, and it's easier to use on the less powerful species, but they work well for the most part. You might all pass out or something, no big deal."

"What do you want?" Commander Fenix asked.

"You're going to come with us and answer a few questions," Abaddon said.

"Like hell we are."

Abaddon reached down and picked up one of the prone soldiers by the scruff of his neck. "This one lives. I can change that if you'd like? Or I can twist his spirit so he'll be under my control. Or I can ensure his spirit stays in the body and he gets to live. I can heal him. The others are beyond my control to heal; they're already dead. Your choice."

Fenix's eyes grew cold and hard.

"If you're thinking about saying that he knew the risks when he took the job, just remember that I can make him my personal slave for the next century," Abaddon said. "Take his soul, twist it until it's nothing but a raging mass of hate and bile, and then let him loose at a camp."

Kristin walked over to Diana and kneeled in front of her. "You're a big deal," she said. "I've heard stories about you."

"You going to threaten me, too?" Diana asked. "Because I'm not really sure that's wise."

Kristin shrugged, stood up, and planted the heel of her boot in Diana's face. Diana growled and moved to stand.

Kristin ignored the threat and turned to one of Nergal's guards. "If she won't change naturally, stick a sorcerer's band on her. We can't have her walking around in her werebear form." The muscles in Diana's body tensed. "You going to fight me?" Kristin said with a chuckle. She cuffed Diana around the side of the head. "I think you want to stay alive long enough to escape. So, just sit there like a good little . . . bear, and behave."

"You're enjoying this," Jared said. "You look happy."

Kristin looked toward Jared and smiled her brightest smile. "I love my job. And sometimes my job has perks like today. Are you sure you really want to become the target of my attention?"

"You just don't need to hurt anyone," Jared continued. "We're unarmed, cuffed, and of no threat."

Kristin stood over Jared. She looked down at him and wondered what it would be like to smash his face in with a hammer. She turned and walked away. "Get them loaded up," she commanded.

She walked over to the injured soldier and drove her sword into his skull, ignoring the cries of rage from Fenix. "The conversation about his life is now done," she told him.

"You like causing mayhem, don't you?" Abaddon said as the pair walked away.

Kristin shrugged. Killing the soldier had made her feel better. Destroying the BMW had helped, but it was no substitute for flesh and bone. "I'm going to have the prisoners taken to Winterborn. Before I head there, I'm going to bring a number of people to hunt for Caleb and Layla in the wilderness around us. Simple, really." Kristin turned away to walk toward her waiting SUV.

"What about Madison?" Abaddon called after her. "Your sister."

Kristin paused. She turned slowly toward Abaddon, radiating anger. She walked back to the necromancer, all sense that she was vastly out-matched forgotten. "What do you know?"

"Calm, little one. I know because your photo was on the evening news. Nergal might not pay attention to humanity, he might not care, but I find them interesting. I watch the news, I read about them. I like to know what kind of people these creatures became after several thousand years without our guidance."

"Madison betrayed me and needs to die."

"I assume you'll go back and try again?"

"Eventually, yes."

"You let a clone do it, I assume?"

Kristin nodded. "Not a mistake I'll make again. Madison is a personal issue, but personal and work don't mix."

"That's shit, and you know it. Damn, I've killed for personal. I've murdered and slaughtered for personal when I was supposed to be focusing on the bigger picture. I like you, Kristin, but unlike you, when I went out to destroy those who had crossed me, I completed my objective. And I did it no matter what the cost. Next time, just blow up the damn restaurant, or massacre them all in their beds."

"Why are you telling me this?"

"Because eventually Nergal will find out what you did, and he's probably going to blame another failed plan on your lack of focus. I just want you to be aware of that."

Kristin didn't believe that for one second. Abaddon always had a reason for doing something, and she wasn't known for being particularly altruistic. "I'll deal with Nergal when the time comes. He'll forgive me. I'm important to his plans."

Abaddon nodded. "Just like Elias was important to his plans?"

"Elias failed where I won't," Kristin snapped. "Nergal plucked me out of hell and gave me everything I ever wanted."

"Is that why you didn't just kill Madison with a car bomb? You wanted Madison to know, didn't you?"

Kristin maintained eye contact with Abaddon and nodded. "She needed to know."

"No, she didn't. You did. She wouldn't have given a shit, because she would have been dead. And the dead don't care how they died. That sentimental crap only matters to those who live."

"What about spirits?"

"For the most part, spirits are just memories and energy in human form. They don't much care how they died, and even on the occasion that they do, there's nothing they can do to change it. You cared that Madison knew it was you killing her—it wouldn't have mattered to her once she was dead, but you wanted to see the fear in her eyes. The same as when I killed Cronus and Rhea two years ago. You can care how they died, but don't lie to yourself and say it's for them."

Kristin didn't like that Abaddon's words were true. Madison hadn't needed to know. "Are you coming with us to Winterborn?"

Abaddon shook her head. "I have things to do. A friend is coming to visit after some time apart. I think I'll take her to Texas when you finally manage to grab hold of Caleb. I'm sure she'd like to see him.

"In the meantime, it was a pleasure to see you work, Kristin. I hope you don't get yourself killed. Nergal isn't half the boss he thinks he is. He'll be perfectly fine with you doing all the heavy lifting, but don't expect him to think of you as an equal. He didn't think his own wife was his equal; he doesn't think I'm his equal. Women are beneath him, they always have been. That's why eventually someone will surprise him and put a knife in his gut. Probably his ex-wife."

Kristin watched Abaddon walk away and get into a car, which soon drove out of sight. The blood elves who had been reanimated dissolved to nothing. Kristin looked down at her phone. Nergal had been mean to her on one-too-many occasions. She was loyal to the man, but loyalty had a limit. Hopefully, things would get better once Abaddon was gone from Nergal's day-to-day operations.

12

After an hour of running, the group stopped to rest. They had no water, little food, no shelter, and an unsatisfying number of weapons. Harry, Cody, and Malcolm in particular were having trouble keeping up with those members of the group who weren't human.

Layla sat beside Harry. "You okay?" she asked.

"Exhausted from all this running," he said. "It's hard enough to run for an hour at the best of times, but my adrenaline wore off a while ago, and it's cold. And my boots are not made for running. They're made for stomping and keeping my feet dry."

"It's a day's walk from the prison to Winterborn," Cody said. "And that's in good weather. Thankfully we have the whole day ahead of us before we need to camp."

"Hopefully the weather will hold out," Malcolm said. "Do you think your friends are okay?"

"There's no way a bunch of blood elves could take out Diana," Chloe said, "and the strike team are more than capable of keeping themselves alive. Jared will be fine."

"I know," Layla said, hoping her confidence shone through. She really didn't want to start thinking about what Nergal might do to the people she cared about. To Diana. To Jared. "Hopefully Remy got the call out and reinforcements will be on their way soon." She removed the phone from her pocket. "Still no reception."

"We need to keep moving," Kase said as she returned from scouting the area. "There's no one chasing us. At least no one I could smell. We need food, though. There's a fresh water stream about a mile to the north of here. I drank from it and didn't suffer any effects. I checked for dead animals nearby, but it looks good. I say we get there, drink, and see whether or not we can find a way to contact home and let them know what happened."

Harry got back to his feet. "In the meantime, we march until we drop."

"Hopefully it won't come to that," Layla said looking over at her dad. "You coping?"

Caleb nodded. "First time I've been outside of a prison for a while. I'm quite enjoying the freedom. Wish I'd spent more time doing laps in the yard, though. That would have come in handy. Be better if this sorcerer's band could go."

"Not a chance," everyone said in unison.

Caleb sighed, but the smirk on his face suggested that he wasn't overly bothered. Layla wondered how long it would be before he started looking for a way to escape.

"We've got a long trek ahead," Chloe said. "Let's get started."

They walked in silence for the better part of two hours, the wind increasing in strength as the day wore on. Trees loomed high above them on all sides, their leaves a mixture of reds, oranges, greens, and yellows. Layla thought it would probably have looked beautiful at any other moment in time. A large number of leaves littered the ground, making any kind of stealthy approach all but impossible, which was at least a small comfort.

"We have company," Kase said from the head of the group.

"Good company or bad?" Chloe asked.

"Fox company."

Everyone turned as Remy walked toward them. "Hello, people. I checked and you're not being followed."

"You are a sight for sore eyes," Chloe told him. "Any luck?"

"Well, yes and no," Remy said. "I got hold of Hades, and he wants us to head to Red Rock. The plan is to send dearest Papa Psychopath through the realm gate there, and so remove the piece from being played by either side, in the interim, at least. Then they'll destroy the gate. Thunder Bay has been attacked, and even though they're putting up a great defense while they evacuate, sooner or later it's going to fall, and then Red Rock is next."

Everyone turned to look at Zamek. "I knew about the plan," he said. "I also told them it was only possible in a theoretical sense."

"So, you're going to destroy a realm gate theoretically?" Remy asked.

"In theory, any alchemist should be able to destroy it," Zamek said. "Just because the dwarves built it doesn't mean we have to be the ones to destroy it. You only need to remove the parts of the inscribed runes that allow it to regenerate."

"Which means you need to be at Red Rock," Kase said.

Zamek nodded.

"Irkalla is weakened," Layla said. "Everyone else is close to exhaustion, and my father needs to get to that realm gate; a realm gate we're going to use to strand him in another realm."

"Our options are limited," Zamek said. "I get that you really don't want to make your father the problem of a whole new realm, but what are our options?"

Layla rubbed her eyes. It had been a long few hours. "I get it. I do. But it does mean I'm going to have to go with him. That is something I hadn't really considered. But on the plus side, at least we know exactly where we're meant to go." She looked up toward Caleb, who was being shadowed by Irkalla, Malcolm, and Cody. Layla wouldn't want to be her father if he crossed Irkalla, even in her weakened state. She wondered if he would try to escape once they got to the new realm.

"The good news keeps coming," Remy said, bringing Layla's thoughts back to the present situation. "There's a house about two miles to the west of here; it's in the middle of nowhere. We can rest there and figure out how we're going to get to Red Rock."

"What about the strike team and Diana?" Layla asked. "What about Jared?" His name almost caught in her throat as she said it. She couldn't imagine that Nergal's people would make their stay hospitable.

"If they have Jared and the others, we'll find them," Chloe said. "And then we'll make the bastards regret ever taking them."

"Sounds like a plan to me," Harry said. "And a plan that means we can get out of the cold much quicker than the original plan."

The group moved swiftly with the newly found impetus of avoiding a day-long hike. They walked for nearly an hour before they saw the brick house in the center of a large clearing. It was a lot larger than anything Layla had been expecting. There were three levels; the lowest was a huge garage. Stairs led up from the drive to the front door, and there were many windows and solar panels on top of the roof.

"Ah shit," Malcolm said. "Bill's house?"

"Who's Bill?" Chloe asked.

"He used to be some sort of Wall Street guy," Cody said. "He made a fortune from other people's misery. Now he comes here every summer to be a pain in everyone's ass."

"And they call me a monster," Caleb said, standing close enough that when he spoke the prison guard darted out of the way.

Layla noticed the smile on her father's face. "Why?" she asked him. "Why do something just to get a reaction like that?"

"It's fun," he said with no shred of enthusiasm or enjoyment. "Not as fun as killing those who deserve it, but you take enjoyment where you can get it when you're locked up for twenty-three hours a day."

"You find killing people entertaining?" Chloe asked.

"Don't you?" Caleb asked her. "Killing the wicked, your enemies, people who think that they're predators . . . Don't you get a thrill out of showing them otherwise? How many have you killed since you started working with Thomas Carpenter and his allies?"

Chloe turned to face Caleb. "No, I don't enjoy it."

"I've killed many people in my life, but there was one in particular," Caleb said as if Chloe hadn't spoken. "He was the third person I eliminated on my crusade to remove the scum from this planet. He worked on Wall Street and got away with killing someone with his car. I followed him home and beat him to death with a meat tenderizer."

"How can you say that as if you're talking about making a sandwich?" Layla asked.

"I did actually make a sandwich after," Caleb said. "He had this phenomenal rye bread that I've never been able to find. I think it was homemade. I should have gotten the recipe. That was back in the days when I was more impulsive and always after the rush of the kill. Took me a while to realize it's the buildup that needs to be the sweetest."

"Shut up," Layla snapped. "Please."

"I've seen evil before," Chloe said. "My mum was evil, and you have that same look in your eyes. That look that means you believe you're right, and everyone else is wrong."

"I am right."

"No, you're a psychopath. Just like my mum was."

"Your mom is dead, I suppose? Did you kill her?"

"No," Chloe said forcefully. "Someone did it before I could. Turns out, he did me a favor. The world is better off without her in it."

"Don't antagonize my friends," Layla said. "Or anyone at all. We got you out of prison so you could help us, because it's that or help Nergal."

"Don't bite the hand that feeds you?" Caleb suggested with another smirk. "As you wish." Caleb walked on, leaving Chloe and Layla alone.

"I'm sorry about him," Layla said.

"I'm sorry for you," Chloe told her. "I'd heard stories, but his eyes are just empty. It's like whatever was there—whatever emotion and feeling he had—is just gone. I know this must be hard for you."

"I'll manage. It's that or push him down a ravine."

"We could push him down a ravine," Remy said. "Repeatedly, if it doesn't work the first time."

"Remy—" Layla started.

Remy held his hands up in surrender. "Just kidding. Not a lot of it going around at the moment, obviously. Don't let your emotions get the better of you. I don't want to have to stop you from bludgeoning him because he said one out-of-line thing too many."

"What about your dad?" Chloe asked as the three of them started walking. "Mine died because of my mother, Layla's is—" She waved her hands in Caleb's direction. "What about you?"

"My father is a tale of alcohol, assholery, some more assholery, and a touch more alcohol. He was a mean drunk, and he was drunk all the time. He was a wealthy French aristocrat who married an English woman to gain all of her wealth.

"Unfortunately for yours truly, in the eighteenth century, it wasn't like you could just go and tell someone that your dad was a dick. Your rich, politically connected, highly influential dick of a father. He beat my mother and me, and my brother. Less so my sister; I think she scared him. She looked a lot like his mother when she was young. My father respected, hated, and feared my grandmother. I don't think he could raise his hand to my sister because of it. I certainly never heard of him doing such a thing. My brother was older than both my sister and me by a few years, and my father used to attack him without provocation. Me, he'd wake from my sleep so he could tell me what a useless runt I was and how he should have drowned me in the river when I was born," Remy finished.

"Holy shit," Chloe said.

"Yeah, he was a peach. He died when I was ten. An accident, so I'm told. He accidentally got stabbed forty-two times. Once for every year he was alive."

"Did you do it?" Layla asked. "Sorry, that's none of my business."

"It's fine. And no. My brother and sister did the deed. She was seventeen, and my brother nineteen. My brother joined the army, and I never saw him again. My sister married a wealthy landowner, had lots of children and seemed to be happy with her life. I envied her that. It took a few years, but I became a drunk reprobate, who either spent my wealth in brothels or . . . actually no, just brothels. I liked brothels. They were, frankly, awful places, but it was better than being at home alone. My mother re-married and moved to Ireland, leaving me to deal with my own shit at the tender age of sixteen. Which I did: drunkenly, and with as many naked women on top of me as possible. Unfortunately, it was nowhere near as fun as it sounds."

"I didn't exactly expect that," Chloe said. "I knew you were the son of someone rich, but the rest of it was awful. I'm sorry you had to go through that."

"Turned out okay in the end," Remy said. "I pissed off more than my fair share of people and had to flee to England, where I resumed the duty of trying to kill myself through alcohol. From there, it all went a bit crazy. I got turned into a fox by a witch coven for sleeping with someone I shouldn't have and then spent a few centuries becoming a damn sight better with sword and pistol. I was lucky in a way. My father could have killed me, or he could have lived another decade and pissed all the money away, instead of allowing me to do it; or he could have just murdered everyone in the house in a rage because my mum did something that displeased him. He's dead, screw him."

"Damn, Remy, that's an exceptionally crappy upbringing," Chloe said.

"We all have our highs and lows. It's just that my lows were the entire first few decades of my life. I learned a lot during that time, although mostly I learned not to piss off women who can do powerful magic."

"You didn't know that before then?" Layla asked.

"I never said I was a smart son of an aristocrat."

A few minutes later, the group arrived at the drive of the house. Kase helped Irkalla up the stairs and into the building while everyone followed soon after.

"That's a bit impressive," Chloe said as she stepped inside.

The entire downstairs was one huge, open room. There was a kitchen at the far end, a large dining room table after that, and then a couch that could have fit a dozen people on it. A TV that probably took three people to carry had been hung on the wall. A set of stairs led to the floor above, and there were three doors underneath the staircase.

"Bathroom," Remy said. He pointed to the door the furthest from the stairs. "Other two are cupboards."

"What's that door?" Kase asked, pointing toward a gray-painted door at the far end of the floor.

"It has trophies in it," Remy said. "Of the hunting variety. Lots of guns, too. Lots of guns."

Zamek walked over to the door and opened it, stepping inside the dark room while Layla flicked on the light switch and looked around at the menagerie of stuffed animals and guns.

"That's a lot of weapons," Kase said from behind Layla as she looked into the room. "And that's a stuffed wolf. That's messed up."

"And a bear," Remy said, pointing to the large animal at the far end of the large room. "Bill has a grizzly bear in there."

"You ever killed for sport?" Kase asked Remy. "You being the son of an aristocrat and all."

"Nothing we didn't eat after," Remy said. "I'm all for hunting, if you eat what you kill. And we used bow and arrows. Try taking down a grizzly with a bow and arrow, and I'll be impressed with your hunting prowess. Shooting an animal from hundreds of yards away, from the safety of wherever you're holed-up, doesn't strike me as very sporting, or as much of an interesting experience. But to each their own."

The four of them left the room, switching the light off as they went.

"Where's my dad?" Layla asked.

"Malcolm and Cody took him to the back room," Harry said. "I, for one, am happy about that situation."

"I remember hunting as a young woman," Irkalla said from the sofa, changing the topic. "It was called surviving. You didn't hunt, you didn't eat."

Everyone looked toward Irkalla, who'd been considerably quieter than her usual self up to this point.

"I'm fine," she said. "Just getting used to the idea of the power I took. My body is adapting to it, trying to make sure I don't blow up a city block if I use it. I've never taken the spirit of an oni before. I do not wish to have this experience again."

"We'll try very hard to not let you kill an oni," Remy told her.

Irkalla smirked. "I'm sorry, I interrupted your conversation about hunting and the like. Please do continue."

"Pretty sure I was done," Remy said.

"I'm going outside to try to contact Tommy," Layla said, checking her phone and finding it still had no reception. "Or not."

"Use the Wi-Fi," Harry said.

Layla changed the settings on her phone and left the house to make the call, sitting on the stairs and dialing Tommy's number.

"Layla, everything okay?" Tommy asked, his voice slightly frantic.

"We're okay. Have you heard from Jared, Diana, or the other members of the strike team?"

"I'm sorry, Layla, but it looks like Nergal's forces took them. We'll get them back, I promise."

A hollow feeling hit her in the gut and she was glad to be already sitting down. "I know. We're going to Winterborn, and from there we'll head to Red Rock. We think Winterborn is Nergal-controlled."

"That's our assessment, too. Before we discuss the next step, how are you doing?"

"My boyfriend has been kidnapped by insane fanatics hell-bent on killing a large number of people, my father is a psychopath, who I'm certain will kill his way across the country if he ever gets free, and somewhere Nergal's forces are waiting for us. No one appears to have followed us from the prison, although it's entirely possible Nergal's people have someone else who can hide them from us. Either way, Nergal doesn't strike me as a just-give-up kind of person. If we can go around Winterborn, that would be helpful. Any chance you guys can get a Black Hawk to this location?"

"Is there enough room?"

"We can make room, Tommy," Layla told him. "It would be safer than going through a town that's under enemy control. And going around it will take too long."

"If you stay where you are, we'll sort something out," Tommy said. "Won't be until tomorrow morning, though—there's too much bad weather around here to take off at the moment. I'll get Hades to talk to people in Red Rock, hopefully divert something your way."

"Thanks, let me know," Layla said.

"Take care, Layla. We'll get you back here and then we'll find Jared, Diana, and the others. Commander Fenix is with them, so wherever they are I'm certain he's making his captors' lives hell. And I can't imagine a single situation where Diana's captives would be happy to have her. Go rest. We'll speak tomorrow."

Layla stared at the phone for several seconds. She hoped it would work out. Or she hoped that they could at least save those Nergal had taken. She looked out through the forest of tall, thick trees, and then down at the large drive. Landing a helicopter was going to take more space than they had. At least everyone was going to be kept busy.

13

Layla relayed what she and Tommy had spoken about, and the team immediately started figuring out how to remove enough trees to let a helicopter land.

"I'll do it," Irkalla said. "I need to get some of this power out of me. I'll walk into the forest and let loose. Should clear enough of a space, although it's not exactly going to be scientifically done. We might still have to clear stuff out, and there's a good possibility I'll need to rest afterwards."

"It's not like we're inundated with ideas," Kase said. "Who goes with you? Because I'm damned if I'm letting you go alone."

"I'll go," Remy said. "Worst case scenario, she kills me, and I come back to life. Besides, I'll be able to smell anyone coming. You're about to kill a lot of wildlife."

"Can't be helped," Irkalla said. "Hopefully, once I start dumping the power created by this oni, most things will get the general idea and run for it."

"We seem to be missing the most important part of all this," Zamek said. "We're officially at war with Nergal. Which means we're officially at war with Avalon. Thunder Bay will fall, and Red Rock soon after. We need to get to Red Rock as quickly as possible."

"We were already at war," Harry said. "It's just that it's not a war people hear about on TV. If there's one thing Avalon is good at, it's keeping information out of public consumption."

"What about those of us who were taken?" Kase asked.

There was silence for several seconds. Layla could feel everyone looking at her, and she knew what they were thinking: they could either save her boyfriend and the people who had sacrificed themselves so they could escape, or save thousands of innocent lives from Nergal's war machine as it headed toward Red Rock.

"Shit," Layla said softly. "We can't leave them in Nergal's hands. I *won't* leave them there."

"You have a plan?" Chloe asked.

"We split up. The helicopter comes and takes Caleb, Zamek, Irkalla, and Kase to Red Rock to help with the defense. Everyone else gets moved somewhere safe—Greenland, a hidden fortress, wherever is best. I'll go to Winterborn. One person will be better than a crowd."

"I'll come with you," Harry said. "Humans aren't exactly seen as threatening to these people."

"Me too," Chloe said. "No arguments."

"Then that's the plan," Layla said. "Hopefully we can at least figure out where Nergal is keeping them so we can help Hades' forces launch a rescue."

As the group discussed further ideas, Irkalla left with Remy to go and destroy part of the forest. It was going to take her half an hour to clear the area, so everyone sat around and tried to rest. Layla found her father handcuffed to a bed at the rear of the property. Malcolm and Cody sat beside him.

She looked at the two prison guards. "Can I have a moment?"

The guards left, and Layla took the chair furthest from her father.

"I haven't tried to kill anyone yet," he said with an almost jovial tone.

"It's the word 'yet' that I'm worried about," Layla said.

"Do you plan on talking to me?" he asked. "Actually talking to me. About anything, not just hating me."

"I wasn't planning on it, no."

"I loved your mother."

Layla turned away. "You loved yourself. That's all you've ever loved, Dad. You loved killing people, and you loved the way it made you feel powerful and in control. I've read the psychologists' reports. I've read everything about your case. If you'd cared about me and Mom, you wouldn't have forced me to do military training at the age of five, and you wouldn't have made her scared of you."

"She was scared of me?"

Layla turned back to face her father, anger blazing on her face. "You don't even see it, do you? You don't even see the hurt you caused to your own wife and child." She breathed deeply. "No, I'm not doing this. Everything you say is a manipulation."

"Why would I want to manipulate you?"

"Because that's what you do all the time. You manipulate to get your own way. It's almost like breathing to you."

Sadness passed over Caleb's face and left as quickly as it arrived, but Layla noticed it and wondered if maybe there was more to her father than what she remembered. More than what she'd read about.

"Is there no part of your childhood with me that you remember fondly?"

Layla wanted to make sure she gave away no more of the anger and disgust she felt. "I hid from the FBI agents who came to get you because I thought they were the monsters you always told me were out there. You pretended to be my father. You pretended to be a good man. Any good memories of you are tainted by the shit-show you managed to create."

Before Caleb could reply, Harry opened the door. "Irkalla is about to let go."

"You hate me. You really do hate me. Not just what I did. But me as a person," Caleb said as Layla got to her feet.

"Yes, Dad. I hate you. I hate everything about you. What you did, why you did it, how you thought of nothing but yourself. How you didn't even show remorse. How you never once cared that everything you did affected me and Mom. The fact that I have to spend time with you makes my skin crawl." She looked down at him and wondered if there was anything left of the conscience he might once have had. Or if he was just pure evil. At one time, she'd wanted to see him, to ask why. But now, now she just wanted to forget him.

Layla left the house just as the ground began to shake and smoke rose out of the forest. "Stay here, Harry," Layla told him.

"Not going to argue, trust me."

The rest of the group ran into the forest. Kase sped away from the remainder of them, her werewolf-enhanced speed one of the few perks of the species that Layla envied; that, and the healing. A werewolf's ability to heal was legendary, even amongst other non-humans.

They smelled the devastation before they saw it; the burning wood was difficult to mistake for anything else. The clearing that Irkalla had made was big enough to land two or three Black Hawks with little difficulty. She sat in the center of the area, taking deep breaths.

Remy stood beside her, his fur a little singed, but otherwise he looked okay.

"If I make another stupid suggestion," he said, "stop me."

"She okay?" Nabu asked.

"I think so. Have you ever seen her do anything like that before?"

"Once. We were at war and during the fight she absorbed hundreds of spirits in the space of only a few hours. She had to release so much unspent energy at the end of the battle that it basically tore the earth apart. I haven't heard of her having to do anything similar for thousands of years."

"Hundreds," Irkalla called out. "I had to take the spirits of several trolls a couple of centuries ago. Long story short, there's a mountain that's now a bit smaller than it was before I started."

"You okay?" Chloe called over.

Irkalla nodded. "I'm going to feel it tomorrow, but other than that, I'm all good." She struggled to get to her feet and Kase ran over to help her up.

"We have to clear this area of anything that might cause problems for a landing helicopter," Zamek said. "Mostly the larger bits."

"I'll take Irkalla back to the house," Kase said. "Get her something to eat."

"Thanks for doing this," Chloe said, and Irkalla gave her a thumbs-up.

Layla thought it was odd to see her so weakened. She'd watched Irkalla defeat a troll alone; hell, she killed the oni by herself, and seeing her so depleted and exhausted was a difficult thing to compute.

Once the team was back in the house, everyone tried to rest for what was going to be a difficult few days. The sun soon set, and Layla decided to get some air, leaving the building and walking down to the driveway below, where she found Harry leaning up against a wall.

"You okay?" he asked as she approached.

Layla nodded. The smell of burning wood was still heavy in the air. Kase had helped put out the fires with her elemental powers, but the scent still lingered.

"Smells like the bonfires we used to have as kids. Like Bonfire Night."

Layla smiled. Harry and Chloe had taken her to a fireworks display a few years ago to celebrate Guy Fawkes Night. It had been a cold November evening, and despite having lived in England for over a decade, Layla had never really understood why the British celebrated the failure to destroy their entire Parliament. But the display was nice, and she had eaten a lot of food and drunk a lot of ale.

"I'm thinking of the first fireworks display you took me to," Layla said. "You remember it?"

"The one with the cider and ale festival?" Harry asked. "I remember you getting very drunk on ale that was a lot stronger than you expected. I remember you trying to hit on that big, bearded dude who was very confused by the drunk American who kept asking him if he was in a gang."

Layla laughed. "Oh God, I did, didn't I? He looked like Charlie Hunnam."

"He did. I assume that's why you also asked him if he'd ever piloted a giant robot."

Layla laughed again. "That was my first ever fireworks display. Mom didn't like big crowds, so we only used to have little ones in the garden."

"You want a hug?" Harry asked.

Layla smiled and nodded. Harry hugged her. He wasn't much of a hugger, and so Layla appreciated the gesture.

"We'll be done with all of this soon enough," he said.

"You hope."

Harry looked at Layla, his expression serious. "You've got to have hope, Layla," he told her. "Otherwise, why are we even bothering?"

Layla shrugged. "Fair point."

"We'll get our people back. I have no doubt in my mind about that."

Layla nodded. "Thank you for being you," she told Harry.

"Being this perfect takes a lot of work," he replied, making her laugh.

"You two having some kind of secret meeting?" Kase said as she descended the steps toward them.

"We're just deciding on the handshake," Harry said.

Kase joined them at the bottom of the stairs. "You both needed a time-out, too?"

"Is that what we're calling it?" Layla asked.

Kase nodded slowly. "I like my alone time," she said. "I love my friends and my family, but I also just need to chill out sometimes and not hear anyone."

"You want to be left alone?" Harry asked.

"No, no," Kase said, "it's fine. It's quieter out here than it is in there. There's lots of discussion about what to do once we've deposited your father. I thought it best to beat a hasty retreat."

"You're welcome to join our gang of people who hide in the dark," Harry said, and then paused for a second. "That sounded more ominous than I meant it to."

Kase laughed and leaned her head against Harry's shoulder. He put his arm around her in turn. Kase was most definitely a hugger, and one of the few people who managed to get a hug out of Harry on a regular basis.

The three of them remained quiet for what felt like a long time, but whenever Layla started to relax, she remembered those who weren't with her and she immediately began feeling anxious again.

"You want a drink?" Kase asked Layla. "There's vodka in the freezer. Good vodka, too."

Layla shook her head. "Not tonight, thanks."

Kase froze and then immediately stepped away from Harry, sniffing the air. "Get back inside," she said, any trace of fun and relaxation gone.

Harry and Layla moved up the stairs as Kase followed behind, smelling the air every few steps until they were all back in the house.

The din of half a dozen people all talking at once immediately stopped as Kase entered the house. "We have company," she said.

Irkalla turned off the lights, and Remy ran to the window, drawing the blinds and peering through two of them.

Layla told Cody and Malcolm to stay with her father, and neither of them complained.

"Harry, guns," she said.

Harry ran off to the room that passed for an armory and returned a few minutes later with several rifles and boxes of bullets. He ran off again and appeared a second time with shotguns and a few handguns.

"At least Bill was prepared for a war," Harry said after his third trip to bring more bullets.

"What are we facing out there?" Chloe asked.

"Can't tell," Kase said. "Multiple scents, a few hundred feet out."

Remy ran to the door and pushed it open a few inches, taking a long smell. "At least a dozen. Can't tell much more than that."

Lights ignited in the driveway below the house, and everyone looked over at Zamek, who'd activated them. "We can see them easier, and they already know where we are," he said by way of an explanation.

A few seconds later, Kristin stepped out of the tree line and moved in front of the driveway lights. Her arms were raised, and she carried a megaphone in one hand. "I'm going to put my hands down now," she said into the megaphone.

Harry took a rifle and crouched beside Layla, passing the weapon to her, but she shook her head. She still had the Glock on her hip, and still hoped she wouldn't have to use it.

"We need to get out of here," she whispered to Chloe.

"There were cars in the garage below," Zamek said. "We checked them over earlier. There's a set of stairs that leads down there and then out to the rear of the property."

"Okay, so how do we get them out of here with Kristin and her friends parked on the front lawn?" Chloe asked.

"We moved one of the jeeps to the rear of the building," Remy said. "We wanted to make sure we had an easy escape should it come to it."

"We're not all going to fit in one jeep," Layla said.

"Kind of my point," Remy told her. "Kristin wants you and your dad. Getting you gone is the most important part of this mission now."

"No, it bloody well isn't," Layla snapped.

"Are you going to talk to me, or what?" Kristin shouted.

"What do you want?" Kase bellowed out of the front door.

"Caleb. The rest of you can go. I'll even drop off your friends." Kristin clicked her fingers and Diana was brought out of the darkness and forced to kneel beside her. "See, I brought a gift."

A low growl escaped Kase's mouth.

"You okay, Diana?" Remy shouted.

"I'm grand," Diana called back. "Don't you worry about me. I'm having a whale of a time."

Several more people appeared out of the dark woods. Layla counted nine behind Kristin; six men and three women. They all wore the same gray uniform and none of them showed any outward emotion. They just stood still and stared at the house.

"Layla, get Cody, Malcolm, and your father out of here," Irkalla said. "We'll keep them busy."

"This house isn't going to stop them for long," Layla said, irritated that people were trying to get her to leave instead of letting her help.

"Long enough," Kase said.

"So, how do you want Caleb?" Remy called out. "He's a little indisposed at the moment: bad food. I figured that maybe we can wait until his stomach settles and then we'll send him on out."

Layla glanced out of the window at Kristin, who looked angry.

"You have sixty seconds, and then we kill your friend," Kristin said. "And after that, we'll kill all of you."

"I have another plan," Layla said.

"Layla, we need to get you out of here," Irkalla said softly. "Your father trusts you, and only you. He'd escape anyone else, and he might hurt someone doing it. He won't hurt you. I don't think he believes he's done anything wrong."

"So I just run out back with him and the guards, and we drive away?"

"Actually, no," Zamek said. "Get out back and run into the woods."

"What about the car?" Remy asked.

Zamek looked at Harry. "Harry is going to drive it away from here. Loudly. They'll think Caleb is escaping and go after him."

"I'll go with Harry," Chloe said. "Best case scenario, we'll give Layla some time to run and split Kristin's forces. Worst case, they all run after us and we have to fight for our lives."

"That's not a good scenario," Layla pointed out. She glanced out of the window again. "The man behind Diana has a dagger in his hand. Any chance we can eliminate him, get Diana free, and then do the car thing? We've got maybe twenty seconds before Kristin's deadline."

Chloe sat next to Layla and picked up one of the rifles Harry had found. She opened the window a fraction and placed the tip of the barrel just outside of it. "These aren't silver," she said. "This won't kill him unless he's human."

"Time's up, people," Kristin called out. "Time to watch your friend die."

The bullet left Chloe's rifle and hit the man behind Diana in the throat. A second bullet smashed into Kristin's knee.

Diana took no time in launching herself away from her captives, sprinting toward the house, and around the back of the building.

"Everyone go," Kase said as flame leapt from the tree line, engulfing the entire front yard. Chloe fired again, and the fire stopped.

"This isn't going to hold them for long," Chloe said. "These bullets are hurting them, but that's about it."

Layla wished she'd taken an MP5 from one of the strike team back in the prison. It would have come in handy right about now.

"Get going," Kase said. "We're running out of time."

Despite hating the idea of leaving her friends, Layla also knew that letting Caleb fall into enemy hands would have catastrophic consequences for everyone. She ran to the bedroom at the rear of the property where Malcolm and Cody had removed the handcuffs from her father and were helping him up.

"We need to leave," she said.

"And how do we do that?" Malcolm asked.

Layla walked to the window and looked out at the ground below. She could drop the thirty feet without injuring herself, and her dad probably could too, but she doubted Cody and Malcolm would be able to. She wondered if she should just leave them both here, but didn't want to be solely responsible for her father if they were outside for long. At some point Layla would need rest, and she couldn't guarantee that Caleb would be where she had left him when she woke up.

She reached out with her power and pulled apart the metal-framed furniture that sat in the back garden. A dozen chairs and two long tables. The metal slinked up the side of the building, stopping at the window, which she opened.

Layla looked down at the ladder she'd made and then turned to Malcolm and Cody. "I'll go first, then my dad, then you two. You both need to move quickly; this ladder will hold you, I promise."

Layla climbed out of the house as the sounds of gunfire resumed. She didn't bother with the ladder and dropped down, landing on her feet and walking away from the window. Someone slammed into her from the side, driving her up against a nearby tree. Layla reached for her Glock, but it was batted away by the woman who was assaulting her.

Layla headbutted the woman, before driving a knee into her stomach and punching her in the jaw, knocking her aside.

Kristin looked up at Layla with rage in her eyes. "You going somewhere?" Kristin snapped. She tackled Layla to the ground and rained down punch after punch on her, biting Layla's hand when she tried to push Kristin away.

Layla saw her dad land on the ground close by, which drew Kristin's attention and allowed Layla to punch her in the throat. She pushed

Kristin off and used a nearby wooden table to get back to her feet. Layla looked over at her dad, who was staring at Kristin with an unpleasantness in his eyes.

"Don't," Layla said, bringing his attention back to her. She turned to Kristin and kicked her in the side of the head with as much power as she could, knocking the woman out and hopefully removing her as a problem. She picked up her Glock, along with a dagger that Kristin had been carrying, as Harry climbed down the ladder after the two guards. Chloe launched herself out of the window a second later.

Chloe took one look at Kristin and drew her gun, but Layla stopped her. "You two need to go, as do we," Layla said.

Chloe and Harry climbed into the 4x4 Dodge truck, and Harry turned over the engine. "Be careful," he told Layla, before she ran off into the dense woodland at the rear of the property with her father and the two guards and Harry floored the truck to make the big diversion.

The four of them ran for an hour before resting next to a pair of large trees. There was a road nearby, and the sounds of cars driving past at high speed made Layla hope that none of the occupants were searching for them.

"Let's rest for a few minutes," Cody said. "We need to catch our breath."

Layla nodded and motioned for her father to sit down. His hands were still cuffed in front of him, and he'd said nothing since leaving the house.

Layla turned back to Cody and felt the sting in her neck before she realized that he was pointing a gun at her. She blinked, felt woozy, then collapsed to her knees, watching in horror as Cody then shot Malcolm in the head with a decidedly more lethal gun. She was on the ground, the forest spinning, as he also shot her father.

"You and your father have been shot with tranquilizer darts," Cody told her. "It contains a very small amount of Gorgon venom spliced with some things Nergal's people put together. Just enough to paralyze and relax." He slipped a sorcerer's band on Layla's wrist, and she felt her power vanish.

She slurred something and watched Cody walk away, then closed her eyes, but didn't pass out. Instead, she listened to the sounds around her: a car stopping. A man and woman talking to Cody. A scream. Layla blinked as Cody picked her up and put her in the back of a car that she hadn't remembered seeing before. "I'll be right back with your dad."

As Layla watched Cody go, rage filled her. She was going to get out of the sorcerer's band, and she was going to inflict untold chaos on anyone who had helped Cody do this. But her anger fought a losing battle against the drugs; the next thing she knew the car was moving slowly, and then nothing.

14

"You're awake. That's good," Cody said from the driver's seat of the car.

Layla blinked. She was still lying on the back seat, but she had no idea where she was or even what day it was. "Where?" she managed. Her mouth was dry and tasted funny.

"There's water next to you," Cody told her. "Just to emphasize, it's just water, but you're going to want to drink something. The drugs will leave you dehydrated otherwise."

Layla picked up the two-liter bottle and stared at it.

"There is nothing else in there."

"Says the murderous drugger," Layla said, not liking the taste of the words as they left her mouth.

The car stopped, and Cody turned around in his seat, grabbed the bottle of water from her hand, and took a swig. "See, not poisoned."

Layla had concerns, but her need for water was greater, and she drank nearly half of the bottle in only a few seconds.

"You'll feel better in a few minutes," Cody told her. "You've been out for just over an hour, so you're probably not altogether with it. I might have given you a little bit more than you needed. Sorry about that."

"Screw you," Layla said, noticing she still wore the sorcerer's band. "You killed Malcolm."

"I did, that's true. I was trying to think of a way to get you and your father to Nergal, and when Kristin turned up, I thought my dreams had come true. Then you wanted to leave with me and Malcolm, which was even better, so I was just going to hand you over to Kristin's clone in the garden. But then Chloe and Harry left with us, and your other friends would have caused me problems, so I needed to get you away from it all. And running with your dad was your own idea; I didn't even have to try and involve myself in the planning. You trusted me exactly how you were meant to. Real shame I had to kill Malcolm, though. Cody liked him."

"Aren't you Cody?"

"Sort of," he said with a chuckle. "Not going to ask about your dad?"

"I assume he's in the trunk."

"Good guess. Drugged, just like you. Pissed off like you, too. Luckily, I had a sorcerer's band, so you'll be less of an immediate concern to me while I'm driving."

"Lucky me. Where'd you get the car?"

"Had to flag someone down. A nice elderly couple stopped, and I told them about how my wife and I had been in an accident."

"They're dead, aren't they?"

"Of course. Couldn't let them go."

Layla swallowed her anger. It would do no good in her current circumstance. "What are you?"

"Shapeshifter. I can kill someone, change myself to look like them, and take their mind too. Means I get all of their memories, but the longer I stay as a person the less I remember of my own life. I've been doing this so long, I don't even remember my true name. It's funny when you think about it."

"Not really."

Cody paused. "No, I guess not."

Layla looked out of the window at the darkness outside. She craned her neck a little and saw that it showed just after midnight on the car's dashboard clock. "They're going to come look for me," she said.

"Yep. That's why we're in a car. I'd like to see them track me over such a distance. It's normally only a few hours' drive to Winterborn from that cabin, but the weather hasn't exactly helped matters, and I didn't want to crash or anything."

Layla managed to get into a seated position behind the shotgun seat. Slushy rain fell heavily in the darkness outside, and the headlights showed the rapidly worsening conditions on the road.

"Don't think about attacking me," Cody said. "You've got a sorcerer's band on, so no powers, remember, and I'm almost certain that if I crash, we all die."

"And that includes you," Layla said. "So you're not impervious to injury?"

Cody laughed. "Ah, you got me, but I don't think I want to talk to you about how you can and can't kill me."

"Shame. It sounds like a nice conversation to have. What does Nergal want with me?"

"You escaped his clutches. He wants you so that Caleb does what he's told. Also, because he hates the idea of someone getting away from him."

"So, you knew that we were going to get my dad out of prison?"

"No. I was put there a few weeks ago because Nergal was going to finally deal with Hades. He was moving his people up to Winterborn for months and months until he was ready. He wanted someone at the prison because he was interested in using the inmates to cause panic in Thunder Bay. Didn't work out, but a few days ago I found out about your dad being there. I notified Nergal, who had heard from someone in Hades' organization that you were going to be getting him out.

I was the backup in case Kristin failed, which is unfortunately what happened."

"And you murdered Cody because?"

"Yes, it is a shame I had to kill him, but it's my job. What can you do?"

"You didn't need to slaughter the prisoners."

"Not my call. I didn't have anything to do with that. Blood elves will do what blood elves do best. Personally, I'd have just gassed you all in the solitary wing, and then dragged you out without any trouble. But Kristin is more of an explosions and drama kind of person."

"So what happens now? We drive to Winterborn, you hand me over to Nergal, and then get to run off to your next thrilling murder assignment?"

"That's about the size of it, yes. I think I was English when I was born. Sometimes I remember it, but it was so long ago. Hundreds of years. Dozens of people. I should have written down the information about myself when I was younger."

"Am I meant to feel sorry for you?"

"Not really. I get paid an obscene amount of money to do my job. I'm just trying to stay awake by talking. It's been a long few days. I wasn't sure I was ever going to be able to get you both out of there. I mean, I knew I could take your dad, but you, too? I didn't know about that. I wondered whether or not to kill one of your friends, become them, and get you that way, but, frankly, I didn't want to be one of your friends. Besides, I can only take the place of a human, so it would have to be Harry. And to be completely honest, I didn't want to be in that little geek's head. He probably thinks about Dungeons and Dragons, and how to kiss his first ever girlfriend."

"Dungeons and Dragons is awesome."

"Ah, you're one of those geek people too, are you? You need to grow up, the lot of you. Playing with children's toys, pretending to be soldiers and warriors. Pathetic."

"Not as pathetic as not knowing who I really am."

Layla saw anger flicker over Cody's face before he responded to her taunt. "Not nice to mock people who have been kind to you."

"You drugged me, kidnapped me, and murdered people. I think we can forgo the idea that you're a good person."

"I am a good person. I'm one of the nice guys. I always tell women that. Women like to be told that they're dealing with a gentleman, that they're dealing with one of the good guys."

Layla laughed. "You don't get laid a lot, do you?"

"Shut up," Cody said. "I'm not going to discuss my personal life with you."

"You have to pay for it more often than not, though, right?"

"I said shut up," Cody almost shouted.

"Women think you're creepy, no matter how nice your outside face might be? Could be because you're just a creepy little asshole. I mean, you can act not-creepy, but then none of us have spent more than a few minutes with you since the prison. I'm guessing any more than that, and the creepiness just shines through."

"Look, you want me to stop this car and throw you in the trunk?"

"Sure, if it means I don't have to listen to Don Juan de Douchebag anymore."

The car screeched to a halt, slamming Layla into the seat in front of her. Cody turned to face her. "We don't have far to travel, but I'm beginning to dislike your attitude. I didn't have to behave so nicely toward you. I could have been rough, could have hurt you. I didn't because I'm not that kind of person. Now, just stop trying to antagonize me, and we'll get along. Deal?"

"You are a great big bag of dicks, aren't you?"

Cody lunged for Layla's leg, but she'd been expecting it and drove the heel of her boot into his nose with a satisfying crunch.

"Goddamn bitch," Cody said, darting away and getting out of the car. He opened the rear passenger door and reached in to grab Layla's legs again. "Come here."

"I don't like that word," Layla told him.

Your sorcerer's band does not appear to affect my presence, Terhal said inside her head. *Cody did not close the clasp properly, so he left a loop. Enough to stop you from using your powers normally, but not enough to stop me from talking to you.*

"I know," Layla said as Cody finally managed to grab one of her squirming legs.

"You know what?" Cody asked. "Doesn't matter. You could have been nice to me. We didn't have to do it this way." He released her leg and pulled a gun from his holster.

"That you're a dumb idiot," Layla said. "All yours, Terhal."

The drenik took control in an instant, and Cody's eyes widened in shock as power flooded out of Layla's body, changing how she looked and tearing part of the car's roof apart. It smashed into Cody's body with enough force to lift him off his feet and throw him back into the night.

Unfortunately, the interference of the sorcerer's band sent Terhal's power out of control. It yanked the steering column to the side and sent the car down a hill. Terhal tore huge pieces of metal free from the car and wrapped them around Layla and, at her request, her father.

There was little time to argue as the vehicle quickly gained speed. It hit something, throwing the car into the air before coming to a sudden stop as a metal-wrapped Layla was thrown into the back of the front seats. Terhal stopped taking control of Layla's body, and the metal encasing her vanished.

Layla touched her head, her fingers coming away wet. She needed to get the sorcerer's band off her wrist, as it clearly hadn't been designed to compensate for Terhal's presence. Since it hadn't been closed properly, she hoped it would be easy to remove. She tried to open the clasp completely, but it refused to budge. *Great,* she thought as she kicked at the door, which swung open.

Layla crawled out of the back seat of the car and dropped the six feet to the wet, muddy ground. She grabbed hold of the rear wheel arch and used it to help her stand. There was a hissing noise from somewhere, but she couldn't concentrate for long enough to find its source.

The front of the BMW had come to rest in a tree, the back hanging down toward the ground. There was an almighty crack, and the tree gave way, dropping the car onto the ground as Layla threw herself aside. She lay on the dirt, looking up at the stars, and concentrated on her breathing. She couldn't access her powers, and there was zero chance of letting Terhal out again after such a short period of time.

Layla forced herself to stand and walked over to the totaled car, finding the trunk empty. Her father had been drugged and dumped in the trunk, so how had he escaped, and just how much trouble was he about to cause? "Shit," she said, slamming the trunk closed. "Good job, Cody, you goddamn idiot."

Her father was free, without a sorcerer's band, and was presumably exceptionally angry about what had happened to him.

Layla took a step around the car toward the driver's seat and felt her legs go. She suddenly felt nauseous and the world started to spin. She stayed on the ground for several seconds, willing it to stop, and eventually it did. She smelled gas escaping from the car and knew she needed to get away from it before it caught fire.

Layla pushed herself up from the floor and took a step away from the car as something smashed into her with incredible force, taking her off her feet and throwing her onto the cold, wet ground. She rolled onto her side just as a boot connected with her ribs, causing pain to rack her body. The foot connected a second time in her side, forcing her to roll over as a third strike landed against the middle of her back.

"You should have behaved," Cody said, dragging Layla by her hair over to the nearest tree and dumping her in front of it. He kicked her in the ribs again, his face contorted with rage. "Now I have to drag you to the town. And your dad is who knows where."

"Bet you wished you'd drugged me with more," Layla said.

Cody grabbed Layla by the throat and lifted her off the ground, slamming her against the tree. "I hope they kill you, I honestly do. I hope they torture you for weeks, slowly take you piece by piece."

Layla weakly put her hands over Cody's, which were still around her throat.

"You're not strong enough to stop me," Cody said. "I could just squeeze the life out of you, and there's nothing you could do."

"Wanna bet?" Layla said, grabbing one of his fingers and snapping it at the knuckle. She drove her foot up between his legs and punched him in the jaw as he started to fall to his knees, sending him sprawling. She might not have much left to fight with, but she was damned if she was going to let someone like Cody take her life without defending herself.

Layla pushed herself off the tree and planted her foot on Cody's mouth as he tried to get back to his feet. He was knocked back to the ground, and Layla used the tree to not fall down. Her body hurt a lot more than she'd realized, and her head still felt strange.

"Come on, Cody, you can do better than that," Layla said as she slumped to a sitting position.

She didn't see her father until he leapt out of the forest darkness and launched one foot into Cody's exposed head. It made a sickening smack as it connected. Caleb then dragged the semi-conscious Cody over to the BMW, propping him up against the rear wheel, before repeatedly kicking him in the head and chest. When Cody dropped to the ground, Caleb began stomping on his head until Layla heard a crunch.

"Stop it," Layla said, her words slurring. Maybe the bump on the head was worse than she'd thought.

Caleb ignored her and continued to attack the utterly defenseless Cody. At some point, Layla noticed that her father had a knife in his hand, and he repeatedly stabbed Cody.

Layla's vision darkened at the edges and she shook her head, hoping it would clear it. She didn't want to be defenseless, not with her father having clearly lost control. Unfortunately, her body didn't respond to her stubborn refusal to faint, and she began to fall to the ground.

She didn't know how much time had passed, but it felt as though someone had injected her with a massive dose of adrenaline as she suddenly sat bolt upright, her head no longer fuzzy, and her body no longer in pain. She glanced at her wrist and saw that the sorcerer's band was no more.

Her father sat a dozen feet away from her, washing his hands with a canteen of water.

"I got blood on them," he said. "Cody won't be bothering us."

Layla looked over at the man who had tried to kill her only moments ago, whose body was drenched with blood. His head was now misshapen, and his neck had been hacked at with something sharp.

"Piece of broken metal," Caleb said. "I wrapped some fabric around it."

"You killed him," Layla said. It wasn't a question.

"It's what I do. He was a threat, I removed that threat. We need to get out of here as soon as possible. There's a lot of blood, and it might attract wild animals."

"You removed my sorcerer's band?"

"I did," Caleb said, getting to his feet and showing Layla that he still wore his. He walked over to her as she stood up and passed her the key for his band. "Your band wasn't properly locked, but I still needed the key to remove it."

"What are you doing?" she asked.

"You don't trust me. So I'll wear a band until you decide to remove it for me. I think that's probably best for us both."

"You're still a murderer."

"That I am. But I'm a murderer who can't use any of his abilities."

"The ability to track anyone anywhere on the planet. Not sure how useful that would be out here in the middle of nowhere."

"The band limits my strength, healing, and the like. Just like it does for you. I don't want you to be afraid of me."

Layla stared at her father for a few seconds and bit back the nastier of the replies that entered her head. "I think we're well beyond that," she said with a slight sigh.

Caleb nodded. "I understand. I've killed a lot of people. That's probably a lot for anyone to take in. Probably a lot for someone to understand. I didn't do it in wartime, or to defend myself. I just hunted people and killed them."

"You killed Cody, too."

"He would have killed you and vanished. He's a shapeshifter; he could become anyone, and no one would ever see him again."

"We need to find somewhere to stay until morning," Layla said. "It's pitch-black, and I'd rather not stumble around in the dark."

"It's clearly not pitch-black," Caleb said.

"It's just a saying," Layla said. "It just means it's really dark. Anyway, I heard wolves in the distance—let's keep away from them." She reached out with her power and began pulling pieces of the car apart, using them to create a rudimentary building that looked a lot like a shed.

"That'll have to do," she said when she was finished, and she stepped inside. She'd created a large enough opening in the roof to let the moonlight in, so she wasn't alone in a small, dark space with a serial killer. She didn't think he'd ever add her to his list of victims, but there was still a small percentage of her that didn't trust him not to try.

When they were both inside, she manipulated the metal to close the entrance, blocking them in.

"Nice workmanship," Caleb said, taking a seat in the far corner. "You want to use your power to put cuffs on me again? I removed them when I was in the trunk. I've picked my fair share of locks over the years."

"Do I need to?"

"No, Layla. You don't."

"He'll kill you, you know," Gyda said, appearing beside Layla.

"Go away," Layla said.

"I can't," Caleb told her.

"Not you. Talking to one of the spirits in my scroll."

"He's as bad as Terhal," Gyda said. "You never listen to me. You never heed my warnings."

"Because all of your warnings end with me being murdered," Layla said. "Now is not the time for any more of them. Please."

Gyda tutted and vanished.

"How many spirits do you have?" Caleb asked.

"Three. You?"

"Two. A man and a woman. I haven't heard from either of them in a very long time."

"The sorcerer's band means you can't talk to them, I guess."

"It's not that. My personality and theirs merged a long time ago. Before I started killing. You know about this, yes? That your personality and that of your spirits will start to jumble around?"

Layla nodded. "It's come up."

"Once it's complete, they vanish. Only appearing when called."

"They never mentioned the vanishing to me."

"They don't know it happens. Once fully bonded, they're only aware of themselves when they're talking to you. The fact that once fully bonded they can't appear without your say-so is neither here nor there. The same thing will happen to me when I die and my spirit joins the scrolls. And the same thing will happen to you, too."

"So, you're not a serial killer? It's the spirit who made you do it?"

Caleb shook his head. "No, I did it. I chose to kill people. I enjoy removing the worst from the planet. It gives me a sense of wellbeing. I was just making conversation about my spirits. They merged with me long ago. You think me a monster because I kill, but I would think of myself as a monster if I let those I kill live."

Layla watched her father as he lay down and wondered whether or not she'd develop more personality traits from her spirits. She wasn't sure she wanted them. Layla thought back to the voice she used to have in her head, the one that told her to hurt the people who threatened her in some way; the one who had told her to hurt Chloe in order to win a sparring match. She'd always thought that it was just the years of training her father had drilled into her. But now there was another possibility.

"Are you sure that none of your spirits were passed on to me when you had me?" she asked him.

"Yes," Caleb said. "Now rest. We need to head out at first light."

For the first time since the day the FBI arrived to arrest her father, Layla felt like he'd said something honest to her. Something real and comforting. She just didn't know if she could believe it.

15

Kristin was furious. Not only had she been unable to capture Caleb and Layla, despite having the shapeshifter known as Cody working for them inside the house, she'd lost Diana, and been injured with a gunshot to the knee. The injury had healed quickly, but she was less than happy with the umbra she'd brought with her, who had been no help when faced with a real combat scenario. It was all well and good to have incredible power, but it was useless if you were unable to use it effectively because you weren't trained to fight.

Kristin had set off to Winterborn, angry and alone, and had contained her rage as she entered the compound controlled by Nergal's forces. A barebones staff, mostly blood elves, guarded the area.

Kristin ignored the blood elves and their message to go and see Nergal and had instead gone down to the prison that had been built underground. She'd walked to the nearby guard station, removed the keys for one of the cells, unlocked it, and stepped inside.

The prisoner had taken the opportunity offered to him to become an umbra, but had refused to cooperate with those who had tried to help him control his newfound power. The umbra had been disruptive, and Nergal had been forced to lock him away until he could be dealt with.

Kristin drew a silver dagger and pounced on the umbra while he slept, repeatedly stabbing him in the head and chest until they were both drenched in blood.

Despite the umbra being dead, Kristin continued the attack until she no longer felt the rage inside of her. She'd picked the umbra because he'd been rude to her several days ago when she'd explained to him that he wouldn't be going home and that it was in his best interest to work with them, not against them.

She stood up and wiped the dagger on part of the quilt that had escaped the spray of blood before sheathing it. She left the room and saw a blood elf standing further down the gray brick corridor. The prison consisted of two dozen doors along either side of the corridor. The doors faced one another, and each led to a separate cell.

"Clean this up," Kristin snapped. "And dispose of the body however you see fit."

The creature's eyes widened in pleasure. Kristin knew that the blood elves left no trace of their food behind. A six-foot umbra would be a good feast.

Kristin walked down the corridor, turning several corners until she reached the cell she was looking for. Two blood elves stood guard outside of the door. "I need to speak to him," Kristin said.

The blood elves stood aside, allowing Kristin to unlock the cell. The blood elves weren't allowed access to the prison keys. It would be like allowing pigs free access to their food.

Kristin stepped inside the cell. She figured the room was approximately twelve feet by ten, with seven-foot-high ceilings. There was a drain in the center that was a foot in diameter: big enough to empty a lot of fluid when the room needed to be cleaned. The floor was bare concrete, but marked where people had carved words or pictures into it. At some point, someone had painted the walls a light blue, although

Kristin didn't know why they'd bothered. It was just going to get splattered with more blood.

A metal table and two chairs sat in the middle of the cell, the former of which was bolted to the concrete. They'd been added to the cell once Commander Fenix had been placed inside. Kristin picked up one of the metal chairs and scraped it along the ground, causing Fenix to wake up and look over at her.

The guards hadn't been particularly kind to him, and he had a nasty cut above his eye that needed stitching. Unfortunately for Commander Fenix, Kristin didn't have any anesthetic to hand. Contrary to what Hollywood would have you believe, there was actually a lot of yelling involved when a wound was getting stitched without anesthetic.

Sweat drenched his blood-stained, white t-shirt. Kristin had the blood elf guards bring in a bottle of ice-cold water. She sat and waited for Fenix to sit in the chair opposite her. The blood elf returned and poured the cold water into a large metal bowl that sat on the table.

"I guess if you were Layla, you'd be able to move the table to kill me," Kristin said. "Or rather, if you were Layla and you weren't wearing a sorcerer's band."

"Your hospitality has been somewhat lacking," Fenix said. "But if you'd like to bring me a cup of tea and some biscuits, I'll consider leaving you a good online review."

Kristin laughed. She hadn't meant to, but the brazen response was something she hadn't been expecting. "You know what, if you answer my questions, you get whatever you like. You want to tell us what that bracelet does? Nergal would like to remove it from you, but he's unsure what the runes inscribed on it do, and we didn't want to cause any little accidents." Kristin hoped that the sorcerer's band and bracelet reacted negatively to one another.

"I don't know what it does."

"That's what you're going to lead with?"

"You can torture me for the information, but I genuinely have no idea. Everyone has to wear one; no one knows why. There are ideas and theories, but nothing concrete."

"Nergal's people will find out."

"Or blow themselves up trying." Fenix leaned over the table a little. "I hope for the second option."

Kristin dunked his head into the bowl of almost freezing water before Fenix had time to react and held it there while she counted to thirty.

Fenix gasped as she released his head; his face was drenched and water ran down his chin onto his shirt, making a small puddle on the table. He moved back in his chair, as if wanting to be as far away from the water as possible.

"I can't abide cockiness," Kristin said. "It's just such a low personality trait. So how about you watch your tongue?"

Fenix spat onto the ground. "Fair enough. I see you're covered in blood. I assume it's not yours."

"Good assumption. Your friend Layla and her gaggle of followers managed to anger me tonight."

"They got away?" Fenix didn't smile.

"Yes," Kristin said. "But their only option is to come here to Winterborn, so I just wanted you to know that you'll be getting some roommates soon."

Fenix's eyes narrowed. "Just tell me what you want already."

"Where is Hades?"

"I don't know," was Fenix's response, and for the merest moment, Kristin thought that he looked surprised at the answer.

"Where is Thomas Carpenter? Or Olivia Carpenter?"

"I don't know."

The surprised look came back, but it was quickly replaced with a smile.

"Where is Hades' base of operations outside of Canada?"

"I don't know," Fenix said, and burst out laughing.

"You think this is funny?" Kristin said, irritated by the man's behavior.

"I really do," Fenix told her. "This is by far and away the funniest thing I've done in some time."

"You want to tell me why?"

Fenix shook his head. "I can't answer your questions."

"Can't or won't?"

"Well, if I could, I still wouldn't. But in this case, can't."

Kristin sat back in her chair. "You're probably wondering if I'm going to torture you. Not the beating you got—that was just a welcome-to-your-new-home kind of thing. I mean torture. Real torture. The answer is no. No, I'm not. I could, and I'm good at it, but I don't think inflicting incredible pain is going to change your mind."

"So do we just sit here and talk?" Fenix asked.

Kristin got up from her seat and knocked on the cell door, which opened a second later. Two more Kristins walked into the room.

"These are two of my clones."

"They have different hair than you," Fenix said. "And that one is a little taller."

"Yes, each clone is slightly different to me, and to the clone before it. Your friend, Chloe Range, killed one of them. And, last night, Layla injured another one so badly that I had to leave her to die. And she's dead now: fractured skull, bleeding on the brain. For someone who isn't supposed to be particularly vicious, Layla did quite the number on her. I'm going to have to have a chat with her about that."

Creating clones meant Kristin had to give away part of her power. For every clone she made, she gave up ten percent of her power, her strength, and her ability to heal. Ten percent of what made her her. It was usually worth the risk, but once a clone was called back, she couldn't recreate that clone unless all nine had been killed or recalled by her. Umbra powers were unpredictable, wild, and sometimes dangerous, but they were always interesting.

"So instead of you, someone else is going to torture me?"

"No, they're just here to keep you from doing anything silly. You're going to want to leave in a minute, and I can't have that." One of the clones passed Kristin a battery-powered speaker, which she placed on the table in front of Fenix.

"You're going to torture me with music? Is this one of those things where you saw it happen on a TV show or something?"

"Not quite," Kristin said, switching on the speaker and filling the cell with the sounds of screams.

Fenix watched the small speaker as the screams were replaced by pleading. "What's your name?" a male voice asked.

"Jared," came the strained reply.

There was the sound of a fist meeting flesh. "Your full name."

"Jared Bray."

"And where is Hades' compound?"

"Canada."

"No, we know it's not. Where is the other compound?"

"I don't know."

"That's a shame, Jared, it really is."

"Please don't," Jared said. "Please. I don't know."

Jared's screams filled the air once again.

"Stop it," Fenix said. "He can't say."

"And why would that be?" Kristin asked.

"I don't know. I didn't even know it was possible until you asked me, and I couldn't tell you. I don't know where Hades' compound is outside of Canada. That information isn't in my head. It's like a black hole."

"That's disappointing," Kristin said, switching off the speaker. "Maybe one of the others knows more, but for now, I'll just leave you here until we have other questions. Or until Jared happens to break. I wonder what will happen first."

Kristin left the room as Fenix called her a string of names. "Keep an eye on him," Kristin told Clone One. She used to give them all names, but had long since changed to numbers. The amount of effort it took to create new clones was a drain on her stamina. It didn't take long to do, but she felt weaker. Kristin didn't get attached to the clones, but she hated when they died because she knew what it would take to recreate them.

"Anything else?" Clone One asked.

"Don't harm him. Even if he's telling the truth, and he can't tell us where Hades' compound is, we can still get a wealth of information about Hades' collaborators."

Clone One nodded and stood guard outside of the room as Kristin and Clone Two walked through the underground maze of corridors to the lift that took them up into the aboveground building in Winterborn.

They were met by Clone Three, who had only four fingers on her right hand. "Nergal would like to see you," she said.

Her last three clones. Kristin could look through their eyes to see what they were doing and learn what they knew almost instantly, but only if required. Most of the time she preferred not to, since the constant updates could be somewhat overwhelming. Instead, she had them act autonomously, downloading their knowledge when she slept. It was only when they were on a mission that she allowed herself to watch them, which was partially why she was so irritated by the failure to kill Madison.

"Go rest," she told Clones Two and Three, and they both went off to sleep. They really didn't need food, or drink, or rest. But the longer they went without the latter, the more quickly Kristin would tire.

While the underground complex was where a lot of the unpleasantness of Nergal's operation was carried out, the aboveground was little more than a large warehouse. Kristin went back to her room and changed, wiping off the blood from her face and arms. She would have showered, but Nergal wouldn't appreciate being made to wait.

When she was no longer covered in blood, Kristin walked across the huge open floor where several hundred agents of Nergal's were climbing into the backs of dozens of large military-looking trucks. She found Nergal upstairs in the largest of the offices, sitting behind a desk, looking through the window at his troops below.

"You really are useless, aren't you?" Nergal said without anger, as if he were just stating a fact. "Dead umbra, dead clones, and no Caleb or Layla. I was going to march to Thunder Bay and oversee the glorious fall of Hades, but instead I'm here having to tell you that you're incompetent."

Kristin bit her tongue. She did not appreciate being blamed entirely for the failed mission. She had no idea that Cody was in the house until an hour before she was ready to go, and she hadn't picked the umbra to take with her; they'd been sent to the prison by Nergal to assist. She wanted to tell Nergal that he could stuff his words up his ass, but instead she remained quiet. She would need to release the rage later.

"We are at war," Nergal continued. "I cannot have this level of ineptitude when I'm in the middle of my greatest accomplishment: removing Hades as a person of power."

"Did Cody complete his task?" Kristin asked.

"Cody was found dead this morning. He left a message last night saying he had both Cassidys, and the BMW he was driving was discovered partially stripped of its metal. A small shed was found nearby. The girl and her father are on their way here."

"How long before they get here?"

"Depends when they left. Cody's body was found an hour ago, at first light."

"Any chance they'll try to avoid us?"

"They will want to go to Red Rock. Hades has a number of his people there, and it's a long trek by foot. They'll need a car, and this is the best place to acquire one."

"So we just wait for them to steal a car and then grab them at the border? Your people are still in charge there, yes? Or we get them at Thunder Bay."

"Unfortunately, I don't think it will be that easy. Layla is much more powerful than she was when I first tried to grab her, and her father is a known problem. I want them brought here, in the town. Letting them get to Thunder Bay when we're about to take the city will create unknown issues. It can't be allowed to happen."

"And how do we ensure they come into town?"

Nergal smiled. "That's where you come in. This is your final chance to get Layla and Caleb. If you fail again, it will be the last time you fail anyone. I gave Elias several chances to capture the girl and he failed, too. I had hoped that sending a woman to capture a woman would bring about better results."

Kristin ignored the remark.

"Women are weak," Nergal continued. "My ex-wife was weak, Abaddon is weak, Layla is weak. I had hoped you would change my thoughts on the matter, but so far, you're just as weak as they are."

"What about Fenix?" Kristin asked, hoping a new topic would stop her wanting to hit Nergal. "He claims he can't tell us the location of Hades' compound. Have the others we took with him managed to give anything up?"

Nergal shook his head. "My people are looking at one of the bracelets we recovered from the dead at the prison, but there appears to be some sort of blood curse mark on it. They're not sure what it does yet and, considering how potent and deadly blood curses can be, no one is willing to start poking at it. We have prisoners who didn't take to the spirit scrolls; we'll use them as guinea pigs when the time comes."

"How many umbra are at Thunder Bay?"

"Enough. Most of the scrolls brought to the Texas compound in the last few shipments have been useless. We managed to get lucky when we found a large number in Turkey, but it appears that most of them were never completed. Out of ten thousand scrolls, maybe a hundred have spirits attached. Of those, maybe twenty will be able to fully bond with a drenik and become a full-fledged umbra. The rest will die before they get close. And with our helpers in Louisiana no longer capable of doing anything, we've lost a large hub for bringing in test subjects and scrolls. We have a sizable number of them here at the compound; I considered forcing the inhabitants of the town to use them, but I'd rather see how the war goes first without having to create a second problem of hundreds of newly-forged umbra."

"I assume Abaddon has gone?"

"She's in the town. At some diner having breakfast, I believe. She brought a masked woman with her. I have no idea who she is, but the pair of them are not annoying me at the moment, so thank heavens for small mercies. Besides, I'm going to Thunder Bay, so they can do what they want. Actually, maybe the diner is a good place for you to talk to them and find out what they plan."

"And what is your plan with Red Rock once we have it?"

"My plan is of no concern to you," Nergal snapped. "You know only what I can be bothered to tell you. I talk to Abaddon because Arthur made it clear I have to. You are an assassin. A delivery person. You are whatever I tell you to be. You are not important enough to know my plans. I plucked you from the prison cell because I wanted to see what would happen when you bonded with a spirit scroll. You were an experiment, nothing more. The fact that you worked is a miracle I hadn't expected. Do not go around thinking you are worth more to me than that."

Kristin bowed her head slightly and left without a word. She usually ignored the way Nergal treated women, and so long as she kept busy, she didn't really consider the way he spoke to her. She thought that he'd picked her from the cell because he'd seen something in her that would be of help to his plans. It had become increasingly obvious to her that she was never going to be the worthwhile member of his team that she'd hoped to become. The thought upset her. She didn't want to be taken for granted. She didn't want to be spoken to like she wasn't worthy of respect. She could not kill Nergal, although the thought had crossed her mind. He was too strong, too dangerous. So Kristin took her anger and frustrations out on others. Maybe she would need to leave Nergal's employ sooner rather than later. But first, she wanted to talk to Abaddon. And she wanted to kill Layla.

Abaddon was closest, so that was her first destination. It didn't take Kristin long to find weapons for the mission and head out in one of the cars in the parking lot. She picked a silver Audi RS5 Coupe because it looked good and had a trunk that was just about big enough to stuff someone in, a fact she knew from firsthand experience.

Kristin pulled into the diner's parking lot, paused, and looked up at the building directly in front of her. The diner resembled something out of the 1950s: all chrome and glass with a red roof and red trimming. The door was at the side of the large establishment. The sign above the diner said *Suzy's*, although Kristin had no idea who Suzy was. With the car window wound down, she caught the smell of coffee and bacon. She hadn't eaten yet, so maybe there was time.

Kristin looked around at the apartment buildings nearby. It was still early, so most people were inside, which was probably for the best. She considered what she was going to say to Abaddon. The spirits in her head no longer talked to her. The force of Kristin's personality had all but swallowed up the two inside the scroll, changing her in only minor ways, so they were no help. She'd absorbed them as soon as she was able; the drenik, too. It had tried to control her and had been rudely surprised to see what the inside of Kristin's psyche housed. She didn't control the drenik—she wasn't sure that anything could—but it appeared to be less than happy to talk to her now, and that was how she liked it.

Kristin pushed the thoughts aside, wound up the window, and opened the car door, stepping out into the crisp morning. She'd been angry when arriving at the compound and angry when leaving it, but the drive had calmed her somewhat, and she now noticed that she was not dressed for a cold morning. She walked to the diner, opened the door, and stepped inside, feeling warmth wash over her.

Apart from two waitresses and the cook, Kristin spotted five people in the diner: one Sheriff's deputy, an elderly couple, Abaddon—who looked up from her coffee and spotted Kristin—and a woman sitting across from the necromancer, who also looked up at Kristin. She wore a black mask with a red slash across her eyes and had no food or drink in front of her. She wore what appeared to be some kind of leather armor.

Apart from Abaddon and the woman, everyone in the diner was dead. Several had slit throats, although, as Kristin stepped over the body of the Sheriff's deputy, she noticed no obvious signs of trauma.

Abaddon motioned for Kristin to sit next to the masked woman, which she did without comment.

"Nergal sent you here," Abaddon said, taking a long drink of her coffee.

Kristin nodded. There didn't seem to be much point in lying to her.

"He wants to know what we have planned?" Abaddon asked.

Another nod from Kristin.

"I want you to work with me," she said.

"Behind Nergal's back?" Kristin asked. She wasn't overly against the idea, she just wanted to know up front.

"Yes. Nergal does not have Avalon's best interests at heart."

"What does that mean?"

Abaddon took another sip of coffee. "He has orders to go to Red Rock and secure the realm gate for Avalon's forces. I believe he wishes to take Hades' territory and claim it as his own. That realm gate is too important to fall into the hands of someone who does not have Avalon's back."

"That would force him to go against Avalon," Kristin said. "Why would he do that?"

"He is arrogant," Abaddon said. "He is unhappy that I have as much influence with Arthur as I do. And I think he's been planning this for some time."

"How do you know this?"

"I have people in Nergal's operation. I've been informed of how he treats you. I thought you might enjoy some revenge."

"Did you get Layla Cassidy?" the woman asked.

"No," Kristin admitted, irritated at having a stranger question her.

"She's a feisty one, isn't she?" the woman said with a chuckle that made Kristin's skin crawl, although she couldn't have said why.

Abaddon stood and passed a small detonator to Kristin. "I've placed the charges. So you're going to use it to prove your worth to me. If you decide not to bother blowing the place, then I'll know you don't want to work with me and will treat you accordingly. And if you do . . . well, if you do, then I'll wait for you outside of Red Rock. At a small town by the name of Nipigon."

"I never said I'd work with you," Kristin said.

"I know, but at some point Nergal will try to have you killed. You failed him twice, and even though it was not totally your fault, he won't see it that way. He'll come for you."

Abaddon and the mystery woman left the diner. Kristin waited for several seconds before leaving. She drove the Audi down the street, stopping at the mouth of an alley. She got out and pressed the detonator, happy to see the diner explode. She wasn't sure if she trusted Abaddon, but she knew not to trust Nergal. At some point, he would decide she was no longer worth keeping around. Before she made a decision, Kristin wanted to know exactly why Abaddon was so interested in the Red Rock realm gate.

16

Layla and Caleb were already in Winterborn when the explosion happened. It felt like the street itself rocked, but the sound, fire, and smoke made sure they knew it could have only been one thing.

"I told you this was a bad idea," Caleb said. He'd been against them going into Winterborn from the beginning, and his arguments hadn't lessened in the hour since they'd arrived.

"We need transport," Layla said. "We needed clean clothes, considering we both had blood on ours. And now we need to figure out a way around the border guards, because there's no way they're not working for Nergal."

"So we need a tank," Caleb said.

"Going around the checkpoint is out. I can't imagine swimming across the river is going to do anything but get us both killed. Umbra or not, we both still need oxygen to breathe. We can't fly, and we don't have a boat to go around. Going through is our only option. And yes, you've mentioned several times that this is Nergal's territory, which is why I told you to behave."

"We're not getting through this town without a fight."

"A fight I'm okay with. A fight after walking through rough terrain is something I'd rather avoid."

They were in an alley behind a row of houses with wooden fences that were easily a dozen feet tall. When they'd first arrived in the town, they'd managed to break into a clothes shop and steal clean clothes and some backpacks to carry supplies when they finally found some. Layla had tried to use the phone in the office, but it hadn't worked, leaving her to wonder if the whole town's communication network had been shut down.

The pair made their way through the early morning streets, as more and more people streamed out of their homes trying to figure out what had caused the explosion. Layla listened to their words of concern, of fear, and more than a few hopes that no one had been caught in the blast.

A crowd had gathered at the end of the street that the diner had been on, and the sheriff and his deputies had placed a cordon around the area so the fire department could do their job. Layla fought the urge to pull up her hood; she didn't want to look suspicious.

They moved around the crowd until they reached the alley on the other side of the street. They ducked down it and jogged toward the end.

"Okay, we need to figure out where to go from here," Caleb said. "Getting out of town isn't going to be as simple as stealing a car."

"This town has the compound where my friends were taken," Layla said.

"You want to go find them? Because that will get us killed." Caleb spoke with real anger. "I raised you to be smarter than that."

Layla stared at her father for several seconds. "Have you always been like this? Were you like this when I was a child? I don't remember. Were you like this when Mom died?"

Caleb's expression grew dark. "Don't."

"Don't what, Dad? Don't talk about Mom? Don't talk about her fear of you, or how she'd be alive today if you hadn't been a psychopath?

Or don't talk about how not once, when you were killing people, did you think about us? Which part shouldn't I talk about?"

"I told you before, I loved both you and your mom. Her death . . . is something I will never stop regretting."

"Death? She was murdered. Don't you know that?"

"Murdered?" Caleb asked, confused. "No, I read the report. It was a car accident."

"She was killed by a man named Elias," Layla told him, wondering how he was going to take the news. "He was supposed to use me to get her to tell them where you were, but she died in the attempt. It was ordered by Nergal."

"And this Elias?"

"My friend Chloe killed him."

"Nergal is responsible for your mother's death, and for you becoming an umbra. For so much pain and suffering. Why have you not killed him?"

"Two reasons," Layla snapped. "One: I'm not a bloody assassin. Two: he's Nergal. Irkalla could do it, probably Diana, Persephone, and Hades, too, but all of those names belong to people who are thousands of years old. I'm not strong enough to fight Nergal. Not yet. He'll get his, though, I'll make sure of it."

Caleb sat down on the sidewalk, his head in his hands. "If we're to do this, I'm going to need my band off. It's not about trying to track anyone; I'll need my strength, my healing. I'm too limited with this thing on."

"No."

"I can kill people whether I'm wearing it or not."

"I just told you Mom was murdered, and you ask me to remove your band. I'm not an idiot. You'll be stronger, faster, less easy to hurt, and frankly a lot more dangerous to everyone in your way. You'll go after Nergal, and now isn't the time. No chance. Get up. We need to go."

"So we just hand ourselves in and hope for the best?"

"No, not so much," Remy said, stepping out of the shadows of the alley beside them.

Layla hugged him. "How long have you been following us?" she asked.

"Since I found out you'd been taken. Kase and I took off after you and found the car and a dead Cody. I assume your dad's work, yes?"

Layla nodded.

"We weren't there long before a bunch of guards arrived, so we followed them back here. You weren't hard to track. I found your scent from the car."

"Where's Kase?"

"Just outside of town with the others. Diana, Harry, Irkalla, Zamek, and Chloe, all of us lived through last night. Most of Kristin's friends did not. Also, we have backup."

"Who?"

"Persephone. She's— Well, the best way to put it would be to say she's angry. Very angry."

"What about Thunder Bay and Red Rock?"

"Thunder Bay is under siege, and Nergal's army is currently moving through the remains of the city killing anyone who isn't on their side. Red Rock is evacuating, but it'll take hours. We're going to head there as soon as we can."

"What about Jared, Fenix, and the others inside the compound?"

"We don't know for certain that they're in there," Remy said.

Layla looked at her father. "You try anything, and Remy will kill you."

Remy smiled.

Caleb held up his wrists. "I have no intention of doing anything at this exact point in time."

She sighed and removed a key from her pocket, unlocking his sorcerer's band. "I want to know where Jared and Fenix are," she told him, still conflicted about having removed his band.

"Do you have anything of theirs?"

Layla shook her head. "If I'd had something of theirs, I'd have gotten you to track them long ago." She passed him Kristin's dagger. "This belonged to a clone of Kristin, I don't know if that makes any difference, but you can see around the person you're tracking, so I'm hoping you might be able to see where Kristin is. Maybe get an idea if Jared and Fenix are in that compound."

She passed the dagger to Caleb, but held on to the hilt. "Don't screw around with this," she said. "Please."

Caleb nodded and took the dagger in his hands. He closed his eyes and opened them a second later to reveal his entire eyes were dark blue, like two perfect oval gems. It lasted a few seconds before they changed back to his normal color.

"And?" Remy asked.

"They're in there. I saw Kristin talking to Jared in his cell. That's it. Only a few seconds, but he's definitely in there. I can't say more, though. I'd need something that the original Kristin held to get a better look, I think."

Layla looked at Remy. "I think I have a plan."

"You're going to get inside that compound, aren't you?" Remy asked.

Layla nodded. "Hopefully, yes. They clearly want us, and I would really like to get our allies free. And maybe give a little back to that Kristin woman."

"Handing ourselves in seems like a bad idea," Caleb said.

"I wasn't going to hand myself in at all."

"Whatever you do needs to be fast," Remy said. "Nergal is heading to Red Rock, and if that realm gate falls, bad things will happen. Persephone didn't go into details, but I got the feeling there's a very good reason they want to destroy the gate. And that reason isn't just to do with the refugees they're sending through it."

"Okay, we need more information about the compound," Layla said. "If we can get our people out as quickly as possible, we can hopefully hurt Nergal here in Winterborn."

"Most of the troops appear to have left already," Remy said. "It's barebones back at the compound."

"Okay, be ready to go on my order," Layla said.

"Going to blow something up?" Remy asked with a grin.

Layla winked at him. "I'll see how it goes. Just how bad is Thunder Bay?"

"You know Nergal has already taken control of Sault Ste. Marie and Copper Harbor, right? So once they have Thunder Bay, they'll have both sides of Lake Superior secured. Persephone said that the airport at Thunder Bay is destroyed. The local news is reporting nothing; it's as if it's not even happening. Thankfully, the city was in the process of finishing off its evacuation when it happened. Even so, there are hundreds of people still leaving, or trapped inside the city."

"Okay, we'll get going," Layla said. "You go get the others ready. Be careful—there are CCTV cameras all over the place, and the Sheriff and his people work for Nergal."

"I got in okay. I'll get out. I'm just a cute little fox, after all." Remy ran down the alley he'd appeared from, almost vanishing from view after a few meters.

"He's a lot more than just a fox/man hybrid," Caleb said.

"Yes, he's been learning what he's capable of. The vanishing trick takes some getting used to, but it comes in handy."

The pair walked over to the warehouse, which was easily visible well before they reached it, as were the armed guards standing at the entrance.

"This isn't going to be fun," Caleb said.

"It never is with these people," Layla told him. "But it's necessary to get our friends back, and to me that's more important than my own safety. If I wanted safety, I'd have never joined Tommy's organization two years ago. I'd have run away and hidden in some tropical paradise."

"They'd have found you eventually."

"I know. Besides, I'm not very good at remaining hidden."

Caleb took another step, and Layla put her hand on his arm to stop him. "We do this quietly," she said. "Get in, release our allies, and let the rest of the group wipe out anything standing between us and freedom. No going off on a blood rage, or something equally stupid."

Caleb sighed. "I do love you, you know. I'm a monster. I murder and torture and revel in the blood I spill. Whatever part of me once hated it, now lives for battle. Lives to bring justice to those who never seem to pay for their crimes. But I never stopped loving you and your mom. I never once wanted either of you hurt by what I was doing. If there's a hell, I know I'm going there. I know it, and I've accepted it. I didn't kill for self-defense; sometimes I did, but mostly it was for selfish reasons, because I needed to. I wish I'd been a better father to you when you needed me."

Layla nodded slowly. "You trained me to hurt people, to be able to defend myself from attacks. To do things children shouldn't be able to do."

"Because I knew my enemies would come for me. Or I thought they would. But I couldn't figure out how, or when, or what would happen if they did. Your mother disagreed with the training, but never tried to stop me. I fear that you were right about her being afraid of me. I was too self-absorbed to see it. Too clouded. I was not a good father, or a good husband. I did what I thought was right."

Layla stared at her father for several seconds. "Unbelievable. You still don't get it, do you? You did what you thought was right? You're still making excuses for being a murderous asshole. You're still making excuses for your actions. You killed because you wanted to kill."

Caleb shrugged. "I needed those criminals to get the justice the courts never gave them. They needed to be removed from the gene pool. They *needed* to be removed to make things safe for law abiding citizens."

"I get that, Dad. I get that many of the people you killed were bad people. But some of them were just small-time nothings. You were indiscriminate."

"So if I'd killed murderers, rapists, and people who ruined lives, that would have been okay? But going after thieves, people who do petty stuff, that's wrong?"

"You killed people, Dad. You did it because you liked it. Their crimes were irrelevant. They just needed to have gotten away with one."

"You kill monsters, too. All of you do. What's different?"

Layla was about to tell her father that she didn't gun down unarmed suspects in the middle of the street, or slowly torture someone to death because they hit someone with their car, when two police cars pulled up beside them. Four deputies got out, along with several blood elves, who quickly pushed Caleb to the ground and placed a new sorcerer's band on his wrist.

"If you do anything, we kill him," one of the blood elves said to Layla.

Layla raised her hands. "You men okay with working with monsters?" she asked the deputies.

"You're the real monsters here," one of them said. "You murder humans. You make us afraid to live our lives. These blood elves are on the side of righteousness."

A second deputy put a hand on his partner's arm to calm him as one of the blood elves forced Layla to the ground, placing silver cuffs and a sorcerer's band on her wrists. He removed the Glock from the holster on her hip, ejected the magazine, and passed it to another deputy.

"Nergal wishes to see you," the blood elf rasped in her ear. "We've been watching you since you entered the town. Where is your fox friend?"

"He ran off," Layla said with a sigh. This wasn't exactly how she'd imagined getting into Nergal's compound, but it seemed like that was where she was headed.

She was picked up and pushed, back first, against the wall. "Nergal will force you to help," the blood elf said.

"How many humans do you kill a day?" She asked it loud enough for the deputies to hear. "You didn't know? Blood elves eat people. You people are idiots."

"It's okay," Caleb said. "Sooner or later people like these will discover the folly of their actions. Hopefully while one of the blood elves is elbow-deep in their chest cavity."

One of the deputies looked a little green at the suggestion, and Layla wondered if her father was right. The human deputies seemed to have no idea what they were sharing their cars with. They thought the blood elves were their protectors, and she didn't think it would be long before Nergal unleashed the elves on the town of Winterborn as a reward for loyal service.

17

The second Layla and Caleb stepped inside the warehouse, her sorcerer's band was removed. But Layla's powers remained blocked and she looked around for the runes responsible as they moved through the building. The blood elves marched them up to the offices above, and Layla took note of how quiet it all was. Apart from a few guards and blood elves, there was barely anyone inside the warehouse.

The blood elves opened an office door without knocking and motioned for their prisoners to enter. Unlike the ones she'd seen at the prison, and in the rest of Winterborn, these elves used rifles and sub-machine guns. They had handguns in holsters on their hips and wore military tactical gear instead of the leather armor she'd gotten used to seeing on Nergal's people.

"They had to modernize," a man said from the end of the office. He was looking out through the windows at the end of the room, watching the few people who remained in his warehouse. He turned and smiled. "My name is Nergal."

Layla watched as her father took a step forward. "You murdered my wife."

"No, Elias did that," Nergal said, as if speaking to a child. "I ordered her and your daughter's kidnapping. Elias no longer works for me. Mostly due to him being dead."

"I still hold you responsible," Caleb told him in a cold, detached tone.

"Frankly, I don't care," Nergal replied. "You're wearing a sorcerer's band, and you're surrounded by armed guards. You won't get within ten feet of me. And you're only about twelve feet away now."

"I'm not wearing anything," Layla said. "What's stopping me?"

"Well, I'm thousands of years old. I'm stronger, faster, and considerably more powerful than you. And, more importantly, I'm not about to be beaten down by some woman with delusions of grandeur. Irkalla couldn't kill me, so you certainly can't."

"Why remove my band?" Layla asked.

"The runes work just as well for your powers. Your father's, too, but frankly I can't take the risk with him, so he keeps his band on. I'm not so concerned about you."

"So, what now?" Caleb asked. "We just work for you?"

Nergal activated an intercom and two blood elves walked into the room. "I think it would be in your best interests to do as you're told, yes." He nodded toward the blood elf closest to Layla, who then stamped on the back of her knee, forcing her to the floor, where he kicked her in the back, sending her to the ground.

Nergal raised a hand and the blood elf stopped. "You see: I have a great many ways I can force you to help me. I was just about to leave when I got word of your capture. I would have had Kristin bring you in, but she appears to have headed out of town, toward Red Rock. I'm sure you'll see her soon enough, Layla."

"So I help you, or you hurt my daughter?" Caleb asked.

"No, you help us, or I feed your daughter to my blood elves. After Kristin breaks her legs. I think you'll find the sight of blood elves devouring someone you love fascinating. And should you decide to call my bluff, I assure you that I could keep your daughter alive for a very long time once the elves start. Maybe we'll remove a hand first, or her whole arm? What do you think?"

Caleb just stood and stared at Nergal, who walked around to the front of his desk and loomed above Layla. One of the blood elves forced her to stretch out her arm, and Nergal placed his foot just above the elbow, applying enough weight to make Layla yell in pain.

"Enough," Caleb said. "I'll help you."

Nergal walked over to Caleb and punched him in the kidney, sending him to the floor. "Just remember who I am the next time you decide to wait before answering me. Both of you will be taken to your new homes," Nergal said, sounding cheerful. "I hope you enjoy your time with us."

Layla and Caleb were led out of the office by the blood elves who had brought them in and back down onto the warehouse floor.

"Nergal had runes drawn on his wall," Layla whispered. "They're stopping my power."

"You can read runes?" Caleb asked.

"One of my spirits is from the realm where the scrolls were created," Layla continued. "Gyda can read some rudimentary runes. The ones in his office count as rudimentary. Someone with little experience did them quickly. Presumably someone Nergal told to get on with it. They work, but they're not going to stop anyone with real power."

"Nergal must know that."

"I doubt he cares," Layla said. "He's arrogant, and I don't think he's all that concerned about someone with power coming at him."

"His arrogance will be his undoing," Caleb said forcefully.

"Stop talking," the blood elf closest to them said, shoving Layla in the back. "Over to the elevator, now. You're going to the crypt."

"This place has a crypt?" Layla asked.

"It's what we call the maze of corridors below," the blood elf told her with an evil smile. "Once down there, you don't come back."

"You came back," Layla pointed out.

The blood elf looked confused. "Prisoners don't come out. We can come and go as we like."

"I think they're mocking us," the second blood elf said with a slight sneer. "I think they believe they're better than us."

"Better than blood elves? Never," Layla said.

"I had never seen a blood elf until you attacked the prison," Caleb said. "Didn't even know that other realms existed. You like chaos, violence, and blood, and the ability to make people afraid of you. I sort of wish I'd known you were around before I went to prison. I would have enjoyed hunting you."

The closest blood elf leaned in toward Caleb. "I would have enjoyed you trying."

Layla tensed, wondering if her father was going to launch himself at the blood elf and start a fight, but instead he just turned and stepped into the now open elevator.

Layla and Caleb stood at the rear of the large elevator while the two blood elves waited by the doors as they closed. One of the elves pushed a button on the console beside him and the lift began to move down.

"You're going to like it here," the elf closest to Layla said with a laugh.

"Question for you," Layla said. "Who did your runes?"

The blood elves looked at one another. "Abaddon," one of them almost whispered.

"The Abaddon?" Layla asked, noticing the recognition in her father's eyes.

"I find that hard to believe," Rosa said from beside Layla. "Did you know there are no runes in the elevator, or the elevator shaft? Sort of seems like an oversight to me. Not exactly the kind of thing a thousands-of-years-old necromancer like Abaddon would do."

Layla looked at Rosa, and then back at the blood elves. "Sorry, guys, but I think your tour is going to have to wait." Thin, razor-sharp spears of metal struck out from either side of the lift, puncturing the skulls of the blood elves, killing each of them instantly.

"How long have you been able to do that?" Caleb asked.

"Long enough," Layla told him as the lift stopped and the doors opened.

"There are marks out there," Rosa said. "I can almost feel them."

"Me too," Layla said.

"You're talking to your spirits, aren't you?" Caleb asked.

"Why would Abaddon post such sloppily-drawn runes in the warehouse, and nothing in the elevator?" Layla asked, ignoring her father. "It seems like something that someone with her power would be able to correct. From what I've heard about her, sloppiness isn't in her vocabulary."

"She wanted a place she could access her power," Gyda said from the corner of the elevator.

"You're talking to me now?" Layla asked.

"If you die, I have to wait around for another person to take control of the scroll. And next time, they might be someone I really dislike."

Layla stepped out of the elevator into the gray corridor and the spirits vanished, along with her connection to her power. The dim lighting was enough to see the rune on the ceiling. It was about a foot long and drawn in bright-blue paint.

"Okay, there's no way you can't see that," Layla said. "Is Abaddon just trying to see how much she can piss Nergal off?"

"It does seem like she's not all that bothered about him noticing."

Layla removed a dagger from the belt of one of the dead blood elves and threw it up into the ceiling, destroying the rune. Her power immediately returned to her.

Caleb and Layla searched the maze of corridors for any of Layla's companions and found nothing except empty cells, some of which smelled of blood and death. She marked each one they searched by partially crushing their metal doors. They found Fenix and Jared just as the alarm went off throughout the complex. They were in a single cell, and both of them looked like they'd been through hell, with bloodied and bruised faces.

Jared and Layla embraced. "It's good to see you," he said.

"I thought we had a date tomorrow. I didn't want to get stood up," she told him.

"There are two dead blood elves in the elevator," Layla told them. "Both have weapons, and this place is currently under assault. Get what you need and get topside. I'll find anyone else and join you."

"What about your dad?" Fenix asked, wincing as he got to his feet.

"He stays with me," Layla said.

"Your trust in me is adorable," Caleb said.

Layla ignored him. "You two going to be okay?"

Both nodded. "They wanted me to give them intel on the Greenland compound, but I couldn't do it," Fenix said. "I think our blood curse mark makes it impossible somehow."

"We'll figure it out."

"They asked me the same thing," Jared said. "Like Fenix, I couldn't say anything. They killed the others. No one could tell them anything, so they killed them. There's no one else to save, Layla. I'm sorry."

Layla kissed Jared on the cheek. "It's okay. We'll get you both home."

Jared rested his head on Layla's shoulder, and Layla hugged him tight. "I didn't think they would kill the other prisoners," he almost whispered. "Diana is gone."

"Diana is with us," Layla said. "I'll explain later, but she's fine."

Jared smiled. "Good."

"We'll stop Nergal and his people," Layla promised, releasing Jared. "Diana and co. are probably tearing this place apart at the moment."

The four of them went back to the elevator as quickly as they could. Layla used the console to select the warehouse floor, and they were soon traveling upward.

"I expected more guards," Fenix said.

"They're attacking Thunder Bay," Layla told him. "There seems to only be a handful of people left here."

"Nergal hates Hades, doesn't he?" Jared said.

Caleb stared at Jared for several uncomfortable seconds before he nodded. "Nergal wants to be the strongest, but he knows he isn't. He can't accept the idea that he can be beaten, but deep down, he knows. He just won't admit it to himself. Nergal is frightened of Hades. I've seen people like him before. They know they're not the 'baddest', so they do everything they can to prove how scary they are."

"Nergal isn't going to enjoy meeting Hades in combat," Fenix said. "I can't think of anyone I'd rather fight less than Hades. Maybe Persephone. She might be more powerful than Hades."

"She's upstairs," Layla said.

"Then we might live through this," Fenix said with a smile.

"That's the plan," Layla told him as the elevator stopped and the doors opened to a world of violence and death.

The bodies of blood elves and human guards were scattered around the outside of the elevator, and the sounds of battle raged throughout the warehouse. Layla spotted Diana—in full werebear beast form—tearing into several blood elves, who were powerless to stop her rampage.

"Even with the runes removed from the compound, none of you are in any condition to start fighting," Layla said, motioning for the occupants of the elevator to follow her and stay low until they reached the rear of a large truck.

Layla didn't need to worry about the runes in Nergal's office, as they only took effect over people inside it, and considering she had no intention of going back in there, she was able to use her powers as she wished. However, that didn't mean she wanted those she'd just saved running around when they were in no condition to help.

"Keep your heads down, I'll be back soon," Layla said. "If my father tries anything, shoot him."

Layla ran off toward the melee, using her power to tear apart any guns or swords in nearby assailants' hands.

One blood elf screamed and charged at her, but was soon stopped when a fist-sized piece of metal tore free from a truck and slammed into his head, knocking him to the floor where Zamek drove his battle-ax into the prone elf's skull.

"Good to see you," Zamek said with a smile. He absentmindedly threw a knife into the chest of a nearby blood elf, before catching it in the throat with his ax as it fell toward him. "Thought you weren't going to turn up."

"Looks like you made short work of the remaining elves," Layla said. She walked over to the dead blood elf and removed the sheath from around its waist, taking its silver dagger as her own.

"There are a few stragglers, but it appears that elves die a lot quicker than I was expecting. Your father still alive?"

Layla nodded. "Over by the truck with Fenix and Jared."

"I'll go check on them. Persephone must be outside. She'll want to say hi."

Layla ran through the warehouse and spotted Diana, Chloe, and Kase dealing with the stragglers. She stepped outside where Irkalla was kneeling on the ground, a dark red glow all around her. Layla took a step forward, and Harry stopped her.

"Don't step in there," he told her.

Layla looked down at the circle that pulsated on the floor. "What's she doing?"

"A lot of these blood elves are reanimated corpses. They're a product of Abaddon's power. Irkalla is going to stop it. You step in that circle and you're probably going to wish you hadn't. She said something about how it'll fry the brain of anyone who isn't a necromancer."

Layla took a step back as the power from the circle vanished and Irkalla stood up. "It's done," she said and then smiled at Layla as if seeing her for the first time. "Ah, you're here. The blood elf zombies are dealt with. We shouldn't be finding any more of them here."

"That's something good," Layla said. "My father is still alive. They killed some of the people they took. Only Jared and Fenix remain. Both of them look . . ." She paused as her emotions threatened to overwhelm her.

"We'll get justice, Layla," Irkalla said. "Do you need some time?"

Layla shook her head. She wasn't about to allow Nergal and his people the chance to hurt anyone else. "Where's Persephone?"

"She's out there," Chloe said as she walked over to the group and hugged Layla. "She started throwing the earth around. She literally tore the earth apart and flattened a truck full of blood elves. Diana went out to join her. I didn't want to be in their way."

Layla wasn't sure how to respond to that. She'd seen impressive levels of power before, but throwing around several hundred tons of rock went beyond anything she expected to see.

Layla ran over to the gap in the wall and found the truck outside buried under several tons of rock. Persephone stood beside it, wearing dark gray leather armor. Layla looked down at her bare feet.

"Remind me not to piss you off," Layla said.

Persephone smiled. She walked over to Layla and hugged her. "It's good to see you in one piece. I trust you got out everyone who was able to leave?"

Layla told Persephone about what had happened since she'd given herself up to Nergal. "Nergal was about to leave. He wants to get to the battlefront. We need to let Red Rock know what's happened."

"We will," Persephone said. "Remy has headed off toward Red Rock to aid in its defense, and that's where we're all going next."

"What's at Red Rock?" Layla asked. "The realm gate? Where does it go?"

Persephone nodded. "I guess you all should know. The realm gate leads to Norumbega."

"Never heard of it," Layla said. "What's in Norumbega?"

"There's an old prison in that realm," Persephone said. "We think that Abaddon believes one of her comrades is being held there."

"Are they?"

Chloe, Irkalla, Harry, and the others joined them, as Diana returned to the group from her hunt of whatever unlucky soul had been on her radar.

"Yes. It was the safest place to put him at the time."

"Who is he?" Chloe asked.

"His name is Mammon."

"Oh shit," Irkalla said. "The Mammon?"

"Who is Mammon?" Harry asked.

"Mammon is one of the seven original devils," Irkalla said. "The same group that Abaddon is a part of."

"Asmodeus was their king," Persephone began, "and Abaddon essentially their queen. They were to be the most powerful weapons of their day, meant to conquer all in the name of their lord. This was thousands of years before the Titans, Egyptians, or anyone else people considered mythological. They were sent to the Earth realm to defeat and rule us, but they were crushed and separated. Thousands of years later, they attacked again. Lucifer—the man you know as Grayson—betrayed them and aided us in a war we might not have won without him. Asmodeus was executed, but Abaddon retrieved his soul and used it to create her ultimate weapon: Arthur.

"Asmodeus and Arthur are essentially one and the same. Sathanus was killed by Lucifer centuries ago. That leaves three others: Mammon, Belphegor, and Beelzebub, none of who are in this realm. They're not literal devils or anything with religious attachments. They're just an exceptionally powerful species like myself. And Abaddon wants them in this realm, by Arthur's side."

"Wait," Harry said. "Grayson is Lucifer?"

"You didn't know?" Diana asked.

"I haven't seen Grayson . . . sorry, Lucifer, in two years, so, no, it didn't come up."

"He's helping to fight the tide of Arthur's corruption in other realms," Persephone said. "I'm beginning to wish he was here, though. We're too spread thin; too many of us are in other realms trying to stop Arthur and his people from taking control of the various pantheons. And too many of us are around the globe, trying to help his enemies escape."

"That might be why this attack was suggested," Layla said. "They know we're spread thin."

"Abaddon wants her kin back," Persephone said, "and she will do anything to achieve that goal."

"We need to get to Red Rock then," Layla said.

They heard the sound of a truck before it appeared through the front gate of the warehouse. Fenix leaned out of the driver's window. "You need a lift?" he said as a second truck drove out of the entrance, with Jared behind the wheel.

After grabbing as many of the blood elves' MP5s and Glock handguns as possible, everyone piled into the back of the two vehicles and sat on benches opposite one another. Caleb sat in the cabin next to Persephone and Fenix, who continued to drive. The arrangement ensured Caleb wouldn't try anything, unless he wanted to learn how quickly an earth elemental could drag him underground and leave him there until he learned to behave.

Layla was glad to be done with her father for the short journey north. She sat beside Chloe, who had a smear of blood on her cheek.

"It's not mine," Chloe said. "And you can't talk—you have some on you, too."

"That's not mine, either," Layla told her. "So, if we weren't all here trying to stop Nergal from taking control of a city and its realm gate, what would you be doing?"

"I planned on having a date with that lovely red-headed teacher at the school."

"There's a school in the compound?" Layla asked.

"You've seen the children running around, yes? Of course there's a school."

Layla hadn't spent much time considering it before. "So, you have a date with one of the teachers?"

Chloe smiled and nodded. "Her name is Piper. I've spoken to her a few times at one of the bars not frequented by off-duty guards. She's really cool, so I asked her out."

"And she said yes?" Harry asked, sounding surprised. He sat across from Chloe and Layla.

"No, Harry, she said no," Chloe said sarcastically. "I just decided that when someone says no, I'm going to stalk them."

"At least they won't have to put up with your personality if you hide in bushes and watch from a distance."

"Funny guy," Chloe said. "And for your information, Piper was excited to see me. She texted me and everything."

"That's just because she doesn't really know you yet," Harry said.

"You're grinning," Layla pointed out to Chloe. "You like her, don't you?"

"A little," Chloe said. "I don't think I'm going to make the date, though. Which sucks."

"You can reschedule. I'm sure she'll understand that you are in a life-and-death struggle to save those who need your help."

"That is literally what I'm going to tell her I'm doing. I'll leave out the zombie blood elf killing. I'm here to save lives and kick ass."

"If you're not careful, someone's going to write a song about you," Harry said.

"I'm okay with that," Chloe told him. "I could do with having a song."

"You okay, Harry?" Layla asked him.

"Yeah, Persephone made me stay back when they attacked. I . . . I sometimes wish I wasn't human so I could help more, and then I saw the zombie blood elves, and was all, yeah, I'm good, thanks."

Layla and Chloe laughed, and Layla felt happy that she got to spend a few moments with her friends while going from one dangerous situation to the next. She looked out of the truck as Nergal's compound exploded.

"We set some charges," Chloe said. "Down in the cells, too. No one is going to be taken back there anytime soon."

The compound was far enough away from anything residential that there was no concern about the buildings closest to it being damaged. After a second explosion, the entire structure was in flames, and Layla smiled. If Nergal was going to try to take Canada from Hades, it was good to know they'd taken something of his in return.

When they'd left the town of Winterborn, Layla looked out of the truck's plastic window and saw smoke rising from the city in the distance. She sighed. It was time to go to work.

18

The truck pulled to a stop as they entered the city of Thunder Bay, and the hatch separating the cabin from the rear opened. Persephone's face came into view. "We're going to have to get out," she told everyone, and they quickly piled out of the back of the truck.

The battle had been completed in a matter of hours. Layla had known that Hades had been preparing to evacuate the town, but the speed at which Nergal had attacked was too quick to get everyone out.

The second truck stopped and everyone inside got out. Persephone, Fenix, and a less than happy Caleb joined them.

"What's going on?" Kase asked.

"We have a problem," Remy said, appearing as if out of nowhere. "I never got to Red Rock. The fighting is intense at the edge of Thunder Bay, and there are still people in the city who need help to evacuate."

"Where are they?" Layla asked.

Remy nodded. "There's a large office block that something has torn apart, but there are people in the apartment next to it. Families. Our people are trying to get to them, but the fighting is intense. There's another oni there. This one is a bit bigger than the last. Until that's gone, those people are stuck."

Layla looked around at the ruined buildings and cracked roads. "What caused all of this destruction?"

"Nergal's people," Remy said. "They came, they saw, and they got pissed off that the evacuation had already started. There are bands of his thugs roaming the city, searching for the unlucky few who haven't been evacuated yet. Most of his force went on to Red Rock. Nergal is with them."

"That's to be expected," Irkalla said. "He always did like to take part in a fight he was certain to win. Thunder Bay is an easily taken gift."

"Any chance some of those trapped are human?" Layla asked.

"It's certainly possible," Persephone said. "This town had a large human population."

"Right, in that case, Remy, Harry, Chloe, and Kase, you're with me," Layla said. "We're going to go help those people. Between us, we should be able to take out an oni, even a really big one. Zamek, you need to get to the realm gate and help destroy it. Diana, take my father, I know that he'll behave himself if you're there. Jared and Fenix need medical attention."

"We have facilities at our compound north of Nipigon—it's a town an hour and a half north of here," Persephone said.

"Right, then the rest of you head there. You're all powerful enough to fight back and not get killed if Nergal's forces cause you any trouble."

Layla grabbed one of the MP5s and checked the magazine. It was full of silver bullets. That left half a dozen MP5s, the same number of handguns, and her dagger.

Layla had at one point been scared of becoming her father. Caleb had tried to link his crimes with what Hades and his people did, but that was horse shit, and Layla knew it. The difference between what they did and what her father had done was that he had enjoyed it. He killed and hurt people for pleasure, no matter how much he liked to suggest he was making the world a better place. Layla killed and fought because she had no choice. She took no pleasure in it. She knew that the realization made Rosa smile. It had been a long time coming.

"Take some weapons," Layla said. "I think we're going to need them."

"Is Thomas Carpenter at Red Rock?" Caleb asked as Chloe and Harry both picked up an MP5 and Remy took a Glock to go with his silver daggers.

"My father will be wherever the fighting is most fierce," Kase said.

Layla saw the fear on her father's face.

"My father scares you," Kase said, having noticed his expression.

Caleb said nothing and climbed back into the truck, followed quickly by most of the others.

"We'll leave this truck here," Irkalla said. "Just in case you have casualties to ferry. We'll try to make sure the main entrance into Red Rock is free of attackers, but there's no guarantee."

"We'll get into the town," Chloe told her. "One way or another."

Everyone said their goodbyes, leaving Jared and Layla alone. "This isn't how I imagined our reunion," Layla said.

"Keep safe, Layla," Jared said, kissing her. "I don't want to see what life is like without you in it."

"You too," Layla told him, and they parted ways. She'd tried not to show the worry she felt at the group splitting up. She knew that Jared was more than capable of taking care of himself, but the concern was still there.

"I guess we leave the truck here," Harry said. "I don't think risking its destruction is a good idea."

"I'll show you where the fighting is," Remy said. "Then Harry can always double back to get the truck if it's safe."

"Truck driving Harry," Chloe said enthusiastically as the group set off after Remy, who was bounding away across the rubble of a partially destroyed neighborhood. More than one car was a simmering wreck and they occasionally came across bodies, both from Nergal's forces and of those who had defended the people who remained in Thunder Bay.

"It's awful to see how much destruction has happened in less than a day," Layla said to no one in particular.

"Nergal's forces were prepared to tear this place apart," Chloe said.

It took only a few minutes for the group to spot the defensive force fighting several of Nergal's guard. Both groups threw magic around like it was confetti, tearing apart buildings and roads. Gaping holes had been ripped in the side of buildings, exposing the apartments within, and the air smelled of burned plastic and wood, an acrid scent that Layla found repugnant.

"I see why there was so much destruction," Layla said as the sounds of fighting intensified the closer they got.

"Sorcerers, elementals, and the like—there are good reasons so many fear them," Kase said.

Remy stopped up ahead and crouched down, waiting for the others to catch up. "Right, Harry, no offense, but this is where you go back to the truck. You need to bring it down that road there, as slowly and as quietly as possible. These magic-flinging bastards won't care about tearing both you and the truck in half."

"That's the worst pep talk in the history of pep talks," Harry said.

"Okay. Don't get killed, you colossal asshat," Remy said. "Sound better to you?"

Harry ignored him and ran back toward the truck as the rest of the group peered over the remains of a stone wall to watch the battle a hundred feet in front of them. Fire and lighting met ice and water with devastating results.

"I count four," Layla said. "Those two in the uniform of Hades' people, and those two, I assume, work for Nergal."

"Where's the oni?" Kase said. "Never mind, I see it."

Everyone followed where she was pointing to the ten-foot-tall oni who was fighting off eight people all at once. They were a few hundred feet away from the fight between the sorcerers.

"Looks like werewolves," Chloe said. "An elemental, maybe an umbra or two. They're holding their own, but they don't have an Irkalla, so I'm not sure how much longer that's going to last."

"Sorcerers or oni?" Layla asked. "I'm going after Nergal's sorcerers. If either of them get past the two on our side, we're all screwed." She hoped that the oni could be kept busy until everyone was done with the sorcerers. The smell of the magical fight made her wish she'd brought a mask.

"I'm with you," Kase said. "Sorcerers first, then oni."

"So we're all in agreement?" Remy asked. "Sounds good to me."

"We need to get around the back, through those houses down there," Kase said. "If we can get behind them, we should be able to box them in. Attack from all sides. The oni is . . . a future problem."

"Where are the people?" Layla asked Remy.

He pointed to a ten-story building next to a slightly taller, partially destroyed office block.

"Okay, so we need to make sure the people inside are alright."

"That's me," Remy said. "I can get in and around quicker than the rest of you, and if there's anyone inside who shouldn't be, I'm okay with teaching them the error of their ways."

The group split, and Layla, Chloe, and Kase followed the road, staying far enough back to keep out of the sorcerer's line of sight. They crept through the remains of a house that had been blasted apart by magic.

Layla had gained a newfound respect for sorcerers after meeting a few during her time opposing Avalon. Most of them were at least centuries old and appeared to be more focused with their magic use, and less interested in causing mass devastation, a marked difference to the sorcerers fighting near Layla and her team.

Some of the buildings that had been damaged by the magical blasts started to collapse, spilling furniture and bricks onto the street close by.

Once outside the house, they moved to the edge of the exterior wall and Kase looked beyond it as a bolt of lightning smashed into the rock above her head. She leapt back, avoiding the powerful magic, and scowled at the destroyed brick wall close to where her head had been.

"You okay?" Layla asked.

Kase nodded. "Errant blast. The two enemy sorcerers are about twenty feet in front and to the right of this house."

"Can we get to them without them noticing?" Remy asked as he appeared out of nowhere.

"How is everyone in the building?" Layla asked, trying not to show Remy that his new ability to appear in a puff of smoke was unnerving.

"Scared. There are twenty-six people in there. Eight of them are under ten."

"Oh shit."

"Pretty much," Remy said. "Considering where they are, they're all being incredibly brave. No idea how long that will last if those sorcerers or the oni get to them. Everyone's human."

"So, back to my question, can we get to the sorcerers without them noticing? The second we open fire on them, they're going to know where we are, and they're going to come for us. We have to do this quickly, or we're going to have a serious problem on our hands, silver bullets or not."

Kase shrugged. "We have to try." She was the only one not carrying a silver weapon: weres of all kinds hated silver with a passion, so Layla could understand Kase's reluctance to use it.

Remy ran to the end of the alley and vanished from view, leaving small traces of smoke behind. He reappeared a moment later on the other side of the street.

"I'll never get used to the fact that he can do that now," Chloe said.

"I'm so glad I'm not the only one," Layla replied as she moved around the front of the alley and crouched behind a partially destroyed car.

She reached out with her power just as a jet of flame slammed into the house next her, turning it into an inferno. Chloe crouched beside her. "Our sorcerers need to learn some control," she said.

Layla kept a hold of her power as it wrapped around the door of a barely recognizable coupe nearby. She couldn't move anything that was larger than her, but weight didn't appear to be a factor. She watched for Remy as he and Kase—now in full werewolf beast form—charged into the enemy sorcerer closest to them. Layla tore the door off the coupe and threw it at the second sorcerer with incredible force. He had turned to see what his friend was doing and didn't notice the door as it smashed into his head at high speed.

It would have killed a human. No question about it. And even the sorcerer was knocked to the sidewalk, blood pouring from a deep gash in the side of his head. Layla raised her MP5, and the hours of training that her father put her through, coupled with all of the training she'd completed since joining Hades' organization, kicked in. She fired a three-round killing burst into the closest sorcerer. Two of the shots hit his hastily assembled shield of air, and the third struck him in the shoulder. Layla continued to fire, keeping the sorcerer's attention on her, but none of the other bullets got through his shield.

The sorcerer moved away from the sidewalk into the middle of the road, keeping his shield up at all times. Layla fired another round, which was easily deflected by the shield, but had the advantage of keeping the sorcerer's attention firmly on her, and not on Chloe, who ran around the nearby building.

Layla fired another round as Chloe came into view, staying low as she crept along the wall closest to the sorcerer. The shadows kept her from being seen until she fired into the man's exposed flank. He whipped up his shield to stop them, but Chloe and Layla kept firing. All of the bullets just fell to the ground as if they'd struck a wall, but the damage Layla had done to the sorcerer's shoulder was going to take its toll sooner or later. Eventually his shields faltered and both Chloe and Layla fired at him: two bullets, both headshots. The sorcerer crumpled to the ground as Remy drove a silver dagger into the heart of the second sorcerer, who had been dazed and unable to defend against the attack. Both were dead in seconds.

Layla looked over at Hades' sorcerers, who'd been fighting Nergal's men; one of them had collapsed onto the ground. She ran over to him, but he died before she could do anything to help with his injuries.

"They shot him with a silver round," the other sorcerer said sadly as he got back to his feet from behind the ruins of a nearby brick wall that had once been part of a house. He looked bloodied and banged up, but otherwise seemed okay. "There's no coming back from that. He wasn't even a hundred. He still fought, though."

"I'm sorry," Layla said as a cheer went up from the group fighting the oni—who now fled through the city, knocking down pieces of building to stop anyone following it.

"My magic is running low. Any chance of one of those guns?"

Remy handed his Glock to the sorcerer.

"We'll get the people out of the building," Kase told him. She'd remained in her werewolf beast form, which was the only way she could use her elemental powers. Layla hadn't met another werewolf-elemental hybrid, and if Kase was the only one, she was glad she was on their side.

"Thank you," the sorcerer said. "I'll go check on everyone." He ran off toward his companions, who'd given chase to the oni.

On their way to the residential block, Layla checked her MP5 and found it empty. Chloe was also out of ammunition, so they dropped the weapons on the sidewalk. They didn't expect to need them now that Nergal's forces had been dealt with, and they were empty anyway, so were no longer of use. At the apartment building, they found most of the people huddled together in the foyer.

"You're going to get us out?" an elderly woman asked as a small child clung to her leg.

"That's the plan," Layla told her. "Is anyone in this building injured, or need help getting out?"

"We'll all be fine," she said. "We just want to leave."

"Why didn't you evacuate with the others?" Chloe asked.

"We were supposed to, and trucks arrived to get us out of town, but the street turned into a war zone. Hades' soldiers told us to wait in here. I assume the rest of the city got out okay?"

"Looks that way," Layla told her. "We'll wait for our friend to return with a truck and load you all onboard. It might be a rough ride out of town, but it's better than staying here."

"What about the monster?" the little girl clinging to the elderly woman asked.

"It ran away," Chloe said. "That's how good we are at defeating monsters. They run away as soon as they see us."

The little girl beamed. "My name is Summer."

"That's a beautiful name," Layla said, crouching in front of her. "How old are you, Summer?"

"I'm this old," she said, raising three fingers.

"Three? That's very old. Can you drive yet?"

The little girl laughed. "No, I'm not old enough to drive."

"You sure?" Chloe asked. "You look like someone who likes taking her granny's car out for a spin."

Summer looked serious. "That's bad," she said at almost a whisper.

Layla heard a scream from outside the building. "All of you go into one of those rooms." She pointed to the doors at the end of the foyer. Each had a number on them. "I'm just going to go make sure that was only someone doing something stupid."

Layla and Chloe shared a look of concern as Remy ran into the building. "I think we might have a problem." They followed him out and immediately saw the problem.

Nergal had arrived and defeated Hades' people, who had been fighting the oni. Their uniformed bodies were strewn around the area. He half-dragged, half-carried one by the neck as he walked up the street toward Layla and her friends.

When Nergal was about fifty feet away, he dropped the struggling man on the ground and crushed his skull with his boot.

"Who screamed?" Layla asked.

"He was dragging a second person," Kase told her. "He killed her just as he came into view. She was terrified."

Layla knew that Nergal's ability to siphon life energy from people was limited to using humans, but she also knew that his power could spread fear throughout both humans and non-human, alike. It was like an aura that surrounded him, making him incredibly difficult to fight. Irkalla had told her that he'd only lived this long because anyone who tried to kill him up close was too scared to act once he activated his power. Layla wondered if there was any way to take him out from afar, and immediately wished she'd found more ammo for the gun she'd discarded.

"I decided to wait around in Thunder Bay," Nergal shouted. "I wanted to bask in the glory of my victory. And then I saw you people, so I thought I'd come say hello."

A man rushed at Nergal from behind the remains of a car, a sword in one hand. Nergal looked over at him, stepped aside, and punched him in the stomach, sending the man to the ground. Then Nergal reached down and picked him up by the throat. "Come out quickly and I won't kill him," he shouted.

"Bullshit," Remy replied.

"Humans think they can kill me. I've killed a lot of them today." Nergal kept hold of the man, who was now shivering and screaming in pain. A second later, Nergal dropped his mummified corpse and smiled. "Dozens of dead, maybe more. I've taken this one's life force. I'm now stronger, faster, and more dangerous than you can ever imagine. My advice is to surrender."

"My advice is to shove it up your arse," Kase shouted back.

"Good comeback," Remy said.

"I've been practicing," Kase told him.

"Nergal will kill the people in this building," Layla said as she walked away from it, crouching down behind a collapsed wall.

"We're not going to let that happen," Kase said, standing beside her.

"The five of you against me?" Nergal asked, and started to laugh. "My word, you are going to die quickly."

"Everyone you've sent against me and my friends hasn't fared well," Layla said. "You're older, more powerful, and certainly a much bigger sack of dicks than anyone I know, but I think you'll find us more than ready to do what needs to be done."

Nergal laughed. "You are children. I am a god."

"You were never a god," Remy shouted. "You just played one until everyone woke up and realized you were just a douchebag with power. Like all douchebags with power, you think a lot of yourself."

Nergal's eyes narrowed in anger. "I wanted you alive," he told Layla. "I wanted to use you to make your father work for me. But I see now that you're just going to cause me problems. So, dead is fine, too. I'm going to kill you all, and then I'm going to kill your families, your friends, and the people you're helping. I'm going to burn down your entire resistance and piss on the ashes."

Chloe stood up and motioned with one hand for Nergal to get on with it. "Come try."

19

Nergal shrugged off his long coat and laid it on a nearby bench, before removing the cufflinks from his white shirt and slowly rolling up the sleeves.

Layla knew that none of the group would attack him, not while he was clearly trying to get them to do so. Nergal was many things, but she doubted an idiot was among them.

He turned back as Remy appeared out of nowhere, slashing at Nergal's face with his sword. Nergal grabbed Remy out of the air and dumped him on his back, on the ground. He went to stomp down on the dazed fox-man as Chloe charged Nergal, punching him in the face.

Nergal staggered back, but grabbed Chloe's arm, swinging her face-first into the brick wall beside him, then launched her across the road and through the window of a nearby house.

Kase opened her mouth, pouring more and more ice over Nergal. But he charged through it, punched her in the face and stomped down on her knee. Layla heard the crack as Kase cried out. Nergal lifted Kase in the air by her throat, but Layla punched him in the stomach with a metal wrapped fist, sending him sprawling.

Layla dragged Kase away, and the team regrouped as Nergal watched from the other side of the road. "We can't win this," Layla said.

"No shit," Kase replied, her body already healing from Nergal's attack.

Layla looked over at Nergal. There was no point in holding back. She needed to fight with everything she had, with no second-guessing. Either Nergal died, or they did, because there was no way he was going to allow himself to be taken captive.

Nergal cracked his knuckles, and Chloe sprinted toward him, punching him in the face with her ability to absorb kinetic energy. Nergal flew into the wall behind him, knocking it to the ground, but a second later he tore through its remains, hitting Chloe hard enough to send her reeling. Even her considerable power had its limits.

Layla used her power to reach for the dozens of tiny metal pieces around the area and flung them all at Nergal. Screws, nails, and shards of metal slammed into him, causing him to cry out in pain as blood began to flow from the many wounds. Then he laughed and tore off his blood-drenched shirt, showing the metal pieces being pushed out of his body, and his wounds closing almost immediately. He shut his eyes and sighed, his skin glowing before the screams started inside the apartment building.

"You can keep hurting me, and I can keep siphoning the life-force from those around me to heal," Nergal told everyone. "The added benefit of terrifying the rest of them is a beautiful bonus."

Kase's leg had healed and she ran toward Nergal with Layla right behind her, pulling small pieces of metal from around her and wrapping them around her arm. Kase swiped at Nergal's chest with her razor-sharp claws, but Nergal moved too quickly, putting distance between him and her.

Kase piled on the pressure, forcing Nergal further and further away from the residential building, until Nergal grabbed her arm, headbutted her, and threw her into Remy, who had run up to stab Nergal in the back. Both clattered to the ground as Layla struck, changing the metal in her arm into a spear and puncturing it up into Nergal's chest, piercing his heart. Chloe hit him with a blast of kinetic energy, throwing him back into the wall of another nearby house, pinning him in place for a second before Nergal's considerable power won out, and he threw a large piece of wall at the group, forcing them to scatter.

Everyone was ready to continue fighting when the truck, driven by Harry, appeared at the end of the road, smashing through debris and pulling up outside the apartment building.

Most of the group ran into the building while Remy remained outside with the truck. He was covered in small cuts and had a nasty wound on his head, but he was alive and looked exceptionally angry.

The residents ran out of the apartment building toward the truck, each of them terrified. Nergal moved his hands and several of the adults dropped to the ground, mummified.

"Keep going," Layla shouted as cries and screams filled the air. Layla sprinted back toward Nergal, who smiled. She pushed out with her power, grabbing hold of a nearby car door and flinging it at him with everything she had. Nergal caught it in one hand, doing little more than taking a few steps back to absorb the power. He threw it back at Layla, who stopped it in midair, then let it drop to the ground. She stepped over it, dragging the metal from the car door and wrapping it around her arms.

Kase let loose a jet of ice, which Nergal sidestepped, putting himself closer to Layla. He moved faster than Layla had expected, and she went down quickly from a punch to the stomach. Only a second jet of ice slamming him down the street kept him from following it with a knee to her face.

Layla wasn't sure what else they could do. Nergal had an answer for everything they threw at him. There was no attack he wasn't capable of ignoring, countering, or avoiding altogether.

"We can't beat him," Kase said as Harry's truck took off with the residents inside.

Remy and Chloe charged Nergal, trying to catch him off guard. Layla took the opportunity to gather a bunch of metal behind him, then yanked it toward her with incredible force. Nergal kicked Remy into the path of the metal, forcing Layla to throw it all aside to avoid her friend.

Nergal kicked Chloe in the ribs as he moved past her, and she retaliated by blasting him in the chest. Layla sprinted forward and, with a fist wrapped in metal, punched Nergal in the face with everything she had, snapping his head to one side. He grabbed her wrist and headbutted her on the nose before kicking her in the chest so hard she thought he'd broken her sternum.

Layla landed on the ground next to an injured Chloe as Remy stood in front of them, his fur matted with his own blood and his sword pointed at Nergal. "Come try," Remy said.

Nergal's laughter was all Layla could hear. She forced herself back to a kneeling position as her body began to heal itself. All four of them were hurt, all four had thrown everything they had, and Nergal had barely suffered a single injury.

He walked slowly toward the three of them, but when he was two feet away, a slab of rock the size of an SUV smashed into Nergal's side, throwing him across the street. He landed on a patch of soil that quickly exploded as roots buried deep beneath the topsoil shot up and wrapped around him, keeping him in place.

"Who dares?" Nergal demanded to know, screaming in rage as he used his considerable strength to rip free from the roots, only to find fresh ones wrapping around him.

"You four did well," Persephone said as she walked toward Nergal. "But now it's my turn."

Persephone tore huge pieces of earth from the ground and threw them at Nergal, who managed to dodge most with ease even as he struggled with the roots. But with each piece thrown, Persephone got closer and closer to him until she dropped to the ground and the concrete beneath Nergal's feet split open, swallowing him up in an instant. Persephone sank down into the dirt a few seconds later.

Layla and her friends didn't bother trying to help. The best thing they could do was to heal the myriad of injuries they'd suffered. Otherwise they were just going to get in Persephone's way. Layla's chest still felt on fire, and she wondered just how long it would be before she was able to take a breath without it hurting.

"How are you doing, Remy?" Chloe asked.

"I ache," he told her. "Until a while ago, I could only heal about as fast as a human, so even with my newfound abilities, this is going to take a while. I could kill myself and be back in no time, but that seems excessive. Or, I could turn into my human form and heal instantly. But then I'm stuck as a human for several hours."

Remy had managed to learn how to turn back into his human form just over a year ago. Once he was human, his power to heal was incredible, but that was pretty much all he could do. As a fox, Remy was stronger, faster, and much more dangerous.

"How long have they been gone for now?" Kase asked.

"Two and a half minutes," Chloe said as the ground shook.

"That didn't feel good," Remy said. "We should leave the street."

A hand punched through the dirt close to where they sat, and a second later the dirt exploded all around them, revealing Nergal. Persephone crouched beside him, her face a picture of terror.

"She forgot about that," Nergal said, looking up just in time to see Chloe's fist coming for his jaw. He fell to the side, rolling across the dirt as Chloe stalked after him. She took one step and crashed to her knees, screaming out in fear. Nergal kicked her to the ground, but was tackled by Remy before he could do anything else. Remy drove his sword into Nergal's chest, but Nergal flung Remy off, pulled the sword out, and threw it at Layla as she got to her feet.

Kase ran forward and collapsed mid-step.

"Just you left now," Nergal said.

Layla took a deep breath. She couldn't win this. If Persephone couldn't beat him, she had no hope. She sought out Terhal in her mind. If she was going to die, she was going to go down swinging.

"You need some help?" Terhal asked with a slight chuckle.

Layla was about to tell her to take control when the earth shifted and Nergal sank into it up to his knees. "Maybe next time," Terhal said before she vanished from Layla's mind.

Persephone punched Nergal in the face, ripping his lips open and causing him to spit blood over the dirt. She went to hit him again, but immediately crashed to her knees, scrambling away in fear.

"There is nothing quite as pleasant as a woman knowing her place," Nergal said as the dirt around him fell away. He looked over at Layla and waved his hand toward her. An overwhelming sense of terror smashed into her, almost knocking her over. She wanted to run, to hide, and to scream out in fear. She forced her mind to think of the spirits who resided inside, but each of them gave off wave after wave of fear, none answering her call. Even Terhal, who normally reveled in fear, was uncontactable.

"The spirits not responding?" Nergal asked Layla with a laugh. "They don't like the fear. It moves through you to them. I discovered that a few years ago when testing on the subjects we brought in to make into umbra. I find it quite interesting."

Nergal clenched his hand into a fist and turned it slightly, causing the abstract terror she felt to take on a more solid definition. She was back at the day her mom died. The day Nergal murdered her. Layla's mom and her husband were forced off the road and killed in the accident. She relived the moment she was told, the moment her world crumbled around her, and she almost couldn't breathe. And as quickly as the fear started, it stopped.

Bathed in sweat, Layla tried to figure out what was going on, and saw that Nergal was no longer standing close by. She blinked and heard voices. Anger and hate mixed with the sounds of someone being hit over and over again. Layla shook her head and forced herself to her feet, to see what had happened to Nergal.

Irkalla had happened.

"Your fear doesn't work on me," Irkalla said as she blocked his punch and broke his arm, throwing him over her shoulder and through a nearby wall.

"Ah, wife of mine," Nergal said, getting to his feet, his face a mass of blood. He threw a rock at her and charged, but Irkalla caught the rock in mid-air, crushing it with her hand as she drove a fist into Nergal's face, spinning him around and dumping him on the dirt.

"This has been a long time coming, Nergal," Irkalla told him.

"I knew you couldn't stay away," Nergal said as Irkalla took one step forward. He hit her hard enough to send her flying back toward Layla, who caught her friend at the same time as the sound of a gunshot reached her ears. Layla kept hold of Irkalla as she dove behind a mass of rubble, putting them both next to Chloe and Remy, who looked as though they'd had better days. More shots rang out.

"How long before the fear goes?" Chloe asked through gritted teeth.

Persephone was on her feet, creating a thick wall of stone that separated them all from their surroundings. "The shot came from the larger building at the end of the road," she said. "I hate this fear shit. It makes me see things I don't want to see."

Irkalla coughed up blood, and everyone moved toward her, thankful that their heads were clearing of Nergal's muck.

"Silver bullet," Irkalla said through pain-clenched teeth. "Needs taking out. It hit a lung, went through some ribs, I imagine."

Everyone looked at Layla.

"I've never removed a bullet from someone before," she said.

"No time like the present," Persephone told her. "We'll go hunting for the shooter, you help Irkalla."

Layla risked peering around the edge of the rubble and watched Nergal run toward a building at the end of the street. There was another shot, and another, and Nergal crumpled to the ground.

"Nergal's been shot," Layla told Persephone.

"I'll check," Kase said, running off toward where Layla had seen Nergal collapse.

"I'll go with her," Remy said. "Make sure there are no more bullets heading our way."

Layla looked down at Irkalla. "Right, I guess we need to get that bullet out. Will you be able to heal once this is done?"

"I have a lot of souls stored up," Irkalla said. "They'll heal me fine once the bullet is gone."

Layla got Persephone and Chloe to help move Irkalla onto her side so that she could cut away the leather straps of her armor. The rune-inscribed armor was designed to stop normal bullets and some magical attacks, but the armor had a weakness. A silver bullet hitting the runes at the right place would shatter the protection and allow the bullet through. It was deemed an acceptable risk as the odds of such a shot were astronomical, but unfortunately the bullet that had hit Irkalla had torn through the outer part of the rune. Thankfully that meant it had only lost some of its power and didn't just plow into her, but it still had enough force to do considerable damage.

Once the armor was off, Layla cut through Irkalla's t-shirt and took a look at where the bullet went in. It had struck her friend in the rib-cage about halfway down, just under her bra, causing a hole no bigger than Layla's thumb. The bottom of the bra wasn't going to do anything but get in the way, so Layla cut through it, causing Irkalla to groan in pain. Blood pumped from the hole and Irkalla couldn't stop a cry from leaving her lips.

Persephone moved the earth around Irkalla, propping up the injured woman's back and supporting her.

"This is going to hurt like a son-of-a-bitch," Layla said.

Irkalla reached out with one bloody hand and retrieved a piece of rubber hose that probably belonged in someone's garden. She put it between her teeth and bit down. Layla placed her hands just above the bullet hole and reached out with her power. Silver felt different to her than other metals. Getting it into her system would kill her, just as it would kill a sorcerer, were, or necromancer, and just reaching out for it felt hot. Not burning hot, but the kind of residual heat found in a fireplace after it's been out for a while. There was no mistaking it.

She wrapped her power around the bullet, and Irkalla screamed in pain and shock.

"I can't possibly find the same path that the bullet took," Layla told her. "And pulling it back toward me is a bad idea, so I'm going to push it out the other side. It's close to your ribs on the other side of your body."

Layla gathered more power around the bullet, wrapping it around the projectile as smoothly as she could manage so that it caused as little discomfort as possible given the circumstances.

When she was certain that she'd used enough power, she took a deep breath and snapped it forward with everything she had, pouring more and more power into the wound to push out the bullet with as much force as she could manage.

Layla sensed that the bullet had fragmented slightly after hitting Irkalla, forcing her to reach out and control all of the pieces. Layla felt the bullet leave Irkalla's body a second later, but it went through another rib. Irkalla's hand crushed the rock she had been holding.

Layla felt the bullet fragments strike the dirt. Persephone removed the earth keeping Irkalla propped up and lowered her to the ground. Irkalla's skin was clammy, and she'd lost a lot of blood, but Layla hoped she'd be okay.

She picked up the largest piece of flattened projectile, turned it over in her hand, and saw a red marking on it.

"Rune," Persephone said. "That's what's on there, yes?"

Layla passed it to her. "Shooter gone?"

"Long gone. Chloe and Remy are scouting still, but there's no trace of them. They got into a car further up the road." Persephone looked down at her friend. "The armor saved her life. Without it, this would have done a lot worse." She picked up the leather and turned it over, removing a portion of the bullet and dropping it onto Layla's hand. "The bullet partially fragmented in the armor, so only a part of it went into Irkalla."

"It destroyed a few of her ribs and did a lot of internal damage, too," Layla said. "Can she heal that?"

Persephone nodded. "She's too stubborn to let a bullet kill her."

"It's silver and fragments upon impact. This wasn't designed to be a kill shot. She was meant to die from the dozens of tiny fragments of silver in her body. It was supposed to be a slow, painful death. What does the rune do?"

"Bypasses the armor protection runes. I've seen their kind before."

"So even if the bullet hadn't hit the rune itself, it still would have gone through?" Layla asked.

Persephone nodded.

Irkalla let out a gasp, followed quickly by a groan of pain. "I want to tear the throat out of whoever shot me," she said softly.

"Told you she was too stubborn," Persephone said. "Can you stand?"

Irkalla nodded. "I've used up every spirit I have to heal myself, so I'd rather not fight again for a while."

"We'll get you out of here," Persephone told her. "There are a few cars at the end of the street, in a parking lot behind the houses. They all seem to be untouched. If we can get one working, we can move Irkalla out of here, and hopefully go help everyone in Red Rock."

"How bad is it there?"

Kase reappeared with Remy. "Nergal is dead," she said.

"What?" Persephone asked. A second later, she was running up the road with everyone but Irkalla, who was being helped by Layla. Irkalla practically had to shove Layla to go and see what had happened.

Nergal had two bullet holes in his head and one in his heart. Layla reached out and found the fragments of the bullets that had been used. The first two were the same as the ones that had hit Irkalla, but the last was of a different caliber. She handed it over to Persephone.

"Gorgon venom," Remy said. "I can smell it. It's from a handgun. I tracked the scent of the killer to a car further up the road, but they sped off, so they could be anywhere now."

Kase rolled Nergal onto his stomach, revealing that most of the back of his head was missing.

"That was close range," Remy said.

Layla stared at the body for several seconds without saying a word. Nergal had been responsible for her mother's murder and for the murders of countless innocent people, including friends of hers. Because of him, Layla was now an umbra fighting for her life against Avalon. Because of Nergal, everything Layla had ever known had fallen apart. She thought she'd be happy to see him dead, but instead she just felt hollow. It didn't feel like much of a victory.

"Someone did us a favor," Chloe said. "Why shoot Irkalla, too?"

"They weren't doing us any favors," Layla said. "They want us all dead."

"Abaddon," Persephone said. "She's always hated Nergal. I'd put large amounts of money on her involvement."

Irkalla had made it to the group by then and glared at anyone who offered her assistance. "Well, the bastard is finally dead."

Remy handed her the Gorgon-venom-coated bullet.

"Good," Irkalla said. "He was an evil bastard."

"I'll go find us a ride," Chloe said. "Hopefully there's something that still works." She ran off with Remy into the ruins of the town.

"We need to get to Red Rock," Irkalla said. "Nergal was arrogant; he would have wanted to lord it over his enemies. Abaddon will just kill them all."

"You think that was her game?" Kase asked. "Take Nergal's forces for her own?"

Persephone nodded. "From what I understand about her, yes. She'll have been working at this for some time. I don't know just how much of Nergal's force came up here to join the war. Avalon would certainly have sent people to help remove our influence from this place. It could make things more complicated now that he isn't there to second-guess Abaddon's plans. For the moment, though, I suggest we stick to the plan we have."

A gray Honda SUV rolled into view with Chloe behind the wheel.

"Are you okay?" Rosa asked from beside Layla.

She nodded. "It wasn't a fun experience back there."

"I do not like being made to feel afraid. Even spirits have their weaknesses. It was like I was alive again, but everything was wrong. It was . . . unpleasant."

Servius and Gyda appeared beside Rosa. "Let's not do that again," Gyda said. "It turns out there are more evil things than Terhal."

"Not evil," Terhal said from somewhere in her head.

Gyda opened her mouth and closed it as the Honda pulled level with Layla. The spirits vanished, and Remy opened the rear door of the SUV.

"You stole a car," Layla said, sounding somewhat impressed. Neither Remy nor Chloe had ever shown any ability to hotwire.

"I have skills," Remy said from the front passenger seat. "Many, many skills."

Layla smiled. "The keys were in the car, weren't they?"

Remy nodded. "Yes, yes they were."

"You good?" Chloe asked.

"It's been a long few days," Layla told her. "I need some vodka."

"A bottle of vodka," Remy said, "and a second one to chase down the first."

It took them a while to get Irkalla in the back seat of the SUV, her head resting on Persephone's lap and her feet across Layla's on the other side.

"I do not like feeling weak," Irkalla said as Chloe drove the Honda through what had once been a main street of Thunder Bay. She drove slowly to avoid craters in the road, passing more ruined buildings—some of which had collapsed onto what used to be a sidewalk. It looked like a bomb had been dropped on the town.

"No shit," Remy said.

"It's a good thing I like you," Irkalla told him.

"You like me? I figured we were in some kind of feud."

Irkalla laughed. "Ouch. You did that on purpose."

"But you like me," Remy said with a wink. "Just so you know, I think it was Kristin who took the shot. Smelled like her. Why would she kill Nergal? I thought she worked for him?"

"She got a better offer?" Chloe suggested.

"Thunder Bay was destroyed in a matter of hours," Layla said as she looked out of the window. "What hope is there for anywhere else if Avalon's army can do this to a place that was under our protection?"

"We will fight back," Persephone assured her.

20

Kristin had intended to go to Nipigon where Abaddon was staying and stop at Red Rock on the way to find answers from one of Nergal's people about why that realm gate was so damn important.

The drive through Thunder Bay had been fine. She'd been stopped several times by Nergal's people and had to have the same conversation about who she was and why she was there. Most of them had heard of her and turned pale when she identified herself.

She saw more than a few of the residents killed as she drove; some were executed in the street, their bodies dumped in the back of huge trucks, while others were marched away to be executed in the forest surrounding the city.

As magical battles broke out around Thunder Bay, Kristin had taken more than one detour to avoid the worst of the fighting, but she'd left the town soon enough and had gotten on the main road up to Red Rock. She was exactly one mile out of Thunder Bay when she saw the large truck barreling up behind her Audi. At first, she assumed that they were working for Nergal, shipping troops to Red Rock. She started to pull over when the truck smashed into the back of the Audi, spinning the car off the road and slamming the passenger side into a large tree.

Kristin blinked. Her head had struck the driver's side window hard enough to cause the glass to spiderweb. She shoved open the door and almost fell out onto the cold, hard earth as the truck stopped and two men got out. Both held AR15s in gloved hands, and when they opened fire on the car, tearing it to shreds in moments, Kristin threw herself behind the nearest large tree.

In her dazed state, she created a clone, which made her momentarily weaker as her body adjusted to the loss of power. Kristin sent the clone around to the far side of the car to run into the forest. The two men shouted after her, and the gunfire erupted once again; a few seconds later Kristin felt the loss of her clone. She moved to the side of the tree and came face to face with one of the assailants.

"Nergal says you're a disappointment," the man said. "You screwed up when you went after your sister. The second you did that, your life was forfeit."

A car screeched to a halt nearby and the man turned to aim his gun at it, but the masked woman from the diner opened the car door and shot him through the head before he could fire a single bullet. She climbed out of the car, crossed the road, and put two more in the man's skull before walking into the forest, where Kristin heard more gunshots.

The woman returned a short time later, carrying the decapitated head of one of the attackers by the hair. She tossed the head toward Kristin. "You're welcome," she said. "Get in the car."

Kristin's body had begun to heal the damage done to it by the impact with the tree and her head felt less fuzzy. She crossed the road and got into the black BMW.

"You know they work for Nergal, yes?" the woman asked as she slid into the driver's seat, put the car into drive, and set off at high speed.

"Yes," Kristin said, not daring to say more in case her temper overrode her mouth.

"Did you know the two men?"

Kristin shook her head. "No idea who they were."

"They were umbra," the woman continued.

"Who are you?" Kristin asked, feeling less than happy about her current predicament.

The woman said, "Either you'll find out or you won't, but my identity is not important. We need to get you to Abaddon—she'll want to talk to you."

The rest of the drive was done in silence, and it took less than an hour's travel along the Trans-Canada highway to Nipigon.

The woman stopped the car outside of a school. "The town is empty," she said. "We evacuated it. See those soldiers there?" The woman pointed.

Kristin followed her finger to look across the school field at the dozens of armed men and women standing outside several large tents.

"They're using the school and its grounds as a command center," the woman continued. "Avalon sent them to help Nergal. Nergal has refused their assistance until this moment. Abaddon will explain more. She'll want you to do something, too."

Kristin said nothing and exited the car. She closed the door behind her and ran up the steps to the school. A woman in combat fatigues told her to follow the yellow line on the corridor floor to the school gym, where she'd find Abaddon. Kristin did as she was told and a few minutes later arrived at the gym, which was empty except for Abaddon, who was throwing basketballs into a hoop.

"This is a weird sport," she said without looking back. She threw three balls, one after the other, taking a step back after each throw. Each ball went through the hoop without touching the sides. Abaddon turned to Kristin. "It's too easy."

"Humans aren't capable of throwing a ball halfway across a basketball court with the ease you do it," Kristin said. Basketball had been her father's favorite sport, and he'd once taken Kristin and her sisters to a game. It was one of the few memories she had of a time when her family wasn't trying to screw her over.

Abaddon held the final basketball in her hand and looked back at the basket. "Dull," she said. She squeezed the ball and popped it before turning back to Kristin. "Nergal tried to have you killed."

Kristin nodded. "He sent umbra after me."

"Nergal ordered your death not because you went after your sister, but because you failed, and could have brought on unnecessary interest in you. No matter his reasons, I thought that maybe you'd like some payback for that."

"You could have warned me," Kristin said, angry that Abaddon would keep that information to herself. Her desire to hit the woman was great, but it would also be the last thing Kristin ever did. She dug her nails into the palms of her hands until the rage passed.

"Could have, but didn't," Abaddon said. "I'm here to give you a second chance. I'm not here to wipe your nose and keep you safe."

"What do you want me to do?"

"You're going to do three things," Abaddon said. "If you complete those three things, I will consider you one of my most useful allies. Fail, and you'll be dead, so it won't matter."

"What three things?"

"You're going to kill Nergal. And when you're done, you're going to come with me to Texas and we're going to take Nergal's compound for Avalon. I want the spirit scrolls he keeps there. I want them in my possession, and any umbra he created that are loyal to him, I want dead."

"Why would you want to waste the power they possess?"

Abaddon smiled. "I note that you're not opposed to killing him."

"He tried to kill me," Kristin said. "I think it's only fair that I get a turn." Killing Nergal and moving on to work with Abaddon was just the next step to her destination. And if Abaddon ever betrayed her, then Kristin planned to do exactly the same to her. Hopefully, Abaddon would allow her the time for personal projects. And if not, then she'd just be much more careful about what she did and where she did it.

Abaddon laughed. "I like you. And to answer your question, they made their bed. I will kill them, and anyone else who is unable to control the spirits. They should be given to those who deserve them, who will use the power to do great things. Nergal gave that power to transients and anyone who needed a warm bed and meal. You destroyed the thousands that were in the cave, yes?"

Kristin nodded. "Nergal was less than happy about their discovery."

"Well, Nergal will be unhappy about me taking his compound and everyone in it."

"What about Caleb Cassidy?"

"We'll find him, don't you worry. I have something he will want very much."

"You have Layla?"

Abaddon shook her head. "Something much more important to him. I'll explain all once you return after killing Nergal. Come walk with me."

Kristin followed Abaddon out of the gym and onto the school field behind the main building. "The third task is the most dangerous, and the most important. I will tell you about it if you kill Nergal. Obviously, if you betray me, your life will be forfeit."

"Obviously," Kristin said, angry that Abaddon was manipulating her, but glad to get the chance to gain justice for what Nergal had tried to do. "Where is Nergal?"

"Thunder Bay. My assistant who saved your life will give you all you need to get the job done. Kill him and come back to me. There is no room for error on this."

Kristin's flesh tingled at the thought of killing Nergal, the thought of getting revenge on him for trying to murder her. She left Abaddon alone and walked to the front of the school where the masked woman was still beside the BMW.

"There's a SIG Sauer SIG516 rifle on the passenger seat," the masked woman said. "It's fitted with a magazine of specially designed, explosive, silver-tipped ammo. There are runes on the bullets that will allow them to bypass the armor runes. If they hit a non-armored part of the body, they will enter and then explode."

"What's the handgun for?" Kristin asked as she looked through the driver's side window.

"In case you screw up," the woman said. "Glock 30. It's fitted with the same modified ammo as the rifle, except this is .45 ACP. Either way, you'll kill him."

"And he's in Thunder Bay? Any idea where in Thunder Bay?"

The woman removed a small device from her pocket and passed it over to Kristin. "Abaddon put a tracker in Nergal's pocket the last time they spoke. Do you need anything else, or will this be sufficient?"

Kristin got into the car and drove away without saying anything. She didn't like the masked woman; there was something about her that made Kristin's skin crawl, and that wasn't a feeling she was used to.

She emptied her mind with regards to the masked woman and Abaddon and focused on the task ahead: killing Nergal. Nergal had given her the spirit scroll that had created her, he had given her freedom and power, and had then tried to snatch it all away because of a personal issue that had nothing to do with him.

She passed hundreds of troops on her journey and was slightly concerned that one of them might realize who she was and kill her for Nergal, but no one stopped.

By the time she'd reached Thunder Bay, Kristin had convinced herself that Nergal's death was necessary for her to move forward with her life. She stopped the car and used the tracker that the masked woman had given her to find Nergal. His signal was strong, and she slowly drove the car down ruined streets. Only a few hours had passed since she'd watched the destruction of the city. To see it now, after most of the troops had left, filled her with an odd feeling.

She ignored whatever emotions stirred inside of her as she slowly turned a corner and stopped the car. The sounds of battle could be easily heard. Kristin kept the vehicle out of sight and switched off the engine before grabbing the rifle and making her way into an abandoned house nearby. She set up a vantage point in what had once been someone's front room and watched Nergal as he fought a group of people several hundred feet down the road.

She looked down the scope at the battle before her, and the second she spotted Layla, a cold rage filled her. Layla had been responsible for the death of one of her clones and the suicide of another. Kristin's finger caressed the trigger. She paused and spotted Chloe, who had also killed a clone. She wondered if she had time to deal with both them and Nergal.

Nergal was fighting Irkalla, a woman that he had mentioned hundreds of times during Kristin's employment with him. He mostly hated her because she had left him, and the thousands of years since their divorce had done nothing to reduce his anger. Sometimes Kristin wondered if everything Nergal did was to get revenge on Irkalla and those who had stood beside her.

Kristin aimed the rifle at Layla and pulled the trigger, but Irkalla was kicked into the path of the bullet and it struck her armor.

"Damn it," Kristin snapped, firing off another bullet at Layla, who dragged an injured Irkalla behind a large pile of rubble. "Damn it, damn it."

She fired at Chloe, who was already moving behind the debris, then swung the rifle back toward Nergal, who was running her way.

She kept her rifle on him until he was only thirty feet away. He called out something, but Kristin wasn't listening. She fired twice and caught him in the head and throat, sending him to the ground. Vaulting over the remains of the front room window, she drew her Glock. She ran toward Nergal and stood over his dying body before putting another round in his skull. She spat on him, ran back to her car, got inside, and sped off.

Kristin's elation was intense. She'd never felt anything like it. *To kill a god.* Okay, not a real god, but someone who had once been considered a god. She would have to find more of this ammo; *god killer ammo*, it had a nice ring to it.

She drove back to Nipigon at high speed, completely ignoring anyone else on the road, and pulled up outside the school. She climbed out as Abaddon exited the reception and descended the dozen steps toward her.

"It's done," Kristin said.

Abaddon smiled. "Excellent. I want you to come with me to Texas once we have Red Rock."

Kristin nodded. She hadn't felt happier than this in a long time. "So, what do you need me to do as the third thing?"

Abaddon led Kristin across the street and into a small cafe with wooden tables and chairs. The masked woman sat in a booth, a Glock resting on the table. She'd removed her mask, and Kristin thought she looked familiar.

"I think it's time you learned a few things," Abaddon said, motioning for Kristin to sit at the table next to the masked woman.

Apart from the three of them, the cafe was empty. A small counter lay at the far end of the shop and dozens of cakes sat inside a glass display dotted with small colored stars showing their prices.

"You can take one if you like," Abaddon said. "No one will mind."

"I'm not a thief," Kristin said.

Abaddon laughed. "Murder is okay, but stealing isn't?"

"Yes," Kristin said as if anything else was unthinkable.

"So you will come with me to Texas, yes?"

Kristin nodded. "You already mentioned Texas."

"I want you to send one of your clones to Red Rock. Unfortunately, they are giving us quite the fight, despite the damage we're doing to the town. We will be unable to take the city before they destroy the realm gate, which I've been reliably informed is their plan. They have a Norse dwarf with them, and since the little bastards were the ones to create the gates in the first place, it's perfectly plausible to assume they can destroy them. Also, there's no way I can push my entire army through that gate when I don't know who or what is on the other side. So we're not going to try to take the gate—we're going to make it look like we are, but we're actually going to get your clone into the city. Once there, the clone is going to join the refugees who are being sent through it."

"I'll lose contact with my clone once it's through the gate," Kristin said.

"Then you'd better make sure it understands what needs to be done once it's out of command range."

"And what needs to be done?"

Abaddon leaned back in her chair. "My brother is in that realm. Mammon. You will find out where he is being held and report the location back to me. That is all."

"Your brother?"

"Not literally my brother," Abaddon said with a wave of her hand. "A brother-in-arms is more appropriate. We were born at the same time, although to different parents. He was imprisoned in another realm thousands of years ago, and all the evidence I've gathered points to Norumbega as being the place where Mammon is kept. I believe that Hades will destroy the gate before I can get inside, so I need someone to do it for me, and your clone is the perfect choice."

"How will they get out again if there's no gate?" Kristin asked.

"There is a second gate. Evidence suggests the people who live there know of its location, but no one in the Earth realm seems to. I've checked and asked a lot of people who were unfortunately unhelpful. Your clone will find Mammon, get out of Norumbega, and relay the information it discovers. If Mammon is not there, then this is a moot point."

"Finding him could take a long time," Kristin said, being careful with her words. She got the feeling that failure in this job was not something Abaddon would accept or tolerate.

"It will take as long as it takes," Abaddon said. "He's been waiting for thousands of years—a little more time is unimportant. But I cannot have the realm lost to me. Do you understand?"

Kristin nodded. With five dead, and one made to go through the realm, it would mean that she only had access to one more clone to create, but it would have to do. Sometimes she wished she could just create the clones and kill them herself, but she'd tried that in the past and found it impossible to accomplish. The clones could not harm her or each other, and she could not harm them. It was, frankly, infuriating.

"Everything is working out how I foresaw it," Abaddon continued. "Nergal left a lot of his people back in his Texas compound, and used Avalon's forces and my own blood elves to carry out this war. Thankfully, with his death, that now means I am in full control of this army. With Hades' territory under Avalon's control, we will be one step closer to stopping Hades and his people from being a thorn in our side."

"I have a question in return," Kristin asked.

Abaddon raised an eyebrow in surprise. "You think you are allowed to question me?"

Kristin shrugged. "Allowed is not exactly a term I'm concerned about. You either answer me or you don't."

Abaddon smiled and looked over at the woman in the corner. "It's about her, isn't it?"

Kristin shook her head. "I want to know what it is you have on Caleb that you think will make him come to you."

"Caleb believes that Nergal killed his wife, and until he discovers that Nergal is dead, he will continue to do so. My people tell me that his escape is being arranged. He will head toward Red Rock as they made suggestions to him that Nergal is there. He will go there to get revenge."

The masked woman walked over to Abaddon and Kristin. "He will find me," she said.

Kristin paused for a second. "You're his wife? You're supposed to be dead."

The woman nodded and offered Kristin her hand. "Elizabeth Cassidy, wife of Caleb, mother to Layla."

Kristin kept eye contact with Elizabeth. "I tried to murder your daughter several times. She's a pain in my ass that just won't go away. Is that a problem?"

"Layla is tough. Tougher than you give her credit for. I think you'll find we Cassidys are made of stern stuff."

Kristin noticed that Elizabeth hadn't said anything about being unhappy with her attempts on her daughter's life and shook her hand. "I guess I'm all yours then," Kristin told Abaddon.

Abaddon smiled at Kristin. "You always were, my dear."

21

As they got closer to Red Rock, it became apparent that the offensive by Nergal's people was happening in earnest. Smoke billowed from the fires that had been set around the outskirts of the town, turning a normally idyllic spot into an inferno.

Persephone told Chloe to turn off and up a road toward the town of Nipigon. The car stopped, and everyone piled out.

"What happens now?" Remy asked. "The guardians of the realm gate are essentially immortal when they're close to it, but how are they going to hold a whole town?"

"They're going through the realm gate, too," Persephone said. "Zamek will be able to keep the gate open and go through by himself. He's practiced doing it before."

"No one will be able to use that gate until they make new guardians," Irkalla said, still sounding as though she were not in the best of shape. "That could be a long time."

"The realm gate is underground, which is why they're going to blow the building above it," Persephone said.

"What about everyone who left Thunder Bay on the first truck?" Layla asked, worried about those who had gone ahead.

"They went to Pine Portage," Persephone said, dialing a number on her phone. "I want an update on what happened to the trucks we sent to you." Her expression darkened as she ended the call. "Harry arrived with the refugees only a few minutes ago. The first truck with Diana, Fenix, and the others arrived earlier. Your father was not among their number. He escaped just outside of Nipigon. Jared and Diana got out at Nipigon to track him down. Zamek has gone south to the tunnels to try to get into Red Rock."

"The tunnels?" Layla asked.

"There's a stretch of land to the south of here." Persephone brought up a map on her phone. "A few streets with some apartment buildings that have been evacuated; it's now controlled by Avalon. There's a tunnel that runs from the basement of a house there, right up into Red Rock. It's only on the outskirts of the town, but it'll get Zamek and anyone who goes with him past the roadblocks. You going?"

Layla nodded. "My father won't know that Nergal is dead and will want revenge for what he did to my mom. As far as Dad knows, Nergal is in Red Rock. It's a few hours' run through the forest, so he's probably close to Red Rock by now."

"What if he finds out that Nergal is dead?" Kase asked.

"He'll become a ghost, and we'll have to hunt him down. I'd rather not, if it can be avoided."

Persephone's phone rang, and she answered it. "Shit," she said with a sigh.

"Diana and Jared tracked your dad to Red Rock—some Avalon forces have grabbed him," Persephone told Layla. "The pair of them are going to meet you at the tunnel and go with you to Red Rock. Rendezvous with them at this apartment building." She showed the exact spot on the map on her phone. "Diana should be able to track Caleb down once you're all in Red Rock, but the objective is still to get the refugees through the realm gate and then destroy it."

"I'll go with you," Remy said. "You could use my nose. Also my winning personality."

Layla nodded. "Thank you. What are the rest of you planning?"

"We're going to head to Pine Portage," Persephone said. "Once Hades, Tommy, Olivia, and the others are through the gate, they'll get the refugees to New York through a second realm gate in Norumbega. The rest of us are going to use the planes waiting at Pine Portage to fly to New York, where we'll meet you and the others who are going through Norumbega.

"When you reach New York, contact Felicia Hales, the woman who gave you the equipment for your trip to the Sawbill prison. She'll arrange transport back to Greenland. Be aware: time in Norumbega works differently than it does in this realm. A few hours there will be a week here, if not longer."

"Okay," Layla said, looking over to Remy. "You ready?"

"You get in—do what you need to do—and you get out," Persephone said. "No screwing around. I don't know how long it'll be before Nergal's people realize that he's dead but once they do, Abaddon will almost certainly be in charge. If you see her, do not engage. She is more dangerous than you can possibly imagine."

Chloe walked over and hugged Layla. "Please be careful," she said. "I don't want to have to come find you." She looked at Remy. "Either of you."

"In and out," Remy said. "No one else is dying today."

Remy and Layla left the car and moved into the dense forest as the others sped off. "You got a plan?" Remy asked.

"It's a ten-minute run from here to the tunnels, but we'll have to go through a defended area." She wondered how Jared and Diana were faring in their trek across the wilderness. Hopefully they'd meet up with them soon enough. "We also need to wait for Diana and Jared before we do anything. There were three apartment buildings in that area. I can't imagine that any of them will be without soldiers."

"So, we need to wait for allies, find the apartment with the tunnel, and clear it of enemy forces?"

Layla wondered about the clearing part of the idea. She wasn't against it, but the discovery of the unresponsive soldiers they'd leave behind could be a giveaway to their plan. "I think we might need to clear all of the buildings. We can't leave any indication that one of them was our target."

"Hopefully, there won't be too many soldiers. At least they'll be easy to deal with."

"Persephone's map showed a bunch of roadblocks along the street that led past the apartments and the tunnel entrance. I don't think they'll post many guards outside these blocks since the apartment build-ings aren't near any strategic entrances to the town. Even so, let's be careful."

The pair moved through the forest, stopping only when they saw four men in combat fatigues standing beside an armored vehicle on the side of the road. Each one held an M4 carbine, and a patch depicting a red dragon was sewn on each of their shoulders. They were Avalon's forces. The three five-story apartment buildings further along the road were Layla and Remy's target.

"You think they're human?" Remy whispered.

"I don't know. Avalon uses a mixture of humans and non-humans. But the humans only seem to be used for the less important parts of their plans. These guards could be a patrol."

The pair crept closer to the soldiers until they were just out of sight and stopped behind a huge boulder at the bottom of a slight embank-ment, twenty feet away from their targets. It was winter, and the lack of foliage meant they would be seen when they got to the top of the bank. Remy and Layla remained where they were and looked around to ensure they weren't about to be spotted by anyone else.

"I don't see any others," Remy whispered, before raising a finger at Layla to stop her from replying. A few seconds later he continued.

"They don't have great hearing. A were would have been able to hear what I said." He sniffed. "They smell human."

"What do non-humans smell like?" Layla asked before she could stop herself.

"Depends," he said. "You smell human most of the time. So maybe they're umbra."

"That would be bad," Layla said. As every umbra had their own unique power, there was no telling what the four soldiers would be able to do. "We need to separate them."

Remy picked up a rock and threw it into the forest behind him. It hit a large tree and spooked something unseen that ran further into the forest.

"What was that?" one of the soldiers asked, raising his M4 in the direction of the sound.

"Probably a deer," a second soldier told him. "There's nothing here. We were told to hold this road, and that's what we're going to do."

"What if some of Hades' forces are going around the city to attack from the north?" The third soldier asked, a tinge of fear in his voice. "I knew we were left behind because we're human."

"We were left behind because, as humans, we can help settle the human population of the town and get them somewhere safe," the first soldier said. "Hades has brainwashed these people into thinking he's one of the good guys. Avalon knows better, and now so do we. We stay, we help keep the peace while Nergal and his people deal with the corruption in Red Rock, and then we all go back to Texas for some well-earned R&R before we're deployed again."

"I never realized just how much these bastards had infested our world," the fourth soldier said. "They've been hiding in the shadows, pulling our strings for so long. The fact that Arthur and his people want us to work together makes me feel less concerned about the future."

The first soldier fist bumped the fourth. "And I don't care how scary they are—these silver rounds will take them down good."

The four men laughed, and Layla felt a pit of anger open up inside of her.

Remy picked up a second rock and threw it after the first, where it hit the same tree.

"There's something out there," said the nervous soldier.

"Go look then," the second soldier told him.

He raised his M4 and set off into the forest.

"If you piss yourself because you find a squirrel, you're never going to live it down," a soldier shouted after him, causing the others to laugh.

"I got this," Remy said, darting off into the forest.

There were no noises to signal what Remy had done, but when he returned he passed Layla the M4 and drew the two daggers he'd taken earlier.

She switched the firing mode onto single shot and raised the rifle at the soldiers. Layla could take all three out before they had a chance to respond, but that would alert everyone who heard the gunshots, turning their stealthy approach into something a lot less pleasant.

She placed the M4 up against the tree and reached out with her power, wrapping it around the weapons carried by the soldiers. Their M4's fell apart as she turned her hands. The soldiers were baffled for an instant, which was all the time Remy needed to dart among them, killing all three with the twin daggers before any of them could call for help. When it was over, Remy and Layla dragged the bodies into the forest, where Layla took a dagger from one of the soldiers and slid it into a sheath next to the one she already had.

Layla ignored the M4's, which she wasn't going to need, but retrieved a Glock .22 that was loaded with silver-tipped bullets. She removed the hip holster the soldier wore and put it on. "That's much better," she told Remy, and grabbed two magazines of bullets from one of the soldier's pockets.

"It's about two hundred feet from here to the first building. Best course is to go through the trees until we get there. It won't take long before someone comes looking for these assholes, so I'd rather not be here when that happens."

"Can you smell Jared or Diana?"

Remy sniffed the air. "Nothing, sorry. Hopefully I'll pick something up when we get closer to the town." Remy had scooped up his own holster and Glock, and a belt for the two daggers. "This is going to get messy."

Layla nodded that she knew. "My father can't be allowed to stay in Avalon's hands, and we need to destroy that realm gate."

"And if that means . . ." Remy trailed off.

"Whatever it takes. My father escaped our custody. If he can't be removed from Avalon's hands, or he refuses to come with us . . . I'll do what I need to do."

Remy rested a hand on Layla's. "You sure you can do that? I don't know many who could."

"My father, or the thousands of innocent people he'll help Arthur kill. It's . . . I don't exactly have a choice." Inside, Layla wasn't at all sure she could do it. How could she kill her own father? Even a father as evil as hers? She wasn't sure that she could go through with it. And even if she put their relationship aside, she would only be killing him so that he didn't fall into enemy hands. There was a big different between killing in self-defense, killing on a battlefield, and straight-up execution.

"Layla, I hated my father," Remy told her. "He was an awful, awful man. But I'm not sure I could have killed him. My brother had to do that for me. You can't help who your parents are, and although some people have parents who should have been placed in a deep, dark hole a long time ago that doesn't make it any easier to remove them from this world."

The pair moved through the forest in silence until they reached a burger restaurant that appeared to be closed.

"There are no lights on in there," Layla said, looking through the windows facing her. "No cars in the lot. No semblance of life."

Remy sniffed the air. "We've got friends coming."

Diana and Jared crept through the forest toward them. Layla's elation at seeing them both was short lived.

"Two dozen soldiers at least," Diana said, nodding toward the apartment buildings. "There are prisoners in there. No sure how many, but I saw some people handcuffed and left on the floor of their apartment. I climbed one of the trees and took a look. I think some of them put up a fight."

"You got a plan?" Jared asked Layla.

"There's a building to the east of here," Diana said. "Seems like some kind of storehouse. There are a few soldiers there—I think that's where they took most of the prisoners."

Layla thought for a second. "Jared and Diana, go to the storehouse. See if you can free the people there. If any of these assholes get a shot off at me or Remy, I don't want them to be able to use the prisoners as target practice."

"On it," Jared and Diana said, running off into the woods.

Remy and Layla moved slowly through the forest, keeping along the treeline until they came to an alleyway between two of the five-story buildings. A fire escape sat on the side of one of them, the ladder hanging down as if recently used.

"How many soldiers do you think there are at the front of these apartments?"

Remy ran to the end of the alley and peered around the corner before running back. "Half a dozen," he said. "It sounds like the third apartment building is their main base of operations. There's an APC outside of it. My guess is more human soldiers. They smell human, anyway."

"We need a prisoner," Layla said. "Hopefully we can find out anything we need to know about their attack on Red Rock."

"Like where they would have taken your father?"

"That would be helpful, yes."

Remy and Layla found the building in question without any trouble. There was a ten-foot-tall fence and fifty feet of open space between the building and the forest. They stopped behind a large tree and watched. A small balcony led to an open set of French windows on the fifth floor. A soldier stood there smoking a cigarette while he looked out at the mass of greenery in front of him.

"My guess is the soldiers here don't expect trouble. They seem quite relaxed."

Layla had to agree, considering the amount of raucous laughter coming from the back of the building. "Any way we can get in there without them noticing?"

"I doubt it. And I don't think we're equipped to deal with what could be dozens of soldiers until we're sure the prisoners are safe." Remy took a long sniff. "At least a dozen in there. It smells like a gym locker room."

"We only need one," Layla said.

"My vote is for the smoker on the balcony."

"He's forty feet above the ground. I'll have to get him from the roof."

"You could always get captured and have them take you to wherever the others are."

"Not more than once per war."

"Fair point."

Layla looked back over to the first building they'd passed. "I have a plan."

"Is it a stupid one?"

"Probably, yes."

"My kind of plan. What do you need?"

"On my signal, give me a distraction."

"What kind of distraction?"

"One that involves a lot of noise."

"Should I go back and get the M4 that still works?"

Layla thought about it. "Actually, that's not a bad idea. The rest, I'll leave to your devious little mind."

Layla ran toward the apartment building with the fire escape and quickly scaled the wooden fence, climbing the fire escape to the roof as quickly as possible. She stopped just before she reached the final flight of metal stairs and peeked over the top of the roof.

Finding no snipers keeping an eye on things, Layla climbed onto the roof and ran over to the side. It wasn't too far to jump, but the other buildings all had slanted roofs, so getting it wrong would cause her to slide off the side of the building.

It didn't take her long to bend the metal railings circling the roof into a walkway to the next building. She made an ever-changing path until she was directly above the smoking soldier and anchored part of the railings to the roof. Then she made a harness that wrapped around her torso and waist and slowly lowered herself headfirst down the slope of the roof. Layla stopped when she reached the gutter and looked down at the soldier. He was still leaning over the railings of the balcony, and for a moment she considered just making the railing grab and drag him to the roof. But that might cause noise and alert the soldiers inside the building. She didn't want to give any of them a reason to come searching.

She waited, hoping the smoker wouldn't look up, as the sound of an M4 burst through the chatter of the soldiers below. It sounded like Remy had emptied the entire thing, and the noise was quickly followed by two loud explosions. Remy had found grenades, a fact that the rising smoke gave testament to.

Layla immediately lowered herself as the soldier leaned out to look at the spectacle. He flicked his cigarette butt over the balcony and turned to go back in just as Layla grabbed him by the neck and wrapped the walkway she'd been using around his body and mouth. Then she descended gracefully to the balcony.

Layla placed the tip of a dagger against the soldier's cheek, only an inch from his eye. "Don't try to be clever," she said. "I have questions— you answer them, and you get to live."

The walkway dragged the soldier off the floor and onto the roof as he struggled in vain to get free. By the time Layla joined him on top of the roof, the metal from the balcony had cocooned the soldier like he was a spider's prey. She returned to the flat roof of the neighboring building the same way as she'd gone across. The metal cocoon deposited the soldier on the ground with a less than pleasant thump, then crawled up and over Layla's arms, forming gauntlets.

She kept the metal wrapped around the soldier's head, but opened a hole over his face so he could talk and breathe normally.

"If you scream, you die," she told him. "You're human, yes?"

The soldier nodded, abject fear in his eyes.

"You work for Avalon?"

"Avalon," he repeatedly quickly. "Inter-species Task Force."

"Never heard of it."

"It's new, only a few months old. We're tasked with helping Avalon do what they need to do to keep the world safe from people like you."

"People like me?" Layla sighed. "You think I'm a terrorist?"

Despite his obvious fear, the soldier nodded. "Terrorist, murderer, you can pick whichever word you prefer. You are the reason humanity is afraid."

"Probably, although not for the reasons you think. Anyway, there's no reason for me to try to change your mind. My friend is down there pissing off your buddies, so I'll keep this quick. Where will your friends in Red Rock have taken prisoners?"

"There's a large playing field at the edge of town. To the east of here. Not far inside Red Rock itself. They've set up a command base there. Lots of tents and the like. Prisoners are taken to the camp."

"What about high value ones?"

"The police station next to the camp. There are runes on the walls that stop powers."

Layla hadn't been expecting to get so much, so easily. "Aren't you meant to tough it out for a bit first?"

"Why, so you can torture me? You're going to go over there and you're going to get yourselves killed. The ITF are taking orders from Abaddon, and she doesn't play nice."

Layla wrapped all of the metal around her fist and punched the soldier out, leaving him safely on the rooftop before climbing down the fire escape to where Remy was leaning on his rifle, waiting for her.

"You look proud of yourself," she said.

"I'm having fun. You know where they are?" he asked. "Those soldiers marched into the forest like little baby lambs into a fox's den. They won't be bothering us again."

"We need to get to those tunnels. You heard of the ITF?" Layla asked.

Remy nodded. "I heard rumors about Avalon setting up a task force to come after us. Looks like they want humans to do the grunt work. Makes it easier for Arthur and his people to say, 'Look at us, working with these lowly humans. Aren't we the good guys here?' I assume they're also great cannon fodder."

"So now we have to put up with being hunted officially by the people we're meant to be saving?"

"Isn't being the good guys a huge barrel of laughs?" Remy said with a large amount of sarcasm.

"So far, all I can see is that being the good guys just means we get shot at more," Layla said. "And that we have to hide from the world. It sucks, and I'd like it to stop now."

"Can't disagree with that," Remy said. "But at least we know that we're in the right."

"I knocked out a guy who was terrified because he thought I was going to kill him. This whole thing just feels twisted. Helping serial murderers, having to fight people who are just terrified of us because they've been conditioned to believe it. Having to kill people because they think we're evil and would give no second thought about killing us."

"It does suck, but it will get better."

"How do you know?" Layla almost snapped, before being able to stop herself.

"Because what else am I meant to think? We do this because we need it to get better."

Layla nodded. "I know. It's just . . . it's just shit."

"And it can always get shittier. We have to keep fighting to make sure it doesn't."

"Can we win this? Or are we just treading water?"

"Yeah, we can win," Remy said. "I've been in unwinnable situations before and managed to win. I fought a goddamn dragon in central London. I got my arse kicked, but, damn it, we won in the end. Nothing is unwinnable. Nothing is so ingrained that it can't be changed. Sometimes change is hard, and sometimes you have to fight for it."

Layla smiled. "When did you get smart?"

Remy shrugged. "I've always been smart. I just hide it under a veneer of barely-concealed rage and resentment."

Diana and Jared walked out of the tree line and jogged over to Remy and Layla. "Soldiers are dealt with," Jared said.

"Prisoners are released," Diana said. "We told them to come with us into Red Rock, but they're not exactly keen on that idea, so they're going to head north to Pine Portage. There are only half a dozen of them, and they took weapons from the soldiers, so hopefully they'll be okay. Besides, they stole one of the APCs in town. It'll take them a few hours, but they should be safe now. You want to deal with the rest of the soldiers and go find your dad?"

"The soldier part of that question is already done," Remy said smugly.

"Let's get moving then," Layla said.

22

They found the entrance to the tunnels with relative ease. The basement of the apartment building where most of the soldiers had been contained a mark made by a conjurer; a species who used illusion and manipulation similarly to how sorcerers used magic. They were rare, but Diana had worked with a few over the years and managed to remove the mark without it exploding, revealing a steel hatch in the otherwise concrete floor. She pulled the hatch up and a rush of warm air greeted them.

Layla looked down into what was a surprisingly bright tunnel. She climbed down the ten-foot ladder and found that black, gothic lamps were hung from the ceiling. They ran off electricity, and someone had gone to a lot of trouble to ensure that the supply wasn't dangerous. The tunnel smelled damp and stale and condensation dripped on the stone walls, but other than that it wasn't the least pleasant place Layla had been in the last few days; certainly no worse than traversing the swamps of Louisiana. A large mine cart had been placed close to the ladder, and she walked around it, noticing that the tracks it was on disappeared into the gloom further ahead.

"I think we can use this," Layla said once Remy, Diana, and Jared had all climbed down. "It looks like there's a motor on the cart."

The four of them climbed inside the cart. There was enough room for all of them to sit down, although Layla wouldn't have wanted more than four of them in it at a time. A control panel held two buttons: one red and one green.

Remy pressed the green button and the cart slowly trundled down the tracks, lights flickering to life along the way.

"This is going to take forever," Jared said. They'd only managed to go a few hundred feet in a minute.

"I don't think this is used for a fast getaway," Remy said. "Maybe we can get a bit more out of the motor."

Layla used her power to push the cart, gently increasing the speed. "Better?" she asked.

Jared nodded a thank you and kissed her on the back of her hand. "Much."

Layla winked at him. She was glad to be in his company again, even if it was to complete a mission to reclaim her father from Abaddon's clutches and destroy a realm gate. Neither would be considered fun times.

"We should go on a date when this is all done," Jared said. "A nice date that isn't cold or dirty, and where no one shoots at us."

"Well, someone clearly doesn't understand romance," Remy said, getting an elbow in the ribs from Diana for his comment. "Hey, I'm just saying. Bullets flying past your head, people trying to tear you limb from limb: sounds pretty romantic to me."

Jared shook his head and rolled his eyes.

"It would be nice," Layla said. "A little normality would go a long way at this point."

The cart stopped with a bump as it hit the buffers, signaling the end of the track. It was lifted up from the rails before dropping back down again, jarring everyone inside.

"I think we discovered why it moves slowly," Diana said, climbing out.

Layla rubbed her back and followed Diana out. "Okay, yes, that was my fault."

"Can we go faster next time?" Remy asked. "I want to see if we can get some serious air."

"In a tunnel?" Diana asked.

"You only live once," he told her.

"You live twelve times in total," Jared said. "Actually, how many lives do you have left now?"

"Okay, well you guys only live once," Remy corrected, pointedly ignoring the question about lives left. "And if you all die, I promise to tell everyone you went doing something awesome for science."

"For science?" Layla asked.

Remy shrugged. "Better than doing something for stupidity."

Diana rolled her eyes at Remy and pointed to a ladder. "I assume we need to go up there," she said. "I doubt once we're out of here we'll be having as much fun as Remy did riding in that cart."

"You don't know that," Remy said. "I'm quite looking forward to blowing up a realm gate."

"Did you mean to sound so happy about that?" Jared said.

Remy made a sad face. "I promise I'll look like this when it happens," he said.

Diana was already at the top of the twenty-foot ladder, pushing open the steel hatch, when she looked back at the other three. "You all coming, or what?"

They climbed out of the tunnel and found themselves in a small wooden hut that was just about big enough to fit all four of them. Layla concentrated on the lock for a few seconds, and when she felt the lock click, she pushed the door open. She paused and then stepped outside into a large field. The dozens of buildings close by had suffered some sort of damage or were on fire. The field around her was scorched and smoking, as the remaining flames that had consumed it died away, but the wooden hut was completely unaffected. The smell was intense, and Layla wondered just how many people had died defending the town.

"Someone really put effort into fireproofing this hut," Remy said.

"There are conjurer marks inside, so it was probably invisible," Diana said. "Looks like more runes outside made it pretty durable."

"Shame they didn't use those marks on the other buildings," Jared said.

The four of them heard voices and darted behind the nearest building away from the hut. It was three stories high, with one wall completely collapsed, along with part of the roof. It gave the impression of slowly folding in on itself.

"What the hell is that?" a man asked.

Layla heard footsteps coming toward them. She felt the metal in their weapons as they got closer and closer, until they were only a few feet away. Layla tore the weapons apart as Diana and Remy killed the six soldiers before they could react.

Layla stepped around the corner of the building. "We need to split up," she said. "The realm gate is to the south, and the prisoners are kept to the east next to a police station."

"I'll come with you," Jared told her. "Not that you can't do it alone, but I'd feel better if you didn't have to."

"We'll meet you at the realm gate," Remy said. "Get your father to the gate as quickly as possible. This town is only a few miles in length, so hopefully it won't take you long to get to us, but if we get swamped, we're going to blow the gate. You do not want to get stuck out here."

"I'm coming with you," Diana told Layla and Jared. "My nose will help you find your father quicker than just searching for him."

Layla nodded. "Thank you."

"I'll go let Zamek know not to blow anything up," Remy said, and sprinted off into the town, vanishing from sight after a few feet.

"I wish I could do that," Layla said.

The three of them moved as quickly as possible. There were multiple Avalon patrols, and it was soon evident that fighting one would bring many more down on top of them, so going through the houses became the best way to get around. It helped that the streets were all in parallel lines, allowing them to run through one house, across the street, and straight through the front door of another.

The people had been evacuated quickly and most of their belongings had been left behind. It was what Layla assumed the apocalypse might look like: cups of half-drunk coffee left on tables next to half-eaten food.

A huge rock wall had been created around the realm gate at the end of the town. It wasn't visible from where Layla and the team had first entered, but the further east they went, the more impressive the two-hundred-foot-high structure looked.

"How are we going to get in there?" Layla asked, pointing to the mass of gray-and-brown rock.

The three of them were hiding in the front room of a house missing most of its upper floor. It looked like something had ripped it apart and strewn most of the belongings across the road.

"Who made it?" Jared asked, sounding genuinely impressed with what he saw.

"Besides Zamek, there were a number of earth elementals here," Diana said. "Zamek told me that he was going to do something big if the need arose. I didn't expect that wall, though. Hopefully he'll know we're there somehow and let us in."

"And that we can avoid the army outside it," Layla finished.

There were tanks and military personnel all around the section of wall closest to them, but no one appeared to be fighting.

"I did notice the lack of noise," Layla said.

"It looks like they're waiting," Jared said. "Any idea what for?"

Diana shook her head. "Let's not be here when it arrives."

They ran from house to house and stopped behind rubble or bushes to hide from the patrols, which lessened the closer they got to the police station. The three of them ran into a sporting goods store, which had been hit with a large blast of magic that had almost taken off the entire front of the building. Layla moved first, running through the store and hiding behind a large wooden counter before motioning for the others to join her.

"They must not like tennis," Jared said. "The entire section is just a big puddle of melted goo."

"The police station is across the street," Diana told them after looking over the counter.

"The command center tent is exactly where that soldier told me it would be," Layla said. "My dad is inside the police station, but we can't use any powers once we're inside the building."

"I'll check the perimeter," Diana said. "Remove anyone who might become a problem. If there are prisoners in those tents, I'll see what I can do to help them. Maybe create a Remy-sized distraction."

Diana sprinted across the empty road, vanishing from view behind a hedgerow that was still intact. Apart from the sports shop, most of the street appeared to be in one piece; maybe Jared had been right, and someone just really hated tennis.

"You ready?" Jared asked.

Layla nodded, and they ran across the road, up the steps to the police station, and, after looking through the glass doors for any guards, moved straight inside. Layla's power switched off in an instant.

"Shit," she said. "They weren't kidding about the power stop."

The reception area for the police station consisted of wooden desks opposite the front door. The desks were placed on either side of another door that lead further into the station. Various police notices were placed on the wall, and a corkboard held several announcements for fundraisers that were about to take place in the city. Layla pushed the door open to reveal a large open-plan office. The dozen or so desks inside had been thrown around, and the paper and electrical items that had sat on them were all over the floor. At the rear of the office were three more doors, one with the word "Toilet" on it.

"I think we can ignore that one," Jared said.

"Oh, I hope so," Layla said.

The pair moved through the ruined office, keeping low to ensure that no one outside could see them through the windows, which were mostly intact. There were no bullets in the walls, or blood, so Layla assumed that the invaders had arrived, found it empty, and trashed the place anyway.

Jared reached the middle door first and pushed it open, revealing a long windowless corridor. They reached the end and Jared opened the next door.

"Cells," he said, stepping into the room.

Layla followed him. The cells lay next to one another along one side of the room. There was enough of a pathway for people to stay out of the prisoners' reach. The cells—four in total—stretched to the end of the room and were completely separated from each other. The door to each cell was open, revealing their contents: a bed, sink, and toilet, along with a barred window on the far wall. There was another, larger window on the wall outside of the cells; it too was covered in a crisscross of black metal bars.

"Layla," Jared said, pointing into the cell the furthest from the entrance to the block.

Layla looked inside and saw a pair of cuffs and a sorcerer's band. She went in and picked up the band. "You think this is for my father?"

"No," Jared said. "It's for you."

Layla turned around as Jared fired a dart into her neck. She dropped to her knees, the sorcerer's band falling from her hand.

"You've had this before," Jared said. "You remember Cody the prison guard?"

"The hell?" Layla asked.

A second dart hit her in the opposite side of the neck, and Layla's world began spinning, her entire body feeling heavy.

"I thought one would do it," Jared said.

"Work for?" Layla managed.

"Abaddon," Jared said, kneeling in front of her. "Always been Abaddon."

"Was it her plan to get me here?"

Jared nodded. "She wanted me to ensure you'd come to the prison. She knew that you'd go to Red Rock for your father. Abaddon and I had a nice chat when I was captured. I told her that they'd send your father through the realm gate in Red Rock. She thought it was funny."

"Won't be funny when it's blown up, will it?" Layla snapped.

Jared laughed. "She's sending someone through the realm gate— that's why there's no fighting. They won't risk killing her. Abaddon has a friend you're going to really want to meet. She's able to communicate telepathically; she's an umbra, just like us. She's been talking to me for a long time, relaying new orders and the like."

Layla swiped at him with one hand, but found nothing but air.

"Had to play the part," Jared said, dragging her out of the cell, down the corridor, and back into the main office, where he dropped her on the floor and removed his cell phone to make a call. "No reception in there," he told Layla. "And I can't have you out of my sight, just in case."

Layla tried to listen to what he was saying, tried to focus, but her world was just a swirling mass, and she had to force herself not to fall asleep.

"I have her," Jared said. "I'll bring her to you." He ended the call and looked down at Layla. "I sort of wish it had been different."

He aimed the tranquilizer gun at Layla again, but a roar of anger forced him to spin around toward the door as Diana, still in her human form, charged forward. She moved quicker than Jared could ever hope to match. He threw a dozen small marbles of explosives at her, which Diana promptly ignored.

In a panic, Jared threw more marbles at the closest window, blowing out the glass, and then dived through the opening to the outside.

"You still there?" Diana asked Layla, who nodded slightly.

Diana plucked the two darts out of Layla's neck, before picking Layla up, throwing her over her shoulder, and running out of the police station. She kept running for what felt like hours to Layla, but was probably only a few minutes. Layla remained conscious for the whole journey, as the various spirits inside of her tried to keep her awake.

"Is she okay?" another familiar voice asked as Layla lay on the ground. She looked around to find Zamek and Remy beside her.

"Where am I?" Layla asked, still not entirely with it.

"Those stones we saw," Diana said. "They part if you have one of our bracelets on. Zamek is a smart bugger when he wants to be."

"Jared," Layla said, feeling the anger build inside of her. She reached for Terhal, prepared to release her drenik and destroy Jared, but quickly realized that Jared wasn't there and forced the anger aside.

"Now is not the time," Gyda said. "But we do need to talk."

"Talk," Layla said, reaching out to Gyda. "Talk, talk, talk."

Gyda sighed and vanished from view.

"Gyda," Layla called. "Gyda."

A rush of power flooded Layla's body and she sat bolt upright, screaming at the shock. "Holy shit," she shouted, causing both Zamek and Remy to dart back to her and share a concerned glance.

Layla looked behind her at the realm gate. It was fifteen feet high, and about the same in width, and it glowed a faint orange color. The gate itself appeared to be made of a mixture of wood, rock, and metal, but she couldn't tell where one part started and another stopped. In the center of the realm gate was black space, just nothing there at all. "I thought you were going to destroy this?"

"What the hell just happened?" Zamek asked.

"My spirits are vanishing," Layla said. "My power is increasing. I don't really know how."

Zamek touched the realm gate and it ignited bright orange, its black center now showing the realm beyond it. Dozens of people stood there, including Hades and Tommy. Layla took a step forward and looked back at Zamek.

"I thought you were destroying this building?" she asked.

The room they were in looked like something out of NASA's launch control, with banks of computers all pointing toward the realm gate. Large explosive charges could be seen on the walls around her.

Remy led Layla through the gate, and instantly her body disliked the experience. She dropped to her knees on the other side and tried to stop her insides from wanting out.

"First time always sucks," Olivia said, helping Layla to her feet and moving her away from the gate.

She sat Layla down on a chair as Zamek ran through the gate, which immediately switched off, but not before Layla saw the explosion inside the room.

"Buried the gate on their end," Zamek said, patting the armor on his forearm, which was smoldering a little. "Just have to destroy this one."

Layla looked around at the familiar faces; she wanted to tell them what Jared had said about Abaddon sending someone to the realm, but instead she pitched forward and fell asleep.

23

While Layla slept, she found herself sitting up against a large oak tree; it's huge number of leaves kept the rain off. Gyda sat opposite her. Servius sat beside Gyda, and Rosa sat next to Layla.

"You vanished," Layla said to Gyda.

"You knew it would happen eventually," Gyda said. "We're still here, though. We just can't be called when you're awake."

"So, I'm going to pass out when you two go?" Layla asked.

"Depends if you've been dosed with enough drugs to knock out a rhino," Rosa said. "You'll wake up soon. You have to get going once you do."

Layla nodded.

"Your father attracts evil and hate," Servius said. "It's drawn to him. Wherever he goes evil is never far behind. I wonder if that's because his own evil soul attracts that in others."

"Evil begets evil," Rosa said. "Always has."

"And vengeance begets vengeance," Gyda replied, appearing beside Layla. "I've heard this all before."

"I believe that jibe was aimed at me," Rosa said.

"You killed out of vengeance, which caused more vengeance to be given back in return. Violence is born out of violence."

"Not always," Layla said. "Some people take peacefulness as a sign of weakness. Some people believe that only the strong can survive and that anyone else is inconsequential."

"Abaddon certainly seems to believe that," Servius said, "as do the drenik."

Gyda sighed. "I saw so much death and pain in my short life. I created a lot of it when I bonded with the drenik. I do not wish to be the creator of more. I do not wish to surround myself in war."

"So what should I do, Gyda?" Layla asked.

"Run. Run far away and hide," she said.

"I won't run from my friends. I won't run away while there are innocent people dying. I'm not going to give in to those who want to control and rule with an iron boot. That's not happening on my watch."

"It's already happened," Gyda said. "Now you need to run from it."

"Sorry, Gyda. I agree with you about violence begetting more violence. It does. But that doesn't mean you shouldn't fight back when you have to. It doesn't mean you should bury your head in the sand and hope like hell that it just all goes away. That's not the kind of person I want to be."

"So you'll fight Abaddon and you'll die. Is dead the kind of person you want to be?"

"If I die fighting her, I will have died doing the right thing. Anything else is allowing evil to win. And they've won enough over the centuries. I have to try to stop them before it gets worse. And, frankly, it's more than a bit shitty at the moment."

"We fight for what's right because we have the power to do so," Servius said.

"You fought because you enjoyed it," Gyda snapped back. "All of you enjoy it."

Layla shook her head. "I don't like hurting people. I don't like getting up at four in the morning to go on a mission to find the body of someone who was helping us. No one likes it. But sometimes what you like and what you have to do are two different things."

"Take care," Servius said, and vanished from view.

Gyda got up and walked over to Layla, taking her hands. "Do better with this power than I did." Gyda vanished, too.

"So, just us two," Rosa said.

Layla lay back on the grass, listening to the rain. "When I'm done with all of this, do you know what I'm going to do?"

"Bathe?" Rosa asked.

Layla laughed. "With bubbles. Like all of the bubbles. But, no, I'm going to get my nails done."

Rosa raised an eyebrow in question. "Really?"

"I know, it's a little thing, but I used to enjoy having them done. Being able to make them unique. It was fun. I haven't done it since we moved to Greenland. I mean, what was the point? I'd like to do that again. I miss it."

"Anything else?"

"Getting dressed up to go out. Chloe would badger me into a night out, and I'd end up loving it and having a lot of fun. Not much to do night-out-wise in the compound, except use the practice range or hope the satellite is picking up TV shows." Layla sighed.

"When I was out on a mission, the thing I missed was feeling sexy," Rosa said. "I liked dressing up in nice clothes and feeling like a million quid. It's hard to dress up for yourself when all you're going to be doing is killing someone and splattering blood on yourself. When I got back from a mission, I'd bathe—good suggestion, by the way—and then I'd dress up in clothes that made me feel good about myself. And I'd just go out to eat or see a friend, anything normal. It was a kind of therapy, I guess. I had a beautiful green dress that I'd had made so that I could keep a throwing dagger belt hidden in the waist. It was my favorite thing in the world."

"I have a pair of jeans and a Lord of the Rings t-shirt that I adore. Clothes were never my thing when I was little. I didn't care one way or the other. My mom used to be furious at me because I'd go out and get covered in mud, climb trees, tear my clothes; you know, the usual kid stuff. She'd sit me down and tell me that I had to be careful with things purchased for me, that I had to treat them with the respect they deserved. If someone chose to buy me something, it was to be cared for. Not sure how much she was trying to instill a sense of value in me, and how much she just didn't want to spend hundreds of dollars on new clothes every few months."

Rosa laughed. "You haven't spoken to any of us much recently."

"No, it's been beyond crazy. I've barely had time to think. My father said that once I fully merged with the spirits, one of them would become more prevalent than the others. And that you know nothing about it."

"He's not wrong. I don't. I can't remember it happening before, but then it's certainly possible that there are some things we spirits aren't allowed to remember, for one reason or another."

"Umbra are weird things, aren't they? Complex and simple, all at once."

"You're tired, Layla. You haven't stopped in days, and before that you ran yourself ragged. You need to rest. And I don't just mean get a few hours of extra sleep because someone dosed you with drugs. I mean rest. Proper, full-on resting."

Layla felt angry. "Jared."

Rosa placed a hand on hers.

"No one gets the time to rest," Layla said. "We're being hunted."

"I know, but you're the one who asks for extra training, you're the one who stays up long after everyone else to practice with your powers.

You're preparing for battle, but just make sure that when it comes you're going to be able to fight."

Layla nodded. "I know. I know all of this. I know I need to sleep. I know I need to take a step back and stop pushing myself, but, damn it, I just can't. Not while people I care about are in harm's way. And certainly not while my father is out there. He will escape again. He will murder again. I don't think he could stop himself, even if he wanted to."

"You want to talk about Jared?"

"I cared for him," Layla said after a few seconds of silence. "Really cared for him, and it was all a lie. I don't want to talk about him at the moment. I don't want the anger I feel to cloud my judgment. Tell me something, Rosa: were you ever in love?"

"I miss the woman I love," Rosa said sadly. "I had one great love, and her name was Gwendolyn. She was a few years older than me and lived alone in a house in London. Law forbade our relationship. I couldn't marry her, I couldn't show affection in public, and I certainly couldn't let on how much it irritated me when men asked for her hand on a semi-regular basis. She was a wealthy woman, having been married to a man who died several years before I met her, and a number of men thought themselves suitors.

"If I'm being honest, irritated doesn't begin to cover it. I hated it. I hated that our society dictated how she had to behave. I hated that she allowed herself to be dictated to. I loved her in secret because we weren't allowed to love each other in public. And then one day, one of the suitors didn't take kindly to being rejected and he got a little physical. I almost beat him to death right there and then in the drawing room. And when I was done, I saw the look of horror and fear on the face of the woman I loved, and I fled. I never went back."

Flickers of memories arrived in Layla's head. The rage, hate, and sorrow of what Rosa had done, the smell of blood, the sounds of Gwendolyn begging Rosa to stop. Layla remembered it all. "I'm so sorry. What happened after?"

"You could just reach into your memory and find out for yourself."

"I could, but some things are important enough to hear it directly from the person."

Rosa smiled and patted Layla on the hand. "I fled. I ran and ran and didn't come back for two years. Upon my return, I discovered that Gwendolyn had died about a year after I'd left. She caught pneumonia and never recovered. Her banker thought I was running a con to get part of her estate, but all I wanted was the locket she owned. It had a picture of me in it, and she wore it until her dying day. I took the locket and anything else she'd left me, including a large sum of cash, and soon after I became an umbra.

"Two years after that, I killed the man who had hurt Gwendolyn with a hatpin. He was one of my many targets, and I felt a slight happiness at his death, after the misery he'd caused in his vile life. I had many affairs, with both men and women, but I only loved Gwendolyn. I was grateful for every single day that I had her in my life. Even for as short a time as it ended up being." Rosa took hold of Layla's hand. "Can I give you some advice?"

Layla nodded.

"When you find a person you love—and you will: one day someone will appear in your life, and you will love them—don't run. Don't try to push them away. Just be happy you found each other. My one regret is that I ran from Gwendolyn because I was terrified that I would no longer be good for her, that she'd seen the real me. I hated myself for it for a long time."

"Thank you," Layla said. "For telling me that, for keeping my mind off where I currently am, and for generally being a good friend."

"I try," Rosa said with a smile.

"Jared will be dealt with," Layla said after a few seconds. "He . . . What he did, it hurts. Like someone ripping my insides out. I just . . . I know he's the enemy now. I know that everything we had is a lie, and the anger I feel threatens to overwhelm me. I have to push it down, keep it locked up. Because it'll cloud my judgment if I don't."

Rosa nodded. "Deal with it soon, though, because you won't like it when your emotions crash down over you."

The world vanished, and Layla opened her eyes, staring up at the wooden beams above her head. "How long was I out?" she asked.

"Half an hour," Tommy said from the chair beside her. "I thought it best that someone stay and wait for you to wake up. You actually fell asleep. Not knocked out, or passed out—just fell asleep. How are you feeling?"

"Jared betrayed us all. Betrayed me."

Tommy nodded and there was a look of anger in his eyes. Layla hoped that Jared got to feel that anger first hand.

"Abaddon has sent someone through the realm gate," Layla told him, sitting up.

"Kristin's clone. We know," Olivia said from the corner of the room. "We spotted her coming in. She seems to have been under the impression that if she came through with the flood of refugees we wouldn't notice her. She took off toward the prison."

"Prison?" Layla asked, swinging her legs out of the bed.

Olivia and Tommy motioned for Layla to join them, and the three walked out of the single-story wooden building and down the steps to a small garden where Diana, Remy, Hades, and Zamek were waiting.

"What's this prison?" Layla asked.

"You know about the seven devils, yes?" Olivia asked.

"About Lucifer and the like?" Layla asked. "Yeah, it came up."

"Mammon is here," Hades said. "In this realm. He was imprisoned many thousands of years ago, but time in Norumbega moves differently, so it's probably only been a thousand years to him."

"Only," Remy said with a shake of his head.

"Where's the prison?" Layla asked.

"It was built into the mountain by the dwarves who brought him here," Tommy said. "Abaddon cannot be allowed to find out that this is where Mammon truly is. She suspects it at the moment, but if she discovers that the other realm gate is in New York, we're all screwed."

"So where is the Kristin-clone?"

"At the prison," Hades said. "About three miles north-east of here, on the other side of the wood. She's been followed by several of my people. No one has been inside the prison for millennia, not since Mammon was placed there. There's no telling what traps have been left behind by those who created the place."

"I'll go get her," Layla said, looking around the town. It was like something out of a painting. All of the wooden bungalows along the perfectly maintained, snow-covered streets were beautiful. Large creatures that looked like a combination of ox and horse—but were much larger than either species—pulled massive carriages up and down the roads. The beasts were different shades of black and brown and all had huge antlers on their heads. People milled around as if they didn't have a care in the world. It was tranquil, peaceful, and beautiful. Layla looked up at the crisp blue sky with not a cloud in sight, her breath visible in the cold.

"If possible, we want her alive. But if you can't get her back here, kill her. Those are pretty much the only choices we have."

Olivia's words brought Layla back to the here and now. "I never assumed otherwise."

"But she can't be allowed to get to the second realm gate on the other side of the forest," Tommy said. "Olivia, Hades, and I will go to the second realm gate. If she gets past you, she won't be getting past us."

"She's one clone," Remy said. "How long was she around before you spotted her?"

"A few hours, why?" Hades asked.

"You sure she's the only one?" Remy asked.

Hades shook his head. "We thought of that, too. Those in charge of this town are going through all of the refugees and trying to find out who is, and isn't, on our side. It's a long process, but they're not allowed to leave until we're satisfied."

"And where are they being kept?" Layla asked.

"There are plains to the west of here, hundreds of miles of nothing. They've been taken there. They'll be allowed to stay or leave the realm as soon as we can vouch for them."

"The realm gate we came through is destroyed," Zamek said. "So at least we know no one else is coming through. I'm not sure how long it'll be before the gate heals itself—only the ancient dwarves knew that secret—but it's going to be a while. Like all of life's problems, everything can be solved with alchemy."

"All of them?" Layla asked with a slight smile.

"All the ones that dwarves care about," Zamek replied, wearing a smile of his own. "We'll find this clone and stop her from escaping, but if she's not the only one who came through the gate, we might have some problems in town."

"Best of luck," Hades said.

Layla was introduced to one of the giant creatures—called a bordox. A carriage with a single female human driver took her, Zamek, Remy, and Diana out of the town. The carriage was painted black and gold, and the interior had the same color scheme. It moved slowly at first, and Layla got to look out of the open window at the town around her. All of the two-story buildings, most of which appeared to be Victorian in design, sat apart from one another, each with their own snow-covered gardens. The Victorian theme stretched to the clothing, too, although the women and men wore similar outfits: trousers and shirts, with thick winter jackets of various colors.

Children played in a snowy park close to the houses, and, to Layla, no one seemed to mind that thousands of refugees were just a short distance away.

"It's nice here," she said. "Peaceful."

"These people have lived here for thousands of years," Diana said. "They're probably living in the most peaceful realm I've ever been to.

They really seem to believe that they can do great things if they work together. It's a big change from Earth, or Olympus, or frankly any realm."

The moment the bordox left the town limits, it opened up its trot to a full-on run, throwing Layla back in her seat. "Holy crap," she said, grabbing the belt that was attached to the soft seat. "I guess I now know why these are necessary."

They sped past countryside. Open fields of wheat changed into orchards of large fruit trees, all under a beautiful blue sky. After a few minutes, the bordox reached the huge, dark forest that had been in the distance and shadow engulfed the carriage. Layla could no longer make out anything but a blur of trees and the blanket of multi-colored leaves that littered the forest floor. As small drops of water began to pelt her through the open window, Layla pulled the blinds. Partially to stop getting wet, and partially to ensure she didn't have to see just how close to the trees the bordox was getting.

A short time later, the bordox stopped and the occupants of the carriage stepped outside.

"Holy shit," Remy said. "That's a prison?"

The building was a mass of gray-and-white stone and glass and gave the appearance of being carved from solid granite. To Layla, it was beautiful. A dozen huge columns—each one fifty feet tall—were carved from a rock almost blue in color. Glass domes crested the part of the prison that was outside of the mountain. Layla couldn't tell where the prison ended and the mountain started, so good were the architects.

"The dwarven ancients did this," Zamek said. "It's like nothing I've ever seen."

The entrance to the prison was behind two thirty-foot-high metal doors. Even from where she stood, Layla could tell that one of them was ajar. "The clone is here already."

There was a roar from somewhere inside the prison, and the bordox kicked at the ground, scared of whatever had made the noise.

"Get it out of here," Remy said to the driver. "We're going to need Hades, Tommy, and anyone else you can find."

The driver didn't need to be told twice and took off back toward the town.

"Okay, she could have at least tried to talk us out of this," Remy said, only half mocking.

One of the doors to the prison moved slightly, and a huge hand appeared around it. The skin was yellow and red, as if there were fire just beneath its surface. It took hold of the door and tore it free, then threw it at Layla and her friends with enough force to land it only a few feet away from them.

"It threw that door two hundred feet," Diana said. "What the hell can do that?"

"I have a very bad feeling about this," Zamek said.

The creature stepped out of the shadows of the doorway and roared in anger. It was twenty feet high with yellow-and-red skin all over its body. Its eyes blazed orange and it cracked its knuckles as its gaze settled on the four people in front of it. The top of the creature's skull was ablaze, as if it wore a crown of molten rock.

"That's an eldjötnar," Zamek said.

"A what?" Layla asked as the creature roared again: a noise that she could feel in her bones.

"A fire giant," Zamek said. "A species who aren't exactly known for their intelligence and easiness to get along with."

"So we need to take it down?" Remy said. "You got a nuke in your pocket?"

The giant took one huge step toward them.

"Oh good, it's seen us," Remy said.

"They're slow and strong," Zamek said. "We need to find a way to cool it down."

"And then what?" Diana asked.

"It'll be calm once cooled," Zamek said. "A lake or stream would be great."

"I'll get right on it," Remy shouted.

The giant tore free one of the pillars and hurled it at the group, who scattered to avoid it.

Layla looked up at the snow-covered peaks above the jail. "Avalanche," she shouted.

"That'll do," Zamek said.

"You two keep it busy," Diana said. "Layla and I will go get the snow."

"Be fast," Remy shouted, avoiding a slow-moving arm as the fire giant reached out and tried to grab him.

Layla ran toward the prison and saw Kristin's clone leave. She looked at Layla and smiled before running off into the woods.

"Go get her," Diana said. "I'll deal with the avalanche."

"I have a better idea," Layla said. "Get to the columns."

Diana did as Layla suggested, and Layla reached up with her power, taking hold of the metal inside the rock above the prison. There was so much there; so much metal, so much that she could do with it. She felt the power flow through her, reached down, and touched as much of the metal as she could. She knew she didn't have to move a lot, but the rock was a hundred feet above her head; she'd never managed to manipulate metal from such a distance before.

She twisted the ore in the rock and heard it groan, heard the very mountain complain, then felt the metal give way. The avalanche began slowly, just a few rocks tumbling down the mountain and hitting the glass domes with enough force to break them had they been made of normal glass, and not created by powerful dwarfs.

"Remy, Zamek," Diana shouted.

Both Remy and Zamek had been running circles around the lumbering giant, trying to throw it off balance, but with every blow that landed on the ground, a small fountain of fire erupted around it. Zamek and Remy needed to be extra careful.

"What about the clone?" Diana asked Layla, who was about to reply when the most awful sound she'd ever heard shook the very slabs of stone she stood on.

The snow moved quicker than Layla had anticipated; it flowed down the mountain like a raging river. Zamek and Remy made it to the prison's columns just as the snow smashed into the ground before them. Huge pieces of rock hit the landscape as the snow continued to rush across the clearing in front of them, tearing up the nearby trees and carrying them off as if they weighed nothing at all.

As powerful as the giant was, it was defenseless against the force that smashed into it. Its red-and-yellow skin dulled, becoming a light gray as it was buried under the snow.

The whole thing lasted only a few seconds, but when it was over, the clearing before them was buried a dozen feet beneath thick snow, rock, and ice. The giant was on its back at the far edge of it, no longer able to cause a problem.

"Well, that was terrifying," Remy said.

Diana sniffed the air. "I can't track the clone—she has no scent."

"Zamek, can you clear a path?" Layla asked.

Zamek placed his hands on the stone in front of him and the earth shook as steps erupted out of the snow, forming a bridge.

Layla ran across it, dropping down beyond the snow to the part of the forest that they'd arrived through. The clone had fled that way, but Layla knew she couldn't have gotten far on foot through dense forest, especially with an avalanche right behind her.

"Clones can bleed," she said.

Remy sniffed the air. "Fresh blood at three o'clock," he said.

"I'll stay with Zamek," Diana said. "We're going to need to put the giant back in the prison. I think it's still alive. You two go find the clone."

Remy smiled. "Let's hunt."

24

Layla and Remy ran through the forest: Remy slightly in front as he tracked the bleeding clone toward the second realm gate. Layla was more than a little impressed that, despite suffering an injury, the clone had not only managed to survive the avalanche but continued to run without pause. On the plus side, she knew that the clone wouldn't be able to keep its pace up forever, and when she'd fought the last one, it had gone down just as easily as a human would have.

True to Layla's thought, the clone started to slow after a few hundred feet. Remy stopped and held up a paw for Layla to follow suit.

"What's up?" she asked.

"I smell something. Oil. And something else." Remy sniffed the air. "Explosives."

Layla flooded the area with her power and found the thin wire that stretched across two trees. She crouched down and pointed it out to Remy.

"She must have come this way before going to the prison," Remy said.

A bullet smashed into the tree beside them. They flung themselves low as a second bullet slammed into the tree just above Layla's head.

"You ever wonder what happened to the people Hades sent after me?" Kristin's clone called out.

"I assume you killed them," Remy said.

"They woke the giant," the clone shouted. "Something had to. It was guarding Mammon. Did you kill it?"

"Go back and poke it," Remy said. "Find out."

"I'm getting through that realm gate," the clone said. Her voice had changed place.

"She's circling around," Layla whispered.

Remy nodded. "I don't like that idea," he said. "Let's piss her off."

Remy was up in an instant and vanished from view as he ran around the tree.

"Nice trick," the clone said.

Layla concentrated and searched for the gun that the Kristin-clone was using. She found it quickly and pulled it apart.

"Goddamn it," the clone shouted.

Layla kept searching and found a second gun on the clone's hip. Layla forced the gun to fire three times: each one coincided with a scream.

Layla stepped over the wire and found Remy, his sword drawn and pointing at the clone's throat. She was bleeding heavily where the bullets had struck her in the leg.

"Kristin will kill you," she told Layla.

"She can try," Layla told her. "I think she might find it harder than she would have a few days ago."

"You caused the avalanche. I hadn't expected that."

Layla shrugged. "Is Mammon in there?"

The clone nodded. "He's in a state of suspended animation."

"We're going to check, you know," Remy said.

"The dwarves built that place to last," the clone said. "You know that Kristin is with Abaddon now."

"Kristin killed Nergal, didn't she?" Layla asked.

The clone nodded again. "Nergal tried to kill us. Abaddon gave her a way to avenge that insult."

"How altruistic of her," Remy said.

"They're going to take Nergal's Texas compound."

"When?" Layla asked.

"Once Canada is Avalon's."

"Why tell us this?" Remy asked.

"Because I know that you'll go there, and Kristin will get her chance to kill Little Miss Perfect here."

"Little Miss Perfect?" Layla asked.

"Loving parents, loving friends, loving life. You had everything. Your father loved you; he trained you, made you better. You are what I would have been if I'd had that love."

Layla wasn't really sure how to respond to that statement. "My father is a serial killer."

"Who still loves you," the clone said. "He helped you become what you are. And you want to know something even better? Abaddon has a surprise for you. A big surprise. A masked surprise."

"You want to tell me what it is?" Layla asked.

Kristin's clone shook her head. "You'll find out. And then you'll die. Nice knowing you." She snapped her head forward, as fast as possible, onto the point of Remy's sword and fell back dead. Her body dissolved a few seconds later, until there was nothing left on the cold forest floor.

"Well, that could have gone better," Remy said. "At least she didn't get to the other gate."

Layla continued to stare at where the clone had been; she knew that this was far from over. She sighed and went back with Remy to find that Hades, Tommy, and Olivia had arrived at the prison. With Zamek and Diana, they'd managed to pull the giant back inside.

"How did it go?" Olivia asked Remy and Layla.

275

"Better than having to drag a giant back inside there?" Tommy said, jerking his thumb toward the prison. "I'm going to smell like a giant's loincloth and feet for weeks."

Zamek was using his alchemy to reattach the door as Hades walked out with Diana.

"The people I sent to track the clone were killed by the giant," Hades said, "but the ancient runes used to keep the giant in suspended animation were still there. We shouldn't have any more problems. Fire giants aren't naturally evil or anything, and it looks like it was just a guard doing its job, so I'm glad you didn't have to kill it."

"It took a mountain to hurt it," Remy said. "I think the poor injured fire giant is fine."

"It's not as good as it was," Zamek said. "But the door will hold."

"We need to get back to the Earth realm," Olivia said. "Did the clone say anything?"

Remy and Layla relayed her words.

"We have to stop Abaddon from getting that compound, if we can," Hades said. "All of those spirit scrolls, all of those innocent people nearby."

"Do we even know where exactly the place is?" Remy asked. "Texas isn't what I'd call small."

"I know where it is," Hades said. "It's about thirty kilometers south-east of a town named Cornudas, in Hudspeth County."

"Okay, and where is that?" Diana asked.

"The closest big town is El Paso," Olivia said. "I've been to El Paso. It's Avalon-controlled. And not in a small way."

Hades nodded. "That's true. And we have to go through El Paso to get to Nergal's compound?"

"That seems like a bad idea," Remy said.

"I'd agree, but I have some friends in Las Cruces, New Mexico who owe me more than a few favors. If we can get to them, we can get anything we need before we drive the rest of the way."

"What about Avalon?" Tommy asked.

"Avalon's influence in New Mexico is minimal at best," Olivia said. "Same with Arizona. They concentrated on California and Texas when it first became apparent how important they were, and sort of ignored the bit in the middle. It's a trend that continues to this day. We'll have to go through El Paso, but if we keep our heads down and don't draw any attention, we should be okay."

The group returned to the village and, upon arrival, Hades walked off to talk to the elders about leaving the realm, while everyone else loaded into two of the bordox carriages. Tommy, Olivia, and Zamek were in Layla's carriage.

"You okay?" Tommy asked her.

Layla nodded. "Do you think this is ever going to get better?"

Tommy smiled. "Yeah, it will eventually. We've lost people, good people, people we love, and we're still fighting. We will beat Arthur. We will show the world what Avalon has become."

Tommy spoke with such conviction, such utter assurance that Layla couldn't help but be boosted by his words.

Hades arrived at their carriage window. "We're good to go. I'll have to send these people some troops to help keep order. With so many extra people, they want to ensure there are no problems."

"I have a question," Layla said.

Hades nodded. "What's up?"

"Now that Jared's joined Abaddon, won't he be able to tell everyone where we are in Greenland? Are we going to get back to the Earth realm and find our home a smoking ruin and our friends imprisoned? Or worse?"

"Your bracelet is linked to the blood curse mark on the back of your shoulder," Hades said, pointing to her wristband. "Without a bracelet, no one has power in my compound, and they are unable to tell anyone its location. It's just a safety feature. And even if he has a band, you can only talk about it with someone who has the same blood curse mark."

"Jared can't tell Abaddon where we all are?" Olivia asked.

Hades nodded. "We'd have had a whole new war on our hands if he'd been able to say anything. And since he appears to have always been under Abaddon's command, he would have revealed our location a long time ago if he could. So, until he finds someone else with the same mark, who is also wearing a bracelet, he's mute concerning our home."

"So, he's still a threat that needs to be resolved," Zamek said. He turned to Layla. "Sorry."

"No, you're right, he does," Layla agreed.

The group set off a few minutes later, with Layla feeling slightly better about what she was going to find in the Earth realm.

The guardians at the realm gate let everyone through and Layla found herself in a room almost identical to the one in Red Rock, except that it was full of people who were happy to see them. Felicia Hales strode toward them, hugging Tommy, Olivia, and Hades in turn. She kissed Diana on each cheek, and high-fived Remy as he walked past. Zamek shook her hand, and they nodded toward one another.

Felicia stood in front of Layla and sighed. "I'm glad you're okay— you had people worried." She embraced Layla and nodded. "Go on out. We have some people waiting for you."

Layla thanked Felicia and exited the realm gate control room. Harry, Chloe, Persephone, and the rest of the group were waiting for her.

"I'm sorry," Chloe said, hugging Layla tightly after she'd said her hellos. "About Jared."

"How'd you know?" Layla asked.

"He went on national TV and told the nation that he was working with Avalon to stop the spread of terrorism in Red Rock. They treated him like a damn rock star. It's been a few days since you left."

"Only a few hours for me," she said. "It's like a raw anger bubbling just under the surface. I'm going to find Jared and I'm going to hurt him very badly."

They took some BMW SUVs to a disused airfield to the north of Westchester County Airport. Half a dozen Black Hawk helicopters sat on the tarmac, along with a C-130 Hercules. Several more members of Hades' security force waited for them, including Commander Fenix, who came over to Layla as soon as he saw her.

For a moment, she thought he was going to ask her how she could have missed Jared being a lying sack of shit. But instead he offered his hand, which Layla shook.

"I'm sorry about Jared," he said. "We all thought he was one of the good guys."

Layla just nodded, unsure what else to say and unwilling to open the emotional can of worms. It had been a long few days, people she cared for had been hurt, and Jared's betrayal was just one more thing on the shit heap of recent events. She would have to deal with her feelings about it sooner rather than later, but for now she just wanted to get ready to fight.

Harry led her into a nearby building. "You doing okay?" he asked. Layla sat down on a red cushioned sofa as Harry placed a thermos in front of her. "Figured you could need this."

Layla unscrewed the lid and inhaled the beautiful coffee aroma. "You, sir, are a god amongst men."

"Hell yeah, I am," Harry said, making Layla laugh.

Tommy entered the building and placed a sandwich and chocolate bar in front of her. "Eat. You're going to need it." He left before Layla could reply.

She bit down reluctantly on the bacon and egg sandwich and soon found herself shoveling in the rest as fast as possible. She hadn't realized just how hungry she was. When she'd finished the food and three cups of coffee, Harry placed a small ring in front of her.

"Are we to be wed?" Layla asked, picking up the black ring and turning it over, looking at the runes inscribed underneath. "I have to warn you, I expect my husband to stay at home and keep the house clean."

"You're a witty woman," Harry said.

"Yes, yes I am. Also, I need a dowry."

Harry stared at Layla for several seconds. "You done?"

"I have more, but you go ahead."

"It's a sorcerer's band, but in ring form. Oh, and without the built-in magical napalm."

"How did you make this?"

"Zamek and I have been working on it for a while. I want one that lets me create things from my mind."

"I heard you wanted Green Lantern's ring."

"Doesn't have to be green. I'm okay with any color."

Layla chuckled. "That's big of you. How's that going?"

"It's in the planning and never-going-to-happen-in-a-million-years stage."

"Sorry."

"That's okay. I'll just have to keep trying to get super powers the old-fashioned way."

"Get bitten by something radioactive?"

"Or blinded, blown up, shot in space; basically, I figure I hang around radioactive material for long enough and I'll die or gain superpowers."

Layla raised two thumbs in support. "Good luck with that."

Harry smiled. "The ring doesn't do anything until you activate it."

"So I can wear it all the time and not lose my powers?" Layla slipped it onto the index finger of her left hand. She used her power to change the shape of the metal thermos cup into a bird. "How do I activate it? Also, why would I even want to wear this thing if it takes away my powers?"

"We'll get to that in a second. Pinch above and below the ring and squeeze slightly."

Layla did as she was instructed, and the effect was immediate as her powers just vanished. It was an unpleasant sensation. She pinched it again and they returned.

"Okay, yes, the ring will nullify your power," Harry said. "I know it's difficult to feel like you've lost a limb or something, but we're working on it. But that's not the cool thing about the ring. When you activate it, it disables the powers of everyone in a fifty-foot radius. So, yes, you'll be human when you've activated it, but so will anyone else near you."

Layla stared at the ring. "Holy shit, that's useful. How?"

"Zamek and I managed to cobble together some runes that make it work. Short periods only, and by that I mean ten to fifteen minutes. Then the ring burns out and won't work for several days. I figured if you're going after Abaddon, you could use something to equal the odds. This is a prototype, Layla. There are no others out there, and we're not sure we can recreate it. It took me a year just to figure out the right type of metal to use—titanium, by the way."

"Why black?"

"The runes turned it that color. I'd advise you to not use it often."

"You're like Q."

"I'm not giving you an exploding pen. Or an Aston Martin."

"Spoilsport."

"You ready to go see everyone else?"

Layla got up from her seat. "How bad is it out there?"

"It's not brilliant," Harry admitted. "We lost Canada, but most of the people in Hades' strongholds got out. So, not great, but it could be worse."

They found the rest of the group on the runway.

"You feel better?" Chloe asked Layla.

"I've eaten for the first time in what feels like days," Layla said. "So not bad."

"We had a platter," Remy said. "In the car on the way here. An actual platter of food. It. Was. Amazing."

"Right," Hades said, and everyone quieted down. "We're going to go to New Mexico and then head to Nergal's compound near El Paso. This is not a search-and-rescue mission. We're going to stop Abaddon from claiming any of the spirit scrolls that are still there. We have word that she left from a private airfield just outside of Winterborn two hours ago. Thankfully, my people were able to cause enough trouble that she was delayed for the few days I wasn't around."

"So Abaddon is just going to turn up at Nergal's and take over?" Zamek asked. "I don't see Nergal's people being happy that she had him killed."

"Abaddon is going to march in there and murder every single person loyal to Nergal," Sky said. She'd been waiting in New York with several members of Hades' team for everyone to join her and get ready to go after Abaddon. "She has an army of blood elves at her disposal. This is going to get messy and we can't just wait until one side wins. There are inhabited places in Texas that neither side will have any problem with destroying when the fight spills out of the compound. And it will."

"And once Abaddon has those spirit scrolls," Hades said, "she's going to be a lot more pro-active with them than Nergal was. If anything, he was too cautious about using them. We want this fight to be contained, but getting those scrolls before Abaddon is the focus of the mission here."

"One other thing," Persephone said. "We need to strike back. We lost Canada. We lost our home. We lost friends. Now we're going to show Arthur and Avalon that this is far from over. Once we do this, Avalon will double its efforts to find us. So let's make it count."

"We need to destroy Nergal's factory and help the people he's abducted," Sky said. "Abaddon will kill them all. I don't think anyone here thinks otherwise."

"And what happens to the people he's turned, who don't want help?" Harry asked. "Didn't mean to interrupt, I just thought of it."

"We need to give them a choice," Hades said. "They either come with us, or we're going to send them to Shadow Falls. After Arthur tried to kill us all a few years ago, we evacuated the entire realm of Shadow Falls. As far as Avalon knows, it's empty, and after we destroyed an elven realm gate we found there, we've been using it as a sort of makeshift prison realm. We'll take the umbra there. We'll try to rehabilitate anyone who has been brainwashed by Nergal and Avalon."

"And if they're not brainwashed?" Layla asked.

"We'll try them as criminals," Persephone said. "And they'll be dealt with according to Avalon's rules of law; the old ones that we adhere to. Those who have committed war crimes under their own volition will be dealt with accordingly."

"Meaning what?" Layla asked.

"I have a prison that is unknown to anyone but myself," Hades said. "Avalon still doesn't even know it exists. War criminals will be sent there. Any more questions?"

"How are we going to fly those things to Texas and back?" Irkalla asked.

"They're all modified," Hades said. "The Black Hawks can fly about five thousand kilometers without a refill, and the Hercules can fly about seven thousand kilometers before it needs to refuel. We'll be just fine. They've been designed to be slightly larger than a standard one too, so it can carry more people."

Layla looked past the Black Hawk at the Hercules. She'd gone to an air show years ago, just her and her mom, and seen one fly. It had been awe-inspiring, and for a while she'd wanted to be a pilot. Life had, obviously, had other ideas, but the grace and power of the massive machine was something that still made her smile.

"You all ready?" Hades asked.

"Let's go piss off Avalon some more," Remy said. "It's becoming a hobby of mine."

People moved away to get ready and Layla climbed into one of the Black Hawks, strapping herself in.

"Nervous?" Remy asked her, after she'd been looking out of the window for several minutes. They'd all been given headsets with microphones so they could communicate over the sounds of the powerful engine.

"A little," she told him.

"I figured I'd be on the frontline charging in," Harry said. "I'm going to go commando on all their asses. The movie, you understand, not the lack of underwear."

Kase placed a hand over her mouth to stifle her laughter.

"You're going to stay in the car," Chloe told him. "You don't heal from bullets."

"Neither do you, if it's the right bullet," Harry pointed out.

"Harry, I admire your courage," Diana told him, "but please don't do anything stupid. You deserve a spot with us. You've proven yourself, and you're providing intel on this mission. We need someone who can stay back and keep us informed about incoming troops, or escaping troops, or anything that will screw us over."

"The cavalry then," Harry said with a wink. "I need a horse and a sword."

"You do not get a horse," Remy said. "If anyone gets a horse, it should be me."

"You're a fox," Chloe said. "Why do you need a horse?"

"To look majestic," Remy said, as if the answer was obvious.

"Have you ever looked majestic for a day in your life?" Harry asked.

"My coat is soft and glossy. Can you say the same?"

"Is now the time to explain that I'm not a fox?" Harry asked.

Remy stared at him for several seconds. "You don't know what you're missing out on."

"Well, I know you're missing out on being able to go on the big kids rides at theme parks," Harry said quickly.

Everyone in the Black Hawk laughed and even Remy smiled. "You're a terrible person, Harry. A terrible person."

25

Four days after she had killed Nergal and joined Abaddon, Kristin was beginning to feel as though she might have made the wrong decision. Abaddon had stayed in Canada to oversee the fall of the towns belonging to Hades, and while some small groups continued to resist, the necromancer had been mostly satisfied with the outcome. Humanity had praised them on the news. She was meant to feel happy that she'd picked the winning side. But she didn't.

Her clone had died earlier the day before. She had been cut off from communicating with it since it vanished through the realm gate and had also felt a loss of power. For two days that absence of power remained. And then on the third day, the power pinged back into her. Her clone was dead.

She'd lost all of her clones in the last few days as the enemy continued to fight, and with each death she regained more of her power. With the death of the last living clone she was now able to recreate them all as needed, but she would wait until she needed them.

Kristin knew that telling Abaddon about the death of the clone in the other realm would be a bad idea. Abaddon would be less than happy that Kristin's clone had failed, and she wondered if the necromancer's disappointment would be taken out on her. They had no way of getting through the realm gate in Red Rock, even after they'd dug it out. And they had no way of operating the gate in Red Rock, no Guardians to turn it on. It would take time before they were recreated, and Kristin wondered how long she had before the death of the clone was discovered.

Thankfully she had been sent to deal with the aftermath of Red Rock and hadn't seen much of Abaddon or Elizabeth since murdering Nergal. But now, on day four of the taking of Canada, the necromancer had finally decided to head to Texas to deal with Nergal's compound.

Abaddon had managed to keep Nergal's death a secret from Avalon, but someone loyal to Nergal had managed to take control of his compound, which had gone into high alert, now expecting an attack: an attack that Abaddon was all too happy to provide.

Kristin, Abaddon, and Elizabeth reached a disused airfield close to Winterborn and climbed into a private jet. Kristin had been ordered to join them. Jared—a man that Kristin distrusted after she'd discovered he'd been working for Abaddon all these years—sat in the rear of the jet.

Jared stood and bowed his head to the necromancer, who nodded in return before taking her seat. The jet was large enough to fit twelve and it had a bedroom in the rear. Kristin sat across the aisle from Abaddon and Elizabeth.

"You don't like me a whole lot, do you?" Jared asked Kristin after the jet had taken off and he'd caught her scowling at him.

"We had you in custody," she said. "We beat you. You didn't give up where Hades' main compound is, and not once did you let us think you might be working with us."

"I wasn't working with you," Jared told her. "I was working for Abaddon. Like I have been ever since she found me."

"Found you?"

"I was a soldier in the British army. We were training in Turkey and my squad and I came across an old vault buried in the ground. We found some scrolls, but there were people who didn't want us to have them, so they attacked us. Killed most of my squad, but I accidentally activated a scroll, and now here we are."

"You said Abaddon found you?"

"She was watching the force attacking us—they'd been interested in the scrolls, and she was interested in where they were. She interjected once the fight was over and offered me a job. The old me died, and I was reborn. After a few years I was placed in a position where Tommy could find me by accident and offer me a job."

"Your entire past is a lie, I assume."

Jared nodded. "My age, my upbringing, everything was a fabrication. I wasn't meant to get close to Layla. It just worked out that way."

"Did you genuinely like her?" Elizabeth asked.

"Yes," Jared said. "But I owe Abaddon everything, and that's more important."

"So why didn't you tell us where Hades is?" Kristin snapped.

"He can't," Abaddon said absentmindedly. "There's a blood curse mark on his back, and it's linked to a bracelet he's no longer wearing because you took it from him. He can't tell you anything, because without them both he genuinely can't remember anything about it."

"So we need to get him a new bracelet," Kristin said.

"Doesn't work like that," Abaddon assured her. "Needs to be a specific bracelet with the exact runes on it. We'll just have to find them the hard way."

"What about Caleb?" Kristin asked. "Will you be using him to track down Hades and his people?"

Abaddon nodded. "Eventually, yes. They will come to me first, though. I've taken their home. I've killed their people. They will want revenge for that. In the meantime, Caleb is safely unconscious in the room at the rear of the jet. We captured him with ease outside of Red Rock. I think he wanted to be caught so that he could get to me."

Kristin looked over at the closed wooden door and felt a little uncomfortable having someone like him on the flight, although she didn't want Abaddon to know that. "Does he know his wife isn't dead?"

Elizabeth smiled. "We haven't spoken, so no. When the time comes, my ex-husband and I will talk, and he will realize exactly what he stands to gain by helping us."

"I'm curious about something," Kristin said. "What actually happened with you? I've read the police report. You died when your car left the road at high speed and ploughed into a tree. Nergal was furious because you were meant to be taken alive. Elias checked your pulse and breathing. He said you were dead, and if there's one thing that Elias was genuinely good at, it's knowing when someone is dead."

"I knew of Elias' plan," Abaddon said. "He was going to ram the car off the road, grab both Elizabeth and her new husband, and drag them to face Nergal. The speed limit was just over thirty due to road works in the area, and it was a wet night. Elizabeth's car was going three times that in an effort to trick Elias into thinking he'd been identified. They chased, and in the wet his car touched hers. The car was never supposed to go into the forest; she was meant to make the bridge, where the car would have lost control and gone over into the water below. I had people down there waiting.

"When Elias' car sped across the bridge alone, I knew something had happened, and so I went and found the car. Elizabeth was irrefutably dead. Her chest had been destroyed from the impact. All kinds of things inside her body that would have kept her alive had been torn apart. Immediate hospital care wouldn't have saved her."

"You healed her?"

"That's part of it, certainly. I used one of my stored spirits to heal her flesh, and then I reached out and took her spirit. The spirits of the dead hang around for a while before going wherever they go, so I had plenty of time. But there were two problems. One, the longer a spirit is out of the body, the more traumatic it is to put it back in. And two, when a person dies due to a violent act, be it murder or accident, their spirit is somewhat . . . tumultuous. Forcing it back into a body causes more psychological issues. I took her to my home in the eastern mountains of Siberia, where I was searching for blood elves."

"And you healed her back to health, and all lived happily ever after?" Kristin asked.

Abaddon laughed. "While there, it became apparent that the damage the accident had done was going to take more than my healing could offer. She was delirious most of the time, and barely spoke. I bonded her with a spirit scroll, and her body healed in its entirety in only a few days. Unfortunately, it did little for the state of her mind, which was quite fractured after putting several spirits inside of it. She needed time to learn, and she needed time to heal. Time we didn't have."

Kristin looked at Elizabeth, who stared out of the jet window. "What did they do to you?"

Elizabeth turned to Kristin and smiled. "Harbinger trials."

Kristin had heard of the trials before. They were an old Avalon secret. Once someone had reached a sufficient age and level of power, they were allowed to undergo the trials. They were placed in a comatose state and forced to live decades in their minds, while only a few months passed in real time. While comatose, they were made better, their use of their abilities became more powerful and focused, their bodies trained during the night when the mind slept. It was an incredibly dangerous thing to do to someone, even more so when the participant was only human up until a short time before.

"You're thinking me cruel for doing it," Abaddon said, noticing the expression of shock on Kristin's face.

"I think Elizabeth is lucky she isn't sitting in the corner lobotomized."

"A fair point," Abaddon said with a wave of her hand. "It was dangerous, but I had little choice. I enlisted a friend of mine to help maintain the constant psychic link necessary, and we set about molding her into the weapon we needed. She and the spirits lived their lives inside her head, eventually merging with her and forming a whole, and, more importantly, stable personality. She went through ten years of life in a year. It took her a while to get used to life outside of her head again, as it does for everyone who undertakes the trials."

"I am Elizabeth Cassidy," she said. "But I am not the same woman Caleb or my daughter would recognize."

"How do you think Caleb is going to react if the truth comes out?"

Elizabeth shrugged. "I do not care. I was afraid of him when I was married to him, but I knew how important his work was. I knew that Layla would need to be ready to face the enemies that his work would bring. Unfortunately, she has grown into someone who needs to recognize her position in this world and accept that Abaddon is going to win."

"And if she doesn't?" Kristin asked.

"Then I will kill her," Elizabeth said. "It's a mother's duty to take care of her children, after all."

Elizabeth's cold and detached tone made Kristin shiver inside. It wasn't a feeling she was used to.

"I make you uncomfortable," Elizabeth said.

Kristin nodded. She saw little point in lying about it. "A little. I'm more curious about how you're going to break the news to your husband that you're alive, well, and an umbra working with Abaddon."

For the first time since Kristin had met Elizabeth, real emotion showed in her eyes. "I don't know," she said. "There was a time when I was unsure how he would react to my appearance. There are memories of me loving him, but there are memories of me hating him too. I'm unsure whether I should kill him or be happy to see him."

Abaddon placed the ring that Caleb had been carrying on the table between her and Kristin. "When we found him, he had this in his pocket. I want you to take this to him."

Kristin stared at the ring. "What's the significance of the ring?"

"When I was reborn, the ring still connected with the old, dead me," Elizabeth said. "I've been wearing this since we took control of Caleb. It should give him the information he needs to realize I'm alive."

"And what then?" Kristin asked, looking between Elizabeth and Abaddon. "Because I'm thinking he's going to want to get to her, and we're on a jet, thousands of feet in the air. I'd rather he didn't cause a commotion up here."

"There are runes drawn on his chest that render him unconscious," Jared said. "They take a while to prepare, and they don't last forever, but he'll be out for a few hours yet. And he's wearing a sorcerer's band. He's no threat."

"You clearly haven't read his file. Or seen what he did to Cody."

"He scares you," Elizabeth said.

"Concerns me," Kristin corrected. "He's a noted serial killer, with hundreds of victims. He has no qualms about murdering anyone in his way, and that more than likely includes anyone standing between him and you. You want him to work for you, and with you, and hunt people down so you can kill them, but I'm not sure he's a work with people kind of person. Nergal never understood that, and I don't think I did to begin with. But after seeing how he acted with his own daughter, I'm sure there's no one on this earth who can force him to do anything he doesn't want to do."

"He'll come around," Abaddon said.

"That's what Nergal said," Kristin told her, noticing the irritation on Abaddon's face at being compared to him. "I don't think he will. He will, however, eventually escape, or try to escape and kill a bunch of people. His file said he killed over a dozen men in the first prison he was put in."

"He never tried to escape from jail," Elizabeth said.

"He never had reason to. His wife was dead, his kid didn't give a shit, and he had hundreds of the type of criminals he used to prey on within a few hundred feet. He escaped from his cell a dozen times just to go kill someone, before they finally put him in solitary in a prison designed to minimize his powers."

"He's not your problem," Abaddon said, making it clear that the conversation about him was over. "We're going to burn Nergal's whole operation to the ground."

Kristin had to admit she didn't mind the sound of that.

"Every last piece of it," Abaddon confirmed.

A short time later the jet landed on a runway full of Abaddon's blood elves fighting Nergal's loyal defense. Kristin knew for a fact that most of Nergal's people were highly trained warriors, but they were being easily slaughtered.

"This is what happens when the attack is a surprise," Elizabeth said. "We had several hundred blood elves among Nergal's forces inside the compound just waiting for their chance to butcher Nergal's people. They spent years together, but the blood elves care little for such things. As soon as I sent word to their commander that we were on our way, they turned on those who had been comrades."

"They won't stay surprised for long," Kristin pointed out.

"Long enough to get what we need," Abaddon told her as the jet door was lowered and the sounds of battle drifted through the opening.

The pilot came out of the cockpit, explaining that they needed to refuel.

"I'll ensure that's possible," Abaddon said. "My blood elves will clear the runway of Nergal's forces so you have time to do what you need."

Kristin stepped out of the jet and watched as those loyal to Nergal were cut down.

"We had to make sure the airfield was ours," Abaddon said. "The main attack will be much harder, but we're not here for that."

"The umbra," Kristin said. "They'll be in this wing of the compound. There's a door there that will need to be bypassed, along with security."

"But you know the codes for such things, yes?" Abaddon asked.

Kristin was aware that she was only there to help Abaddon get what she wanted from Nergal's compound. She wondered if Abaddon would have helped her if she wasn't useful to her plans to destroy her enemy. Probably not, she decided. Kristin looked over at Abaddon and Elizabeth as they spoke in whispers, and she knew that they'd kill her the moment they had a chance, especially once they discovered her clone had failed. That meant Kristin had to figure a way out of this predicament without causing the power of Abaddon to come crashing down on her head.

She walked with Abaddon, Jared, and Elizabeth into the hangar, ignoring the stench of blood and death that hung around after the short-lived battle. Blood elves approached Abaddon, and Kristin took that moment to walk away down a corridor, creating a clone of herself and leaving her in there as she ducked into an empty room.

"What are you doing?" Jared called from behind Kristin's clone. Her eyes were a different color, but Kristin hoped that no one was paying much attention.

"Checking for survivors," the clone said.

"Well, we're going to the main compound. There are miles and miles of buildings to search, and you know it better than us, so can you leave this to the blood elves?"

The clone shrugged and followed Jared without complaint. Kristin slipped out of a window and hurried around to the side of the building where she watched Abaddon and her entourage set off toward the main complex a few thousand feet in the distance. The sounds of battle were easily recognizable, and she wondered how the blood elves would do against the majority of Nergal's forces. It would certainly be a much closer fight.

When she was certain she'd put enough distance between the two of them, she created a further seven clones and told them to search out enemy placements and relay the information back to her. Something felt wrong about everything that happened.

After her clones had walked off to fulfill her orders, Kristin ran back across the runway to the jet, discovering two dead members of Abaddon's crew inside the fuselage and Caleb sitting in one of the chairs with a bottle of vodka and a single glass. He pointed a gun at Kristin and motioned for her to sit down.

"Me and you, we're going to have a chat," he told her.

"I thought you were unconscious; there's a rune or something," she said.

"The man who put the rune on me worked for Nergal," Caleb confirmed. "Apparently, he wasn't thrilled about Abaddon wiping out the people he liked. Or you killing his boss."

"Your wife is alive," she said, taking a seat and placing the ring that Abaddon had given her on the table between them. It wasn't like she had unlimited options.

"She's not my wife," he told her, raising his hand toward Kristin, showing the lack of sorcerer's band. "The pilot had the key."

Caleb picked the ring up, his eyes turning white for an instant before going back to normal. "Nope. She's got my wife's body, but whatever is inside of her is no longer the Elizabeth I knew. They killed her, took her spirit and forced it back into her body. She's a revenant now, a revenant with the powers of an umbra, and the training of a harbinger."

"You heard everything?"

Caleb stood up and knocked back a vodka. "I also know that Nergal didn't order your death. I heard Jared talking to the pilots about it."

Kristin nodded. She had suspected as much for a few days and had originally been angry with herself for falling for Abaddon's lies. "I figured as much. She set me up thinking I'd help her."

"You tried to kill my daughter."

"She got in the way."

Caleb nodded. "Because, frankly, I don't want to waste any more bullets, and you're probably more useful alive than dead, this is the only time we'll meet and you don't die." He pointed at the two men, both of whom had bullet wounds to the throat. "Shot them when you went into the building. Abaddon is playing you, and me. I'm going to go after her for what she did to Elizabeth."

"What am I meant to do?" Kristin asked.

Caleb motioned toward the seat opposite him. "Sit and don't get in my way."

Once Kristin had sat down, Caleb left the jet. She poured herself a glass of vodka and knocked it back. So many of the people in the compound wanted to kill one another, and most of them were a thorn in Kristin's side, or could soon become one. Maybe today was going to turn out well, after all.

26

Half a dozen black Audi SUVs drove through the State of Texas toward their destination: Nergal's compound. Unfortunately, the moment that they saw the pillars of smoke coming out of the compound, it became quickly apparent that Abaddon's forces were already trying to burn the whole place down.

"You ready?" Chloe asked from beside Layla.

The SUVs had modified interiors so that two rows of up to three people could face one another in the back. There wasn't a lot of boot-space, but seeing how everyone was already wearing rune-inscribed combat armor and most were carrying at least one type of weapon, the roomier seating space made more sense.

Layla nodded. "My father is in there somewhere. Abaddon's people took him outside of Red Rock and I plan on finding him."

"And Jared?" Remy asked from next to Chloe.

"We'll see what happens with that little toad," she said, gaining a smile from Sky and Diana sitting opposite her.

The remaining journey was done in silence, until the convoy drove through a pair of ruined gates and halted as gunfire smashed into the side of the reinforced doors. A group of soldiers were firing semi-automatic weapons at them. The glass spiderwebbed from the impact, but didn't shatter.

Layla wrapped her power around the door and tore it free from its hinges. She pushed it out in front of them like a shield as everyone got out and huddled behind the SUV next to her. Layla gathered as much power as possible and threw it all into the door as she flung it at the soldiers with terrifying force. The makeshift weapon slammed into them, bowling over anyone who hadn't moved.

Several of Hades' force took the opportunity to deal with the other soldiers, while Layla pointed toward the large number of steps leading up into an almost cathedral-like building at their top. There were no soldiers on the stairs, but there wasn't anywhere for anyone to hide if some happened to appear.

Layla, Chloe, Sky, Remy, Diana, Tommy, and Zamek all ran up the stairs as quickly as they could, waiting at the top while a second group, including Irkalla, made the journey to join them. Once the group of over twenty soldiers had gathered at the mouth of the building, Layla wrapped her power around the metal door and threw it into the room beyond.

"You're getting good at that," Remy said as the soldiers entered the room first. There was gunfire, and then a shout of "All clear!" from one of them.

The rest of the group moved into the room and discovered it had a high ceiling and huge, stained-glass windows.

"What is the stained glass depicting?" Remy asked.

"Nergal," Irkalla said, in a tone that suggested she was less than surprised to see her ex-husband had portrayed himself in stained glass.

"In that window, he's a king with his people bowing before him," Diana said.

"I know this has probably been said a lot over the centuries," Remy said, "but he really was a massive bellend, wasn't he?"

Irkalla raised an eyebrow in question.

"A very British way of calling someone a dick," Chloe clarified.

"Yes, yes he was," Irkalla said.

The soldiers opened the two doors at the end of the chamber and stormed into the rooms beyond, preceded by more gunfire. They moved from room to room until they came to a large courtyard with half a dozen identical doors on either side of it, and another three opposite where Layla stood. The doors were Gothic in design, and the courtyard was paved with white brick. The lack of roof meant that the sounds of battle were easy to hear.

"It's like Nergal recreated the Coliseum, but made it really Gothic," Chloe said. "It's a bit weird."

"We'll take the left, you the right," Diana said, pointing to the soldiers and Sky. "We're all wearing mics, so stay in contact."

The groups split, with Chloe, Diana, Remy, Tommy, Zamek, and Layla taking the first door that led to a long empty corridor with another door at the end of it.

"This is becoming more and more maze-like," Tommy said. "I'm beginning to wish we'd brought a ball of wool or something in case we get lost."

Tommy's joke made Layla smile and eased some of the tension. She looked back as the rest of the group split into their various teams. They hoped that a small force could get in and out with what they needed, while Abaddon's and Nergal's forces kept one another busy. Layla just hoped they stayed that way until they had the chance to get out again in one piece.

The door at the end of the corridor opened into a large room with yet more doors.

"This is getting silly," Diana said. She took another step, pulled the tactical vest she was wearing over her head, and turned into her werebear form, her other clothes shredding as she did. She sniffed the air. "Those two are empty," she said, her voice a low rumble. She kicked open the closest door, causing it to disintegrate from the impact, to show them the empty room behind it.

The next door was the same, but the last two doors both opened into stairwells, one going up, and the other down.

"I'll go up," Layla said.

"I'll join you," Tommy told her. "Zamek, you care to help out?"

Zamek cracked his knuckles and drew his battle-ax. "I've been waiting all day for this."

The other three went downstairs, and Layla, Tommy, and Zamek took their time ascending, pausing outside the door at the top of the staircase. Tommy counted down on his fingers from three to one, before opening the door and revealing a huge hallway.

"This man liked his pomp," Zamek said, pointing toward the dozen suits of armor that stood at attention along the hallway. A red-and-white rug on top of a black-and-white carpet ran the length of the hall, and the windows along one side looked down over the rear of the compound and across dozens of smaller buildings. The compound looked big enough that some might have called it a town.

"This was built with alchemy," Zamek said, sounding angry. "I can sense it. It's everywhere. Dwarves built this place."

Tommy stood beside Layla. "There's a runway over there," he said, pointing. "The Hercules and Black Hawks will meet us there, but we'll need to clear it for them once we're done here." He looked back at Zamek. "You think the dwarves are prisoners?"

"I don't know of any dwarves who would have willingly helped Nergal and his people, but then I can't speak for all dwarves. It's perfectly reasonable to assume that some will see his way as the right way. That some will ally themselves with the bastards who caused us to lose our own realm. It's unforgivable, but reasonable to assume."

"How are we going to get the umbra out?" Layla asked.

"That depends on their number," Tommy said. "Hopefully, we can commandeer transport for them. That hangar at the side of the runway looks big enough to house some impressively-sized planes."

"One thing at a time," Layla said. "I know."

"There are three doors up here," Zamek said. "I say we each try a door and see where they go. Then we're not far away from one another if it turns out we've opened a door into hell or something."

"A door into hell would be a step up right now," Tommy said, placing his finger to his ear. He said little, but the expression on his face told the story.

"How many dead?" Layla said when Tommy lowered his arm.

"Hades found a building not far from this one, and in the rear of it, a prison. There are hundreds of bodies. Diana said maybe five hundred people are buried in the pit at the back. She thinks they were all umbra who didn't accept their powers or refused to deal with what they'd become."

"Damn him," Layla said softly. "Let's just get what we need and leave. This place makes my skin crawl."

Tommy and Zamek walked over to their doors, which were close to one another on one side of the hallway, while Layla's was on the other side. She opened her door without pausing and found a room full of old weaponry and armor. Most of it hung on the walls, but there were pieces on mannequins that made Layla double-check to make sure they weren't real.

She turned back to Tommy and Zamek as several orange marble-sized balls landed on the rug between them. She didn't even have time to shout a warning before they exploded. Layla was flung back into the doorway as the ceiling between her and her friends collapsed, making it impossible to get to them.

Layla's ears rang and her head felt dizzy as dust clouded her vision. She blinked and looked around as a golf ball-sized red marble stopped at her feet. She had the wherewithal to use her power to drag the metal armor in front of her. It shielded her from most of the blast, but it was still powerful enough to throw her through the window behind her.

She fell twenty feet onto the roof of a much smaller building below. She landed on her back, feeling several ribs pop, and slid down the roof tiles, unable to stop until she managed to turn a suit of armor that had fallen with her into an anchor. She wrapped a part of it around herself and stuck the rest firmly into the roof.

For the first time, she realized that she couldn't hear anything, but unfortunately Layla had bigger issues to deal with. Her legs dangled off the side of the building, and she looked down to see that it was a good forty feet to the ground below. The towering building that she'd been blown out of stretched another hundred feet above her, and she could smell the stench of burning wood and plastic.

She grabbed hold of the hastily made chain and pulled herself up onto the roof, stopping only when she reached its peak and could finally lie down to rest. She removed the earpiece and tossed it aside after discovering a crack in its casing. It was pretty much useless to her now. And it wasn't like she would hear anything even if it did work. Her body was already healing any internal damage, but it would take time before she was back to full health; time she probably didn't have.

She didn't see Jared jump from the shattered window above, but she felt the impact on the roof as he landed a dozen feet from her. She looked up at him and saw his lips move, and a hot rage filled her. What had once been the face of someone she cared about, someone she thought cared about her, was now the face of her enemy, a face of lies and betrayal. Layla had wondered how she'd feel seeing Jared again. As it turned out, all she really wanted to do was break his jaw.

The ringing in her ears hadn't quite stopped. She tapped her ears to indicate that she couldn't understand a word he was saying and wondered whether or not she was meant to care anyway.

"I said," he shouted, the words getting through to Layla as her ears repaired themselves, "that I'm glad to have found you."

"You lied to me about everything."

"That is true. I did."

"You made me think you had feelings for me." In that moment, she wasn't sure she'd ever been so angry with someone she'd cared about. She sucked down the hurt and pain, the feeling of shame that she hadn't seen through his lies. She took it all and turned it to rage. She wasn't going to let him manipulate her emotions ever again.

Jared smiled. "That was my job. I wasn't meant to get into a relationship with you; it just seemed like the easiest thing to do when it became apparent that you liked me. If it's any consolation, I quite enjoyed playing the part of your boyfriend."

Layla looked beyond Jared and tried to figure out if, in her injured state, she could get to him and throw him off the roof before he overpowered her. "So, what's your play? You going to take me to Abaddon?"

"That's up to you. If you don't think you can behave, I'm happy to drag your corpse over to her, too. Your father will help us either way. He's here, by the way. Hopefully where I left him, but who knows with your dad, am I right? I'll give you one chance to behave your blasted self, or I'll kill you and be done with it. Doesn't bother me one way or the other."

"If you can't kill him, I'll be happy to," Terhal said from beside Layla. "I can peel the skin from his body."

Layla shook her head. She didn't trust herself to speak; she didn't want words to just tumble out of her mouth, to scream at Jared about how she felt. She wanted to show him.

A huge explosion tore through one of the buildings close by, and the power of it threw debris high into the sky, scattering it all over the massive courtyard below them. It took Jared's attention away for just a second and gave Layla the chance to turn the metal anchor into a pad around her shoulder and arm and then launch herself into Jared's stomach.

The pair fell from the roof. Layla headbutted him, changing the metal into a chain that hooked into the brick wall. The momentum carried Layla toward the building, and before she could do anything to stop it, she crashed through a window. She landed on a table and rolled over it onto several chairs before hitting the hardwood floor.

She exhaled and wished she hadn't. Pain wracked her body, and it took a count of thirty to realize that she was in a classroom. There was a whiteboard on the far wall next to the window she'd destroyed. The desk she'd slammed into looked like one she'd had back in her childhood school. And there were a dozen small tables and chairs facing the whiteboard. There were no drawings or pictures on the walls, only a map of the world with various parts of it circled in red pen.

Layla got to her feet and, after managing to stay upright, got closer to the map. The red circles didn't seem to have any real pattern to them, but she saw one in Red Rock and wondered if they were realm gate locations. If so, there were hundreds of them all over the globe.

"You sow," Jared said from the open doorway. Blood covered half of his face, and he limped as he stepped into the room.

"Feeling pained?" Layla asked.

Jared's face changed; his eyes turned deep red, and the skin around them went orange and started cracking, as if the power inside was forcing itself out. His hands became claw-like, with talons replacing fingernails, and two huge horns grew out of his head. He charged Layla, picked her up and ran with her into and through the exterior wall behind them. They fell ten feet to the ground with Jared on top, who then threw a punch at Layla's head, which she caught in her own taloned hand.

Layla kicked drenik-Jared in the stomach, sending him sprawling, and got to her feet. She'd allowed Terhal to take control of her body the second Jared had grabbed hold of her. Now, like him, her eyes were red and the cracked skin on her body glowed orange. She reached up and tapped the ridge of hardened bone that ran the circumference of her head. That was new.

"So, the bond between us is strengthening," Terhal said. "That's nice to know."

Layla activated the ring on her finger and she felt her power vanish, but drenik-Jared continued unaffected. Layla immediately switched the ring off.

Drenik-Jared was already back on his feet, throwing ball after ball of orange explosives at Terhal, who gathered metal from the legs of the tables and chairs around the room for a shield. She was considerably more powerful in their merged form, but that power wouldn't last long. She had to make it count.

Drenik-Jared threw a dozen small explosive balls at her, and Terhal flung herself aside. She wrapped her power around the door of a nearby car and threw it at her opponent as he dove through the window after her. Jared managed to avoid it at the last second before it smashed into the wall with enough force that it disintegrated in a cloud of red brick dust.

Terhal used the distraction to get in close, smashing her fist into drenik-Jared's stomach and following up with a knee to his face. He grabbed hold of Terhal's foot and dragged her off balance, punching her in the stomach as she fell toward him. Drenik-Jared stood and grabbed Terhal's hair, intending to pull her up to face him, but he didn't get a good enough hold, and Terhal twisted aside, pushing his hand away and whipping her head up as quickly as possible, cracking Jared on the nose with the back of her skull.

In response, Jared smashed Terhal face first into the wall before darting away to put distance between them.

Terhal dropped to the ground, feeling the blood stream from her busted nose, but had no time to think as several marbles dropped beside her and exploded before she could use any metal to shield herself.

Drenik-Jared stood above her, a triumphant look on his face. "I beat you," he said, spitting blood onto the ground. "I assume you're not going to give in?"

Terhal was about to reply when there was another huge explosion from behind her. She turned and watched in horror as a third explosion blew out the side of a nearby building. Black smoke billowed from the gaping hole. A helicopter that had been too close was caught up in the blast and began to fall toward Terhal, flame trailing from the tail rotor.

"I'll leave you to this," Jared said, having shed his drenik form. He kicked Terhal once in the face and ran away.

Rage tore through Terhal's mind and she reached out with all of the power at her disposal. She couldn't stop the helicopter from falling; she didn't have enough power for such a large machine moving so fast. Instead, she adjusted its position, moving just the nose of the helicopter so that it fell straight down, slamming into the ground. The metal frame of the craft bent and broke with an ear-splitting noise. It exploded a second later, raining pieces of metal all around. Terhal managed to deflect anything coming her way, and then looked over at Jared, who just stood there, smiling.

Part of the main rotor tore free and Terhal moved it, mid-flight, toward Jared with enough speed and power that he had no hope of avoiding it. The rotor hit him in the chest like a spear, throwing him back and pinning him to the wall.

Terhal got to her feet and walked toward him. When she was close enough, she allowed Layla to take back control. "You won't die," she told him.

Jared looked up and opened his mouth to speak, but only blood came out.

Layla nodded. "Not silver, so you won't die, but I bet it hurts like hell."

Dozens of marbles dropped from Jared's open hands onto the floor beside Layla, who sprinted away before they exploded. Jared vanished as part of the building collapsed on him.

"You think he's dead?" Rosa asked.

Layla wasn't sure. She took a step toward the rubble and heard the shouts of combat further inside the compound. She couldn't search the rubble for Jared and go help her friends. She sprinted off toward the sounds of fighting. If Jared wasn't dead, she was certain she'd get a second try later.

27

Layla discovered that the sounds of fighting belonged to Abaddon's and Nergal's people trying to kill one another. Layla ignored them and continued on, avoiding large groups of soldiers from both sides, who were mostly too interested in killing each other to bother with her. She only had to dispatch one blood elf who decided to come at her with a sword. She took it from him mid-swing and threw it back into his skull as he turned to run. She was in no mood to play nice.

She didn't know where any of her allies were, and she was in enemy territory. Her options weren't exactly brilliant, and she half expected to run into Abaddon at any moment. Layla's only thought was to find her friends and make sure they were okay. She opened a set of doors and discovered only dead blood elves and soldiers. Scorch marks littered the walls and ceiling of the room, and more than one blood elf had been burned so badly it looked like it had been in a furnace.

She opened the only door leading from the room and stepped into a huge hall, which had a table that ran its length. Dozens of chairs had been destroyed in the fighting. Bodies littered the floor and the stench of blood and death was so thick Layla had to take a moment and center herself so she wouldn't vomit.

Tommy and Zamek burst through the doors, both covered in blood and sporting a few injuries. Tommy had removed his armor and was bare-chested, his trousers ripped. He'd turned into his werebeast form at some point.

"Did you do this?" Tommy asked, pointing to the bodies.

"They were like that when I got here," Layla told him. "Jared is out of the picture."

"He's dead?"

"I'm not sure. He got impaled by a helicopter rotor, and then a building fell on him. You look like you had fun." She expected to feel sorrow for what had happened to Jared, but she just hoped that his physical pain matched how he'd made her feel with his betrayal.

"Nergal's people still don't like us, despite him being dead," Zamek said.

"You heard from the others?" Layla asked.

"They're meeting over by the domed building close to the runway. I've heard they found a lot of blank scrolls there," Tommy said. "We were trying to get you on your comm earpiece."

"It broke, so I threw it away," she said. "You see the explosions earlier?"

Tommy nodded. "No idea what happened there, but hopefully it did something awful to our enemies."

The three of them left the building only to run into a large number of blood elves, who were searching for survivors.

"Well, shit," Tommy said, transforming into his werewolf beast form and charging into the pack of blood elves. Zamek waded through what remained, killing several before they had a chance to fight back.

Layla stood for a moment, reached out with her power, and found each and every blade that had been dropped by its dead owner. She wrapped her power around them all and flung them at the mass of blood elves. Dozens of weapons found homes in the flesh of their enemies, and half a dozen blood elves fell at once.

"Move," Layla shouted to Tommy and Zamek, who did exactly as she suggested just before she flung a second round of weapons into the remaining blood elves. Those still alive turned to run and found themselves between a rock and hard place, as Irkalla, Diana, Sky, Chloe, and Remy stood in their way. The thirty or so remaining blood elves were decimated in minutes.

Hades and Persephone walked out of a nearby building after two sorcerers. Hades avoided a jet of flame, moved closer, and touched one of the sorcerers on the chest. A second later the sorcerer fell to his knees as Persephone opened the ground up beneath the second sorcerer, crushing him as he fell in.

"Have I ever said how scary they are?" Chloe asked Layla as Olivia joined the group.

"I think it could stand to be repeated," Layla told her. "You okay?"

Chloe nodded. "You?"

"I'll be fine."

"She maimed Jared," Zamek said.

Layla explained what had happened.

"You pinned him to a wall with a rotor blade?" Remy asked.

"I didn't have a lot of other choices at the time," Layla said. "He was trying to kill me."

"Even so, that's badass. Remind me not to piss you off."

Layla smiled. "I'm sure that's advice you'd only ignore."

"True, but that's because I'm clearly more awesome to have around than Jared." Remy placed a paw on her hand. "I'm sorry about what you had to do. That must have sucked huge amounts of balls."

Layla laughed. "You have a way with words, Remy. A terrifying way, but a way nonetheless."

Remy winked.

"What's the plan?" Tommy asked Olivia. He'd turned back into his human form, and she walked over and kissed him without a word.

"This place is a torture factory," Irkalla said. "They experiment on people—both human and otherwise. I had no idea Nergal had gone this far. He was trying to find the perfect candidate to turn into an umbra."

"There are several buildings we haven't searched," Hades said. "And the fighting appears to be centralized to the west and south sides of the compound. I say we look east, at that large building over there. It has several floors and is quite close to the runway. Hopefully, we'll find some more scrolls, or more of the umbra we came for. The umbra we have found, we've sent to the Hercules on the runway."

"How many?" Layla asked.

"Several dozen at the moment," Olivia said.

Everyone set off together and were soon joined by a company of Hades' security force who had been clearing out several of the smaller buildings. They included Commander Fenix and Kase, the former of whom nodded hello to Layla. He told her that the explosions had been caused when a sorcerer had used a glyph to blow himself up with his own magic. It was an act that several of them had used in the past and was one of the ways Arthur and his people were able to convince humanity of the threat of his enemies and use their fear to come to power. To have humanity welcome them with open arms.

Layla happened to glance over at a single-story building that was several hundred feet long, and saw her father go inside. "I'll catch you up," she told Kase and Chloe, who were beside her.

"Layla, what's wrong?" Kase asked as Layla began to head toward the building in question.

"My father went in there," she told them, feeling apprehensive about whatever was going to happen once she confronted him.

"What's your plan?" Chloe asked.

"Take him down, bring him to the runway. Hopefully he'll surrender."

"Is that likely?" Fenix asked.

"I have no idea," Layla told him.

"You want backup?" Kase asked.

Layla shook her head. "I need to do this alone. He won't hurt me."

"You sure?" Chloe asked, not a hundred percent certain about that.

Layla nodded. "Give me five minutes and then, if I'm not out, come get me."

Kase and Chloe looked at each other, but nodded. "Three minutes," Chloe said, passing Layla a new earpiece. "I had a spare. Stay in contact."

"If you're not out by then, my parents will drag you out," Kase told her. "No arguments."

Layla sprinted across the open space, almost barging through the door, into a long, empty chamber where floor-to-ceiling red and black drapes covered the tall windows, bathing the room in gloom.

"Hello, Layla," Caleb said. He sat on a chair at the far end of the chamber, two dead men at his feet. He dropped a bloody knife onto the floor, making enough noise for Layla to hope that no one else came to see what the problem was.

Layla tapped her earpiece. "I don't think my dad is in the kind of mood to come quietly."

"We'll be there," Chloe said.

Caleb started to get up, but Layla wrapped the metal in the chair legs around his arms, dragging him to a kneeling position on the floor. "We wait," she told him.

"Whatever you wish," Caleb said with a smile.

The rest of the team burst through the doors behind Layla. "Are you okay?" Chloe asked Layla, who nodded.

"Do you know where Abaddon is?" Irkalla asked.

"Dad?" Layla said.

"Sorry. No idea. She really wants to tear this whole place down, though." Caleb looked over at Layla. "We have things we need to talk about."

"You guys go, I'll stay," Layla said. "I need to talk to him."

Chloe sat on a chair next to her. "Don't you dare tell me to go, too," she said. "It's not happening."

"Get what you need, then meet us at the airfield," Hades said. "If we're not there when you arrive, wait. Don't split up again. I'd rather we didn't hang around."

"Be careful," Layla said.

"You, too," Persephone told her. "Irkalla, you feel like staying here and helping?"

Irkalla picked up a chair and sat down.

Layla waited until everyone had gone before she relaxed the bonds keeping her father in place. "You're coming with us," she told him.

"Just so you know, your mother is alive. Sort of."

Layla didn't remember sitting down, but the next thing she knew, she was. "What?" Her emotions ran from disbelief to confusion, and then finally settled on anger. "Don't you dare start making up shit about her."

"Abaddon found your dead mother, forced her spirit back into her body, and then made her an umbra. She looks like your mom, but . . . but she isn't."

"Abaddon did that?" Layla asked, not wanting to believe him. "Why? How?"

"The *how* is because she's a powerful necromancer. The *why*? I don't know. But I am going to kill her for it."

"Is that how you deal with people who hurt you?" Chloe asked, taking a seat beside Layla and holding her hand.

"It's what I'm good at. Killing my enemies is the best way for me to get the job done."

"You won't kill Abaddon," Irkalla said.

"I'll try."

"You are an arrogant little prick," Chloe snapped.

"You are not the first one to tell me this," Caleb said. "I am sorry for all the hurt you've gone through in the last few days. It seems that removing me from prison was meant to go a lot smoother than this."

"Good people died because of you," Layla said. "Don't belittle them."

"I'm not," Caleb said with a slight sigh. "One thing you should understand, though: your mother, Elizabeth, she knew all about my crimes. She was scared of me, yes, scared that I'd go too far and kill an innocent, but she always helped me cover up what I did. Helped me remove evidence and gave me alibis if needed. She wasn't innocent; she just didn't wield the deathblow herself. Honestly, I think she found it a little exciting to be married to someone like me."

"You liar," Layla shouted, almost jumping to her feet with fury.

"I'm not, Layla. You were young, but you can remember your mother telling you to say I'd been there when I hadn't, wanting your help to move things. The amount of time you spent digging up the back garden with her."

Layla opened her mouth to argue, but found that she couldn't. She remembered little things her mom had done, things that over the years she had ignored, but looking back they now felt like things that might add up to something unpleasant. Layla remembered finding blood-stained clothes, and her mom telling her that her father had cut himself, but that he was okay. She remembered whispered conversations, remembered her mom telling her not to go into her father's locked room; but then seeing her mother go in and out of there herself. "You were both monsters." The realization of those words threatened to push Layla over the edge, and she leaned up against the wall, feeling as though the weight of the world were pushing her down.

"Yes, to one degree or another. Your mother was a good woman, though. I loved her very much. This new version of her is not your mother. She will kill you. I'm sure you'll be seeing her before long."

"You didn't know all this time?"

Caleb shook his head. "Sorry. Wish I had—I'd have broken out and dealt with it. Did you kill Jared?"

Layla shook her head.

"Hard to kill people you care about, isn't it? Even when that person betrays you. My uncle betrayed me when I was only twelve. He attacked a woman in our street. I thought he was this awesome guy who would never hurt anyone, but I found out that he was just a thug. He got away with what he'd done. Not enough proof, they said, even though they had evidence. He was my first kill. I was fifteen. I beat him to death with a metal bar while he slept. I found out he was friends with the arresting officer, and that certain items of evidence had vanished. The cop was my second kill."

"And it never ended," Chloe said.

"It probably never will," Caleb told her, before looking at Layla. "Good to see you again."

Layla re-formed his metal restraints. "No more chances, no more games. I'm done with this shit."

Caleb beamed as if proud of his daughter.

The door to the building burst open and Kristin entered, firing a rifle. Layla stopped most of the bullets mid-flight, flinging them back at her, riddling her with her own ammunition. Layla saw another Kristin creep slowly outside of the building; she also had a rifle slung over her shoulder.

"We'll be right back," Layla told Irkalla, who nodded.

Chloe motioned for Layla to move to the rear window and climb out. When Layla opened the window, it made a squeaking noise and the Kristin who was outside spun around toward her, rifle raised high. Chloe dove through the window onto Kristin, tackling her to the ground, and then kicked the rifle away.

Four of Kristin's clones appeared around Chloe and began stamping on her as Layla charged forward, smashing her forearm into the face of the Kristin she'd tackled to the ground: the original Kristin. One of the clones vanished as Layla followed the hit with a knee to Kristin's gut, before smashing her face into the brick wall.

Layla went to use her ring, but Kristin blocked her hand and punched her in the kneecap, dropping Layla to one knee, where Kristin applied a quick arm bar, threatening to snap Layla's limb.

After finally getting to her feet, Chloe blasted the nearest clone in the chest with enough power to put a giant hole where her heart should be. A second blast was aimed at the original Kristin's head, but Kristin released Layla, rolled to her feet and fled.

"I'll get her," Layla said, already giving chase as Chloe dealt with the last two clones.

Layla tackled Kristin to the ground, where she smashed her forehead onto the concrete, giving Layla time to straddle Kristin's back and rain down punch after punch on the back of her head and neck.

Kristin's body began to change as she allowed the drenik to take control, but Layla rolled off and used the ring on her finger. Suddenly, she lost her power. But thankfully so did Kristin, judging from the confusion on her face as the other clones vanished. Just in time, as Layla saw several blood elves join the fight against Chloe.

"I'm going to tear that damn thing off," Kristin snapped.

Layla motioned for Kristin to come try.

Kristin roared with fury as she ran toward the younger woman. Layla blocked her punch, grabbed her wrist and stepped in, twisting to lift Kristin off her feet and dump her on the ground.

Layla kept hold of Kristin's wrist and broke it at the joint, ignoring her opponents' scream of pain as she wrenched back on the elbow joint until she heard it crack.

Layla released the limb and drove her knee into the side of Kristin's head. Kristin rolled to her side, her ear bleeding, and Layla punted her in the ribs with as much power as she had. She did it a second time as Kristin tried to crawl away toward a dagger that she'd dropped.

"You want this?" Layla asked, picking up the sliver dagger and turning back to a still prone Kristin.

"Bitch," Jared screamed as dozens of marble explosives suddenly littered the ground near her and Kristin. The bombs sizzled and vanished the second they touched the field of powerlessness that surrounded Layla.

Layla ignored the seriously injured Kristin and sprinted toward Jared, who was limping badly and still bleeding from the horrific wounds he'd sustained earlier. He looked like something out of a zombie movie that just wouldn't die. The marbles in his hand disintegrated as Layla got closer and panic hit his face. The look didn't last long as he threw a weak punch at Layla, who easily avoided it before driving the dagger up under his chin and into his skull, killing him instantly. She pushed Jared away and noticed that she was covered in his blood. It was all too much, and she spun back to Kristin with thoughts of rage, but discovered her gone. She searched around, expecting to see her wounded frame limping off, but Kristin was nowhere to be found.

28

Kristin was seriously hurt, and she knew it. Even when she was out of range of Layla's blasted ring, her body was going to need a lot of time to heal itself. Time she didn't have.

She limped along and spotted several blood elves coming toward her, each of them bloody from battle. She instructed one of them to give her a silver dagger before ordering them to stop Layla from following her, so that she could report back to Abaddon. They did as they were commanded, and Kristin wondered just how much time she'd bought herself.

She made it to the building beside the runway, just able to stay upright without swaying, but she was still forced to stop every few steps and cough. She was bringing up a lot of blood.

Kristin leaned against the wall to rest for just a moment as a Hercules sped past her and took off at the end of the runway. It started to climb until a blast of energy leapt up from the ground and smashed into the plane's engine and wing, causing them to explode. The Hercules continued to gain altitude as a second bolt of power smashed into its rear stabilizer. It lost control and plummeted toward the ground, just out of sight. The explosion lit up the sky and thick black smoke billowed into the air.

For a moment, Kristin stared in disbelief; she'd seen some unbelievable things since becoming an umbra, but nothing quite like that. She couldn't imagine just how much power it must have taken to bring down an aircraft of that size. She looked over to where the energy had come from and found Abaddon walking across the tarmac toward her.

"You did that?" Kristin said, still partially impressed at the enormous display of power. Another part of her, a part she tried to ignore, was telling her to run, to get as far away from Abaddon as she could. Kristin knew that was pointless. This was where her path had taken her, and this was where she would see it through, no matter how it ended.

"I killed an oni," Abaddon said. "Needed to get rid of the power from its spirit somehow."

Kristin noticed her bloody hands for the first time and a need for answers crept up inside her. "Did you set me up?"

"Excuse me?" Abaddon asked, incredulous that someone would take such a tone with her.

"With Nergal? Did he really try to kill me, or did you just set it up so I'd betray him?"

Abaddon laughed as if she'd been told something hysterical.

Fury at being mocked filled Kristin and she dove for Abaddon, driving the silver blade toward her stomach. "Don't you dare laugh at me," Kristin screamed at the necromancer. "No one gets to laugh at me."

Abaddon punched her in the face, sending Kristin to the ground. She kicked her in the ribs, before picking the silver dagger from the tarmac and tossing it further away. "Yes, I set you up," Abaddon told her. "You were wasted working with Nergal. He didn't value your contribution, he didn't care that you had so much more to give. He just used you as an extra body, and when he eventually got tired of you, he was going to discard you like he has so many others."

"He treated me like dirt," Kristin said. "You didn't have to lie to me. You could have just told me that you wanted me to help you."

"I had to know that you would be loyal. Unfortunately, it seems you allow your anger to override your common sense."

"The clone died," Kristin said with a slight laugh, as she summoned three of her clones, who all appeared between her and Abaddon.

"The one you sent through the gate?" Abaddon asked, anger in her voice for the first time. "You didn't tell me."

"Wasn't sure how'd you'd take it. Jared is dead, too," Kristin said. "Most of Nergal's forces are dead. The umbra are missing."

"The umbra were on that Hercules, along with the scrolls. If I can't have them, no one else will." Abaddon took a step toward the clones. "As for these." Abaddon moved toward the first and blasted it in the face with her necromancy power. The clone died before it hit the ground, followed a moment later by the second as Abaddon tore out its throat. The third clone, Abaddon punched, knocking it to the ground; then she stamped on its knees, breaking its legs. The clone screamed in pain before it died.

Kristin lay back, expecting death.

"What are you doing?" Abaddon asked. "I'm not going to kill you. You're the first person to get close enough to stab me in hundreds of years. I'm sort of impressed. You'll have to re-earn my trust, but I don't really want to kill people who are useful to me. We can teach you how to make yourself even better: even more powerful. But you will have to prove yourself, too." Abaddon took several steps back.

Kristin's head started to swim, and a green fog swept over her body and inside her as she inhaled. The clone beside her died as nausea swept over her. "What the hell are you doing to me?"

"Not me," Abaddon said. "Elizabeth. You're going to prove yourself to me by killing her. You live, and you get to come back to the fold."

Elizabeth stepped in front of Kristin with a smile on her face. "I'm an umbra, remember? I can mess with people's heads. Head spinning, nausea, and weakness: it's all one big package of awfulness. Even Abaddon isn't immune to it."

Abaddon said. "She's my very own pestilence. Which is funny, because the last person who called themselves that was not someone I'd want to work with."

Kristin noticed that Abaddon had moved several feet further back than she had been only a few moments ago; Abaddon was going to let her die.

"You know when I said that I didn't care that you tried to kill my daughter?" Elizabeth asked Kristin. "Well, I lied. I did care. Cared very much. It filled my bones with rage and took everything I had not to tear your face off. She is my blood and she is not yours to kill."

"She's alive," Kristin said, her vision darkening as she found it harder and harder to think.

"My power renders people almost defenseless," Elizabeth said. "You should have just stayed loyal. Not questioned what we told you."

"I will," Kristin said, her voice barely above a whisper, but it felt as though each word boomed inside her head. Then the sickness vanished, but Kristin remained on the floor, panting as sweat drenched her body.

Elizabeth dropped a knife by Kristin's head. "Come kill me. See if you're good enough. I'll give you a chance."

Kristin got to her knees and picked up the knife. She tossed the leather sheath aside with shaking hands. "Give me a second," she said. "World still spinning." No one complained as Kristin stood and slowly walked away from Elizabeth. She looked back at Abaddon. "Why do this? Why not just kill me?"

Abaddon took a step toward Kristin. "This is more fun."

"Should have paid more attention to my clones," Kristin whispered as one of them appeared next to Abaddon and stabbed the necromancer over and over again in her side. Abaddon picked the clone up by its neck and crushed its skull before punching Kristin in the chest hard enough to collapse her sternum, sending her flying through the air to crash onto the runway.

"How dare you?" Abaddon screamed in rage, her face contorted with pain and fury. She walked over to Kristin, who struggled to breathe, and kicked her in the ribs over and over again, each blow breaking more bones as Elizabeth watched.

After what felt like an eternity, Abaddon stopped and ripped off her shirt, tossing it aside to examine her multiple stab wounds. Kristin looked up at Abaddon and watched as she used her power to heal herself. Kristin had hurt her. Abaddon should have been honest; people who lied to her deserved to die. Deserved to be hurt. Abaddon had to feel Kristin's wrath, no matter the outcome. She smiled.

"That used up every last bit of energy I had," Abaddon said. "I have no more souls in my body. Do you know how long it took me to take some of those souls?" She stamped on the side of Kristin's head, bouncing it off the tarmac.

"Just kill me," Kristin said breathlessly, barely able to form words.

Abaddon reached down and picked up Kristin by her hair, holding her up. "Kill you? You little asshole, I'm going to keep you alive as my new personal stress ball."

"You're such an idiot," Kristin said, spitting blood all over Abaddon's face.

Abaddon unleashed her temper and threw Kristin on the ground, repeatedly attacking the defenseless woman until she no longer moved. Then Kristin's skin began to glow as her drenik took control of her body.

Abaddon watched with a fascinated expression as Kristin's body healed itself. Drenik-Kristin got to her feet and a dozen clones appeared beside her.

Abaddon turned to Elizabeth. "Kill Kristin. Frankly, she's not worth my time." She walked away, closer to the hangar.

Drenik-Kristin got her feet and stared at Elizabeth as she walked closer. Drenik-Kristin smiled. "I'm going to tear your throat out with my teeth," she said.

Elizabeth stepped forward, raised two silver daggers, and started cutting through the clones in an attempt to get to Drenik-Kristin. She spread her power, weakening the clones and making them easy targets. The clones died, but came back in an instant. After some time watching this, Abaddon raised her hand and blasted a large number of clones with her necromancy.

With the path clear, Elizabeth moved quickly, slashing the silver blade across Drenik-Kristin's throat before burying it to the hilt in her forehead and pushing her down onto the tarmac without a word.

Kristin took control again as she died. She watched Elizabeth turn and walk away, watched her talk to Abaddon—although she couldn't hear what they said. Abaddon waved at her, and Kristin felt nothing but fear of whatever was going to come next. She closed her eyes and saw the spirits who she'd once bonded with come toward her.

An elderly man whose name Kristin didn't remember stood before her. "I guess you get to join us," he said. "Maybe you weren't better than us, after all?"

Kristin smiled. "I did more with my life than any of you. I had the courage to use my power to its fullest."

"And now you get the chance to wait with us until someone else comes along and picks up your scroll."

Kristin looked at the emptiness all around her.

"Hundreds of years. Maybe longer, maybe shorter. We have no way of knowing."

The fear of the situation overwhelmed her, and Kristin desperately tried to figure out how to escape.

The elderly man laughed as the scenery around them changed hundreds of times, showing snippets of her life. "You think you're better than us? Well, now you're one of us. You're just one of the spirits in the scroll waiting for a new host." The old man faded away, leaving Kristin alone in the cell where Nergal had found her.

Kristin regretted little of her life, but as the memory of Nergal stepped through the cell doors and offered her a chance at a new life, she tried in vain to say no, and when she couldn't, she finally realized what her hell was going to be.

29

Layla sat on her knees on the grass close to where she'd fought Jared and Kristin. She breathed in and out slowly. Jared was dead, Kristin had escaped, and her father had also broken free the first chance he'd got.

Chloe sat beside her. She'd been fighting blood elves while Layla killed Jared.

"You think Kristin's dead?"

"She was badly wounded," Chloe said with a slight sigh. "Also, that ring on your finger, that actually works. Good job you were far enough away from me it didn't affect my powers."

Layla looked at the ring. "It burned out. Doesn't activate at all anymore. I think Harry will have to work on it again." She stood and looked over at the runway as a Hercules took off.

"I'm glad someone managed to get out of here," Chloe said.

When the first blast of energy hit the engine, both Chloe and Layla were on their feet, staring at what was happening, hoping the aircraft could get away. The second blast, and subsequent crash, horrified them.

"How many people were on that plane?" Layla asked.

"I have no idea," Chloe said softly. "Those poor people. They didn't deserve that." She tapped her finger against her ear. "Did you see that?"

There was a pause as Chloe listened to whoever was talking on the other end. Layla tuned out while the conversation continued and watched the black smoke. People had been on that plane. People who were trying to escape had died. She took one step forward.

"You need to be careful," Rosa said from beside her. "You can't use Terhal again so soon. And we both know that if Abaddon was responsible for that attack, you can't beat her."

"Thanks for the pep-talk," Layla said.

"Just being realistic."

"Your mother is out there somewhere," Servius said as he appeared next to Rosa, before taking a step away. "She does not appear to be the virtuous woman you remember."

"Apparently not," Layla said.

"You honestly believe that?" Servius asked.

Layla shook her head. "It was meant to be a simple mission. Just get my father back to the compound to ensure that Nergal didn't reach him first."

"Jared would have still betrayed you," Rosa said. "But he might have killed someone close to you. Your father might have escaped a long time ago. You can't live on what ifs. What you know is that Abaddon is over there, and your mother is probably with her."

"And they're going to get away if someone doesn't stop them," Servius said.

"Meaning Chloe and me."

"You don't have to stop them," Servius said. "Just keep them occupied. The other choice is to wait and lose them."

"Abaddon was once considered a god," Layla said. "How the hell do I keep a god busy?"

"With stubborn tenacity," Rosa said. "You're good at that."

Layla smiled, and the three spirits vanished. She turned back to Chloe, who looked less than thrilled about the conversation she'd just had.

"They'll join us on the runway," Chloe said. "Fenix is already there with a few of his people."

"What's wrong?" Layla asked. "Any sign of my dad?"

Chloe shook her head. "Sorry."

"He's a problem for later. I assume you want to come with me while I piss off a god?"

"Of course," Chloe said, her expression brightening up. "What else am I going to do today?"

The pair set off toward the runway and noticed four blood elves running toward them at full speed.

"I've got this," Layla said, and once the elves were only a few dozen feet away, she reached out to take control of their swords, dragging them clear of their sheaths and driving them into the blood elves' chests. They dropped to the ground, dead.

Layla released her hold on the power and staggered forward a little. Chloe was immediately by her side. "You okay?" she asked.

"Lot of power used in a very short period of time," Layla explained. "Probably should have just used a gun. Probably need to find a gun."

Layla stopped by the blood elves and pulled one of the swords from the closest body. "Until then, this might come in handy." She passed it to Chloe and removed a second for herself.

"I hate these things," Chloe said, making a disgusted expression as they ran toward the airfield. "Blood elf weapons creep me out. It's the black metal, and the fact that they just look like some sort of torture implement more than an elegant blade."

Layla knew how Chloe felt, as her own feelings weren't far from her friend's, but the sword was necessary, and the quicker she could get rid of it and scrub her hands clean, the happier she'd be.

The pair ran onto the tarmac and saw Kristin's broken body, her ruined face, and the silver dagger embedded in her skull.

"I know she was an evil piece of crap," Chloe said, "but that's harsh, even for her."

"She really pissed someone off," Layla said.

Chloe looked all around. There were several destroyed cars and more than one helicopter on the runway, but most of it was clear, even with the burning wreckage of the Hercules in the distance. A second Hercules sat at the far end of the runway, next to two Black Hawks, although Chloe or Layla could see no one close by.

"You think Abaddon has already left?" Chloe asked.

Layla pointed to nearby hangar where a white-and-yellow Cessna sat out in front. "Looks like someone is planning an escape. We should go look."

"This is beginning to feel like one of those horror films where the pretty girl goes into a house with no lights on and doesn't even bother trying to turn them on."

"The pretty girl? Really?"

"Well, I figured I'd make myself feel better before I get my arse kicked by someone who just killed Kristin and blew up a Hercules."

Chloe and Layla moved toward the hangar and were about fifty feet away when gunfire erupted from inside. They ran toward the noise as two of Hades' Special Forces ran out of the building, firing at some unseen foe inside. Commander Fenix was the last to leave. He turned back to his people as a blast of energy struck him in the chest, knocking him to the ground.

Two of his team ran over to help him, but a masked woman stepped out of the hangar, and with a wave of her hands they both dropped to their knees. She wore a black mask with a red slash across one eye, faded jeans, and a gray hooded top. She held a sword by her leg as she stepped around Commander Fenix, who was crawling away, and killed the other two soldiers with quick swipes of the blade. She looked up at Chloe and Layla and walked back toward Fenix.

"Don't," Layla shouted.

The woman turned back to the two women and shrugged. The commander had moved behind a nearby truck that was mostly in good condition, and Chloe ran over to him, keeping an eye on the mystery woman.

The masked woman moved around the Cessna, her eyes never leaving Layla.

Layla hoped she was wrong about who the woman was. She hoped that her father had been lying, but then she saw the small Celtic cross on an index finger, and her chest filled with hurt: it felt like she'd been hit by a car. Her mother was alive. She opened her mouth to say something, but found that the words wouldn't come.

The woman removed the mask and dropped it to the floor. "Hello, my dear."

Layla had tried to prepare herself to see her mom for the first time since that fateful night when she was killed. She remembered the early morning phone call from the police, the feeling of helplessness, of pure disbelief as her brain tried to come to terms with what the officer was telling her.

Whatever Layla felt when she noticed the tattoo on her mother's finger was amplified tenfold when she removed her mask; and for the briefest of seconds, Layla wanted to run to her. Seeing her mother's face again, hearing her voice, it was almost too much to bear. She closed her eyes and tried to ignore the hurt she felt.

"So Dad wasn't lying. You're not dead," Layla said.

"No," Elizabeth said. "I'm very much alive."

Layla was about to say something when her father's warning came back to her. "You're not really my mom."

"What a horrible thing to say to your mum. Aren't you happy to see me?"

"You died. We buried you. I wept over your coffin. I saw your body."

"Not me," Elizabeth said. "We got a shapeshifter to take my place. Unfortunately, that meant killing him once he'd done it. Elizabeth Cassidy is officially dead."

"You don't sound like her."

"I am her."

Layla shook her head. The woman standing before her looked like her mom; her voice was the same, but her mannerisms, her tone, were all wrong. "What did Abaddon do to you?"

"Made me better. Now, come with me and we can be a family again."

Layla couldn't stop the tears from falling down her cheeks. "No," she shouted. "You're not her. You're just wearing her face."

Chloe ran over to stand beside her, grasping Layla's hand and squeezing a little. "Fenix is hurt," she whispered. "But he'll be okay."

"You going to introduce me to your friend?" Elizabeth asked, her voice angry.

"I'm Chloe, and you're meant to be dead."

"Abaddon saw to my continued existence."

"She made you an umbra, too," Layla said, feeling better at having Chloe beside her. "I saw Dad. He's not exactly thrilled about your continued existence."

Elizabeth chuckled. "No, I don't suppose he is. I assume you're here to stop Abaddon. Or try, because there's no way you'll defeat her."

"Just here to say hi," Chloe said. "Wanted to see how the queen of the shitheads is getting on."

Elizabeth's eyes narrowed in anger. "Your friend has a smart mouth. It will get her in trouble."

Layla shrugged. "She's been okay so far. There was a time I thought you might have agreed with us, but you know what, I'm not sure you were ever the person I remember. I think you were a little too helpful where Dad was concerned. You aided him in committing the murders."

"Occasionally, yes," Elizabeth said. "I worked in a law firm. I had access to clients who were guilty and got away with their crimes. My boss even helped me on occasion."

"I wonder: just how much has dying and becoming an umbra honestly changed you?" Layla asked. Whatever she'd once thought of her mother, whatever memories she'd had of her kindness were tainted by the idea of her helping her father all along. The anger and betrayal she felt at what she'd discovered boiled over. "You're not my mother," Layla snapped. "You're just wearing her skin. My mom was a lot of things, and maybe she did help Dad, but she was also sweet and kind, and she loved me. She would never have hurt my friends. She would never have chosen to help Abaddon."

Elizabeth shrugged. "Enough. I think, before this happened to me, I'd have found it impossible to kill you. Now, I'd simply rather not, but if you push me, you'll both die here."

"Where's Abaddon?" Layla asked.

"Resting. She got injured when Little Miss Prissy over there stabbed her with a silver blade. It's going to take her a while to heal, especially after using so much power to bring the aircraft down. She's unlikely to join in, my dear; it's just you two against me. I think I'll manage."

Layla used the metal of the sword blade to cover her fist and forearm, creating a black gauntlet with spikes on the knuckles.

"You have some power," Elizabeth said, waving a hand at Chloe and blasting a green fog at her. Chloe tried to dodge out of the way, but the fog washed over her with incredible speed and a second later she dropped to her knees, crying out in pain.

"Pestilence is my gift," Elizabeth said.

"Stop it," Layla demanded.

"Make me," Elizabeth said.

Layla darted forward, throwing a punch that would have caught Elizabeth in the jaw if she hadn't moved so quickly. Instead, Elizabeth grabbed Layla by the arm, dragged it back over her head, and kicked her legs out from under her, sending her to the ground with a hard impact.

Layla rolled to her feet as Elizabeth moved away.

"I wonder how long it will be before your friend dies?" Elizabeth asked. "I've forced her organs to shut down; it's a painful process and takes a long time. I used a lot less on Kristin—your friend got a far more powerful dose. You'll have to get better if you want to stop me."

Layla crouched beside Chloe, who was sweating and shivering with her eyes closed, muttering something that Layla couldn't quite make out.

"She got quite the blast of that stuff," Elizabeth continued taunting Layla.

Layla got to her feet and ran toward her mother, throwing another punch that Elizabeth easily avoided: exactly as Layla had planned. The metal on her gauntlet sprung out in one long spike, stabbing Elizabeth in the shoulder. Layla pulled the spike free, re-formed the gauntlet, and punched her mother in the face with everything she had. Elizabeth fell to the ground, blood pouring from her broken nose as Chloe gasped.

"Your mother is a real bitch," Chloe said through pained breath.

"I can't kill her, Chloe. I can't do that. I can fight her, I can hold her off, but I can't go further. You need to get someone who can."

Chloe looked up at Layla. "I can't leave you here."

"She'll use you against me. Please go get help. Bring them here."

"I'll help," Fenix shouted, getting unsteadily back to his feet.

"See, Fenix will help me," Layla said.

"Fenix can barely stand," Chloe pointed out.

"I'm fine," Fenix said, swaying slightly when he was upright.

Chloe tapped her earpiece. "Is anyone there? We need help here. Anyone there?" She removed the earpiece and tossed it on the ground. "It's not working. I'll find someone and come back. Can you keep her busy until then?"

Layla looked over at her mother, who was back on her feet, smiling through her bloodied mouth. "Yes. That I can do."

"If Abaddon makes an appearance, run," Chloe said. "You promise me?"

Layla nodded. "I promise."

Chloe sprinted away a second later.

"She's not staying to play?" Elizabeth asked.

"Go get the plane ready," Abaddon said as she exited the hangar behind Layla.

Layla turned to see the approaching necromancer and then looked back at her mother. She had nowhere to go.

"You're not healed," Elizabeth said.

"Do as you're told," Abaddon commanded. Elizabeth bowed her head and started to run. But Layla transformed the metal on her wrist into a whip, tripping her before wrapping it around her feet like shackles. More metal flew from the SUV nearby, covering Elizabeth's hands and pinning them against her back.

"This won't hold me," Elizabeth shouted.

"Long enough, it will," Layla said. "And it means you can't use that toxic shit cloud."

Abaddon picked up the blade and continued on toward Layla. "You can't win," she said.

"I know," Layla told her. "Doesn't mean I'm not going to try."

Fenix raised his rifle toward Abaddon and fired three bullets, each one striking the necromancer in the chest. Abaddon roared in anger and blasted Fenix with an incredible amount of power, killing him instantly.

"No!" Layla shouted.

"I am not here to play," Abaddon said, wincing with every step. "Silver is not a fun thing to have inside of me." Her eyes flickered for a moment. "Damn it, I'm having to use more power to heal myself."

"You don't have a lot of power at the moment, do you?"

Abaddon's face clouded with rage. "I don't need power to kill you, girl."

Layla ran toward Abaddon, creating a new blade from the remains of the SUV and bringing it up toward Abaddon with incredible speed. Abaddon parried the attack, dodging back, but Layla created a second blade as she spun. It bit into Abaddon's bicep, drawing a thin trail of blood.

"These aren't silver," Layla said, moving back.

Abaddon looked at the wound for a few seconds as it refused to close.

"Looks like you lost a lot more than you would like to admit," Layla said.

A second later, the cut closed, and looked as if it had never been there. "My power will return before you kill me," Abaddon said. "And then I'm going to bounce you all over this runway."

She moved in for the attack, forcing Layla to parry and dodge blow after blow, each one delivered with more strength and speed than the last as Abaddon's power seeped back into her.

Layla managed to avoid a swipe that would have cut across her face, but Abaddon was too fast and instead kicked Layla in the chest hard enough to smash her back against the SUV, knocking the wind out of her.

Abaddon struck toward Layla's heart, but Layla used her power to rip the door of the SUV free and use it as a shield, deflecting the blow. She dumped as much power into the door as she could and flung it at Abaddon, who dove aside, getting back to her feet as Layla wrapped more metal around her fists and forearms.

Layla raised her fists in a fighting stance and moved toward Abaddon, who swung her blade at Layla with nothing but power. Layla easily avoided it and struck Abaddon in the stomach with her spiked knuckle gauntlets before following up with an uppercut to her jaw, snapping Abaddon's head back and staggering her.

Layla wrapped metal around Abaddon's left foot, which was the closest to the SUV, holding her in place, then drove a fist into the side of her head, releasing the metal cuff so Abaddon could hit the tarmac.

Layla stepped closer, but Abaddon kicked her in the knee, forcing her back and giving herself a chance to charge. She tackled Layla to the ground and started punching her with as much force as possible.

Layla deflected most of the blows that rained down on her, managing to use the metal around her arms as shields. One punch got through and connected with Layla's jaw, opening her up to a second and third, until she slammed the metal in her arms into Abaddon's chest like a battering ram, knocking the necromancer to the ground.

"You should join us," Abaddon said with a smile.

Layla got to her feet and felt the anger burn inside of her. She extended her power, wrapping it around the silver blade in Kristin's head and pulling it into her right hand.

She looked down at Abaddon and wanted nothing more than to end her existence right there and then. She took a step forward as Abaddon remained lying on the ground with a smile on her face. Layla lunged, but the necromancer grabbed her by the wrist, squeezing it tightly before throwing her back across the tarmac.

Layla hit the ground hard. Abaddon ran to Layla's side and kicked her in the chest, causing all of the air to leave her body at once. Elizabeth used Layla's momentary lapse of concentration to tear herself free from the softening metal.

"Kill her," Abaddon said, placing a sword in Elizabeth's hand.

Elizabeth nodded and darted toward Layla, who was still dazed. She rolled away from the swipe of the blade at the last second, and instead of cutting through her torso, the sword bit into her forearm, just below the elbow, severing the limb.

Layla fell to the ground as blood poured from the wound, and she screamed in shock and agony.

Abaddon got back to her feet and kicked the severed forearm away. "You should have joined us." She turned to Elizabeth. "Let her live. Let her remember what happened here today."

Elizabeth nodded and passed the sword to Abaddon. She turned to her daughter. "Your power should make sure you survive. This is your only warning."

Layla didn't see what happened next as her entire world centered on trying to stop the bleeding.

Rosa appeared beside Layla. "Stay calm," she said. "Keep your arm up. You'll be okay."

Layla could tell that Rosa wasn't convinced by this statement and vaguely noticed that there was a plane taking off close by.

She had no idea how long she had been lying there when an SUV screeched to a halt beside her and Harry jumped out. He took one look at Layla and grabbed a medical kit from the car before crouching beside her. "You're going to be okay," he said, his voice full of confidence.

Layla looked up at Rosa.

"He's a good man," Rosa said to her.

Layla stared at Harry. "Yes, he is," she said, and then she passed out.

30

Layla woke up feeling groggy and disorientated for several seconds, until she realized she was in a bed and not on the tarmac of a runway. Machines beeped beside her and she went to sit up, but immediately thought better of it. She'd been in enough hospitals in her life to know that she was in one at the moment. She looked up at the familiar gray-and-white walls and suspected she'd been taken back to Greenland.

"Hi," Chloe said from beside her. "You feel okay?"

Layla sighed and looked over at her friend. She had no obvious injuries, but she did appear exceptionally tired. "How long was I out? You look like you need a rest."

"I'm fine," Chloe told her. "You were out for a few days. The blade was coated with Gorgon venom, but we had enough anti-venom here to treat you. Your own body did most of the work, and it kept you alive on the exceptionally long flight from Texas back to Greenland."

Layla raised her right arm. It was covered in thick bandages, and she almost cried when she focused on the fact that everything from her forearm down was missing.

"I'm sorry, we couldn't re-attach it," Chloe said. "Your body had healed the blood loss and wound too much; it would have been impossible to do it. Not even magic could make it happen, and trust me we tried."

"It's okay," Layla said, feeling like it was anything other than okay. "My fingers itch. I don't have fingers, but they itch."

"I've been told that's normal."

Layla looked over at Chloe. "Not a whole lot about this feels normal. So that simple mission turned out to be a bit crap."

"I distinctly remember telling you not to go after Abaddon alone."

"Are you blaming me for what happened?"

Chloe laughed. "Now you're just being an arsehole."

Layla smiled. "Abaddon didn't give me a lot of choice. I couldn't let her escape when I realized she'd lost most of her power. Unfortunately, it came back."

"She took your hand?"

"No, my mother did that."

"Your parents are screwed up. It's a miracle you're not more of a mess than you are."

Layla laughed. "Yep, that's me, the poster child for dysfunctional families everywhere: one serial killer parent, the other working with a despot who wants to control the world. I bet they're so proud of me."

"Yes, that's why your mum almost killed you. Pride."

"I never said it wasn't weird. How is everyone else?"

"We lost people at Nergal's, and not just on the Hercules. Two hundred people died on our side in the assault. Another hundred in Canada."

"How many did they lose?"

"Thousands of Nergal's people are dead thanks to the blood elves. Maybe five or six thousand in total: it was not a good day for team Avalon. Although considering they're the ones who started all of this, maybe it was. I'm not sure how they deal with such things."

"Damn it," Layla said, closing her eyes and taking a deep breath.

"Harry saved your life, you know," Chloe said.

Layla opened her eyes. "I remember him coming to my rescue. He told me to put my arm up and made a tourniquet."

"Used his own belt. Kept you stable until Irkalla arrived and used her necromancy to heal you enough that you could survive the journey back here to get the anti-venom."

Layla went to rub her face with her hands and stopped. "Shit."

"People tell me you'll get used to it," Kase said as she entered the room with Harry, Remy, and Diana.

"I hope so," Layla said. "I also hope I can learn to write with my left hand."

"Do we need to get you a blue disabled badge now?" Remy asked. "What, too soon?"

Layla chuckled. "You're an asshole, Remy."

"But a loveable one," he said, patting her on the shoulder. "I'm glad you're okay. The mission sure didn't go well, did it?"

"It was not a textbook mission," Layla said.

"Depends on the screwed-up textbook," Harry said.

"Right, people," Grayson said as he entered the room. "Everyone who isn't currently in a hospital bed, out. I think she has some more visitors."

Diana took Layla's hand in hers. "We'll make this right. Your father escaped the compound. We haven't found him yet, but we will. I promise you, Avalon won't get away with what happened."

Layla nodded. She wasn't sure what else to do. "One thing. My mother worked for a law firm in New York. I'm not sure of the name off the top of my head, but her boss was helping her get information on targets for my father. Can you find out who it was and keep an eye on him? I'm thinking my father might want to have a chat about a few things."

"You think your dad will kill him?" Remy asked.

"Depends on how deeply he was involved in Elias and Nergal finding out where we were all those years ago. Caleb isn't someone who lets things go. And he's going to need to be caught before his murder toll starts up again in earnest."

"We'll take a look," Diana said, and everyone left the room.

"It's been a while, doc," Layla said. "How's things?"

"Busy," Grayson told her. "I've been moving between realms to make sure that we don't lose the people who are keeping us from defeat against Avalon. I was only back in this realm to see Hades, but he said you'd been hurt, and I thought I'd come take a look."

"So you're really Lucifer?" Layla asked Grayson. "The Lucifer?"

"Ta da," Lucifer said. "You want the short version or the long one?"

Layla smiled. "Persephone told me all about it when we were in Canada. Why the name Grayson?"

Lucifer shrugged. "Sounded like as good a name as any other." He checked several charts on the end of the bed. "I'm sorry for what happened to you. If it helps, once we're sure the venom has gone, and we've checked for infections and the like, you'll be free to go. On the plus side, you heal many times quicker than a human, so I'm optimistic that you'll be out of here in a few hours."

Layla looked at the stump at the end of her arm and unfastened the bandage, removing it with a mixture of fear and anger about what she was going to see. When she was finished, she stared at the scarred limb where her forearm used to be.

"We're already working on a prosthetic," Lucifer said. "State of the art, I promise."

Layla nodded without paying much attention to what he said. She just continued to stare at her limb. Lucifer left soon after, leaving Layla to think about what he'd told her. She lay there, looking at her arm, wondering how the hell she was ever going to do the things she'd taken for granted before.

"You know you're not dead," Terhal said from the chair beside her. "Self-pity doesn't suit you."

"I had my arm cut off."

"Part of your arm," Terhal corrected.

Layla looked over at the drenik, who was wearing a smart black suit. "Why the black suit?"

"I assumed we're having a funeral for your arm," she said. "I'm welling up just thinking about it."

"You know, sometimes you do remind me that you're just a massive twat."

Terhal laughed.

"Where are Rosa and the others?"

"You don't know? They're your spirits."

Layla began to feel irritated. "Just tell me."

"They're gone. Not gone, gone, but gone from being around during the day. You merged with them quite a lot during your near-death experience. It boosted your power and made me feel all tingly."

"Gone?" she asked, sad at the news.

"Were you not listening? Not gone, gone. You can speak to them when you sleep, just like what happened with Gyda. I assume you're dealing with your arm's loss a lot better than someone without three spirits' life experience, and you're less worried about killing the people responsible than you were when we first met?"

"I decide what I do," Layla snapped. "I'm not accepting that my actions aren't my own responsibility. That's not how it works."

"I know. I just like screwing with you. You're right. Your mind, your rules. Too many umbra don't accept responsibility for their own actions, like Gyda for example. She hated me for what I did to the people in her village, but she hated those people, too."

"I know," Layla said. "She couldn't accept it, but I knew. I just didn't want to argue with her about it."

"And she knew that you knew. That's why she kept away. I'm guessing your next chat will be interesting."

"So you're still here."

"I'm the source of your power. I can still be let out to hurt people, but the days where I can take complete control of your mind are gone. Considering that I've been living in your mind quite happily for a few years now, it's not exactly a big change. Just one thing, we both know you can't kill your mom. And you can't kill Abaddon. So what's the plan?"

Layla shrugged, swinging her feet out of the bed and standing up. "Imprison both of them. Somewhere deep and dark, where I can throw away the key. She's not my mom. You know that, right?"

Terhal nodded. "I do. I believe her mind was a mess before the drenik was placed inside it. It's difficult to tell exactly, but I think your mom's mind merged with the drenik's. The rage and hate I got from her certainly makes that a possibility. She's a very dangerous woman. And there's no chance you're killing Abaddon. No offense, but you're not in her league."

"Thanks for the vote of confidence."

"Layla, I've come to like and respect you over the last few years, but you got lucky on that runway. You fought a barely powered Abaddon and she still kicked your ass. She brought down a Hercules and survived being shot with silver rounds. No umbra is going to match that level of power."

"So what am I meant to do, leave it?" Layla felt the anger build up inside of her again. She closed her eyes and forced herself to calm.

Terhal laughed. "So your options are to leave it or get killed fighting Abaddon? That's it, no other alternatives?"

Layla opened her eyes and sighed. "What do you suggest?"

"Abaddon has a power base. It includes people such as your mother. You go after them, you're going to make Abaddon very angry and, more importantly, you're going to disrupt Avalon. Pissed off people make mistakes, and the next time Abaddon is there, maybe you can make sure you have your heaviest hitters with you."

"In other words, there's a lot more I can do other than trying to kill her."

"That's about the size of it, yes."

Layla removed the various tubes and wires that were connected to her as Chloe walked into the room and Terhal vanished.

"Going somewhere?" Chloe asked.

"Out of this damn bed for a start," Layla said. "Can you please help me?"

Together they managed to get Layla disconnected from everything and Chloe fetched her some clean clothes. "Shower in there," Chloe said with a smile.

"What?"

"When you're done, come to the command room underground. Room 614. I think there's a conversation happening there you'd be interested in. But first, shower. Enjoy the hot water and try not to freak out about your arm."

"I'm not freaking out," Layla said. "I'm just . . ."

"Angry," Chloe finished for her.

Layla nodded. "My mom tried to kill me. I know she's not my mom, not really, but even so . . . she sure looks a hell of a lot like her."

Chloe sat on the bed next to Layla. "I get that. My relationship with my own toxic mother is well documented."

"How'd you deal with it?"

"Deal with having a mother who'd like to murder me? Well, I'm not sure I did. Not really. Avoiding her like the plague did the job. And then she got killed, so it all worked out in the end."

"You think that?"

Chloe nodded. "My mother was a murderer who tried to kill me because of who my friends were. When I first told her I was gay, she told me it was a phase and called me ridiculous. She made sure my father was murdered and is personally responsible for helping Arthur murder thousands of people so that he could take control without humanity realizing what he is. She is better off dead. The world is better off with her dead.

"Are you upset that your mum is walking around, even though she's not the woman you remember, or are you upset that the woman you remember was helping a serial killer find targets and get away with his crimes?"

"Both. The latter more, I guess. I've seen and heard some crazy shit in the last few years, but my mom coming back was not something I expected. Learning that she helped my father was unexpected, too. It's tainted her image in my mind. I'm not sure if she did it because she loved me, or if she did it to help my dad." Layla got up. "I'm going to have a shower, and then I'll come find you."

Chloe stopped in the doorway. "Would it help if I told you that I rearranged my date?"

"Piper? The redhead?"

"That's her. After fighting Abaddon and Avalon, getting a date didn't feel so intimidating. Besides, I'm a war hero now."

Layla laughed. "Please don't tell me you used those exact words."

"She did, and frankly I'm not sure I want to correct her. I don't feel like much of a hero. I wonder if this is how soldiers feel when people say they're heroic, and the reality is that you only did something because you didn't want your friends to die. Doesn't feel heroic, just feels necessary."

"You expected more?"

"I expected to be swollen with pride at my own awesomeness. Honestly, I just feel like this whole thing is the start of something much worse. So I'm going to go on a date with a beautiful woman, drink some vodka, and watch shitty films with my friends. Not necessarily in that order."

"If you need to talk," Layla said. "Don't try to get through anything alone."

"That's what everyone has said so far. I've been talking to Diana. For someone thousands of years old, she's quite easy to talk to."

Chloe left, and Layla wondered just how much worse things were going to get before they got better. She had a shower with water as hot as she could bear, before getting out and drying herself, taking special care with her stump. It didn't hurt and wasn't too sore, but it was quite tender, and probably would be for a long time. Umbra healing was a thing of beauty, but she couldn't regrow an arm. She would have to get used to her new circumstances, and sooner rather than later.

When dressed, she left the medical facility and made her way down to room 614, where she found Hades, Persephone, Sky, Tommy, Olivia, and most of her team, along with several people she couldn't name. They were in a massive auditorium that sat a few hundred people in total.

A man she'd never met stood at the front of the room next to a white board, loudly humming the theme to Super Mario, while several people on the chairs in front of him looked like they'd heard this song more times than they cared to mention.

"Ah, the woman of the hour," the man said, gesturing to Layla as she entered. He was of average height with a bald head and the beginnings of a scruffy beard. He wore jeans and a t-shirt with a picture of Link from Zelda on it. "Please do take a seat."

Layla was motioned toward the front of the room where she sat next to Chloe and Harry.

"I'm sorry," the man said to Layla. "I haven't introduced myself." He came over and offered Layla his hand.

"Layla," she said.

"Mordred," he told her.

Her eyes widened in shock. Everyone had heard about Mordred, the son of Merlin. The man who was meant to be the king of Avalon centuries ago before Arthur, Gawain—Mordred's brother—and their people betrayed him. They sent Mordred to be tortured for decades by blood elves, who broke his mind and sent him on a quest to murder those who had once been his friends. Layla had heard that he was better now, but a few people were still cautious around him, not least of all because he was an incredibly powerful sorcerer.

"I see you have heard of me," Mordred said with a smile.

"A little, yeah," Layla replied.

"Well, I assure you, I'm not quite as crazy as people make out."

"Not quite as crazy?"

"I'm a bit crazy. But it's all my own crazy, so it works out well."

Layla couldn't help but smile.

Mordred walked back to the whiteboard and tapped it, changing it into three parts. "Abaddon," Mordred began. "She's a big pain in the ass. But she's not the only pain in the ass. These three realms are places where Avalon's forces are fighting the Resistance. We are not winning. At best, we're fighting to maintain a stalemate."

There were a lot of unhappy murmurs at that assessment.

"I'm not saying we've lost it forever," Mordred continued, his voice carrying over the crowd, "but we need to make a decision. We need to decide if we want to win this war, or merely maintain this current stalemate. Winning will mean we have to do something that will make a lot of you unhappy. We have to let one of these realms go. At least in the meantime."

"You're suggesting we let that be the Earth realm?" Hades asked.

"I am," Mordred said. "Arthur and Avalon have already taken it. Whether we want to admit that or not, it's true. They own the governments; they control most of the major cities on the planet. Going to war against Avalon on the Earth realm will kill billions of people. There's no other way. We can stay here and we can help people who need it, but the idea of preparing for a war here at the moment is folly. It's simply not going to work and will only get innocent people killed."

"What's your plan, then?" Sky asked from next to her father.

"These three realms are where the fighting between us and Avalon is the most intense. We need to win these realms. We need to force Arthur to take troops from Avalon and send them to these realms because they're losing. Once he does that, we take the realm of Avalon. And we crush him like a Goomba."

A few people exchanged looks of confusion.

"They're the little brown things in Mario," Mordred said. "Not quite mushrooms, but maybe they're like evil mushrooms . . ."

Silence descended on the room.

"I'll move on," Mordred said. "The realms are Nidavellir, Helheim, and Midgard: all Norse realms, because the battle between Arthur and the Norse has raged for centuries. If we can win them, we will get a lot of power on our side. And not just from the Norse; there are a lot of people who went to the Norse's aid. I have been fighting there for the last two years. And we're gaining nothing."

"Where do you suggest we put our forces?" someone in the back asked.

"Asgard and Midgard are connected. What some of you might not know is that Midgard is separate from the Earth realm. To get to Asgard, you have to go through one of the other realms, Midgard being one of them. I suggest we put our forces in Midgard and Helheim. That's where the fighting is most intense."

"And what about Nidavellir?" Zamek asked from across the room after rising to his feet. "My people are there fighting for their lives."

"I know," Mordred said. "I have special plans for them, trust me."

Zamek nodded and returned to his seat.

"Why am I here?" Layla asked. "Why am I the lady of the hour?"

"I'll explain when we're done," Mordred said. "I just need you to hear the rest."

No one else spoke for the hour that Mordred continued, spelling out his plan to force Avalon back and defeat them in the realms that Arthur had put so much time and effort into claiming. It made sense, but no one was happy about leaving Earth with vastly fewer people than were currently here.

When the meeting finished, only a few dozen people remained behind, most of whom had taken part in the attack on Nergal's compound.

"You're not going to Helheim or Midgard," Mordred said. "I need a small number of you to go to Nidavellir. I need to you get those dwarves out and bring them to one of the other realms. There are hundreds of dwarves in Nidavellir and each of them is just as good a warrior as Zamek. We need their help."

"Are you forgetting about the blood elves?" Zamek asked.

Mordred shook his head. "Six months," he said. "You have six months to get something working that will take us into that realm, away from the blood elves."

"We've been working on it for hundreds of years," Zamek said. "Six months isn't going to make much of a difference."

Mordred removed a stone tablet from a bag that Layla hadn't noticed before and gave it to Zamek, whose mouth fell open in shock.

"Can you do it?"

Zamek nodded and ran from the room with Harry in hot pursuit.

"Where does that leave us?" Layla asked.

"In six months, you and your team are going to go to the worst place I've ever been to and you will rescue our allies," Mordred said. "The blood elves there are trapped in the realm, but we took an Avalon stronghold in Midgard and found those tablets. They allow you to go from one realm to another, but, more importantly, they give instructions on how to make your own realm gate. A realm gate that is able to change its destination."

"You're going to build a realm gate in this compound?" Chloe asked. "And then you want us to go back to the place where the worst thing in my life happened?"

"I never said it would be easy," Mordred said. He looked down at the floor for a second, before sighing and looking back up. "There's one more thing."

"And that is?" Layla asked.

"You have six months to find your father, because you're going to need his help tracking people."

"This is getting better and better," Remy said.

"Oh, it's going to get worse," Mordred said. "Abaddon has gone to London, under Hera's protection. We can't get to her without turning the city into a war ground."

"Great, so our enemies are fortified, and we have to go to a place of monstrous evil," Diana said. "Sounds like a normal day."

Layla's mind turned to the six months during which she'd need to find her dad and persuade him to help, and then go to another realm and save a bunch of people. She had no idea if Caleb had enough decency left in him to want to do that, but hopefully they would pass that bridge when they got there.

"I'll do it," Layla said. "Six months. And then we piss off Avalon a lot more than we've ever done before."

Epilogue

Three months later. New York State.

Layla stood on the sidewalk and stared at the place that had once been her childhood home. The house had been demolished. Layla hadn't been told, and no one in the car that had brought her seemed to have any idea why or when it had happened, but the house was definitely not there. It was as if it had been plucked up and then erased from existence.

Three months ago, Layla had asked that her mother's old boss at the law firm be put under surveillance. It hadn't taken long to look into the man's background and discover that he'd given up Caleb to the FBI and was one of the reasons they'd managed to catch him. Layla was convinced that her father would show up to do him harm.

Two days ago, her mother's old boss had vanished on his way home from work. He'd got into his car that evening and no one had seen him since. It hadn't taken long for Layla to think that her father was involved.

Mordred stood next to Layla. He'd been keen on going with her, and despite the fact that Avalon would have liked to kill him—even more than most of the people working against them—he said he wasn't concerned. New York had been independent of Avalon's influence for centuries, and while it could no longer claim that status, there were still enough people there who fought against the oppression in their own way, by turning a blind eye to Avalon's enemies.

"Any idea where your father would take this man, if not here?"

Layla shook her head before an idea formed. "Actually, yeah. I have a plan. There's a cemetery nearby. Mom's grave is there."

"I wonder who is actually buried there?"

Layla hadn't wanted to think about it.

"Sorry," Mordred said as they set off to walk the short distance to the cemetery. "I didn't mean to say anything upsetting. My brain and mouth aren't always in sync."

Layla smiled. "Don't worry about it."

They walked for a few minutes down quiet sidewalks, past dozens of houses in which the majority of occupants were still asleep. It was almost peaceful. The cold night air and the stillness of the neighborhood created something that made Layla feel nostalgic for those childhood evenings when she'd wake up in the middle of the night to watch the snow fall outside.

"How's the new hand?" Mordred asked as they reached the entrance to the large cemetery.

Layla raised her gloved hands. "It's weird," she said. "Really weird, if I'm honest. Stay here, please. I want to go check for myself."

Mordred nodded. Layla found him to be an interesting man, one who had suffered a lot at the hands of his enemies and taken a long time to come to terms with what he'd been forced to become.

She stopped and readied herself. This wasn't going to be a fun meeting, but her dad was either going to come with them peacefully, or in a less pleasant manner. The end result would be the same.

Layla stepped into the dark cemetery, and with a combination of moonlight and the flashlight she'd brought with her, walked along the path between the rows of tombstones. About halfway into the park lay six crypts in a row. She knew that there were six others on the opposite side of the patch of grass that ran in between them. She remembered walking along them after burying her mom.

Layla continued on until she reached the top of a steep slope that led to a large pond. She followed the slope until she was halfway around it, and then continued along the path for a few feet until she came to a wooden bench. The bench had been put there by the groundskeeper as a favor to Layla, and it sat opposite her mom's grave.

A man lay bound and gagged on the grave, next to Layla's dad, who leaned against the tombstone.

"I did wonder if you'd find me," Caleb said. "Peter here, well, he didn't believe. He thought that offering me money was the way to go." Caleb punched Peter on the arm. "Didn't you, Petey?"

Peter made a soft noise, muffled by the gag.

"He sold you out," Caleb said. "Sold you and your mom out to Nergal. I always wondered how they found you after the LOA had taken such pains to keep you safe. Now I know. Your mom had gone to see Peter to tell him she was going, and he sold her out. A million dollars was the price. Which I guess is a lot, but it sounds like small change in comparison to how much this piece of crap is worth.

"He helped me find victims. He helped me dispose of evidence. And he betrays you and your mom like that. I think I'm going to start with his eyes and work my way down, but do you have a preference?"

"He gave evidence to the FBI about you, too; did you know that?" Layla asked.

Caleb nodded. "I don't begrudge him that. I do begrudge him trying to get you killed."

"You're not going to murder him, Dad," Layla said, taking a seat on the bench.

"No intention of doing so. I do intend to make him scream."

Peter's eyes widened, and he thrashed about, showing Layla that his hands and feet were tied with a thin wire that was attached to two metal hooks in the ground.

"Tent pegs?" Layla asked.

"Same principle," her dad told her. "He keeps pulling, and the wire is going to slice through his skin. I assume he doesn't want to lose a hand."

Layla stared at her father for several seconds. "You don't know?"

"Know what?"

Layla stood and removed her jacket, laying it over the bench, before she did the same with her hoodie, leaving her in a t-shirt. Her forearm gleamed in the light.

"What happened to you?" Caleb asked. His voice was soft and appeared to contain genuine concern.

Layla was surprised at his tone; she hadn't heard warmth from her father in a long time. "Mom says hi."

"She cut your arm off?"

Layla raised her arm, moving the fingers on her metal hand. "Yep."

"All the way to the bicep?"

Layla shook her head. "Forearm. I added the extra metal because it means I can make a few things with it. I tried a number of different styles. The first one freaked everyone out as it looked like a skeleton's hand. This is more normal-looking."

"Except it's made of metal."

"Except that." Layla picked up her hoodie and put it back on. "Took me a while to learn to write with it, but I'm getting there. It has most of the function of my normal hand, but it means I have to maintain a constant level of concentration that I originally found hard. It's getting easier, though. Soon it should be second nature, and I won't even think about it."

"So catch up aside, can I assume you're here to take me in?"

Layla nodded. "You're going to help us piss off Avalon."

"And your mother?"

"She's pissed off all the time, I think," Layla said, her tone business-like. "She's not Mom."

Caleb nodded. "She's Abaddon's creation."

"One way of putting it. Look, Dad, I'd love to sit here and chat with you, but you have a bound and gagged man lying beside you and it's cold. Let him go, and then we can move on."

"If I help you, I want you to come see me."

"If that's what it takes to get your help, I'll come see you every week and I'll bring cake and whiskey."

"You seem harder than before."

"My mom cut my arm off, and is a monster created by someone who wants me dead. Oh, and my father is a serial killer who escaped and made me hunt him down again. It's been a hard few months."

Caleb shook his head. "Something else. You fully bonded with your spirits, didn't you?"

"Yes. Is that a conversation to have right now?" Layla looked down at the terrified Peter. "Peter, you're a piece of shit, but my father is not going to kill you, so please stop making that noise."

Peter nodded quickly, and the noise stopped.

"Are you going to threaten me?" Caleb asked Layla.

"No. You help me, or you die." Layla surprised herself with how cold her words sounded. She felt tired and fed up, and was in no mood for her father's games, but even so, her tone surprised her. "No threat, just facts. We'll do it with or without you, but with you would be easier, and fewer innocents might die. We have a plan all in place."

"To kill Abaddon?"

"No, Dad, not to kill Abaddon."

"But she hurt you. She did unspeakable things. How can you not want her dead?" He asked the question in the same way someone might ask why she didn't want ice in her drink on a hot day.

"Because I'm an adult," Layla snapped. "And I have bigger things to worry about than revenge."

"Revenge is sometimes enough."

Layla shook her head. "Killing Abaddon will do what? Make me happier for a bit? It won't remove Avalon, it won't remove Arthur, but it sure as hell will get innocent people killed. You can seethe and be angry that I'm not going to go on a suicide mission to avenge my arm, but I'm still not going to do it. And Mom went to Abaddon first; she made a deal with the devil and the devil is a crappy boss. Who knew?"

"Her living irks me."

"Grow up, Dad. You irk me, but I'm not about to slit your throat and be done with it. Abaddon is a problem for later. She was only a problem then because Nergal decided to try to get one over on her. Mom is a whole separate problem, but we'll get to her when we've dealt with Avalon. This world is a mess. Avalon is in charge, and they're killing innocent people by the thousands. None of the human governments are going to help because they're already under Avalon's control. I figure instead of doing the selfish thing and getting killed, I'd try to help a lot more people. And you're going to help me." Layla extended one of her metal fingers, turning it into a knife, and cut the wire that was holding Peter in place. "Run, Peter. Run very, very fast."

Peter didn't need to be told twice and stumbled away a second later.

"Why are you letting him go?" Caleb demanded, getting to his feet.

"Because he's an asshole, but that doesn't mean I'm going to kill him. Besides, a large amount of information will be passed to the news outlets and the FBI about his crimes. Turns out we still have friends there, and frankly Avalon isn't going to care about whether or not one human gets charged with conspiracy to commit murder. Some DA will take the case because it'll be a big news day when they parade him out as an accomplice to the All-American Ripper. Who, by the way, has escaped custody and is on the run."

"But Peter will say you were here. You're going to let him escape?"

Layla sighed and placed a finger to her ear. "Peter's on the way." She looked at her dad. "We'll make sure he turns himself in."

"That's not good enough."

"Too bad. So are we going, or what?"

"And what if I say no?" Caleb said.

"Then my friend, Mordred, will shoot you. We'll take you anyway, and everyone will get what they want, except you. And I don't care what you want at this exact moment in time."

Caleb held out his hands and Layla detached part of the metal in her arm, turning it into cuffs that she put on her father's wrists.

"I will get out of your custody eventually, you know that, yes?" Caleb asked. "You're my daughter and I care for you, so I think it's fair play that I let you know. I understand that you're angry with me, but at some point in the future I'm going to have the chance to kill someone who deserves it, and I'm going to take that chance. There's nothing you can do to stop it happening."

Layla stared at her father for several seconds before she punched him in the gut, forcing him to his knees, coughing and spluttering. "I can't kill you. I don't think I'm emotionally able to, but if you give me enough time and reason, I'm sure I can build up to it."

"You're going to rough me up first?"

"Dad, I don't think you understand. I'm not you. I'm not like you. I'm not going to become you. You can smirk and make accusations about who or what I'm becoming, but even if I'm forced to hunt you down like a rabid animal, I'm never going to become you. You're going to help me and my friends, and then I'm going to find a deep, dark cell, and I'm going to shove you down there, lock the door, and throw away the key. That's your future. The only way you get out of it is to help in every way you can without making me hate you more than I already do."

Caleb spat onto the grass. "I think I can do that."

"Good," Layla said. "Because we have a lot of work to do, and not a lot of time to do it."

"What does that mean?" Caleb asked as the pair walked back through the graveyard.

"Oh, did I forget to mention? We're going to another realm to free a lot of our allies and in the process piss off Abaddon more than she is already."

Layla and Caleb walked through the cemetery to an SUV waiting at the entrance with several armed men and women standing outside it.

"You brought a lot of backup," Caleb said.

"I figured you deserved it," Layla told him, opening the rear door. She absorbed the first set of Caleb's metal cuffs back into her arm and replaced them with a new pair, along with a sorcerer's band. Then she settled her father into the passenger seat.

Layla closed the door and turned around to find Chloe standing there. "You okay?" she asked.

Layla nodded. "Just glad to finally have him off the street." She sighed and rubbed her eyes with the fingers on her left hand. "So now we prepare to go to war."

"We're already at war," Chloe said.

"Yes, but now we prepare to start winning," Mordred said.

"About damn time," Layla told him.

ACKNOWLEDGMENTS

This will be my ninth published book—tenth if you want to include my novella—and I have no intention of stopping anytime soon. There are a large number of people who help make these books possible, and without their help and support I might not have gotten anywhere near the number of books published that I have.

My wife will always be the first person I thank. She listens to ideas and reads parts of the book I'm unsure about. She allows me the time to sit away in my office without distraction, and every single day I am thankful for her being in my life.

My three daughters are one of the reasons I write. And one day, when they're old enough, they might actually be able to read what I've written.

My parents are some of my biggest cheerleaders, and it's both awesome and a little weird to see all of my book covers on their living room wall.

To my friends and family. Thank you. For everything.

A huge thank you goes out to my agent, Paul Lucas, who is as great an agent as one could hope to find.

A big thank you to Jenni Smith-Gaynor, who has edited nearly all of my books, and I'd like to think that I've become a better writer over the years due to her suggestions and questions.

D.B. Reynolds, Michelle Muto, and a special thank you to everyone who used to be a part of the OWG family. You know who you are, and you're all awesome.

To everyone who works at 47North, you keep publishing my work and being incredibly supportive and helpful, and I appreciate that a lot. Also, they got me whisky and cake, and that goes a really long way to making me like someone.

To all of my fans and the people who love my work, thank you for enjoying the ramblings in my head. A special thank you to anyone who meets me at conventions and says hi. You people rock.

So, that's another book finished. And if you're wondering what's next, well, I can promise you I'm not done by a long shot.

ABOUT THE AUTHOR

Photo © 2013 Sally Beard

Steve McHugh is the author of the popular Hellequin Chronicles. He lives in Southampton, on the south coast of England, with his wife and three young daughters. When not writing or spending time with his kids, he enjoys watching movies, reading books and comics, and playing video games.